To those who thirst and hold fast
to the dream of water

The falling camel attracts many knives.

—ANCIENT ARABIC SAYING

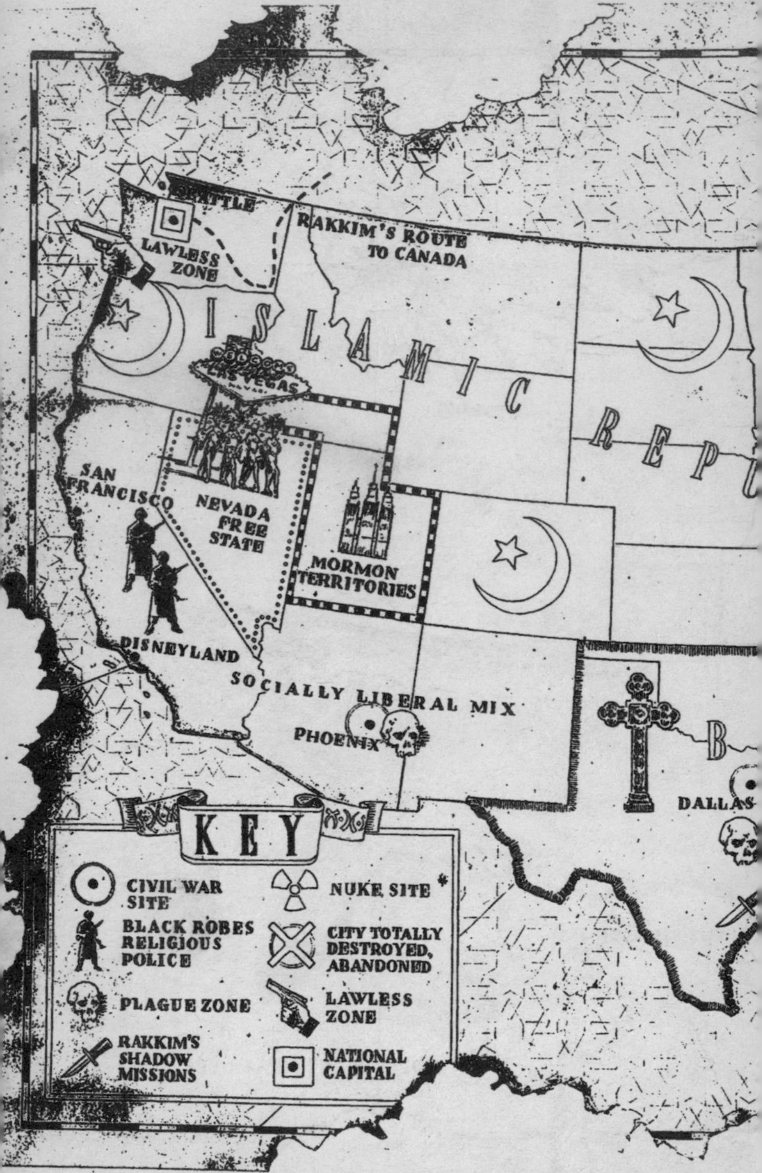

SEATTLE
LAWLESS ZONE
RAKKIM'S ROUTE TO CANADA
ISLAMIC REPU
WELCOME TO FABULOUS LAS VEGAS NEVADA
SAN FRANCISCO
NEVADA FREE STATE
MORMON TERRITORIES
DISNEYLAND
SOCIALLY LIBERAL MIX
PHOENIX
B
DALLAS
KEY
CIVIL WAR SITE
NUKE SITE
BLACK ROBES RELIGIOUS POLICE
CITY TOTALLY DESTROYED, ABANDONED
PLAGUE ZONE
LAWLESS ZONE
RAKKIM'S SHADOW MISSIONS
NATIONAL CAPITAL

CHICAGO DETROIT

B L I C

ST. LOUIS

NEWARK

NEW YORK

PITTSBURGH

WASHINGTON, D.C.

OAK RIDGE

B L E   B E L T

ATLANTA   SAVANNAH

BILOXI

ORPUS CHRISTI

SOUTH FLORIDA
INDEPENDENT UNALIGNED NEW AREA

PROLOGUE

Strange to be lying in the parking lot of a looted Wal-Mart, one leg twisted under him as he stared up at the sky. Jason used to shop at Wal-Mart for jeans and DVDs and Frosted Flakes. Now he was dying here. Crows drifted down from the light poles, black wings fluttering across his field of vision. They seemed to be getting bigger every day. Bolder too. Dying wasn't so bad. There had been pain at first, terrible pain, but not anymore. A blessing, because he wasn't brave. He was scared of spiders and dentists and pretty girls, and most of all, being alone, but he wasn't scared now. Dying in a holy war meant he would immediately enter Paradise. That's what Trey had said, and he knew the Qur'an lots better than Jason. Trey said all that mattered was that Jason make his declaration of faith—*there is no God but Allah, and Muhammad is his messenger*—and everything would be taken care of.

Trey was already dead. Shot through the chest three weeks ago by a rebel sniper as they approached Newark. Jason had bent over him, held his hand, and begged him not to die, but Trey was gone, only his startled expression left behind. The sergeant had ordered the unit to keep moving, but Jason refused, said he wanted to make sure that Trey's body was properly attended, and the sergeant, a former accountant for H&R Block, had given up and moved the platoon out. They were all new Muslims, just like Jason, and unsure of themselves. Jason had waited until the morgue detail had wrapped Trey's body in white cloth, then helped them dig his grave. By the time he rejoined his unit, the sergeant was dead, and now Jason was dying, and there wasn't enough white cloth left for all of them. Allah would understand. That was something else Trey would say when Jason worried because he still liked his pork chops and his bacon too—read your Holy Qur'an, Allah would understand.

Jason could barely see now, but it didn't matter. He had seen enough. The parking lot was littered with bodies, all of Newark a graveyard. Civilians and soldiers, Muslims mixed with rebels from the Bible Belt. Americans against Americans. Both sides battling on their home ground, fighting for every freeway and minimall, cities burning all across the country. Two or three times this last week, the rebs would have taken Newark if it hadn't been for Major Kidd rallying the troops, a black giant leading the attack himself, ignoring the bullets flying around him, utterly fearless.

Jason was just glad that he hadn't been ordered to the Nashville front. His people had moved from there to Detroit years ago to work in the auto plants, and he still had kin in Tennessee, folks who were probably fighting on the other side.

Times had been as tough in the Bible Belt as anyplace else in the years before the transition—people out of work or worried they would be, factories and schools shut down, kids hungry. That hadn't changed their minds though. They just dug in harder. The only places offering comfort during the hard times . . . the only places offering *answers* were the mosques. Anybody could see that. The rest of the country had come around, had converted or at least gone along with it, but not the folks down South. They kept to their old ways, their old-time religion. That's why in spite of everything, Jason couldn't bring himself to hate the rebs. He understood them. They loved a country that had let them down, a country that no longer existed . . . but they still loved her. Holy war and all, you had to respect that.

Even Redbeard would have agreed. The deputy director of State Security was a righteous warrior, but he understood. The rebs' loyalty was misplaced, but Redbeard said such loyalty was honorable and made their future conversion all the sweeter. Jason had seen him all over TV. The grunts liked him almost as much as Major Kidd. Plenty of politicians wanted to burn the Bible Belt down to the dirt, but Redbeard bellowed them into silence. Built like a bull, with angry eyes and a beard the color of a forest fire . . . no wonder Redbeard's enemies were scared of him.

It was pitch-black now. Jason wasn't alone though. He heard the beating of great wings and silently made his declaration again. Dying for the faith meant he got all kinds of virgin brides in Paradise. Jason wasn't one to argue with Allah, but he kind of hoped at least one or two of them had some experience, because he sure didn't have much. Would have been nice to graduate from high school too. He would have been a senior this year. Go, Class of 2017. Picture in the yearbook wearing his letterman's jacket . . . that would really have been something. Oh, well, like Trey said, inshallah, which meant, like, *whatever*. Jason smiled. The sound of wings was louder now, the fluttering of angels come to carry him home.

CHAPTER 1

Twenty-five years later

The second half of the Super Bowl began right after midday prayers. The fans in Khomeini Stadium had performed their ablutions by rote, awkwardly prostrating themselves, heels splayed, foreheads not even touching the ground. Only the security guard in the upper walkway had made his devotions with the proper respect. An older man, his face a mass of scar tissue, he had moved smoothly and precisely, fingers together, toes forward, pointing toward Mecca. The guard noticed Rakkim Epps watching him, stiffened, then spotted the Fedayeen ring on his finger and bowed, offered him a blessing, and Rakkim, who had not prayed in over three years, returned the blessing with the same sincerity. Not one in a thousand would have recognized the plain titanium band, but the guard was one of the early converts, the hard core who had risked everything and expected nothing other than Paradise in return. He wondered if the guard still thought the war had been worth it.

Rakkim looked past the guard as the faithful hurried back to their seats. Still no sign of Sarah. A few aisles over, he spotted Anthony Jr. making his way up the steps. The new orange Bedouins jacket he was wearing must have cost his father a week's salary. Anthony Sr. was too easy on him. It was always the way; the toughest cops were soft at the center.

From his vantage point, Rakkim could see domes and minarets dotting the surrounding hills, and the Space Needle lying crumpled in the distance, a military museum now. Downtown was a cluster of glass skyscrapers and residential high-rises topped with satellite dishes. To the south loomed the new Capitol, twice as large as the old one in Washington, D.C., and beside it the Grand Caliph Mosque, its blue-green mosaics gleaming. In the stands below, he saw the faithful stowing their disposable prayer rugs into the seat backs, and the Catholics pretending not to notice. He could see everything but Sarah. Another broken promise. The last chance she would get to play him for a fool. Which was just what he had told himself the last time she'd stood him up.

Thirty years old, average height, a little heavier than when he'd left the Fedayeen, but still lean and wiry. Rakkim's dark hair was cropped, his mustache and goatee trimmed, his features angular, almost Moorish, an advantage since the transition. Black skullcap. He turned up his collar against the Seattle damp, the wind off the Sound carrying the smell of dead fish from the oil spill last week. He felt the knife in his pocket, a carbon-polymer blade that wouldn't set off a metal detector, the same hard plastic in the toes of his boots.

Music blared as the cheerleaders strutted down the sidelines—all men, of course—knees high, swords flashing overhead. The Bedouins and the Warlords surged onto the field, and the crowd leaped up, cheering. Rakkim took one more look around for Sarah. He saw the security guard. Something had caught his attention. Rakkim followed the man's line of sight and started moving, *hurrying* now, taking the steps two at a time. He timed it perfectly, caught Anthony Jr. as he reached the deserted top level. There was an emergency exit here, a surveillance blind spot not on any of the public schematics—the kid was a lousy thief, but knowing about the exit said something for his planning.

"What are you doing, Rakkim?" Anthony Jr. squirmed, a muscular teenager in a hooded sweatshirt, all elbows and wounded pride. "Don't touch me."

"Bad boy," Rakkim rapped him on the nose with the wallet the kid had lifted. Anthony Jr. hadn't even felt Rakkim take it, patting his shirt to make sure it was gone. Rakkim rapped him again, harder. "If the cops arrest you, it's your father who's disgraced. The Black Robes snatch you, you'll lose a hand."

Anthony Jr. had his father's pugnacious jaw. "I want my money."

Rakkim grabbed him by the scruff of the neck and threw him toward the exit. When Rakkim turned around, the security guard with the ruined face was already there. Rakkim held out the wallet. "The young brother found this and didn't know where to return it. Perhaps you could turn it in for him."

"I saw him find the wallet. It had fallen into a merchant's pocket."

"The young brother must have good eyes to have seen it there," said Rakkim.

The security guard's face creased with amusement, and for

that instant he was handsome again. He took the wallet. "Go with God, Fedayeen."

"What other choice do we have?" Rakkim started back to his VIP box.

Anthony Colarusso *Sr.* didn't look up as Rakkim sat beside him. "I wondered if you were coming back." He guided yet another hot dog with everything on it into his mouth, relish and chopped onions falling into his lap.

"Somebody has to be here to Heimlich you."

Colarusso took another bite of his hot dog. He was a stocky, middle-aged detective with droopy eyes and a thunderous gut, piccalilli dripping from his hairy knuckles. The VIP sections in the stadium were reserved for local politicos, corporate sponsors, and upper-echelon military officers, with Fedayeen given preferential seating. A mere local cop, and a Catholic besides, Colarusso would never have gotten into restricted seating if he hadn't been Rakkim's guest.

The Bedouins' quarterback took the snap, backpedaling, the football cocked against his ear. He double-pumped, then let fly to his favorite receiver, a blur with hands the size of palm fronds. The pass floated against the clouds, and the receiver ran flat out, leaving his coverage behind. The ball grazed his outstretched fingertips, but he hung on, just as one of his cleats caught the turf and sent him face-first into grass. The ball dribbled free.

Boos echoed across the stadium. Rakkim looked back toward the mezzanine again. Still no sign of Sarah. He sat down. She wasn't coming. Not today, or any other day. He punched the empty seat in front of him, almost snapped it off its moorings.

"Didn't know you were such a Bedouins fan, troop," said Colarusso.

"Yeah . . . they're breaking my heart."

The receiver lay crumpled on the grass as the groans of the Bedouins fans echoed across the stadium. Rakkim even heard a few curses. A scrawny Black Robe in a nearby fundamentalist section glanced around, a deputy of the religious police with a tight black turban, his untrimmed beard a coarse bramble. The deputy shifted in his seat, robe rippling, trying to locate the offender. He reminded Rakkim of an enraged squid. The deputy's eyes narrowed at Colarusso and his mustard-stained gray suit.

"I think that eunuch's in love with you, Anthony."

Colarusso swiped at his mouth with a napkin. "Keep your voice down."

"It's a free country . . . isn't it, Officer?"

It still was. Most of the population was Muslim, but most of them were moderates and the even more secular moderns, counted among the faithful, but without the fervor of the fundamentalists. Though the hard-liners were a minority, their ruthless energy assured them political power far out of proportion to their numbers. Congress tried to placate them through increased budgets for mosques and religious schools, but the ayatollahs and their enforcers of public virtue, the Black Robes, were not satisfied.

The receiver slowly got up, blood pouring down his face. The stadium screen showed him coughing out a pink mist to thunderous applause.

"I remember when football helmets came with face guards," said Colarusso.

"Where's the honor in that?" said Rakkim. "A hard hit wouldn't even draw blood."

"Yeah, well . . . blood wasn't the point in the old days."

The deputy glared now at the moderates in the bleachers, young professionals in skirts and jeans, women and men seated together. The Black Robes had authority only over fundamentalists, but lately they had begun hectoring Catholics on the street, hurling stones at moderns for public displays of affection. Fundamentalists who left the fold were considered apostates—they risked disfigurement or death in the rural areas, and even in the more cosmopolitan cities their families ostracized them.

The Super Bowl blimp drifted above the stadium. Emblazoned on the airship was the flag of the Islamic States of America, identical to the banner of the old regime, except for the gold crescent replacing the stars. Rakkim followed the progress of the blimp as it slowly banked in the afternoon sun. In spite of the Black Robes, the sight of the flag still brought a lump to his throat.

"Look who's here," said Colarusso, pointing to a lavish VIP box filled with national politicians and movie stars and ayatollahs. "That's your old CO, isn't it?"

General Kidd, the Fedayeen commander, saluted the network camera and the home audience. An immigrant from Somalia, he was resplendent in his plain blue dress uniform, his expression stoic. Beside him was Mullah Oxley, the head of the Black Robes, his fingers bejeweled, his robe silk, his beard a nest of oily curls. A total swank motherfucker. They made an incongruous and unsettling couple. When Rakkim had retired three years ago, General Kidd would never have sat next to Oxley, or any politician save the president. The Fedayeen were independent, answerable only to their own leadership and the needs of the nation. Three years ago anyway.

"The general looks like a real whip-cracker to me." Colarusso put down the hot dog. "On my best day, young and hung, I wouldn't have lasted five minutes in your old outfit."

The Fedayeen were the elite troops of the Islamic Republic, used mostly on small unit, covert operations against the Bible Belt. The breakaway states of the old Confederacy had a sizable arsenal of nukes, and only the balance of terror kept the two nations from all-out war. Instead there was a constant, low-level conflict of probes and feints, deadly combat without quarter or complaint.

"Best of the best," continued Colarusso. "Heck, they wouldn't even let me in the door."

"What do you want, Anthony?"

Colarusso fidgeted. "Anthony Jr. wants to apply to the Fedayeen. He's nineteen, and all he talks about is the Fedayeen, and that killer-elite strut. He's at the gym now, working on his skills, instead of watching the game with his buddies. The boy is committed."

Rakkim stared at Colarusso. "Tell him to join the army. Even better, tell him to learn a trade. The country needs ironworkers more than it needs Fedayeen."

Colarusso flicked crumbs off his necktie. "My wife wanted me to ask you to put in a word for him. He's planning to convert, but a recommendation from you . . ."

"The standard enlistment is eight years. Thirty percent of those who make it through basic training don't survive long enough to re-up. Does Marie know that?"

"She knows what having a son in the Fedayeen will do for us," said Colarusso. "You've seen our daughters. They're not raving beauties, but if Anthony Jr. gets accepted, the girls won't have to settle for Catholic suitors, they'll have their pick of the litter."

General Kidd's face on the stadium screen loomed over the end zones. "Do your boy a favor. Tell Marie I don't have that kind of clout anymore."

"Decorated Fedayeen officer, retired with full honors . . . no way she buys that story."

"Then tell her the truth. Say that you asked and I refused."

Colarusso looked relieved. "Thanks. I had to try, but thanks."

"You should keep an eye on Anthony Jr. Make sure he doesn't have too much free time."

"He's a good kid, he's just got big dreams." Colarusso sipped his Jihad Cola, winced. "Just ain't the Super Bowl without a cold beer. *Real* beer."

"Gentlemen?" A doughy software entrepreneur seated in an adjacent corporate box leaned over. "If I may, I have a flask of vodka-infused fruit juice."

Colarusso belched, ignored him.

"Sir?" The entrepreneur showed Rakkim the neck of the flask, half pulling it from the inside pocket of his bright green jersey.

Rakkim waved him away. The entrepreneur was one of those moderns who wanted it both ways, wearing a sports jersey and khakis, but sporting an Arafat kaffiyeh to please the fundamentalists. Probably bought an instructional video to show him how to drape the checked head scarf, and still couldn't get it right.

The Warlords had lined up on the Bedouins' eighteen-yard line, players pawing at the turf, when the Bedouins called a time-out.

Rakkim stood up, stretched, took another look toward the mezzanine for Sarah. A *last* look. She wasn't there. Maybe her uncle had requested her presence at the last minute. Maybe her car had broken down on the way to the game, and she didn't want to call him, afraid her calls were monitored. Hey, maybe she *had* called him, but there were sunspots and the call didn't go through. Why not? It could happen. In an idiot's universe.

The Warlords quarterback went into his count. Rakkim looked away from the field, saw a couple of the deputy's morality police barging into one of the segregated sections. The Black Robes whipped their long, flexible canes across the backs of three women seated there, sending them sprawling, herding them up the aisles, the women covering themselves even as they tried to avoid the blows.

Rakkim was on his feet, shouting at the Black Robes, but the sound of his rage was lost in the crowd noise as the Warlords quarterback drove through the line for a touchdown. Rakkim was too far away to help the women, and even if he were closer, there was nothing he could do. An arrest for interfering with the religious authority was a serious offense. The women themselves would testify against him, would do it eagerly.

"Ugly business," said Colarusso, standing beside him.

No telling what the women's crime had been. They could

have shown too much ankle, or their head scarves might have slipped. Perhaps they were laughing too loudly. Rakkim sat down, still shaking with anger as the Black Robes swung their canes. This was the first time he had been at an internationally televised event where the Black Robes had so freely used their flails. Usually they were more concerned about appearances, but today they didn't seem to care. They were almost inviting the cameras.

The deputy a few rows ahead of Rakkim had also noticed the actions of his fellow Black Robes, the cleric's fingers wriggling with delight, keeping time to the lash. Rakkim stared at him so intently that the man must have felt the weight of his gaze and looked over at Rakkim. He inclined his head in acknowledgment, but Rakkim didn't respond, and the deputy turned away, touched his turban as if for protection.

"Risky behavior, troop." Colarusso rooted in his ear. "No sense making an enemy."

"Too late now."

Colarusso examined his finger. "Always a choice."

Rakkim watched the Black Robe. "Yeah, and I already made it."

CHAPTER 2

After late-evening prayers

They came for him just before midnight, Redbeard's men, two of them slipping into the Blue Moon club with the rest of the boozy Super Bowl revelers. Rakkim might have spotted them sooner but he was distracted, sprawled beside Mardi in her big bed, spent and lost in the aftermath. He watched the cigarette smoke drift against the ceiling and thought about Sarah.

"God, I needed that," said Mardi, her head propped on the

pillow. "Been a long time. A *long*, long time." She dragged on the cigarette, her eyes shiny in the candlelight. "I should have ordered more beer." She tapped ashes onto the floor. "I thought forty kegs would be enough."

Rakkim felt her heat where their bodies touched, the long border of their thighs. The breeze through the window stirred the smoke, chilled the sweat along his arms and legs, but he made no attempt to cover himself. Neither did she, the two of them prickling each other with goose bumps, hot and steamy and a million miles apart.

"You're quiet. Something happen at the game?" said Mardi.

"No."

She leaned over, breasts swaying, made the sign of the cross on his forehead with her thumb.

He rubbed away the sign, annoyed. He had told her that he didn't like her doing that, but it had only encouraged her.

Mardi kissed him, slipped out of bed. "I don't remember you being so angry. Not that I'm complaining. I appreciate an angry fuck. Do I have your little Muslim princess to thank?"

"Don't call her that." He watched her walk across the bedroom, push aside the curtains. She stood there overlooking the street, one hip cocked, defiant in her nudity. She was thirty-eight, hard and blond and wanton.

Music filtered through the floor from the club below . . . yet another cover version of one of Nirvana's grunge classics from fifty years ago. Mardi must have seen his expression. "You don't like the music? Enjoy it, Rakkim, that's the sound of money in our pockets."

"Is that what it is?"

"Tourists come to L.A. for chicken mole and mariachi. They come to Seattle for a tour of the Capitol building, a good cry at the Hall of Martyrs, and to listen to grunge."

Rakkim didn't want to argue. He was the minority partner in

the Blue Moon, but it wouldn't have mattered if he held the 80 percent share, and she had 20. Mardi knew what she was doing. She knew the proper configuration of the dance floor to insure maximum profits, and who had the best wholesale prices for beer and khat infusion. She knew whom to hire and whom to fire. Mardi needed Rakkim for his underground contacts and to keep things smooth with the police and protection gangs, but she could have paid him a straight fee for much less than cutting him in for a percentage. An interesting oversight for someone focused on the bottom line.

Rakkim checked the wall of security screens opposite the bed, watched the revelers packed in below. The club was busy most nights, but after a Super Bowl every hot spot in the Zone jumped, the sidewalks filled with revelers in various stages of euphoria. The dining room had a two hour waiting list, the dance floor was shoulder to shoulder, and the bar stacked three-deep with rowdy Warlords fans.

The Blue Moon was located in the Zone, officially called the Christian Quarter, a thirty- or forty-block section of the city where nightclubs and coffeehouses flourished, where cybergame parlors and movie theaters operated largely free of censorship. The Zone was loud and raucous, the streets littered, the buildings marred by graffiti, a morals-free fire area open to everyone — Christian, Muslim, modern, tech, freak, whomever or whatever. Untamed, innovative, and off-the-books, the Zone celebrated dangerous pursuits.

Every major city had an area like the Zone, a safety valve for a population whose previous cultural tradition had been based on extreme notions of freedom, and individuality. The police rotated their uniformed officers out of the Zone after two years, hoping to minimize corruption, but two years was usually enough for beat cops to buy vacation homes in Canada or Hawaii, safe from the prying eyes of Internal Affairs.

Mardi stood at the open window, and the cool breeze blew

the curtains against her. The sound of rain filled the room. Still slick with sweat, her body glistened in the red neon glow from outside. She swayed to the music and the rainstorm, and he could see her nipples harden in the soft red light. It made him think of Sarah.

He had stopped seeing Mardi when Sarah had first contacted him a year and a half ago. Now that Sarah and he were over, he had gone running back. Cowardice and resentment, a lethal combination. He was glad he couldn't see his own face. He would have cut his throat. Taking Mardi to bed . . . letting her take him . . . either way, it had been a mistake. He watched her dance, hair lank around her shoulders, and he wondered where Sarah was, and what she was doing, why she hadn't shown up today.

"I miss him," Mardi said softly.

Rakkim didn't need to ask whom she was talking about. "So do I."

"You remind me of him. Not in looks . . . it's the confidence. Self-assurance . . . it was like a scent he gave off." The wind whipped the curtains, rain splattering the floor, but she didn't move. "Most men spend their whole life afraid, but not him. Not you either."

Mardi always talked about Tariq afterward. Sometimes she talked about the first time they had met, or the last time they had been together, but Tariq was always part of their intimate moments. As though she was trying to explain to herself why she had just made love to his best friend. It didn't bother Rakkim. They were both standing in for someone else, someone better than whom they were with, someone out of reach.

"I cost him a promotion." The curtains billowed around her. "I wouldn't convert. He was told to divorce me, marry a Muslim girl . . . but he wouldn't." She shook her head. "I should have converted." Her laugh was hollow. "It's not as if I'm a good Catholic."

"A promotion wouldn't have saved him."

"He would have been a staff officer, safe behind the lines. He would have—"

"He was a warrior. He died the way he wanted to. He just died too soon."

"You're a warrior—"

"Not anymore."

"No, that's right. You were always smarter than he was. He was braver, but you were smarter." Her face was stretched tight as she turned to him. "I wish it had been you," she whispered. The breeze blew the candles, sent shadows scurrying across the walls. "I wish it had been you who had gotten killed."

"I know."

"You should get married," she said.

"You should get married."

She fumbled for her pack of cigarettes, hastily lit another one. The ancient Zippo snapped shut. Tariq's lighter. "I *am* married."

Rakkim didn't mind the smoke; it seemed to calm her, the routine as much as the nicotine, the slow, steady inhalations and exhalations, the glowing ember at the tip, a beacon in the darkness. He didn't even mind the smell. The raw Turkish tobacco was more acrid than that from the old days, but Virginia and the Carolinas were part of the breakaway Bible Belt, and the embargo was still in effect.

"My grocer was beaten by the Black Robes yesterday," Mardi said, dragging on the cigarette. She must have been waiting for the right moment. "They were waiting for him outside his shop when he arrived before dawn. They broke him up, broke up his store too. He had converted, of course, converted right after the transition. He was just a child but he knew what was good for him. Conversion was good enough before, but not anymore. Now he's just a Jew." Another drag. "I've been buying fruits and vegetables from him for as long as I can remember. He taught me how to tell when a pineapple is ripe. Funny the things you remember." She stubbed the cigarette out.

Rakkim didn't respond. He knew what was coming.

Redbeard had done many terrible things as chief of State Security, but in the early years of the republic, he had insisted that any Jews who converted to Islam must be spared. Though Zionists had been blamed for the assassination of his brother, he refused to initiate a pogrom, had instead cited verses in the Holy Qur'an that said converts were to be welcomed, and none of the Black Robes or politicians had the will to overrule him. Redbeard had been able to insure the lives of the converts, but no one had been able to insure their treatment. Now, things were getting worse.

"Can you help them, Rakkim? The grocer and his family . . . they have to get out."

One of the surveillance screens showed four women seated in one of the side booths of the dining area. College students probably, keeping their purses close, nursing their brightly colored frothies. Each wore a tiny hajib on her head, the latest style among freethinking Muslim women. A head covering in name only.

"The passes are snowed in," said Rakkim. "The southern routes have roadblocks."

"They'll take the chance."

"I won't."

Mardi crossed her arms across her breasts.

"Tell the grocer when the spring thaw hits, we'll go," said Rakkim. "The border patrols will be in their bivouacs, too worried about avalanches to venture out."

"Thank you."

The college girls kept glancing over at the nearby clusters of young men, but didn't accept their offered drinks. They were just dipping a toe into the alluring nastiness of the Zone, the four of them beautiful in their innocence. Enjoy yourselves, ladies, enjoy the visit to the monkey house and take back some tales to the dorm. Let the memory bring a flush to your necks for years to come. There were plenty of other clubs in the Zone, meat racks and psychedelic joints without bodyguards or bouncers, but Rakkim imposed his own rules on the clientele. No narcotics, no fights, no rape rooms. He knew what the human animal was capable of. Pleasure worked best on a leash.

"Mardi . . . what happened tonight was wrong."

She laughed. "That's why it felt so good."

"It won't happen again."

"I'll survive." Mardi's mouth tightened. "You're a romantic, Rakkim, that's your problem."

"I'll add that to the list." Rakkim started to get dressed, then stopped, staring at the surveillance screen. Nothing specific gave the two of them away; they were well trained. Both were medium height, with modified blockhead haircuts and earrings. Total moderns. One wore a Warlords jersey like half the other men in the place, the other had on one of those flex-metal jackets popular with the high-tech types. Just a couple of guys out on the town, looking for action at the Blue Moon club. Like the neon sign over the bar asked: *R U Having Fun Yet?*

They were State Security though. There was an aspect to their posture, a certain arrogance. Small giveaways, but enough. Redbeard, the head of State Security, had trained Rakkim himself. Raised him from the age of nine, schooled him and tested him constantly. They never walked through a crowd that Redbeard hadn't kept up a quiet commentary, teaching Rakkim to read a face and a gesture, to learn from a hastily knotted necktie or the wrong shoes. Redbeard had been furious when Rakkim had joined the Fedayeen instead of State Security, but in time he'd accepted the rejection. What he could not forgive was Rakkim and his niece, Sarah, falling in love.

"What's wrong?" asked Mardi.

Rakkim pointed at the screen. "Those two . . . they're State Security."

"*Here?*" She squinted at the screen. "You're sure?"

"Redbeard sent them." Rakkim watched the agents at the bar. "See how their bodies move?"

"No."

"They're mimicking the flow of the room. They don't even know it. It's called *active observation*." Rakkim was used to official attention; everyone from local cops to liberal clerics to small-time politicos ended up at the Blue Moon sooner or later. Not State Security. State Security didn't ask, didn't bargain, and didn't give warnings. These two were here for a pickup. He scanned the screens, looking for other agents. There had to be more. "Don't worry, they're here for me."

"I thought you and Redbeard weren't speaking."

"I guess he decided to change the rules."

The band finished the song, the dancers clinging to each other in the red and yellow houselights. The lead singer toasted the crowd with a flute of khat champagne, finished it in one long swallow, and threw the empty glass onto the floor. Her fans followed suit. Mardi was going to have to bump up the price to maintain a profit. A spotlight drifted across the crowd and Rakkim tapped the screen with a forefinger. "*There* you are."

Another agent leaned against the back wall, watching the dancers. Rakkim had only glimpsed him for a moment in the spotlight, but it was long enough. The third agent was a slim, pockmarked dandy in red toreador pants, with a cruel face and a pencil mustache. The dandy would have come in earlier; he would have checked out the basement, ambled into the back rooms, pretending to be lost. Now he was waiting for Rakkim to show himself, or try to escape.

"Slip out my private exit," said Mardi. "I'll tell Redbeard's men that I haven't seen you."

Maybe that's why Sarah hadn't met him at the Super Bowl this afternoon. It was almost a relief to think that it was *Redbeard* who had stopped her, not her better judgment. He wasn't worried about

Sarah. Redbeard would be angry with her for disobeying him, but his anger would only go so far. Rakkim had no illusions about his own privileged status. He might call Redbeard his uncle, but that was only a sign of respect. Sarah was the daughter of Redbeard's only brother. She was *blood*, Rakkim was not. He considered taking Mardi's offer; there were a dozen places he could hide in the Zone without fear of being found. He could meet Redbeard at a time of his choosing.

The houselights came up. The pockmarked dandy watched a pretty girl walking across the room. He looked up suddenly, stared at the hidden security camera.

"Get out of here," said Mardi.

Rakkim thought of Sarah. No telling the things Redbeard was saying to her. He headed for the door.

CHAPTER 3

After late-evening prayers

Rakkim removed his shoes, then washed his hands in the lightly scented water of the fountain. He splashed his face, ran his wet fingers through his hair. When he turned, Angelina was there with a towel. He kissed her on both cheeks. "Salaam alaikum."

"Allah Akbar." Redbeard's housekeeper was a short, older woman, her broad face framed by the headpiece of the black chador, the loose robe that fell almost to the floor. It was almost 2 a.m., but Angelina was wide-awake. When he had had nightmares as a child, she had been the one to comfort him, crooning lullabies until his eyes closed. He had grown up believing that she never slept. Twenty years later and he still wasn't sure.

Like Redbeard, Angelina was a devout, moderate Muslim.

She could drive, had gone to a secular school, and had her own bank account. She said her prayers five times a day, kept the dietary law, and dressed modestly. She fasted during Ramadan, donated 2.5 percent of her total worth to charity each year, and someday, *someday*, she was going to make the pilgrimage to Mecca, the hajj that all good Muslims were required to do at least once in their lifetime.

Angelina gently touched the side of his head where the hair had been singed by the pockmarked dandy's stun gun. "We've missed you, Rikki."

He smiled. "Speak for yourself."

"We've *all* missed you."

"How's Sarah? Is she all right?"

Angelina embraced him, robe rustling, and he smelled the spices that clung to her, garlic and cinnamon and sweet basil, cooking smells from childhood. "Worry about *yourself.*"

He kissed her again, then started toward Redbeard's office. When he looked back, she was watching him, hands clutched.

The drive from the Zone to Redbeard's villa had taken forty-five minutes, Rakkim in the back of the ambulance the security agents were using to transport him, siren wailing. The two subordinate agents sat in the front, nursing their wounds, while Stevens, the pockmarked dandy, slouched on the bench seat across from Rakkim, flicking his stun gun off and on. The smell of ozone filled the air. He tried to smile at Rakkim, but his split lip and bloody nose made it painful. Rakkim had smiled for the both of them.

Rakkim knocked twice on the office door, waited, then let himself in. The office was as he remembered: a wood-paneled, windowless room containing a large walnut desk and chair, two computers, a phone bank knobbed with privacy guards, and a leather sofa on which no one had ever sat. Rough, goat-wool tribal prayer rugs from Afghanistan and Pakistan covered the floor, Redbeard preferring their muted natural dyes. A door on one side of the office led out to the water garden. Another led down to the bomb shelter.

No paintings were on the walls, no honoraries, no photos of Redbeard with presidents or ayatollahs. Just a map of North America and three aerial-surveillance photographs taken immediately after May 19, 2015.

Rakkim stared at the stark, black-and-white wreckage of New York City and Washington, D.C., trying to take in the miles of shattered concrete and twisted metal, but it was impossible. The photo from ground zero at Mecca was less dramatic, but equally devastating. The nuclear bombs that had been smuggled into New York and Washington, D.C., had been city busters, but Mecca had better security. The device detonated at the height of the hajj had been a suitcase nuke, a dirty bomb. Over a hundred thousand who had made the pilgrimage died later of plutonium poisoning, but the city itself was intact. The Great Mosque could clearly be seen in the photograph, surrounded by worshipers who refused to leave. Though the city remained radioactive, the faithful still came every year to fulfill their obligations. Rakkim wiped away tears, embarrassed, certain there were cameras in the room and that Redbeard was watching.

At first, the U.S. media blamed jihadis for the attacks, Muslim radicals who had never forgiven the Saudis for their rapprochement with the West. The ruse might have succeeded, but a week later, the FBI captured one of the Zionist conspirators who was truly responsible, and he led them to the others involved in the plot. Their confessions were broadcast internationally. The United States immediately withdrew the defense umbrella that had helped protect Israel since its creation, and within a month the Zionist state was overrun by a Euro-Arabic coalition. Only the offer of sanctuary by Russia saved the Zionists from extinction.

The map of North America showed the same configuration as in the textbooks Rakkim had studied in school—the Islamic

Republic outlined in green, the Bible Belt in red. The red states included all of the old Confederacy, plus Oklahoma, Northern Florida, and parts of Missouri. Missouri had been a trick question on his final exam in history. The map showed Kentucky and West Virginia as red states, but they were still being contested on the ground. The Nevada Free State was white, denoting its unique and independent status. Southern California, Arizona, and New Mexico were green states politically, part of the Islamic Republic, but socially they were extensions of the Mexican Empire.

Rakkim walked to Redbeard's desk and picked up the book left open on the desk, wondering if it was a test or a trap that Redbeard had set out for him. *How the West Was Really Won: The Creation of the Islamic States of America through the Conquest of Popular Culture.* The book had originally been Sarah's Ph.D. thesis, rewritten and published for a mass audience two years ago. It became a bestseller, but her premise was so controversial that the publisher had been wise not to use Sarah's photograph on the jacket—even today, she wasn't recognized on the street.

Historians had debated the transformation of the former United States into an Islamic republic ever since President-elect Damon Kingsley had taken the oath of office with one hand on the Holy Qur'an. Most historians credited the will of Allah, noting that the persistent malaise post-Iraq, and the continuing threat of terrorist attacks, had left the nation ripe for a spiritual awakening. The Zionist Betrayal was the final blow, collapsing the economy and bringing on a declaration of martial law. In the midst of such chaos, the moral certainty of Islam was the perfect antidote to the empty bromides of the churches, and the corruption of the political class. After losing a disputed national election, vast numbers of disaffected Christians migrated to the Bible Belt and declared their independence. In a stroke of political brilliance, the remaining Christians, mostly Catholics, were granted almost equal citizenship with the Muslim majority in the new Islamic Republic. The nation held together.

While recognizing the spiritual dimension of the regime change, Sarah's book had argued that the transformation had been more calculated, initiated by decades of Saudi stipends to American decision makers, and, even more important, a series of high-profile public conversions. Sarah had cited a Best Actress winner who'd shared her newfound faith during her acceptance speech at the Oscars, and a country music star praising Allah at the Grand Ole Opry, for starting a cascade effect that had led to millions of new converts within weeks. The ayatollahs had been furious at her interpretation of history, calling her book blasphemous, but Redbeard had intervened, and the fundamentalists had backed down, issuing a statement that called it "a deeply flawed work of honest intent."

Rakkim thumbed through the pages, finally found her author's note.

I expected neither the degree of success nor of the criticism the prepublication copies of *How the West Was Really Won* engendered. Traditional historians and clerics have charged that my book gave undue weight to shallow secular events and deemphasized the role of divine intervention. The attacks quickly turned personal. I have been accused of trading on my family name. Of being the cat's-paw of my uncle, who was supposedly using me to rewrite history and undercut his political opponents. I have been accused of being a woman, and a *modern* woman at that, doubly unworthy to speak to issues of such importance.

To those who say that my research gives undue weight to secular interpretations of history, I say perhaps Allah, the all-knowing, chooses to unfold his plan within the mundane sphere. To my critics who charge me with nepotism and naïveté, I say that my uncle, the esteemed Redbeard, needs no cat's-paw, nor would I allow myself to be used in such a manner. To those who accuse me of being a modern woman . . . I plead guilty, without excuse or apology.

Rakkim set the book back down on the desk. He loved Sarah's ferocity, but he wasn't sure if he agreed with her premise. He placed more trust in force of arms than movie stars and religious groupies, and the book tended to gloss over the nuclear attack and the social devastation afterward.

He stared at the photograph of New York, drawn to the gray stumps of buildings that dotted the dead city. A boneyard of dreams. His mother had been in New York that day on a business trip, though whether she had died from the bomb blast itself or the fires and panic that engulfed the city afterward, he never knew. Only four at the time, he barely remembered her. He had clearer memories of his father, mostly of the man's anger and frustration, the temper that had gotten him killed three years after the attack, when food was still scarce and opinions were strong. They had been waiting in a soup line, his father holding his hand, telling him to quit fidgeting, *damnit*. A man cut ahead and his father had spoken up, the argument escalating rapidly. Rakkim wasn't even aware of the screwdriver shoved between his father's ribs until he felt his father's hand soften and slip from his grasp. He stood there, alone, while the line moved forward without him. Two year later he saw Redbeard walking down the street, and—

"Am I interrupting, boy?"

Rakkim turned at the familiar, gruff voice.

Redbeard fixed him from the middle of the office, a powerfully built man in his early sixties, his square face deeply lined, seamed to the bone. His reddish blond hair was cut short, his ears flat against his skull, and though his beard was shot with gray now, his blue eyes still burned. A tiny patch at the center of his forehead was callused from years of prayer. He wore a gray cotton sweat suit, looking like the athlete he had been. A former college wrestler, a champion if the biographies could be believed, he retained the thick neck and aggressive intimacy of the sport. Rakkim had often seen him unnerve his political opponents by invading their personal space, an arm casually dropped around their shoulders, intimidating them by the weight of his flesh.

"Uncle." Rakkim fell to one knee.

"Don't call me that . . . and get up, you're not fooling anyone." Redbeard looked him over. "You appear healthy. Wasting your life evidently agrees with you."

Rakkim stood, waiting.

"Two of my agents were limping when they escorted you inside."

"Perhaps their shoes were too tight."

"Stevens has a broken nose. Was his *face* too tight?"

"I refrained from killing them, but I couldn't go quietly. I didn't want to disappoint you."

"Too late for that."

Rakkim kept his head high, but the words stung.

Redbeard leaned forward slightly, and for an instant Rakkim actually thought he was going to apologize. "Are you about to cry, Rakkim?"

"Not if you were to tear my eyes out, Uncle."

Redbeard laughed. Rakkim didn't share the laughter, but Redbeard didn't seem to mind. "You can keep your eyes." He opened the door to the water garden. "We'll talk in here."

Rakkim hesitated, then stepped inside. His shirt stuck to him in the steamy interior, but Redbeard beamed in the moist air, completely comfortable in spite of his heavy clothes.

The water garden was a domed tropical enclave, a half-acre

dense with rubber trees and cloying oleander, lush with bulbous creepers and pink hibiscus. Condensation ran down the glass walls, dripped from overhead as Rakkim followed Redbeard deeper into the green world. Vines and palm fronds brushed against their faces as they padded down the narrow path that wound through the garden. Lit only by moonlight and dim yellow lamps, it was a place of shadows.

Tiny, white snowflake orchids peeked from the foliage as they passed, swaying from their movements. Rock waterfalls, half-hidden misting units, and a shallow brook created a constant echo. No passive or active listening device, no laser microphone, could screen out a human voice from the ambient noise. The tungsten-dusted dome prevented satellite inspections and insulated the plants against cold fronts. The water garden was safe and serene and harmonious, the essence of Paradise to the desert dwellers to whom Allah had first revealed his truth. Redbeard supposedly spent his time here meditating, but Rakkim knew he conducted other business in the garden.

Redbeard clapped Rakkim on the shoulder, kneading the muscles up to and over the pain threshold. "Do you remember the first time I brought you here?"

"It was the day you told me I could stay. That I could live with you and Sarah." Rakkim watched Redbeard's face when he said her name. Redbeard didn't react, but his fingers tightened slightly on Rakkim's shoulders before releasing him, and Rakkim was certain now that Sarah was the reason he had been summoned here tonight. He wondered how long Redbeard had known that they were lovers. Whether he had just found out, or if he had known for months, waiting to see how their affair would progress, weighing the pros and cons of silence.

"What are you thinking about?" asked Redbeard.

"I'm remembering the day we met."

Rakkim had been dressed as a religious student that morning, a schoolboy in a white jerkin, when he'd spotted Redbeard bustling down Pine Street. He knew from the way people scuttled out of his path that Redbeard was a man of importance, but Rakkim had held his ground, the Holy Qur'an clutched to his bosom, lips moving rapidly as he recited the verses he had memorized. Redbeard had stopped, questioned him on some point of Qur'anic law, and not getting the response he wanted, had cuffed Rakkim aside. Rakkim used the blow to pluck Redbeard's wallet, backed away, sniffling phony tears. He almost made it into the alley before Redbeard grabbed him, shook him so hard his teeth rattled.

"See this one?" Redbeard pointed at a tiny frog perched on a blade of grass, the frog almost translucent in the pale light, its throat thrumming with every breath. "His species lives on condensation and algae. The invisible thriving on the ineffable. I treasure his kind—life at the margins of existence shows us the mercy of Allah." He looked up at Rakkim. "That day we met, I saw a skinny thief with steady eyes, a boy who did not shrink from my grasp or beg to be released, but fought until he was exhausted." He smiled. "You were lucky my curiosity was greater than my sense of justice."

"I thought you were going to take me to the children's prison. If I had known who you were, I would have been even more frightened to remain in your company."

Redbeard watched the frog, fascinated, as though he had never seen one before.

"Then I met Angelina and I wasn't afraid anymore." Rakkim knelt beside him, watching the frog breathe, its green skin glistening. "I told myself that if she could survive your foul nature, so could I."

"She spoiled you. She barely left the kitchen that first week, turning out omelets and steaks and fried potatoes—to this day, I never saw anyone eat like you." The frog hopped away, finding refuge in the deeper grasses closer to the creek. "I told her you were a thief, but she just kept cooking, said in the eyes of Allah we were all thieves. I warned her not to get her hopes up, that I wasn't sure you were going to be staying, but she knew that I had already decided."

"So did I. I didn't understand it then, but I was just what you were looking for."

"I thought so anyway." Redbeard raked a hand through his beard. "I never married. I had enough work, more than enough, but a son . . . I always thought a son would be a good thing. A son to stand beside me, a son to carry on afterwards." In the heart of the water garden, a bird cried out, and Redbeard stood up, moving slower than Rakkim expected. "It was a vain and foolish wish."

"Do you regret bringing me home that day?"

"What does it matter now?"

"It matters to me."

"Regrets are for poets and women," said Redbeard.

"It was my fault," said Rakkim, tired of the pretense, the *game*, always the game, a game in which Redbeard got to make the rules. "The Super Bowl was my idea. No matter what Sarah told you, it was *my* idea."

"Spare me the chivalry, Sarah has been ungovernable since she was born." Redbeard wrinkled his brow. "What *about* the Super Bowl?"

Rakkim remained wary. An admission of guilt was never the last word for Redbeard, it was merely a beginning. Each thread had to be followed until all involved were snared, all named, so that new threads could be unraveled and followed in their turn. "Sarah and I were supposed to meet at the Super Bowl. Isn't that why you brought me here?"

"I *wish* it was just a matter of you two disobeying me." Redbeard seemed to lose his balance for an instant, but quickly recovered. "I need your help. Sarah . . . Sarah's gone."

CHAPTER 4

After late-evening prayers

The Wise Old One watched his aide prostrate himself against the carpet, and he couldn't remember the boy's name. *John*, that was it. Named after the prophet that the Christians called John the Baptist. The one who had announced the coming of the Jesus. John, yes, that was the name of this youngster slowly getting to his feet. A popular name. So many aides now, so many more over the years, it was hard to remember all of them. The Old One's birth name was Hassan Muhammad, but he hadn't been called that in many years. The sound of his own name would be foreign to him now, even if there had been someone present who remembered it.

"Redbeard has brought in his nephew," said the aide, his voice soft and uninflected, as though passion would hurt the Old One's ears. So many fools who confused age with weakness.

"His name is Rakkim and he is no nephew," chided the Old One. "He is a pawn raised by Redbeard to be a knight."

The aide pressed himself against the carpet, a sallow intellectual with a scruff of blond beard. His white tunic and baggy trousers were supposed to imply purity, but to the Old One they revealed only a bland adherence to form. In time the boy would learn that though the Old One valued devotion, he valued intelligence even more. Devotion alone limited the ways a tool could be used.

The Old One sat on an embroidered yellow love seat, arms casually spread across the back. His beard neatly groomed, his long, thinning white hair combed straight back as in his youth, the regal elegance of a vain man whose vanity had only grown with time. He crossed his bony shanks, admiring the sharp crease in his cuffs. Many of his aides preferred robes and tunics and slippers, but he preferred suits from Barrons Ltd., and supple, black tassel loafers, a remnant of his British education. The English were a wan and bloodless race, but their tailors were still the best in the world. Today's suit was a dark blue, double-breasted, and a custom, ivory dress shirt with a regimental tie. Windsor knot, of course, and lapis lazuli cuff links. He examined his manicure, then peered down from the dais. "How fresh is this news about Rakkim?"

"We believe he is still at Redbeard's villa," said the aide, still on his belly.

"You *believe*?"

"Yes . . . yes, Mahdi."

Mahdi. His aides had called him that more often lately. The Mahdi was the awaited one, the enlightened one written of in the scriptures. A messianic figure prophesied to appear at the end of time, when Muslims were most in peril. Destined to unite the believers, the Mahdi would lead them to a great victory over the infidels and usher in an era of peace and justice. A one-world caliphate. The first time the Old One had been called Mahdi, he had been annoyed, feeling it was presumptuous, and there had been others thought to be the enlightened one, bumblers like Osama, who had not lived up to the calling. Now . . . the Old One decided that he would leave his naming, as all things, to Allah.

"In deepest secrecy, Redbeard sent a mission into the outskirts of the city earlier tonight," hurried the aide. "Our brothers followed them, but it was a ruse. While we gave chase, a trio of Redbeard's agents stole into the Zone and brought Rakkim to the villa in an ambulance, sirens howling. Redbeard often has ambulances visit, so that we never know his true medical condition."

The Old One rolled his eyes. He did not need this wispy-bearded youth to muddle through Redbeard's strategy for him.

"The deception failed," said the aide.

"The deception didn't fail, otherwise you would *know* whether Rakkim was still at the villa," corrected the Old One. "Who alerted you that Rakkim had been picked up?"

"We . . . we got a phone call from one of our sympathizers in the Zone." The aide's lower lip quivered. "It . . . it took some time for the call to be made, and for the information to be forwarded."

"So we got lucky." The Old One smiled. "Don't look so frightened, I've been lucky all my life, thanks be to Allah." He admired his reflection in the shine of his right shoe. "Still, don't you think we should have had a brother watching Rakkim, rather than depend on the beneficence of God?"

"We did not consider that Redbeard might reach out to him. The two of them have had no contact for years. Rakkim is a renegade who makes no attempt at concealment. He goes about his business—"

"How would *you* know what his business was? Rakkim was schooled in deception by Redbeard himself." The Old One waved the aide away, watched him back out the door of the penthouse. The Old One plucked a speck of lint off his trousers. "Well, now we know."

"Yes, Father, now we know," said his chief counselor—Ibrahim, his oldest son. Oldest surviving son. A tall, slender Arab with a short beard; his skin was darker than his father's, but he was dressed like his father in Western business attire. Fifty-three years old, with a high forehead and dark, hooded eyes, he could have been an academic. In fact, Ibrahim held doctorates in mathematics and international finance, but he had personally killed five people, one a younger sibling with a habit of bragging to blue-eyed rent-wives when he had too much to drink.

"When the girl Sarah disappeared, I hoped she had truly left on sabbatical, but if Redbeard has called in Rakkim, she didn't disappear, she escaped. From Redbeard and from us." The Old

One sighed. "You were right, my son. We should have acted sooner. I should have grabbed her up as soon as we learned of this new book she was writing."

"It is done, Father. Inshallah."

"I should have taken her, just as you advised. Now she is gone and we are vulnerable."

"Knowing the truth is one thing, but proving it is another," said Ibrahim. "If the girl had evidence, the book would have already been written, and the world turned against us. Yet here we are, alive and well—we just have to find her, and the threat will be ended."

The Old One tapped his lip with a forefinger, pleased with his son's spirited response. Over the long years he had groomed four of his sons as potential successors—two had been killed doing the great work, another had proven to be a moral traitor. Only Ibrahim was left. There were younger sons, most of them promising, but none of them capable of assuming the task he had set for himself. He thought of all the things he had done to reach this point, all that he had given up, given up gladly to be sure, but when he had started on this path, he had never dreamed that he might not complete the mission himself.

"Father?"

"Finding Redbeard's niece is only part of our task. As important as she is, the evidence she seeks is even more valuable. We find that, and we end the threat once and for all."

"What if there's no evidence to be found? After all this time, *surely* it would have already been presented."

"Perhaps the time was not right before." The Old One smoothed his necktie, his stomach churning. His digestion had been foul this whole last year as he readied the final stages of his plan. "Twenty years of planning, and now, to be so close . . ." His face darkened and he tasted bile at the back of his throat. "Twenty years and this *bitch* jeopardizes everything."

"We'll find her, Father."

"Your confidence is laudable. Tell me, though, Ibrahim, do you have even a *hint* of where the girl might have gone?"

"The girl . . . she is extremely cautious."

The Old One fixed his son with a stare that had withered lesser men.

Ibrahim inclined his head. "I have no idea where she is, Father."

The Old One looked past his son. They didn't know where Sarah had gone, or even how much she really knew. All they had was a disturbing record of the books she had accessed from the university library, and a single faint impression left on a notepad, a working title for her next book, *The Zionist Betrayal?* That question mark had made all the difference.

A brother working as a janitor in the History Department had found the notepad and brought it directly to him. *More* luck. Without that scrap of paper . . . The Old One felt his stomach lurch again. The brother who found the notepad didn't know what the faint impression meant, but the Old One had him executed anyway. He remembered the brother's willing compliance, praising the Old One even as he bent his head for the blade. The Old One felt a flutter of anger at the memory, the waste of it, and his anger made him feel young, young enough to blow up the world for the chance to remake it in his own image. Blow it up *again*. If he could have killed the book by killing the girl, he would have strangled her himself.

"Redbeard is no better off than we are, Father. He can't find her either. If Rakkim were to have an accident leaving the villa, we will be the only ones looking for her."

The Old One glared at him. "No *accidents*. Not only do I doubt your men capable of murdering Rakkim, but any simpleton could see that we need him alive."

Ibrahim moistened his lips.

"Redbeard thought enough of Rakkim to use him as his blood-hound," explained the Old One. "Well, we shall use him too. I just pray he is as skillful as Redbeard thinks he is." He stood up and walked to the panoramic window behind him. "Join me."

Ibrahim quickly complied, standing a half step behind him.

Spread out below them, the lights of the Las Vegas Strip pulsed with light: blue and green and red strobes on the hotel marquees, arcs of incandescent color, and spotlights bouncing off the sky in a prayer to the gods of greed. The Old One's redoubt was on the top ten floors of the ninety-story high-rise dubbed Colossus by the newspapers, but the name on the deed was the International Trust Services building. Banks and brokerages dominated the floors below, insurance and health care conglomerates, these great marbled institutions grown fat on interest and usury, the very ravening heart of the beast. The Old One never grew tired of the view.

Caught between the Islamic States of America and the Bible Belt, Las Vegas was a geopolitical anomaly, an independent and neutral territory that functioned as a broker between the two nations. With a population of over 14 million and still growing, Las Vegas was the information and financial hub of the continent, beyond doctrine or politics, a useful evil. It suited the Old One's needs perfectly. With no allegiance to any nation or government, faithful only to his divine mission, the Old One had been ensconced in Colossus for the last twenty years, invisible to his enemies, able to operate with impunity. He had overseen the construction of the building, placing numerous safeguards inside the walls and floors and ceilings. It had been his private joke to lease the lower floors to the very moneylenders that were anathema to honorable Muslims. It was camouflage and a sweet irony; a perpetual reminder of the lengths required to fulfill his destiny.

"We must keep track of Rakkim," said the Old One. His right index finger directed the play of colored lights on the Strip as though conducting a symphony, as though the city itself were under his dominion. "*He'll* lead us to the girl, and once we have the girl . . . well, then, Allah willing, we'll find out where the idea for this book came from. She didn't come up with this on her own."

"I'll put a team of our most reliable brothers on Rakkim," Ibrahim assured him. "If he eats a piece of rye toast, and a crumb falls from his lips, you'll know of it. "

"If a crumb fell from his lips, it would be because he knew he was being watched." The Old One followed a helicopter that soared silently over the great black pyramid of the Luxor hotel, tiny blue lights flickering on its fuselage. Helicopters had seemed like dragonflies in his youth, before he knew of their rocketry. They seemed like dragonflies again. "No, I will contact our friend, instead. He is more suitable for the task at hand."

Ibrahim winced. "Darwin can't be trusted."

"Of course he can't. The best always have their own agenda."

"He is a demon, Father."

"Yes, he is. A demon, a devil, a djinn . . . but, Darwin is the only one who can shadow Rakkim. When Rakkim finds the girl, Darwin will be watching. If they locate the evidence they seek, Darwin will be there too." The Old One flicked his fingers at his son. "Now go, I will spare you the ordeal and speak with him myself."

Ibrahim quickly backed away and closed the doors behind him.

Cars made their way slowly through the crowded streets below. The Old One imagined horns blaring, but the thick glass was soundproof. He thought of this boy Rakkim, this street rat grown to manhood now, Redbeard's own creation. He wished he knew more about him. He had read Rakkim's file, of course, but was unsure of how much to believe. Fedayeen files were top secret and notoriously unreliable, used for disinformation purposes as often as not. He wasn't even sure of the boy's real name. Redbeard valued him, that's all that was important.

Redbeard and his older brother, James, had been thorns in the Old One's side since the very founding of the Islamic Republic. James Dougan had been the first director of State Security, Redbeard his second-in-command. James had been the charismatic head of the agency, but Redbeard had provided the steel. At the chosen moment, the Old One had attempted to assassinate both of them, leaving his own mole, the number three man at the agency, to take charge. The attack had been only partially successful. James had died, but Redbeard, though shot several times, had clung to life, fighting off death as though hell awaited him. Stitched together like a stuffed bear, Redbeard had immediately assumed control of State Security.

Within days, Redbeard had ordered the execution of dozens of his own agents, the first of whom was the Old One's mole. Over a hundred police and Fedayeen had also been executed, and even Black Robes had disappeared and never been seen again. Most of them were innocent of anything but the most tangential involvement in the attack, but forty-three of the dead were the Old One's loyal followers. Two of his most trusted aides had been captured, men who had served him for decades. Had they not immediately committed suicide, the Old One himself might have been taken.

Redbeard's brutality had set the Old One's plans back years, and now the niece was threatening everything he had worked for. Truly there was something in that family, some dark seed sent by the devil himself to thwart his noble intentions. After the niece was brought down, incinerated with this new book of hers, then the Old One would send Darwin after Redbeard and put an end to them, once and for all.

The smile faded as he reminded himself of the task at hand. He was not looking forward to speaking with Darwin, but it was necessary. Phone conversation with the man was not dangerous, it was repugnant. The sour taste was back in his mouth. Getting prissy in your old age, he told himself. How many times have you welcomed one beast or another into your home? Pigs and monkeys have you dined with, and treated so graciously that none guessed your true thoughts. How many times have you ventured into the abyss itself, when it suited your reasons? Talk to the man, give him your orders, and listen to that laugh of his. Then wash yourself.

Yes, yes, yes. *Enough.* Doubts weaken the body and the soul, and the Old One could not afford a diminution in either. He watched the wind turbines along the mountains in the distance, the lights from the Strip a mere distraction now, feeling the peace of the infinite descend upon him like a kiss. The hardy nomads of the land of his birth believed that Allah had already written the book of life. Thus prayer to them was an obligation, but they harbored no illusions that God was influenced by their beseechings. He watched the power turbines spin in the cold desert air and thought of Redbeard, who had stymied him for so long. Matching him move for move. Now it was Redbeard's turn to twist in the wind, at the mercy of fate and fearing for the safety of his niece. In this one thing only, Redbeard and the Old One were in complete agreement: they both wished fervently that Rakkim would find her.

CHAPTER 5

After late-evening prayers

"Sarah's *gone*? What does that mean?"

"She ran away two days ago." Redbeard checked his watch. "Make that three days now. She disappeared Friday morning, after teaching her first class."

Rakkim put a hand on him. "You're *certain* she wasn't snatched?"

Redbeard slapped Rakkim's hand away, walked off the main path. He moved a little stiffly.

Rakkim followed him deeper into the garden, ducking his head to pass through the elephant ferns and clumps of hanging lilies, flowers for the dead, cloying. Even with the full moon it was murky in the garden, but Redbeard knew where he was going. So did Rakkim. At a small clearing beside a rock waterfall, Redbeard sat down, supporting himself with one hand for a moment. Rakkim joined him.

Redbeard pursed his lips. "Sarah left on her own. I thought at first that she had gone with you, but she called Friday night. She said she was safe and I shouldn't worry."

"Why would she run away? What did you do?"

"I was looking after her," said Redbeard, glaring. "I had arranged a marriage between her and a suitable man, not an easy thing at her age, particularly after the publication of that damned book of hers. The Saudi ambassador offered his fifth son, Soliman, a petrochemical executive, and I accepted. Soliman has two wives, but they live in the Kingdom, protected from the supposed moral taint of our nation. Sarah was to be his primary spouse and they were to live here in the ambassador's compound. Soliman is well educated, cosmopolitan—"

"How considerate of you." Rakkim had seen them together, followed them without Sarah's knowledge. The Saudi held his coffee cup with both hands while he drank, as though not trusting his own grip. "You found a moderate for her. Sarah could still teach and go to movies. She might even be able to dance at her own wedding."

"Should I have waited until someone discovered the two of you sneaking around in sin? Then Sarah would have had *no* prospects."

Rakkim stayed silent. Rakkim could ignore Redbeard's wishes, but in spite of her age and income, Sarah was expected to obey her guardian.

"I want you to find her."

"You have plenty of agents. What do you need me for?"

"I trust you."

"Why would I bring her back? I'm just sorry she didn't call me first."

"She's going to get herself killed," Redbeard said quietly. "An unmarried woman who leaves home without permission is always at risk, and Sarah's writings have made her a target. She doesn't appreciate the situation—"

"You think the Black Robes would dare go after *your* niece?"

"It would be foolish, but people in power do foolish things all the time."

"Oxley is too cautious, too smart . . ." Rakkim stopped. "What aren't you telling me?"

"Mullah Oxley *is* cautious, but there are others among the Black Robes who do not consider that an admirable quality." Redbeard fingered his beard. "I did my best to cover Sarah's absence. She's taken sudden sabbaticals before when her research required it. The chair of the History Department was fooled. Someone else was not." A vein in his thick neck pulsed. "The day after she disappeared, I got word that certain bounty hunters had been given the commission to find her. Specialists in returning errant wives and daughters. My men intercepted two teams of hunters. One of my best agents, Stevens, whose nose you chose to break, led the captures, but I'm sure there are other teams looking—"

"Who hired them?"

"They were contacted anonymously. Their commission untraceable."

"Don't worry, Uncle, I'll find her. I won't bring her back so you can marry her off, but I'll find her. Then you can send out Stevens to find *us*."

"Spare me your threats. I've already made my excuses to the ambassador. I told him today that Sarah was in seclusion seeking spiritual guidance. That was reason enough for him to call off the wedding. The pious are always suspicious of devotion in others."

"You should have let us marry."

"I should have done many things."

"I was an officer in the Fedayeen then, I had brought honor to you. There was no reason for you to deny us your blessing."

"My blessing seems to be the only thing denied the two of you." Rakkim felt his cheeks flush.

"You were cautious, I'll give you that. I thought once she was married, that would be the end of such foolishness." Redbeard dipped a hand in the stream, let the cold water rush over his fingers, his eyes half-closed. "I spoke with your imam. He said you haven't been to mosque in years."

"Guilty."

"You avoid the company of believers. You spend your days with Catholics and worse."

"Oh, *much* worse."

"Have you become an apostate, then?"

"I believe that there is no God but Allah, and that Muhammad is his messenger. That is *all* I am certain of. I remain a Muslim. Not a good Muslim, but a believer all the same."

"Then there is still hope for you." Redbeard peered at him. "I heard a story that might interest you. It's about a travel agent who takes no money for his services. Imagine that. Emigration without permission is an act of treason. Anyone connected with the act is equally culpable. Yet there is a smuggler who works for free. What would make a man do something like that?"

"A good Muslim is required to feed and shelter those who appear on his doorstep."

Redbeard looked amused. "Ah, but you are *not* a good Muslim. Isn't that what you just told me?"

Rakkim didn't return the smile. "Was I *really* so unsuitable?"

"I had other plans for Sarah. Other plans for you too." Redbeard backhanded the stream, sent water splashing into the foliage. "A lot of good it did me."

Rakkim noticed that the right side of Redbeard's face was slack. He had thought at first that it was just a trick of the poor light. "What happened to you?" He moved closer. "You favor your left leg when you walk, and here . . ." He lightly touched Redbeard's cheek. "A fresh scar. Your beard doesn't grow there anymore. *Something* happened."

"There was an attempt on my life last month. They died. I didn't. That's all."

"The Black Robes?"

Redbeard shrugged. "As you said, Mullah Oxley is too cautious to attack me directly, but it might have been someone in the hierarchy, one of his deputies hoping to curry favor. Or, it might have been another's hand at work. A new player perhaps."

"Who do you *think* was behind the attempt?" persisted Rakkim.

"Find Sarah, and perhaps you and I will turn our attention to that riddle."

There was no sense trying to get more information out of Redbeard. "If Sarah's been gone since Friday, she could be anywhere by now. You should have called me sooner."

"She's still here. Her call Friday night was local. The airports and train stations were already keyed to her profile—"

"There are other ways to leave the city."

"Sarah doesn't know she's running for her life. She thinks she just has to stay gone long enough for me to call off the wedding. She *knows* Seattle. She won't feel the need to leave. She thinks she can call me up in a month and invite me to lunch, and I'll forgive her. I *would* forgive her too, but we don't have that luxury." Red-beard straightened his posture, winced. "I've assembled a complete file for you: her phone logs for the last six months, the memory cores from her computers, a list of her friends." He sounded calm. "Whatever else you need, just ask and—"

"I'll handle it."

Redbeard looked past him. "I promised myself when you quit the Fedayeen that I was done with you. I told myself that you were dead . . . but you were not. The nights seem longer as the years pass. More often now, I wander through the house with only my footsteps to keep me company and wish you were beside me." He swallowed. "Sarah . . ." His voice broke, but he kept his head high. "Now she's gone too. I blame myself."

If Redbeard was waiting for Rakkim to disagree, he would be waiting for a long time.

They sat beside the waterfall, listening to the cascading water, neither of them speaking. Alone in the garden, out of sight of the stars and satellites. Whether God was watching, neither of them knew.

Rakkim pushed his sleeve up, reached through the waterfall, and brought out a couple of bottles of Coca-Cola from Red-beard's hiding place. He handed one to the startled Redbeard, unscrewed the other, and took a swallow. It was so cold his teeth ached. "Ahhh. No matter what they say, Jihad Cola is swill." He clicked his bottle against Redbeard's. "Fuck the embargo."

Redbeard was aghast. "How long have you known?"

"Since a month after you brought me home."

Redbeard shook his head as he opened the bottle. "That's what I get for not counting."

Rakkim had always been careful not to hit the stash unless Red-beard had recently restocked the secret grotto, and though he had shared his pilfered Cokes with Sarah, he had never revealed her uncle's hiding place to her. She would not have been able to restrain herself, would have gotten them caught, not out of greed, but from a sense of joyous abandonment, a deliberate flouting of the rules. He loved Sarah for her sense of invulnerability, but he knew better.

Rakkim drank deep. "Those peckerwoods in the Bible Belt are black-hearted infidels and eaters of swine, but you have to admit, they know how to make soda pop."

Redbeard took a sip. "Peckerwoods have the formula, *that's* the difference."

"Time for our scientists to start working on that formula." Rakkim admired the bottle. "Who could imagine something this good would be illegal?" he asked innocently. "Possession of contraband. Two years hard labor, no parole."

"Don't try to understand the law."

"The law is beyond my comprehension, we both know that." Rakkim took another swallow. "You ever had RC Cola?"

"Long time ago."

"I had some about eight years ago . . . Tennessee . . . my first solo recon inside the Bible Belt. Checking out rumors of nuclear activity at the old Oak Ridge facility." Rakkim took a sip, savoring the taste. "I spent three months blending in, beardless as a newborn. Worked the turpentine trail, fixing home electronics door-to-door, chatting up the housewives and factory workers. Joined the local church. Sat right next to the local sheriff, skinny black man with a wine-stain birthmark on his cheek, the two of us belting out 'The Old Rugged Cross.' I like that hymn." Another sip. "Didn't handle any snakes. Peckerwoods are supposed to do that, but I never saw it. Good people . . . I was surprised at that too. I guess I shouldn't have been. Sarah always said they weren't that different than us. *Read your history, Rakkim.*" He felt Redbeard's eyes on him as he fingered the bottle. "And the food—you have fresh peach pie at a Pentecostal church social, fresh peach with a ball of homemade vanilla ice cream, and you'll think about converting back to that old-time religion. Don't give me that look, it's the truth. I was *there*. The people, the food, the little kindnesses . . . girls in their summer dresses . . . small things, but if it hadn't been for Sarah, the memory of her . . ." He looked at Redbeard. "I didn't find any nukes. At least I never got a hit on my radiation patch." He watched the bubbles rise in the bottle of Coke. "Oak Ridge people are partial to RC Cola. Their roads are worse than ours, and beef is scarce, but they got everything you'd ever want to drink. Bubble-Up, Seven-Up, Everclear moonshine, and bourbon so smooth it's like drinking sunlight. I drank it *all*, Redbeard. I had to. They're on the lookout for infiltrators, and a man who turns down corn whiskey gets a long, hard look. Coca-Cola's still my favorite, though. So you can tell my imam I'm not beyond the light." Rakkim took a long swallow, the icy sweetness like an avalanche down his throat. He stared at Redbeard. "All that fresh-bottled Coca-Cola . . . peckerwood's finest, and none of it tasted as good as what I stole from your secret stash. Why do you think that is, Uncle?"

"Find her, Rikki. Please?"

Try as he might, Rakkim could not recall a single previous occasion when Redbeard had used the word *please*. It was almost enough of a surprise to stop him from thinking. Almost. "Why did Sarah leave *now*?"

"What . . . what do you mean?"

"Why didn't she leave a week ago? Or *next* week? Why now? What was the trigger?"

"There was no trigger."

"That's not what you taught me. You said that whenever someone makes an abrupt decision, a hard choice that changes their life, that there's always a trigger. Find the trigger and you learn the truth, that's what you said."

"This wasn't an abrupt decision, so there was no trigger," said Redbeard. "She fooled me. I thought she had accepted her betrothal, but she was planning to leave all along. She had been taking money out of her bank account for months, small amounts, not enough to get my attention." He frowned. "Twenty-five years old, she should have been *grateful* I could still make a match for her."

"You can't think of any other reason why she would run away?"

Redbeard looked him in the eye. "None at all."

"I'll find her." Rakkim set down the empty Coca-Cola bottle. Redbeard, he knew, was lying.

CHAPTER 6

Before dawn prayers

Rakkim watched the military jets flying formation over the city as he drove from Redbeard's villa, the old, but reliable, F-117 Stealths on their regular patrol over the capital's restricted airspace. The faint thunder of their passage was comforting. He craned his neck for one more look, then headed home, driving east on I-90, taking the roundabout way back to the city in case he was being followed. He wasn't worried about State Security tracking him—the silent-running Ford that Redbeard had loaned him undoubtedly had a GPS unit somewhere on its chassis, probably two transmitters, one to be easily found, the other built-in at the factory. Redbeard would know where the car was every moment, but Rakkim didn't care. He wasn't worried about Redbeard; he was worried about whomever *Redbeard* was worried about. If the villa was under surveillance, any car coming or going might be a subject of interest.

Most of the vehicles on the road at 3 a.m. were tractor-trailers hauling goods over the mountain passes to eastern Washington, and snow buggies on their way to Snoqualmie Summit. Rakkim held the Ford to just above the speed limit and checked the rearview screen. A green delivery van changed lanes when it didn't have to.

Rakkim was still stuffed from the postmidnight breakfast Angelina had insisted he eat, blueberry pancakes and eggs and sausage. While she harangued him for being too skinny, he ate and questioned her about Sarah. The pancakes were more satisfying than her answers—it had been a long time since Sarah had confided in her, she had admitted, wiping her eyes.

Rakkim called Mardi's number at the Blue Moon. "Howdy," he said when she picked up, his greeting alerting her that the call might be monitored. "I'm taking some time off."

Mardi hesitated. "Everything okay?"

"Doing a favor for a friend. I'll see you in a few—"

"I hope it wasn't anything I said tonight."

"I'll survive." Rakkim broke the connection.

The freeway was potholed, the roadway buckled in places from the storms last fall. He took the off-ramp at Issaquah, one of the region's high-tech centers, its office parks and underground research centers protected behind layers of biometric trip wires. The green van took the same exit, turned right at the traffic signal, and kept going. Rakkim watched it leave in his rearview screen, driving on, waiting. A mile later, he picked up a second tail, this one a silver sedan. Even on full magnification, he couldn't see the driver. A family car with full security screen? Right.

A half hour later he was heading back to the city on one of the alternative routes, the traffic thinning out until he was driving in darkness with only his headlights for illumination. The sedan was still a mile or so behind him, its lights only occasionally apparent on the narrow, twisting road. The alternative route was cut through a forest of tall firs and cedars at the foothills of the Cascade Mountains, an old road, pretransition, well made and still smooth. A few housing tracts had been built out here ten years ago, but had failed to sell; the commute was too long and the homes were poorly designed and cheaply built. Squatters lived in the crumbling houses now, without power or sewage systems, roofs leaking, floors cracked, the yards gone to weeds and thorny blackberries. The neatly laid out culs-de-sac were barricaded with junked cars, off-limits to strangers, and ignored by the authorities. Rakkim could see bonfires burning through the trees as he raced by.

A light rain was falling now, the wipers seesawing back and forth across the windshield. The silver sedan had fallen back, careful in the treacherous terrain. There were no streetlights, no shoulders, just a sheer drop-off on one side, and deep woods on the other. The car had a programmable steering computer — all he had to do was key in his destination and sit back, take a nap if he wanted, but he didn't want to input his destination, and the computer didn't know the way through the badlands. Rakkim knew the road, knew where it dipped and fell, where it was underwater in the rainy season. He used the badlands to ferry people out of the country, Jews and homosexuals and runaway fundamentalists, all of them desperate for the relative safety of Canada, or the Mormon territories. He kept driving.

Rakkim had spent an hour in Sarah's suite at the villa, Rakkim dizzy with the scent of her. Her favorite stuffed animal still rested on her bed, a wreck of a calico bunny, ears frayed, one eye missing. It had already lost most of its batting by the time he'd first seen it, right after Redbeard had brought him home. Rakkim had looked at the floppy creature that day and all he could think of were the bodies hanging from bridges after martial law was declared. He had hated that stuffed bunny then, he hated it now, but tonight he had straightened it on her pillow. Then he searched her room: her closet, her desk, her collection of classic Muslim Barbies. He saved her dresser for last, her silky things slipping through his fingers.

The car skidded, kicking up gravel, and Rakkim forced himself to slow down. He didn't know if Redbeard had deliberately lied to him about the timing of Sarah's departure, but he did know she hadn't planned to leave Friday morning. Not when she left the villa. He didn't know what it was, but there *had* been a trigger for her decision. Something had happened after she'd got to the university, something that had compelled her to leave. The proof was in his breast pocket: a wallet-size photograph.

The photo was Sarah's most precious possession, kept tucked away in a secret compartment inside her music box. She had shown it to him once, made him promise not to tell, and he had kept the promise. The snapshot was of Sarah and her father. Sarah an infant, sleeping peacefully in his arms while her father looked directly at the camera. There were many official portraits of James Dougan — the first State Security chief was considered one of the nation's greatest martyrs — but this was the only photo Rakkim had ever seen where he looked truly happy. Rakkim had never asked Sarah why she hid the photo away. Only someone who had not grown up in that house would have wondered — any secret kept from Redbeard was a victory. He patted his pocket for reassurance. If Sarah knew she was leaving that morning, she would never have left it behind.

A clear-cut section of forest gave a brief glimpse of Seattle glittering in the distance, dozens of airships drifting over Queen Ann Hill, guarding the presidential palace. The road curved, the faint lights of the trailing sedan lost to view.

The white-pine desk in Sarah's bedroom had been stacked with real books and yellow legal pads filled with her small printing. She loved antiques, loved computers with keyboards and ballpoint pens, comic books and DVDs. There wasn't a single photograph of Sarah's mother in the room, not now, not ever. Katherine Dougan had disappeared just after her husband's assassination and was widely regarded as having had a part in the conspiracy that had killed him, an attempt by radical Christians to destabilize the new Muslim regime. Despite Redbeard's best efforts, she had not been found, and though the active search for her had long since been called off, Redbeard forbade even her name to be mentioned in the house.

Rakkim remembered wandering through the villa after he'd first arrived, room after room, remembered dipping a toe into the swimming pool and telling himself not to get too comfortable here, that it could all end as suddenly as it had begun. He was barely nine, street-smart and wary; Sarah was five, an orphan just like he was, lively and smart, already reading. The first time they met, she looked relieved to see him, as though she had been awaiting his arrival for a long time.

They had grown up together in that great house, swam laps and splashed in the pool, collected bugs in the woods with their bodyguards, and worked on their homework side by side in the study. A confirmed moderate, Redbeard had insisted that Sarah be as well educated as any male, encouraged to ask questions, allowed to play sports and wear contemporary clothing, except on the Sabbath. After her book came out, he probably regretted not being more strict with her.

The back road gave way to an even narrower road. He kept his eyes open for the glint of broken glass or cables stretched from tree to tree—people traveled here at their own risk. Even the army only drove through by convoy. He didn't mind. In thirty miles the road got even rougher, became a web of winding gravel and dirt roads, abandoned mining paths, railroad rights-of-way, and forest service roads, most of them no longer on any maps.

Maps were only an approximation, that's what he had learned in the Fedayeen. Trust your instincts, trust your eyes, and trust your brother Fedayeen. Only when all else fails should you trust a map. So what was he to make of the map he had seen in Sarah's room tonight? A world map hanging over her desk, colored pushpins stuck in various places, all of them evidently related to her studies in recent American history.

Red pushpins marked the Islamic Republic's early military for-

ays into the Bible Belt: Charleston, Richmond, Knoxville, Abi-
lene, New Orleans. All of their attacks had been rebuffed, the
breakaway Christians fighting like rabid dogs, fighting to the
death, blowing themselves to pieces rather than being captured.
The Bible Belt counterattacks were marked with yellow pushpins . . . Chicago, Indianapolis, Topeka, Newark. What a meat-
grinder Newark had been; over five hundred thousand dead, most
of them civilians. After Newark the calls for an armistice had been
too loud for either side to ignore. The false peace had lasted ever
since.

Gold pins indicated Rakkim's own Fedayeen operations, the
ones Sarah knew about anyway. While the army had been rele-
gated to a strictly defensive role since the treaty, the Fedayeen's
elite units mounted covert operations both at home and abroad.
Gold pins were stuck in the Mormon territories of Utah and Col-
orado, a few more in Idaho and Montana when they had moved
against Aryan Identity holdouts, more pins in Brazil and Nigeria.
There were no gold pins to mark his last six years of service. No
gold pins for his solitary reconnaissance insertions into the Bible
Belt itself. No gold pins for Corpus Christi and Nashville, Biloxi
or Atlanta. It was just as well.

Rakkim had seen something odd on the map in her bedroom.
Squinting. It was only when the angle was right that he could spot
the perforation in the center of China. He had moved closer,
swept his hand across the map, felt the indentation. There was a
pinhole on the Yangtze River. The only hole in the map without
a pin to mark it. It wasn't a mistake or a miss. There were no pins
anywhere in China. Just a single pinhole in the middle of
nowhere. There had never been a military attack on China by the
Islamic Republic. China, the world's only superpower, had maintained strict neutrality during the turmoil that had followed the
Zionist Betrayal. So why had Sarah marked the Yangtze?

Rakkim slowed the car, looking for the spot . . . the cutoff. He had used it before, but it was hard to see in the rain. It was right after a sharp twist in the road, where his taillights would be hidden from anyone following. He crept along. *There.* He braked gently, then backed into the brush, branches slapping the sides of the car as he parked perpendicular to the road. Engine purring. Lights out. He rolled down the window slightly, the damp sweetness of the forest filling the interior. Rain dripped off the trees, sizzling on the hot hood of the car, and he thought of Sarah.

He had been eighteen when things had shifted between the two of them. Excited at leaving home for the Fedayeen Military Academy, Rakkim had bent down to kiss her good-bye.

"I'm going to marry you someday," she had whispered, clinging to his neck. She was only thirteen, thin and gangly, but she spoke with the certainty of a woman.

He tugged at her hair, thinking she was joking.

She clung on to him. "You know it's true."

He laughed it off, but as the years passed, he felt the attraction too. Every time he came home on leave, she was more mature, wiser, still able to get inside him with a smirk or a knowing glance. Their feelings were never acted upon, rarely even spoken of, too powerful for words. Under Redbeard's urging, Sarah had agreed to attend mosque with the son of the Senate majority leader, the two of them going for long walks afterward, chaperoned of course. The courtship lasted four months before she put an end to it. That spring, Rakkim just back from the Bible Belt, they walked into Redbeard's office and asked for his blessing. Rakkim was twenty-five, freshly promoted and with the offer of a staff posting in the city. Sarah had finished university. They were in love. It was time to marry.

"Out of the question," Redbeard had rumbled. Rakkim had argued his prospects while Sarah had assured Redbeard of the purity of their love and the propriety of their behavior. Redbeard dismissed their arguments with a wave of his hand. Then he dismissed Rakkim.

Perhaps if Rakkim had stayed Fedayeen he could have obeyed Redbeard's order not to see Sarah again. Already on the fast track to command, honored for his courage and initiative, he could have married, had children, and continued to serve his country. Instead, after two more lengthy missions into the Bible Belt, Rakkim resigned his commission and moved to the Zone. Every day he thought about contacting Sarah, but she acted first. A year and a half ago, a lightly veiled older woman had bumped into him outside the military museum, pressed a message chip into his hand, and hurried away.

The next day Sarah slid beside him in the back row of a darkened movie theater. "I thought Fedayeen were bold. I kept waiting to hear from you. Were you going to let Redbeard decide your whole life—?"

Rakkim kissed her.

"That's better." Sarah stroked his face.

They had met every week or so for the next year, sometimes in the early evening under cover of darkness, sometimes in midmorning when she didn't have classes, but always carefully—he had conducted military raids with less planning. Their affair was dangerous and doomed to discovery, but sweeter somehow because of it. Once after a policeman recognized Rakkim and shook his hand, they had promised to end the affair. The promise was broken a week later under a crescent moon, a lovers' smile in the night.

"We should get married," Rakkim had said afterward, breathless from exertion and the joy of being with her again. "We don't need Redbeard's permission."

"Of course, we do," said Sarah, always the practical one.

"We should stop then. A woman of your standing . . . what we're doing could ruin you."

"I'm *already* ruined." She had laughed. "Don't worry, Redbeard will change his mind."

It was raining harder now. He remembered the feel of Sarah's lips, and the taste of her, and the way she rubbed her feet against him in bed. He hadn't expected it to last, but the abruptness of the ending still surprised him. He had arrived at the home of a vacationing friend and waited for her. Waited in vain. The next day she had called and said they couldn't see each other anymore. Said the situation was impossible. The phone was almost too heavy for him to hold. He asked if she was sure. She was. That had been six months ago. She had contacted him three times since then; and three times she had stood him up. Now she had disappeared and—

Rakkim heard the silver sedan's engine before its headlights flashed through the trees.

Eyes glinted by the side of the road. A bedraggled deer caught in the light.

Rakkim put Redbeard's silent-running Ford into gear as the sedan slowed to make the turn. Floored it as the sedan passed the cutoff, hitting it broadside and sending it tumbling over the edge of the embankment. He heard it crash through the underbrush and land with a crunch on top of one of the other two wrecked cars down there.

The deer blinked, scampered away.

Rakkim maneuvered the Ford back on the road. No lights behind or ahead. Just rain and him and his memories.

CHAPTER 7

Before dawn prayers

Mullah Oxley opened his mouth so wide when he laughed that Khaled Ibn Azziz could practically see down his filthy gullet, and what he laughed at was filthier still. Oxley was seated at the head of the banquet table, surrounded by high-ranking Black Robes, with Ibn Azziz on his immediate right. A place of honor, but with an abhorrent view.

"Smile, Khaled," said Oxley, head of the Black Robes. "*Smile*. Your face is spoiling the party."

Ibn Azziz did as he was ordered. Tried to, anyway.

"Look at him," bellowed Oxley, bits of roast pigeon falling from his lips. "Fasting, as usual. To look at our emaciated brother you would think that food is an enemy." More laughter. "I expect decorum from my ministers in public, but you are among friends here, Khaled. This is a *party*, a celebration of our growing power, all praise to Allah, and my chief deputy is grim as a Jew on Judgment Day."

The table roared with glee, the other deputies pounding their fists on the table, setting the plates and crystal goblets bouncing. The upper echelon of the Black Robes had been eating and drinking all night. It was almost dawn now, and still they continued.

Ibn Azziz looked down the table, saw only weaklings and cowards in black silk robes, a dozen men grown fat and greedy, forgetting their mission. Only Tanner and Faisal hung their heads, embarrassed for him, their plates untouched, hands folded on their laps.

The leadership of the religious police was infested with hypocrites, men who chose the holy order for personal gain, lovers of luxury who hid their base desires under their robes and thought no one would see. Oxley was the worst offender. His public demeanor was acceptable, but in private he was a drunkard and a pederast. Little girls, little boys, it made no difference to Oxley, as long as there was innocence to be sucked out of them. His perversions were an abomination, but even worse, he was an appeaser to the moderates, eager to make bargains with the secular authorities. Oxley was the third mullah of the religious police in the last twenty years. The last time he had taken a real risk for his faith was when he'd murdered his predecessor.

Oxley waved off the acolytes serving them, picked up a wine bottle and poured into Ibn Azziz's already full goblet, the red wine overflowing, staining the white tablecloth. "Drink up, Khaled. *Drink,* damn you." He kept pouring, wine dripping off the table and onto Ibn Azziz's robe. "I won't have your pinched face mocking me."

Ibn Azziz slowly reached for the goblet, took the tiniest of sips. He wanted to vomit.

Oxley slammed the wine bottle down on the table. "*That's* better." He raised his own glass, waited until the others joined him in the toast, then drained it in one long swallow. He wiped his mouth, belched, his chins jiggling. "There may be hope for you yet, my young skeleton."

Ibn Azziz stared straight ahead. A pale ascetic with bulging eyes, he appeared sickly, but was filled with an unnatural strength, and an even more ferocious temper. His beard was sparse, his black hair tangled around his shoulders, uncombed and unwashed, for he rarely bathed, lest his own nudity lead to impure thoughts. Mocked when he'd first joined the order, he rose swiftly up the ranks. Picked by Oxley to be his enforcer, chosen over numerous older men, Ibn Azziz was Oxley's righteous hammer. All eyes were downcast when he entered a room now. Oxley used Ibn Azziz to cow his political enemies and his own ambitious subordinates, but he had not counted on Ibn Azziz's purity. Ibn Azziz was celibate. He owned nothing other than two robes and a copy of the Qur'an. He could neither be bought nor tempted. He considered moderates and moderns more dangerous than Zionists, the human rot in the perfect Islamic state.

Oxley peered at Ibn Azziz. "I don't know why you aren't enjoying yourself. Today's Super Bowl was a great victory. The cameras caught our brothers whipping some moderns for their immodesty. The whole world saw our rigor."

"The brothers barely drew blood," said Ibn Azziz, wine dripping off his robe.

"Patience, Khaled." Oxley turned to the rest of the table. "Our young brother wanted Ayatollah al-Azufa to lead the halftime prayers rather than the Ayatollah Majani."

Ibn Azziz knew he should remain silent, but honesty was his only indulgence. "Ayatollah al-Azufa is a warrior of God. Majani is a glib entertainer that makes even the moderns feel devout."

Oxley squinted, his face ruddy with drink. "Majani was my choice, as you well know."

The table was silent now. Oxley's two bodyguards leaned forward slightly, hands on their daggers. They stood on each side of him, a stocky, dark-skinned Yemenite and a taller American, a former Super Bowl standout for the San Francisco Falcons.

Oxley smacked Ibn Azziz on the shoulder, laughing, and the others joined in, glad to have the tension broken. "If I had allowed al-Azufa to lead the prayers, he would have railed against the president for a lack of piety and probably stoned to death a few adulterers for good measure. How do you think that would have looked for the cameras?"

Oxley beamed. "Khaled will not be happy until the Super Bowl is played with the heads of sinners instead of footballs." A patronizing pat for Ibn Azziz. "You have much to learn, young brother. Subtlety is the highest form of politics."

"We are charged with enforcing Allah's law," said Ibn Azziz, "not playing politics."

"It will take politics as well as Allah to rid us of Redbeard," barked Oxley.

Ibn Azziz lowered his head, shocked at the blasphemy.

"That is our goal, is it not?" lectured Oxley, as the other deputies muttered their agreement. "It is *Redbeard* who stands in our way."

"Then let us unloose our whips against him." Ibn Azziz looked around the table for support. "An hour ago, a State Security vehicle *deliberately* rammed a car of ours that was tracking it. Three brothers were badly injured." He tapped the table with a fingertip. "This is no time for idleness and frivolity."

"Our brother is eager for battle, but in his haste he would doom us all." Oxley waved a turkey leg at Ibn Azziz, directing him to quiet down. "We must be stealthy," Oxley said, warming to the sound of his own voice. "Just last week, because of my personal intervention, the imam of Redbeard's own mosque issued a fatwa condemning the immorality of popular culture, calling modern music and fashion 'acts of social terrorism as dangerous as any threat from the Bible Belt.' It was a huge embarrassment to Redbeard," Oxley gnawed at the turkey leg. "See, Khaled, *this* is the way to victory: tiny bites. We shall nibble away at Redbeard until there is nothing left of him."

"Tiny bites . . . ?" Ibn Azziz pushed his plate aside. "So, you ask us . . . the instruments of the Almighty, to be mice?"

Oxley threw down the turkey leg. "Are you too good to be a mouse, Khaled? Is that why you disobeyed me?"

The rest of the Black Robes shifted in their seats, and the bodyguards moved slightly away from Oxley.

"Khaled came to me last Friday," said Oxley. "He was convinced that Redbeard's niece had run away, convinced that she had been overcome by lust, eager to join a lover—"

"The slut didn't show up to teach her class. My contact in the History Department said the chairman had not been previously notified. It was an *opportunity* for us."

"An opportunity?" Oxley spread his arms wide. "The bitch has female troubles and Khaled gets cramps."

The Black Robes howled with laughter. Even the bodyguards grinned.

"Our brother asked me for permission to send out men to find the niece," said Oxley, no longer smiling. "What did I tell you, Khaled?"

"You said it was not worth the risk of bringing her to justice."

"I said we are winning the battle. It's not necessary to attack Redbeard directly," said Oxley. "Not as long as he has the president's trust."

"The president is a hollow man," said Ibn Azziz. "Without strength—"

"You asked permission, and I told you *no*. What did you do then? Please, Khaled, share with the brothers how you responded to an order from your mullah."

Ice filled Ibn Azziz, packed his veins until no feeling was left. No pain, no pleasure, only a crystalline certainty.

"We're *waiting*, Khaled," said Oxley.

"I disobeyed my mullah, choosing instead to obey the dictates of Allah."

"You confuse the buzzing in your ears with the voice of Allah," sneered Oxley. "You are a learned cleric, Khaled. Tell us, what is the price of disobedience?"

Ibn Azziz stood up, bowed to Oxley, put his hands flat on the table.

"You have been a valued servant," said Oxley. "Clever and resolute." He beckoned to his guards. "I will reward you with a quick and painless death for your service. May you discover the joys of the flesh in the afterlife that you rejected in this world."

The American bodyguard slid next to Ibn Azziz. "Don't worry, brother," he said softly, a big, blond killer from Wyoming, a faint twang still in his voice. "I'm gonna snap your neck so fast you'll be rolling in perfumed virgins before you know you're dead."

Ibn Azziz was watching Oxley when he heard the American

bodyguard cry out. A soft cry. A baby's cry. Oxley's eyes widened and Ibn Azziz smiled.

The Yemeni bodyguard eased the American to the floor, pulled the dagger out of his broad back.

Oxley tried to stand, but he was slowed by alcohol and surprise, and Ibn Azziz was behind him now, looping a linen napkin around his neck. Tightening it. Oxley tore at the napkin, his nails digging into Ibn Azziz.

Ibn Azziz paid no attention to Oxley's desperate struggles. He just kept twisting the napkin. Oxley was twice his size, but soft with sin. Ibn Azziz was pure in heart, with the strength and clarity of the righteous. *God will call you to account for all that you may reveal from your souls and all that you may conceal,* he recited, tightening his grip.

Oxley gurgled, eyes bulging as he bucked wildly. His black silk robe billowed around him. Tears ran down his cheeks, dripped into his beard.

Ibn Azziz pressed Oxley down. *And Allah said . . . Allah said to Iblis, the Devil, "The path which leads to Me is a straight one and you have no authority over My servants except the erring one . . . the erring ones who follow you. Hell is the promised place for them all."*

Oxley's lips were purple as a ripe grape. He clawed at the tablecloth, sent dishes and glassware tumbling. His movements slowing . . . slowing . . . until he slumped forward.

Ibn Azziz released him and Oxley fell off the chair, lay dead on the floor. Ibn Azziz wiped his hands with the napkin, tossed it aside. He looked down the length of the table. The deputies stared at their plates, trembling, except for Tanner and Faisal, who fingered their prayer beads. Slowly, with great formality, Ibn Azziz took his seat at the head of the table. The Yemeni bodyguard took his place behind him. Ibn Azziz felt surrounded by a pure white light. He was twenty-six years old. There was much work to be done and he had barely gotten started.

CHAPTER 8

Afternoon prayers

The next afternoon, Rakkim sat behind Sarah's desk at the university, looked slowly around the office, seeing what she would have seen. He smiled. Tucked into her bookcase was a photo of Sarah in an orange parka, arms raised in triumph from atop Mount Rainier. If he looked closer, he would see himself reflected in her glacier glasses, Rakkim dressed in a blue parka aiming the camera at her. Another one of Sarah's secrets, another one of *their* private jokes.

Students shuffled past the office door as he riffled Sarah's desk, the second bell warning them they had only five minutes to get to their classes. The university was strict about tardiness, and adherence to the dress code, but they needed a bigger operations and maintenance budget. The campus was immaculate, not a scrap of trash on the grounds, but the waxed wood floors of the buildings were cracked and uneven, the classrooms cramped, the desks and chairs mismatched. The professors' offices were no better, the furniture shoddy, the walls patched. The faculty computers were ancient, without satellite uplinks and only limited Internet access, supposedly to avoid the ubiquitous Russian viruses. Rakkim had been stunned at the neglect the first time he had walked the grounds—Fedayeen training facilities were state-of-the-art, from smart desks to holographic combat training. The university by comparison was haphazard and underfunded. The cheap lock on Sarah's office was an insult, a lock in name only.

Early this morning he had left Redbeard's car at an underground parking garage in downtown Seattle. The summons dawn prayer sounded as he walked outside, the muezzin's call undulating from the minaret of the main mosque—*God is most great, God is most great, God is most great. I witness that there is no God but God. I witness that Muhammad is the messenger of God. I witness that Muhammad is the messenger of God. Come to prayer! Come to prayer!* All across the city, the state, the nation, all across the world, the vast body of devout Muslims heard similar calls and responded as one.

Rakkim stood there in the pink glow of daybreak, trembling with the sound, the perfect resonance. One heart. One soul. One God. He hadn't prayed in three years, but he found himself mouthing the words of the muezzin as people hurried past him toward the mosque, businessmen in three-piece suits, teenagers in jeans, women leading children by the hand, urging them on so as not to be late. Congregational prayers were said to be twenty-seven times better than individual prayers, and greater blessings were given to those who were first inside. In a few minutes the faithful would be on their knees, facing toward the Kaaba in Mecca, a perfectly synchronized wave of submission, selfless and infinite, rolling through eternity. Rakkim watched them rush to mosque and envied them their devotion.

For the next half hour, Rakkim took a series of buses back and forth across the Zone, hopped off in the middle of a block, and slipped into his apartment. No one knew where he lived, not even Mardi. He took a quick shower and slept for a few hours. When he awoke, he ate some cold chicken and swallowed four aspirin. Then he borrowed a stranger's car from a long-term parking lot and drove to the university for a little breaking and entering.

Redbeard said he had gone over the office himself Friday evening when the campus was deserted, but Rakkim had to see for himself. He also wanted to talk to Sarah's officemate, Dr. Barrie. She would probably stop in after her 3 p.m. class. The office had originally been designed for one professor, but either for budgetary reasons, or the moral imperative to minimize private contact between students and teacher, all offices were shared.

Rakkim checked Sarah's desk drawers, mentally noting the items before moving them. There were plenty of yellow legal pads filled with Sarah's notes for her classes "The USA Post-Iraq 301" and "Introduction to Forensic Popular Culture." There were grade sheets and a thick handbook from the administration cataloging in voluminous detail the proper codes of conduct and comportment footnoted with the pertinent Qur'anic verses.

Tacked to the bookshelf, out of direct line-of-sight of visitors, was a copy of the old Bill of Rights. He knew there had been ten of them in the old regime, ten amendments, but it was odd to see them posted like this. He wasn't sure if Sarah was asking for trouble or just wanted to remind herself of how things had changed. The First Amendment had been gutted, according to Sarah, and the former protection of the others limited. Most people didn't seem to mind. Rakkim had once read that burning the flag actually used to be considered free speech. The complete elimination of the Second Amendment had been more controversial. There were old-timers *still* bitching about that, but they had turned in their guns, just like everybody else. No guns allowed, not for private citizens. Rakkim didn't need a gun. He was plenty dangerous as he was.

He went through the bookcase: academic texts and biographies mostly, but the bottom shelf was devoted to Sarah's passion, popular culture of the late twentieth and early twenty-first centuries. Books on *Star Wars*, *X-Men*, *The Lord of the Rings*, books on detective movies and horror movies, romantic comedies and political thrillers. Computer flashloads of fifty years of *TV Guide* and an encyclopedia of comic books. Picture books of fashionable shoes, and street-chic clothes, muscle cars and deco jewelry, anything and everything was of interest to her ravening curiosity. *Everything fits, Rakkim*, was one of her favorite sayings. *Everything fits—it's up to us to see the picture in the puzzle*. She did too. Sarah read the cultural tea leaves at a glance, a mixture of insight and intuition that allowed her to form conclusions before most academics had even analyzed the data.

There were no books on China though. No downloads. He was hoping to find something to explain that pinhole in her world map, a Chinese cookbook or a travel guide to panda breeding grounds, but there was nothing. He had checked a geographical website this morning, found that the pinhole roughly corresponded to the site of the Three Gorges Dam, but he didn't see the connection. Sarah was an expert on American history, and China had little to do with the new America. China was the global powerhouse, while the Islamic Republic was considered a technological backwater, politically fragmented, its former glory a thing of the past. So why was Sarah interested in China? Rakkim shook his head. Maybe it was just a pinprick. A mistake. Focus on the *known*, then allow flights of fancy, that's what Redbeard would have advised.

What he knew was that Sarah had disappeared from the university Friday morning. She had left after her "Pre-War American History" class, abandoning her car in the faculty parking lot. Redbeard said she was fleeing an arranged marriage, but Rakkim didn't believe it. If that was her reason, all she would have had to do was meet Rakkim at the Super Bowl and tell him she was ready to elope. So what was the trigger?

A pink note slid under the door.

It was a message for Sarah from Dr. Hobbs, history, asking her to call him about the presentation to the faculty senate. Rakkim stared at the door. Sarah had missed her Friday-afternoon class, and this morning's "Advanced Methods of Historical Research" seminar, but most of her colleagues probably still didn't know she was gone. So why was *this* the first message she had gotten? He checked her desk again. No notes. Her officemate though . . . pink messages were strewn across her desk.

Four messages for Dr. Barrie, all from other professors in the

History Department; a change in a lunch date tomorrow, an invitation to an academic tea, a request for her notes on French-Algerian emigration patterns, and a *second* reminder to return a book to Dr. Phillipi. Two notes were for Sarah. One from the history department chair asking her to contact him, and another, stamped *Sociology*, from Marian, which said, "Did I get the day wrong? Call me." He tucked the note from Marian into his pocket as he heard a key slip into the door. He had deliberately left it unlocked.

"What are *you* doing in here?" A middle-aged woman stood in the doorway, papers clutched to her chest.

"Dr. Barrie?" Rakkim offered his hand, which she didn't take. "The office was unlocked, so I let myself in. I hope it's okay. I'm waiting to interview Dr. Dougan."

"Are you, now?" Leaving the office door wide-open, Dr. Barrie walked over and dropped her papers onto her desk, sending the remaining pink slips flying. "Well, she stood you up, young man. Welcome to the club."

"I'm afraid I don't understand."

"Her royal highness decided to take off on another one of her research jaunts, leaving me to pick up the slack. No prior notice, no indication of when she'll be back." Dr. Barrie sat heavily, pushed her glasses back with a forefinger. An overworked academic in a long-sleeved dress, her gray hair in disarray. "I have no interest in her so-called area of expertise. My focus is Muslim demographic patterns of the late twentieth century, not the popularist twaddle she promotes."

Rakkim smiled. "I'm not a historian."

"Count your lucky stars." Dr. Barrie looked at him more closely. "*What* interview?"

"I'm writing an article on Professor Dougan for the *Islamic-Catholic Digest.*"

"Never heard of it."

"We're a small publication dedicated to better understanding within the community."

"Which community?" demanded Dr. Barrie.

"Don't ask me. The publisher got a grant, I just do the interviews."

"Maybe when her highness deigns to return, I'll put in for a grant and take a sabbatical to the south of France," Dr. Barrie said. "There are some very interesting census documents I'd love to spend a month examining, and then come back and be interviewed by some nice young man."

Rakkim pointed at the framed photographs on her desk. "Are those your kids?"

"My six beauties, and each one of them brought forth in pain and suffering." Dr. Barrie crossed herself. "Good Catholics like good Muslims are not afraid to do their duty. Are you acquainted with Professor Dougan?"

"Not really. I skimmed her book though."

"I don't really have anything against her. I just think she lacks maturity. I've told her that a woman's first responsibility is to marry and have children. She can pursue her profession once her children are grown. That's what I did." Dr. Barrie wiped her bulbous nose. "I work hard. I go to mass every day. I respect the authorities." She straightened one of the photos, looked up at him. "Are you a moderate or a modern?"

"I don't really know. I just do my best."

"That's an odd answer for your people." Dr. Barrie smiled. Her teeth were large and uneven, but it was a good, honest smile. "You sound like a Catholic. We have doubts about everything."

"I was raised Catholic." The lie came easily.

"Converted, did you? I've contemplated it myself." Dr. Barrie checked the doorway, waited for a chatting group of students to pass. "We're all going to Paradise, but some of us are riding at the back of the bus, if you understand my reference."

"I know exactly what you mean," said Rakkim. "I'm disappointed Professor Dougan isn't going to make the interview. Did something just come up?"

"She was here when I went to my nine a.m. class Friday and gone when I came back afterward. Never said a word to me about taking a leave of absence. I find that rude."

"Did she have any visitors that morning?"

Dr. Barrie peered at him over her glasses.

"I'm hoping to find her. I lose this interview, I'm in trouble with my editor." Rakkim sat in Sarah's chair, scooted it closer to Dr. Barrie. He glanced toward the open door, lowered his voice. "You know how it is. Even with my conversion, I have to work harder than the rest of them." He looked sheepish. "I shouldn't bother you with my problems."

Dr. Barrie squared her papers. "It's the same everywhere. Catholics and Muslims are both people of the Book, children of Abraham, yet when it's time to pass out the earthly rewards . . ." She tossed her glasses onto the desk, leaned forward, whispering now. "I tell my husband, if I was a Muslim, I would be department head, and if I was an *Arab*, I would be president of the university."

"Amen," said Rakkim. "I was just hoping . . . if there's anything you could think of that might help me find her, I'd really appreciate it."

Dr. Barrie rubbed her brow, finally shook her head. "I'm sorry, Dr. Dougan kept to herself. The students liked her, of course, but her colleagues found her . . . unacademic."

"Were there any students in particular she associated with?"

"That's not really encouraged by the administration. Not with an unmarried professor."

"I'm talking about something completely innocent. Coffee in the cafeteria . . . I heard she and Marian in the Sociology Department used to get together."

Dr. Barrie shook her head. "Not that I know of, but then, sociology is just more junk science, if you want my opinion. I didn't keep track of Dr. Dougan."

Rakkim stood up. "Thank you anyway." He was at the doorway when she spoke.

"I *did* see Professor Dougan at the Mecca Café Friday morning."

Rakkim didn't let his excitement show. "The Mecca Café?"

"On Brooklyn Way, a few blocks off campus. A student hangout mostly, although a few instructors will grab a sandwich there. The food at the campus cafeteria is overpriced."

"She was there Friday?"

"Yes, but she wasn't talking with anyone. I was stopped at the traffic light, and I looked over and there she was, typing away on one of the computers in the rear of the café. I didn't think anything of it at the time, but now I wonder why she wasn't using her computer here. They're slow but they're free."

Rakkim forced a shrug. "Thanks anyway. I'll reschedule when she comes back."

"You might think of interviewing another history professor," Dr. Barrie called to him. "Someone with a *real* academic track record."

CHAPTER 9

Before midafternoon prayers

Rakkim walked quickly from the Four Kings department store and stepped onto the Pike Street bus. From a seat at the back, he looked out through the rear window, saw no one following him. He kept watch for eight blocks anyway.

It was a habit, this herky-jerky street ballet, doubling back, cutting through abandoned buildings and open-air markets. He rarely spotted anyone trailing him, but often enough; Redbeard's agents, he supposed, or undercover cops trolling for trouble. Truth be told, he preferred the oblique moves. His caution had saved his life more than once during his first years in the Fedayeen, saved his squad from ambush when he was in combat. The others thought him lucky, favored by Allah, and fought to stay close to him. Rakkim didn't have the heart to tell them that luck was not a fire, warming those around it. Luck, like the favor of Allah, was a black hole. You either fell in or you didn't.

After his conversation with Dr. Barrie at the university, Rakkim had driven to the Mecca Café, had a cup of coffee and some conversation with the waitress, and then drove back downtown. After parking the borrowed car, he took a side trip through the crowd at the public market before pushing through the revolving doors of the Four Kings. He had already decided to contact Spider.

He got off the bus at First Hill, joined a swarm of glum hospital workers starting their shift at the nearby veterans' facility. He stayed with them for a block, listening to their complaints about the hospital administrators, before heading toward the Reservoir District, slogging through the puddles that dotted the sidewalk.

The Reservoir District was a blue-collar section of the city, mostly Catholics and lapsed Muslims, a mix of shabby houses and low-rent businesses. Bulky housewives in plastic coats hurried through the rain, while men gathered around burn barrels, arguing and passing around bottles in paper bags. *Go to Mosque* was spray-painted on the alley wall, *Go to Fuck* scrawled beside it in Magic Marker—a dangerous rejoinder, blasphemy could cost a tongue. An ancient Lexus perched on blocks in the front yard of one house, tires flat, rusting quietly in the drizzle. The sidewalks here were crumbling, the street signs stolen to confound the police or strangers.

The bananas under the awnings of the grocery shops were soft and brown, the apples wormy. A music store blared the latest atonal thrash, the bare-chested redhead behind the counter covered in mirror tattoos. Dog shit everywhere. No matter how poor they were, it seemed every Catholic family had at least one dog, a quiet show of defiance to the Muslim majority, who considered the dog an unclean animal. No devout Muslim would enter a home that had a dog inside—you might as well expect them to kiss a pig. Rakkim stepped onto the grass to avoid a steaming-fresh pile in the middle of the sidewalk and had to agree the Muslims were right.

Rain dripped down his collar as Rakkim stepped inside the three-chair barbershop, the outdated laser shears buzzing away. The mutt beside the door looked up at him, yipped once, then put its head back down. Shaking off the rain, he walked past the waiting customers and took a seat on the shoeshine throne at the rear of the shop. He grabbed a well-thumbed newsmagazine and put his boots up.

"Regular or deluxe?" sniffed Elroy. He had a cold. Elroy always had a cold.

"Why don't you give them that special sealer treatment," said Rakkim, glancing at a photo of the president congratulating troops home from the Quebec front. Someone had drawn horns on the president's head. He turned the page. "The stuff with the mink oil."

Elroy slowly unscrewed one of his tins of paste wax. He was about twelve, small and thin, a surly kid with unruly black hair and hooded eyes. His nose was small, of course, a real button. Rakkim heard that it had been an eagle beak before Spider had it fixed. Spider got all his kids' noses fixed so they didn't look anything like him. Too Semitic, too dangerous. Not that Rakkim had ever seen Spider. No one had, but that was the rumor.

Rakkim had used Spider's expertise five or six times in the last few years, usually to check out the bona fides of people who wanted to emigrate, making sure they weren't setting him up, or to help with escape routes. Once Spider had hacked the municipal computer system of Boise, Idaho, and learned the disposition of the police and border patrol, even came up with a count of their night-vision goggles, including model number and condition of the batteries. Boise had been a good exit point, a regular sieve until another travel agent, a sloppy greedhead, had gotten snapped trying to ease a party of seventeen along the Snake River. *Seventeen.* Idiot must have thought he was leading a wagon train. Donner party was more like it. They were all executed, men, women, and children. Rakkim had seen the live feed at the Blue Moon, not reacting. Boise was finished. You couldn't get a snail darter through there undetected now.

It had been Mardi who had put him in contact with Spider. One of Spider's older kids worked as a dishwasher at the Blue Moon, a myopic fifteen-year-old carrying a double academic load at the high school. Mardi let him sleep at the club when he wasn't with his family. Rakkim had no idea how many kids Spider had. Mardi said they were seeded all over the city, hard workers one and all, smart too. When Rakkim wanted to deal with Spider, he went through Elroy instead of the dishwasher. Another oblique move.

"How's business?" asked Rakkim.

"Too many cheapies." Elroy dipped a rag into the black paste, slowly circling the can. His fingernails were bitten to nubs, rimmed with shoe polish. "The losers around here have no pride in their appearance. They'd wear wooden shoes if they thought they could get away with it." He carefully worked the polish into Rakkim's polymer-toed boots. "These headbangers of yours are all right. Who'd you steal 'em from?"

"Some guy who would have probably given you a huge tip." Rakkim turned the page of the magazine. There was a full-page ad for the Palestine Adventures outside San Francisco, happy families waving to the camera, the kids in plastic suicide-belts, hoisting AK-47s to the sky. "You ever been to Palestine Adventures?"

"Yeah, me and the grand mufti rode the crazy bus together," said Elroy, starting on the other boot. "Great ride. I ate a pork chop and puked all over my explosive vest."

Rakkim looked toward the front of the shop, but no one was paying them any attention. He sat back and let Elroy work, enjoying the slap of the shine rag, and the buzzing of the laser. A game show on the wall screen, no holographic converter. Not worth watching. Besides, the questions were too easy.

"You're done," said Elroy.

Rakkim stared at his boots. "Mecca Café," he said quietly, reaching into his pocket for money. "They have two computers, but I don't know which one I'm interested in, so ask Spider to hack them both. I want anything incoming and outgoing from last Friday, between eight a.m. and ten a.m." He paid Elroy for the shine, tipped him fat.

Elroy sniffed. "Wow, now I can go to the college of my choice."

Rakkim tossed him a ballpoint pen. "Is this yours?" He watched Elroy pin it to the collar of his T-shirt. "There's two memory cores inside that." He had pulled one from Sarah's home computer and one from the office clunker before Dr. Barrie had showed up. "I'd like Spider to take a look at them."

"All this rain we've had . . . you're going to need another treatment in about a week."

"I can't wait a week."

"Could get expensive."

Rakkim stood up. "Whatever it costs."

"Where's Simmons?" asked Mardi.

"Mr. Simmons's in the hospital with an infection of some kind. I don't really know the details." Darwin smiled at her, set his case down on the desk in her office. "I'm afraid you're going to have to settle for me."

"I've been buying my hooch from Simmons since I opened this joint. I trust him. You're just a guy who walked in off the street."

"We work for the same outfit. Same prices. Same high quality." Darwin tapped the case. A tiny blood spot was on it. One of his private jokes. "Same samples case. See the monogram?" He winked at her. "Simmons told me to watch out for you. He said you drive a hard bargain."

Mardi leaned against her desk, crossed her long legs. "I don't like being fucked over."

"I'm not here to fuck you over." Darwin touched his necktie. A real rube gesture, the nervous suitor. She *was* a knockout. Catholic bitch with a spattering of freckles on her bare arms, and fine blond down on her upper lip. A real screamer, he was sure of it. He plucked a bottle from the case, laid out a couple of shot glasses on the desk. "We're introducing a new, high-end product."

Mardi eyed the shots he poured. He was generous. Not like Simmons, who barely wet the bottom of his samples. "Our customers aren't particularly interested in quality." She picked up her glass, held it up to the light. Appreciating the light caramel color. "They're interested in a good time and being able to afford enough hooch to get the job done."

Darwin clicked glasses with her. Filled his mouth, savoring the shot before letting it slide all warm and cozy down his throat. She had done the same thing. He smiled at her.

Mardi smiled back.

"I never tasted real Kentucky bourbon, but I'm told this is almost as good," said Darwin.

Mardi licked her lips. "Not bad."

"Simmons was right. You *are* a tough customer."

"What's a case of this hooch cost?"

"For you?" Darwin looked at the ceiling, calculating. "Seven hundred . . . no, make that six-fifty."

Mardi shook her head. "I'd have to get twenty dollars a shot to make it pay."

Darwin refilled her glass, saw the surprise in her glance. Pleasure too. "Think of it as a loss leader, a specialty item to bring people. All the clubs in the Zone offer the same watery beer and bathtub hooch. The Blue Moon would be a unique destination." He clicked glasses with her, toasted her tits with his eyes. "Like your sign says, *R U Having Fun Yet?*"

Mardi sipped the shot.

Darwin watched her swallow, aroused at the way her throat worked. Hot and excited and utterly focused. If he could kill her right now, things would be perfect. Priorities, though. The Old One had made that clear. Time enough for killing later. Anticipation was supposed to be a boon to pleasure, but there was nothing like a quick kill. A sudden kill. God's own lightning bolt.

"What are you thinking?"

Darwin smiled. "How much I love my work."

Mardi pulled out a pack of cigarettes.

Darwin lit her up. "Where's your partner?"

"He took the day off."

"Too bad. Simmons says he's quite a character." The Old One said Rakkim was tough and full of tricks. A *challenge*, the old man had said, knowing that would set Darwin's mouth watering. The photos sent to his phone showed a knotty, hard-eyed modern, more macho than stylish, a real danger ranger. Just the way Darwin liked them.

He had been lying in bed when the old man called, dream-stating with his happy memories. The old man had offered him the assignment, then wanted to get off the phone as soon as he could, but Darwin had kept him on the line, asking about his health and prize horses and all his lovely children. The old man stayed polite as always, smooth, but with just the faintest edge to his voice. No one but Darwin would have detected it.

Darwin watched smoke trickle from her nostrils. "I'm going to be in town for a few more days. I'd really like to meet him." He laid his card on the desk. "Just give me a call. Not too often I get to shake hands with a Fedayeen."

Mardi shrugged.

Darwin topped up her glass. "Don't tell my boss I'm giving away the profit."

"Are you trying to get me drunk, Darwin?"

"You look to me like a woman who can handle herself. Can I put you down for a case? Or do you need to talk to your partner first?"

Her eyes flashed. "Like I said, I don't think I can make it pay."

"Nonsense. Saint Patrick's Day is just around the corner. It might not be a sanctioned holiday, but you know what they say." Darwin clicked glasses with her. "On Saint Paddy's Day the whole world is Catholic."

CHAPTER 10

After dawn prayers

It sounded like a hailstorm inside the Good Woman net café, twenty women bent over their keyboards click-clacking away, another half dozen standing around waiting their turn. All of them wore chadors, many of them black, but plenty of brighter colors on the younger women. Sarah had unhooked her veil for the freedom of an open face. Most of the time she ventured out dressed as a modern, or a Catholic, in jeans or slacks, her hair loose, with a touch of makeup. When she checked the net, she wore the chador. A fundamentalist café, where the site access was rigorously screened and even potentially inappropriate Web addresses were blocked, was the perfect place for coded contact.

The woman at the next computer, a girl of no more than seventeen, was humming a current pop song as she typed. A song about two teenagers attempting to ski their way to Canada who freeze to death in each other's arms. If the girl's father heard her singing the song, he would beat her until she couldn't walk. Would search her room and see if she had altered her radio to receive obscene stations. The girl had loosened her sky blue chador, her blond hair spilling out. Like all the women in the café, she wore a clearly visible plastic card around her neck from her father or husband granting her permission to be outside the house. Sarah wore one too, a forgery she had bought in the Zone months ago. The permission card felt like a millstone.

Sarah waited for the site to boot up. The computers in the café didn't allow photographs to be viewed, of course, but all the filters made them incredibly slow. Slogans and homilies were written across the walls in pink script: *Obedient Children Are a Mother's Gift to God; Many Children = Happy Heart; Honor Your Husband; A Stern Brother Is a Sword Against Sin.*

She listened to the women chattering away, sensed their limitations, their proscribed life. They seemed happy, though, *connected* in a way that neither she nor any of her modern friends were. She said prayers daily, went to mosque at least on Friday, but faith was merely the trappings of her life, it wasn't the spine and soul of her existence. She was a professional, a free-range academic, but her work didn't give her the deep reservoir of serenity that she saw in the faces of the faithful, the certainty that all things were in the hands of Allah. Just the opposite. In these last few days she had found an odd comfort in the modesty of the chador and head scarf, a joy in the anonymity of the veil. It was embarrassing, and she would never admit it to anyone, even Rakkim, but sometimes she thought she paid too high a price for her intellectual rigor.

Welcome to The Devout Homemaker flashed on-screen in gold letters, startling her.

Sarah scanned the list of recent entries, looking for a question about the proper preparation of a holiday meal involving rabbit, sweet potatoes, and victory radishes. There were plenty of questions on similar topics but none mentioned victory radishes, a term that was twenty years out of date. She rechecked the list. The question, had it been found, would have contained a code that would tell her exactly another site where they could have a private conversation. Still no entry about victory radishes.

Sarah clicked on *Post Question.*

My mother, blessed be her memory, has a recipe that calls for victory radishes, but I am unable to locate them at my market. I would be most interested in anyone who could tell me where to find such vegetables, if that is what they are. I am most interested in honoring my mother's memory by serving this dish to my esteemed father.

The door to the café opened as she hit *Post,* a ripple of anxiety whispering through the room. Sarah looked up, then quickly down, breathing hard now. She faced the computer, slowly lifted her veil into place. She watched the Black Robe pace the room, a short, stout man with small, round glasses perched on the tip of his nose. He would have been comical without the long, flexible cane in his hand, and his aura of power.

Whip. Whip. Whip. The Black Robe flicked the cane back and forth as he walked the aisles. The room was completely quiet now save for the sound of the cane. Whip. Whip.

Women tugged their chadors down, making sure their ankles and wrists were covered. The girl next to her quickly pulled up her head covering, tucked in her hair.

"Sister?" the Black Robe said softly.

An older woman glanced over at the Black Robe, her lower lip quivering.

The cane flicked an inch from her nose. "This site you are visiting is an insult to your husband." The Black Robe's voice was high and reedy, as though strained through his thick, black beard. "'The Marriage Bed' . . . this is filth."

"The advice is offered by the imam of Chicago," whispered the woman.

The Black Robe struck the monitor. "The imam of Chicago countenances abominations."

The woman slid onto the floor and kissed the hem of the Black Robe's garment.

Sarah stared straight ahead as the Black Robe approached. Her stomach hurt from holding herself rigid. He stopped in back of the girl next to her.

The cane tapped the floor.

The girl folded her hands in her lap, shaking so hard that her chador seemed to shimmy.

The cane lifted a lock of her long, blond hair that had slipped out of her head covering. She attempted to tuck in the errant curl, but the Black Robe smacked her hand with the cane, made her cry out. "You flaunt your hair for the world to see," he hissed. "Are you a Catholic whore or a devout Muslim woman?"

Weeping, the girl shoved her hair under the head wrap, a red welt across her hand.

The Black Robe must have felt Sarah's angry eyes on him. He glared at her. "Allah, the all-powerful, *despises* an insolent woman."

Sarah lowered her gaze. Grateful for the veil.

The Black Robe jerked the permission card off her neck, almost pulled her out of her seat. "Abu Michael Derrick," he read, his eyes huge behind his glasses. "Your husband has been neglecting his duties. You are dressed modestly, veiled as befits a proper Muslim wife, yet your eyes betray your true nature. Do you disrespect the Prophet, blessed be his name, or only those who humbly seek to enforce his laws?"

Sarah bowed her head, furious with herself for her lapse in character. Frightened too. The Black Robes' power over moderns was limited, but Sarah was dressed as a fundamentalist. He would be within his authority to drag her out of the café, to whip her in the street and bring her to her husband for further chastisement.

"What is your mosque?" demanded the Black Robe.

"Holy Martyrs of the Motherland," Sarah said, eyes downcast.

"An honorable mosque. Imam Plesa is well schooled." The Black Robe tapped the back of her chair with the cane. "Does your husband beat you?"

"When I need it," said Sarah, acquiescent.

"A good answer, sister, but its merit depends on the strictness of your husband." The Black Robe stood over her. Out of the corner of her eye, Sarah could see his grip tightening on the cane. The cane snaked out, lifted her left hand, drew it closer for him to examine without having to touch her flesh. She was grateful that she had removed all trace of the clear polish she usually wore. Grateful that she had remembered to slip on a wedding band. She had thought of Rakkim as she did so. "Your hands are soft. The hands of an idle, self-centered woman. A woman of many servants, or a woman who does not care about the state of her home." He let her hand fall, disgusted. "Your husband indulges you. Have you manipulated him with your female wiles? Are you a *beauty*, sister?"

"If my husband finds me so, all glory goes to Allah, the merciful, who created us."

"Another good answer." The cane swished. "Are you an *educated* woman, sister?"

Sarah hesitated, unsure of how to respond. She felt the attention of the room focused on her. The other women thankful that the Black Robe had selected someone else.

"Answer!"

The cane slammed onto her shoulder, and she groaned, bit her lips shut. The sound was like her throes of passion with

Rakkim, their cries as intertwined as their bodies. Her cheeks flamed at the memory.

"Have you gone to college? Have you drunk deep from that filthy water?"

"Yes . . . one year, until my husband forbade it. For which I am grateful."

The Black Robe nodded. "There may be hope for him yet." He cleared his throat. "I shall speak to your imam. He needs to discuss your behavior with your husband."

"Thank you," said Sarah, her head still bowed. Her shoulder ached from the cane.

The Black Robe tossed her permission card onto the floor.

Sarah made no move to retrieve it. Her eyes shimmered but she refused to cry. Through slitted lids, she watched the Black Robe saunter down the aisle and out the door.

The whispers started as the door shut behind him. Some of the women giggled, more out of nervousness than gaiety. None of them looked at her, not even the girl beside her.

Sarah heard them clicking away at the keyboards again, but she didn't move. She had known about the brutality of the Black Robes, the beatings and subordination of women, but that was academic knowledge. Her aching shoulder was a true education. Any thoughts she had about the pleasures of fundamentalism were gone. The price paid for such contentment was too high.

History was a messy and treacherous business, her favorite teacher had taught, but the truth was worth it. Sarah had been certain of the professor's wisdom while sitting in the classroom, but questioning the truth of the Zionist attack had given her pause, made her wonder if she should continue. To rewrite history was to invite chaos, with all its attendant pain and suffering. This goggle-eyed Black Robe had ended her doubts. There were things worse than chaos. No matter the risk, she was going to continue her research. The truth, wherever it led.

CHAPTER 11

Before noon prayers

"Rakkim Epps," he repeated to the security guard. "Professor War-riq isn't expecting me. Tell her I'm here in regard to a mutual friend at the university." He waited while the guard spoke on the phone, eyeing him. After another moment, the guard hung up, raised the gate, and Rakkim drove through.

It was Wednesday, five days since Sarah had disappeared, three days since Redbeard had called him in. He had spent yesterday going over Sarah's phone records and electronic receipts for the last year, looking for some pattern that might indicate where she had gone. There was no one and no place she called frequently, but that didn't surprise him—Sarah's calls to him had always been made from disposable phones sold under the counter all over the Zone. The GPS system on her car had revealed in minute detail her driving habits, giving him a color-coded grid of her mileage, but Sarah had always taken cabs to their rendezvous for just that reason, and paid cash. He hoped that she might have been less cautious with her chits, but there were no restaurant billings that didn't jibe with her recorded travel, no shopping sprees off the grid. To his shame, he even checked for hotel receipts, but nothing indicated she was seeing someone else. She was Redbeard's niece, she didn't make stupid mistakes. He checked anyway.

Yesterday he'd called Redbeard, asked him again to input Sarah's iris scans into the transit security system. Redbeard had argued that Sarah was still in the city, and it was too late to implement the procedure now anyway. Enter her data, Rakkim had insisted—if she uses mass transport anywhere in the country, she'll be flagged. Redbeard finally admitted that there had been a flaw in the software; a persistent Chinese worm had crashed the system and no one had been able to debug it. They were going to have to completely rebuild the security matrix. Rakkim asked how long this had been going on, but Redbeard refused to answer. Rakkim had hung up feeling the world moving in slow motion around him. Traffic lights failed for days at a time, new highways cracked at the first frost, and now one of the nation's most sophisticated lines of defense had failed, and there was no timetable to fix it. No wonder Redbeard had brought him in to find her.

Earlier this morning, he had used the pink message slip he had found in Sarah's office and called the Sociology Department, asked to speak to Marian. The secretary said that *Professor Warriq* only taught class on Fridays. Rakkim apologized, hung up, and looked up her address on the database Redbeard had given him access to. He had nothing better to do, and she seemed to be as close to a friend as Sarah had.

Rakkim drove up the winding residential streets, turned left at an elegant, blue-mosaic-tile mosque, and kept going. Marian Warriq lived in an exclusive Muslim enclave high on the hills overlooking the city, the low-slung mansions designed to take maximum advantage of the panorama. A pricey neighborhood for a sociology professor. The streets were nearly empty, the lawns lush, and the sidewalks scrubbed. No addresses on the houses. He would never have found the Warriq residence without the directions from the database. At least *that* still functioned.

A stocky man in a gray tunic opened the Warriq front door before Rakkim could knock. He stayed there, blocking the way, an ugly bruiser with a shaved head, a thick black beard, and the physiognomy of an anvil.

"*Kindly* let Mr. Epps in, Terry," called a woman behind him. The bodyguard bumped Rakkim as he stepped aside.

Rakkim removed his boots and walked into the living room.

Professor Warriq sat on a purple, floral-print sofa, hands clasped demurely in her lap, her head covered. She was a full-faced woman in her early fifties, with dark, clear eyes, dressed in a green chador shot with gold threads. His arrival was a surprise to her, but she was a surprise to him too. Marian Warriq had been Sarah's go-between, the woman who had brought Sarah's initial invitation after Redbeard had banished him. Marian had been veiled that day, but he was certain it was her. Her eyes gave her away . . . and her eyebrows, thick and lightly hennaed in the old style. He inclined his head. "Professor. A joy to see you again."

She lowered her eyes in acknowledgment of his hidden meaning, gestured to the sofa opposite her. "Please."

The living room was filled with antique Italian marble statues and Czarist tapestries, a stone head from Angkor Wat, and a small bronze horse dappled with verdigris, the sculpture so lifelike he almost expected it to gallop away. Terry stood nearby, arms crossed over his broad chest.

"I appreciate you seeing me without an invitation," said Rakkim. "You're probably wondering how I found you. I was in Sarah's office—"

"Sarah told me you were resourceful." Marian watched him. "She missed our lunch engagement on Friday, and she never called to apologize, which is most unlike her, and today *you* show up on my doorstep. What other reason would you have to be here?" Her hands were restless now, fingering prayer beads that weren't there. "Something's happened to her, hasn't it?"

"Not yet."

Marian murmured her thanks to Allah.

"I need to find her, though." Rakkim glanced toward her bodyguard, then back at her. "Perhaps we could talk on the veranda."

"Of course." Marian got control of herself, stood up. "I'll join you shortly."

Rakkim watched her glide out of the living room in a rustle of silk. He was still sitting there when Terry barreled over, jaw thrust forward.

"I see you and I see trouble," said Terry.

"Relax, Terry. I don't want to cause the professor any problems. You have my word."

"Your *word*?" Terry ran a hand across his scalp. With his scarred, flat face and epicanthic folds he looked like a club boxer or one of the Mongolian Muslims who had immigrated after the transition, wanting to be part of the great experiment. He squinted suddenly, pointed at Rakkim's left hand. "Is that Fedayeen ring of yours real?"

"As real as it gets."

Terry looked him over. "I was regular army."

"You look like you saw some action."

"You might say that. I was there at Newark. Every day of it."

Rakkim brought his right fist to his heart in salute.

Terry returned the salute. "Be careful with the lady, Fedayeen," he growled. "I'll hand you your head if you don't."

Marian breezed back into the room with a squat woman who wore a chador the same gray color as the bodyguard's tunic. The woman was carrying a heavy silver tea set as though it were weightless. Terry flung open the doors to the veranda, stood aside as the woman in the gray chador laid the tray on a small table. The woman poured them tea and backed away, closing the doors behind her. No wasted movement.

Marian waited until Rakkim sat down. "I don't know where Sarah is. If that's why you came here, I'm afraid you wasted a trip."

Rakkim smiled. "Gas is cheap. Besides, Sarah trusted you to contact me that first time. Maybe you know more than you think you do."

Marian sipped her tea, her pinkie crooked. The cool breeze rippled her chador, but she sat so that her modesty remained perfectly intact.

It was late morning and the smog from the industrial plants in the Kent Valley was piling up, sulfurous tendrils drifting over into the city. Through the haze he could see dozens of rusting oil tankers in the Sound, supertankers fresh from the Arctic Reserve, waiting to off-load. Looming behind the ships was the aircraft carrier *Osama bin Laden*, the former USS *Ronald Reagan*, now permanently on patrol offshore. Seventeen years ago a group of terrorists, an end-times Christian sect from Brazil, had hijacked a jumbo jet and attempted to crash it into the Capitol. Only the grace of Allah, and the outdated version of Microsoft Flight Simulator that the terrorists had trained on, had prevented a disaster. The tail of the jumbo jet still protruded from the waters of the Sound, out of the shipping lane, left there as a warning to the people to remain vigilant. Rakkim turned his chair toward Mount Rainier, a craggy dormant volcano covered in ice, rosy in the light.

"Sarah used to do that same thing when we sat out here," said Marian. "I like the city view myself. The people. The cars and trucks coming and going. The *energy*. I have no use for nature, but Sarah . . . she preferred to see the mountain, just like you."

Rakkim imagined Sarah sitting here on a day just like today, sipping tea in this exact spot. It had been six months since he had seen her. Six months of broken promises. "Did Sarah visit you often?"

"Almost every week. We met at the university about a year and a half ago. Quite by accident. She sat down at my table in the faculty lounge, and it was as if we had known each other for years." Marian ran her index finger around the rim of her teacup. "I knew *of* her, of course. *How the West Was Really Won* had caused a sensation on campus. You have no idea the resentment that book engendered among her colleagues." Marian kept watching him, then breaking away eye contact, as though not wanting to stare. "It was suggested by my department chair that I avoid her, but I ignored him. To be honest, I was pleased to be in the presence of such an iconoclast. It made me feel like a bit of an outlaw myself."

"When was the last time you saw her?"

"Um . . . two Sundays ago. A lovely day." Marian entwined her fingers. Her nails were clipped, perfectly shaped.

When Rakkim had first infiltrated the Bible Belt, one of the first things he'd noticed was the dirty, ragged fingernails of the women. Muslims kept their nails short and scrubbed, as required by the Qur'an, while women in the Bible Belt preferred their hands to look like talons, their nails often painted garish colors — their flag was a preferred motif, the old Stars and Stripes with a Christian cross in the field of blue.

"Is the tea not to your liking, Mr. Epps?"

Rakkim raised his cup. She looked poised, but weary in the morning light, crow's-feet etched into the corners of her eyes. His arrival must have confirmed her worst fears for Sarah, but she was carrying on, refusing to panic. No wonder she and Sarah were friends. He leaned forward to reassure her, saw Terry react from the other side of the glass. "I think your bodyguard is looking for an excuse to break my back."

"Terry is very protective. He and his wife take care of the house, but they also take care of me. My parents are deceased, and a spinster needs company." Marian smoothed her chador. "As it is written, loneliness is a doorway for the devil, Mr. Epps."

"The devil has plenty of doorways, Professor. Too many doorways and not enough locks. Loneliness is the least of our problems."

Marian smiled, lowered her eyes. "It's strange to be sitting here with you. We only met that once, but I feel that I know you Sarah talked about you *all* the time." Her eyes darted up. "I wish she were here now."

"So do I."

"We were collaborating on a book. Did she tell you that?"

Rakkim shook his head.

"Well, we were. We actually started making notes, gathering

research . . ." Marian adjusted her head scarf, pushed an errant strand of hair back out of sight. "We were going to write about the intellectual deterioration of our society since the transition. A risky topic, but Sarah relished the prospect of further intellectual combat, and I would have been careful to credit the religious authorities for our many advantages." Marian added another lump of sugar to her tea, the spoon clinking against the side of the cup as she stirred. "I was born a Muslim. You have no idea what it was like growing up under the old regime. The taunting, the insults . . ." Her mouth tightened to a thin line. "As a child, I had my hajib torn off my head more times than I can count, and after 9/11, it got worse. I'm not telling you this to elicit pity. The happiest day of my life was when we became an Islamic nation, but as a sociologist, I'm troubled by what I see." She looked directly at him, unflinching. "We used to lead the world in science and technology. Hard to believe, isn't it? Now, every year we have fewer graduates in engineering and mathematics. Our manufacturing plants are outdated, our farm productivity falling, and patent applications are only forty percent of what they were in the old regime." She toyed with her teaspoon, set it down with an effort, forced her hands still. "I'm talking too much, aren't I?"

Rakkim was thinking instead of the iris-scanning security software that didn't function, the weather reports that were mere guesses because the satellites were out of orbit. At least no one starved in the Islamic Republic, or froze to death in winter because they couldn't afford heating oil. The Bible Belt might have Coca-Cola and Carolina broadleaf, but it also had power brownouts and rickets, and unlike Islam, which treated almsgiving as a requirement of faith, beggars in the Bible Belt were hungry and cold.

"Rambling on is an occupational hazard for professors," sighed Marian. "Our students hang on our every word, but they're a captive audience."

"What happened with this book you and Sarah were working on?"

"She changed her mind. Six months ago, out of the blue."

"Was that when she got engaged to the son of the Saudi ambassador?"

"Who told you that?" Marian grimaced. "Her uncle *tried* to interest her in the petro-prince, and the prince was certainly taken with her, but you know Sarah."

"I do." Rakkim also knew Redbeard, which is why he wasn't surprised that the man had lied to him. The reason for the lie made him curious. It was a clumsy lie too. Redbeard must have known Rakkim would find out the truth. Maybe Redbeard had told an unnecessary lie to distract him from a more important one. *That* was Redbeard's style. "Sarah broke up with me about the same time she ended your collaboration. Maybe there's a connection. Why did she abandon the project with you?"

Marian hesitated. "She decided to write another book. She wouldn't tell me what it was about though. She said it was too dangerous."

"Sarah's already outraged half the country. Is she trying for the other half now?"

"She was *frightened*. When was the last time you saw Sarah scared?"

Rakkim stopped smiling.

"She was worried about me too. Taking cabs when she came by, asking me not to call her. We always left notes for each other—"

"You have no idea what the new book was about?"

"She refused to tell me." Marian clasped her hands. The inside of her right middle finger was indented from writing with a pen. A traditionalist. "I don't know if it will help, but one of the reasons Sarah came to visit these last months was to use my library. I have some specialized volumes. They're my father's books, actually. His books and journals."

"Your father was a historian?"

"He was a geological engineer." Marian held her head high. "My father was very bullheaded, but he was a fine engineer. He built dams and bridges and sports stadiums all over the world."

Rakkim remembered the map in Sarah's room, the pinhole on the Yangtze. "Did your father work in China?"

"Yes, for many years."

"The Three Gorges Dam?"

"How did you know?" Marian didn't expect an answer. "Three Gorges is the biggest dam in the world. My father was only part of the engineering team, and not the project chief, but he was very proud of the work he did. They started preliminary studies long before the transition, 1992, I believe, but even after it was completed, his team went back every other year to check the construction. The Yangtze is highly unpredictable, and the engineers needed to monitor the river flow."

"So . . . Sarah's new book was about China?"

"I asked her that. She said it was just a small part of the book, but she wouldn't go into detail. I always thought she'd tell me when the time was right. Is that why she's disappeared? Was it this book she was working on?"

Rakkim stroked his goatee. "Did you and Sarah talk much about your father? Was she curious about his work . . . his politics?"

"Not really. My father was a very private man. In most ways, I barely knew him. I think Sarah was more interested in his books than anything else. She was a brilliant researcher. The best historians are, you know."

"Then, I guess I should look at your father's library. If you don't mind?"

"Of course, but I hope you're not easily bored. After my father died, I went through his journals. He always kept them locked away, so I imagined they contained some dark secret, some profound insight into his soul." Marian shook her head. "I loved my father, but I could barely get through the first volume. There were no insights, just a vast laundry list of banal observations." She smoothed her sea green chador. "I have no idea what Sarah found so compelling in those pages, but she kept at it, week after week."

"I'd like to see them."

Marian didn't seem to have heard him. "You're just as Sarah described you. A warrior with warm eyes. She's very much in love with you. I was envious." Marian's cheeks colored.

"Wait until you get to know me . . . you won't be envious."

Marian smiled. "Sarah said the house she grew up in was quiet until you showed up, and then there was noise and laughter. She said you were the only one who wasn't afraid of Redbeard. Other than her."

"The only way to survive Redbeard is not to be afraid of him. Not to show it, anyway."

"You're a survivor, I can see that." Marian idly tapped her teacup. "I'm not much of a survivor. I've never really been tested . . . I've just been lucky. There was my family, and the income, and the university. It all just rolls along. You were an orphan, living on the streets. I can't imagine what that was like."

"Let's just say you learn not to linger over your food."

"Why did you join the Fedayeen?"

"I wanted to be my own man. I couldn't have done that if I stayed in that house."

"But you left the Fedayeen?"

Rakkim smiled. "Maybe I didn't like the man I had become."

Marian didn't return the smile. "I doubt that."

If Rakkim had known how perceptive she was, he might have kept silent. Then again, maybe Marian didn't need conversation to know who he was. *As if they had known each other for years,* that's how Marian had described her first meeting with Sarah. It would take longer for them, but maybe someday Rakkim and Marian could be friends too.

"Do you believe that each of us has only one true love, Mr. Epps?" Marian played with the spoon again. "One person we're meant to share our life with?"

"I don't know."

"Well, I'm absolutely *certain* of it. Sarah is too." A sudden breeze rippled Marian's chador, and for an instant, before she held down the fabric, it looked as if she were flying. Just an instant, but the impression remained that she was not fully bound to the earth. "I found my true love when I was twenty-two. He was a computer programmer, an honorable Muslim, but my father had other suitors in mind. He would not yield, nor would I. There was a standoff in our house for several years while my love and I met surreptitiously, just as you and Sarah did. I hoped to wear my father down, but then the Zionists upended the world. My love was on holiday in Washington, D.C., when the bomb exploded. I had planned to join him there, but I backed out at the last minute." She dabbed at her eyes. "Not a day goes by that I don't regret that he went on holiday to *that* particular city, on *that* particular date . . . not a day goes by that I don't wish that I had gone with him."

Rakkim touched her hand.

She pulled away. "Find her, Mr. Epps."

"It's a promise."

CHAPTER 12

Before midafternoon prayers

The Wise Old One was getting his blood cleansed when Ibrahim walked into the restoration room. His eldest son was dour today, his eyes hooded. "What bad news do you bring?"

Ibrahim hesitated. "Our brother Oxley is dead. He supposedly had a heart attack, but—"

"He was murdered. Ibn Azziz strangled Oxley himself."

"I . . . I only just got word of his death," said Ibrahim, the faintest edge of annoyance in his voice. He stayed still, lean and dark as his long-gone Arab mother. He always seemed ill at ease in the restoration room, but that was to be expected—he was only fifty-three, with the confidence in the natural scheme of things reserved for the young.

The Old One listened to the humming and the hissing of the machines around him, watching the plastic tubes in his veins pulsing with his own freshened blood. Oxley's assassination couldn't have come at a worse time, but the Old One kept silent. Ibrahim was prone to see the hand of Allah in the falling of a dry leaf, the chirping of a sparrow. He was already unnerved by the death of their cat's-paw Oxley. If he sensed the Old One's concern, fear would spread through the family like a virus. "Oxley shall be missed, but he has already served his purpose. There is no cause for alarm."

"I should not have disturbed you, Father."

The Old One waved him silent. "Nothing to forgive, my son. All is well."

The restoration room was completely white—floor, walls, ceiling, the machines themselves white enamel. It made the space seem limitless. In this world of infinite white, the Old One's blood appeared even redder through the clear plastic. Bright red blood, heated to kill any toxins, then cooled back to 98.6. Hyperoxygenated blood for increased energy. Additional blood added to his own, blood from John, the blond-bearded acolyte with the creamy white skin. His son. Blood of his blood. Returning the favor of life.

The Old One had hoped his airy dismissal of Oxley's murder would be a cue for Ibrahim to leave, but he stayed where he was, hands clasped behind his back—a posture he had picked up from his days at the London School of Economics. Ibrahim was clearly disturbed, but the Old One detected something more. A failure on the part of the Old One was an opportunity for Ibrahim. The burden of an eldest son. The frustration of a chief adviser whose counsel had not been headed. "Speak, Ibrahim."

"Father . . . Mahdi . . . it took us years to secure Oxley's co-operation, even longer for Oxley to ingratiate himself with the Fedayeen commander. How *can* he be replaced?"

"Brother Oxley dwells now in paradise, it is Ibn Azziz we must concern ourselves with."

"Can you not task Darwin with killing Ibn Azziz?" pleaded Ibrahim. "Surely you can orchestrate a more compliant successor to Oxley than this wild child."

"Darwin is engaged in more pressing matters," said the Old One, enjoying Ibrahim's distress. "Don't worry, all men are alike, lost in a maze of needs and desires. Seducing Oxley called for certain . . . *inducements*, seducing Ibn Azziz will merely require different methods. Our challenge will be to discern those methods and then implement them."

"But the *time*, Father, we have no time—"

The Old One jabbed a hand at his son, the tubes thrashing. "Don't speak to *me* of time."

Ibrahim lowered his eyes for a moment, but no longer. Three years ago Ibrahim had argued against selecting Ibn Azziz for the upper echelon of the Black Robes. Ibrahim was smart enough not to bring it up now. Smart enough to know he didn't need to.

The three doctors in the room might as well have been deaf. They paid attention only to the devices they monitored, making minute adjustments as required.

"Take heart. Oxley was docile . . . but overcautious," said the Old One. "Ibn Azziz is hot-tempered and harder to control, but *when* we bring him to heel, he will be infinitely more useful than his predecessor."

"As you say, Mahdi," murmured Ibrahim. His dark eyes lingered on the tubes running into the Old One, but his expression remained unreadable.

"Ibn Azziz's ascetic nature might even appeal more to the Fedayeen commander than Oxley's excesses," said the Old One. "General Kidd is devout. Even with the grand ayatollah's blessing of Oxley, he found the man distasteful. No, my son, in years to come, you shall see that the ascension of Ibn Azziz was a manifestation of the will of Allah, the all-knowing, with whom all things are possible."

Ibrahim held his open hands high, offered his blessing.

"Now go, consult with our brothers among the Black Robes. Find the way into the heart of Ibn Azziz, that we may act accordingly."

Ibrahim backed slowly out of the restoration room.

The Old One lay back on the table. Would that it were so simple. Oxley's murder was a disaster, just as Ibrahim had said. Oxley was profane and corrupt, but a master politician, able to insinuate himself into the halls of Congress, giving their allies the cover of his religiosity, and condemning enemies from every mosque. Now he was dead. The Old One had underestimated Ibn Azziz, thinking him merely another of the fiery young clerics attracted to the Black Robes. Not anticipating Ibn Azziz's boldness was a failure on his part. He had been distracted these last few months, but that was no excuse.

A doctor checked the Old One's cuticles, then made a notation in his chart.

The Old One hated the sight of his feet and hands on the examination table. Steroids and genetic infusions kept him vital, organ transplants kept pace with the passing years, but his extremities were beyond treatment. Reedy and translucent, his hands and feet allowed a glimpse of his true age, gave hope to those looking for infirmity. He glanced toward the door. Ibrahim was restless. The Old One took a risk in ceding a measure of power to him. Without a degree of autonomy, Ibrahim's sizable talents would be denied to the Old One, but too much power would ignite the boy's ambition. That was why the Old One kept his own network of spies, both in Las Vegas, and in the Islamic Republic. The Old One needed to know what was happening and needed to know it first. Ibrahim would bear closer scrutiny in the weeks ahead.

The Old One flexed his fingers, made a fist. He might minimize the consequences of Oxley's murder to Ibrahim, but not to himself. Losing Oxley's influence over Congress was bad enough, jeopardizing the relationship with the Fedayeen was infinitely worse. General Kidd had been repelled by Oxley's excesses, but the Old One's covert intercession with Kidd's imam had slowly overcome his disgust. It had taken years, but when the moment of truth came, General Kidd would send his troops to serve the Mahdi rather than the president.

The army remained loyal to the president, but that was surmountable—though far fewer in number, the Fedayeen were infinitely superior militarily. In a confrontation, the army would quickly capitulate. The problem was that Oxley was the only direct contact between General Kidd and the Old One. His death shook a shaky alliance. If the Fedayeen held back when called upon, if General Kidd harbored any doubts . . . there would be no way the Old One's plan could succeed.

A doctor leaned over the Old One. "Your new kidneys are still functioning perfectly. No sign of rejection, thanks be to Allah."

The Old One ignored him. He was on his fourth set of kidneys. The doctors always emphasized the miraculous over the science, hoping to gain his favor with their flattery.

It was because of the Fedayeen that the Old One hadn't sent Darwin to kill Ibn Azziz. The Black Robes would spread the tale of Oxley's unfortunate heart attack, but General Kidd would find out the truth soon enough. Assassinating Ibn Azziz would cause too much turmoil among the Black Robes and diminish their authority. They might lose General Kidd's support altogether.

The Old One felt his cheeks and fingertips tingling, part of his vast reawakening that signaled the end of his weekly treatment. His vision seemed more acute, his hearing sharper, and there was a fullness in his private parts too, a hunger beyond flesh. He slowly sat up, rubbed his hands together as though he might give off sparks.

It would take time to turn Ibn Azziz, to bend him, but the Old One had no doubt that the young zealot would align himself with him. The Old One was chosen by Allah for this historical mission, the restoration of the caliphate. If Ibn Azziz was truly led of God, he would see that. The youngster just needed guidance. First though, Darwin needed to find the girl. Find her and follow her. A cancer was at the heart of the Old One's plan, and only Darwin had the knife sharp enough to cut it out without causing harm. First find the girl, then the Old One would contact Ibn Azziz. If that didn't work, if the boy refused to accept his dominion, the Old One would reach out to General Kidd directly.

The Old One tore the tubes from his arms, flung them aside, blood dripping onto that pure white floor as he slid off the table.

CHAPTER 13

After late-evening prayers

Rakkim eased out the side door of the Blue Moon, right behind a noisy foursome of oil workers fresh from the offshore rigs, the riggers drunk, staggering as they elbowed their way through the crowd outside. The wind off the Sound made him shiver, but the riggers were in jeans and T-shirts with the sleeves rolled, flashing their muscles to the moderns, who gave them room. Rakkim stayed with the riggers, close enough to smell the petroleum in their shaggy hair, then peeled off into one of the Zone's cobblestone alleys.

He had stopped at the Blue Moon after spending a fruitless afternoon in Marian's library. He and Mardi had had dinner and she'd given him his share of the week's receipts, the part that they didn't report to the tax authorities. She went on about some incredible bourbon the new salesman had let her sample, then asked him again if he could help the grocer and his family escape to Canada. He told him again it would be spring. Maybe when he found Sarah, he would take them *all* to Canada. Winter or no winter, he would find a way.

Rakkim had gotten quiet after that, and Mardi knew him well enough not to try to engage him in conversation. He ate beef stew and thought of geology and earthquakes and load-bearing trusses. Marian's father, Richard Warriq, had hundreds of textbooks in the library, but Marian said it was his journals that Sarah had been interested in. Warriq had traveled to China for over forty years, before and after the transition, one of the few Americans who had such access. Sarah had been looking for something in his journals. She must not have found it, because Marian said Sarah was supposed to visit and do more research last Saturday, the day after she had disappeared.

Three jocks in college letterman sweaters trudged down the alley toward him, half-slipping on the slick stones, wispy beards hanging from their chins like dirty icicles. The wind sent fast-food papers tumbling. Rakkim gave the jocks plenty of room, but they barely noticed him, arms around each other's shoulders, singing some rah-rah song. He increased his pace as he zigzagged through the maze of alleys, the nearby tech shops shuttered this time of night.

Rakkim had no idea what Sarah was researching. Plenty of topics would be dangerous to write about, even for the niece of Redbeard. Any examination of the legal authority of the Black Robes could lead to trouble, and no publisher would dare print an exposé of the finances of the congressional leaders or the army high command. Rakkim kept coming back to Sarah's interest in

China and Miriam's father's work on the Three Gorges Dam—
that was the only connection he had.

Although Russia had given refuge to the Zionists, China, the
richest and most dynamic nation, had aroused the greatest concern
among the Islamic high command. General Kidd, the Fedayeen
commander, had been the most bellicose, particularly when he had
a cheek full of fresh khat. Most Westerners preferred the distillation
of the euphoric stimulant, but Kidd preferred the herb itself, flying
it in daily from Yemen. In private, Kidd had stated that if the Chinese ever signed a pact with the Russian Bloc, or attacked nearby
Muslim countries for their oil, he had a list of prime targets ripe for
destruction. He had never named them, but the Three Gorges Dam
had to be high on the list; six hundred feet high, it allowed ships
direct access from the ocean to the interior. Its destruction would
flood millions of acres and cripple the Chinese economy overnight.

If Sarah was writing a critical book on the Fedayeen, that qualified as dangerous, since most of their covert actions were in vio-
lation of the cease-fire with the Bible Belt. The pushpin in Sarah's
map would have been a visual cue for Sarah, one she had removed
after she'd decided that Redbeard might see it and ask questions.

Rakkim had hoped to find evidence in Warriq's journals, some
indication that he was feeding the Fedayeen information about
China, taking notes for a future attack, or some potential sabo-
tage. Unfortunately, the journals were as impenetrable as the textbooks, Warriq's handwriting neat but cramped, the words pressed
together with barely a break. One shelf of the library was given to
his private journals, thirty-eight of which were devoted to his work
in China. Rakkim had barely skimmed two volumes this afternoon, before his eyes gave out.

Marian was right—her father's journals *were* a laundry list, a
travelogue of useless information. Warriq cataloged every meal,
noted every landmark, accounted for every hour of his schedule.
Page after page, the man's disposition was uniformly foul. The

meat was of poor quality, the tomatoes tasteless, the soup cold. His bed was too hard. Or too soft. Proper hygiene for his prayers was difficult. The roads were poorly designed. The weather was not to his liking. His descriptions of his Chinese employers were equally critical: they were dismissed as "ignoramuses," "atheists," "eaters of pigs and dogs." His superiors fared no better, and the accounts of his engineering work yielded nothing of particular interest. Rakkim found no evidence that the man was a spy, but ample reason to conclude he was a supercilious pain in the ass. Rakkim had asked Marian if he might take a few volumes home, but she had politely refused, said she *never* let them out of her keeping, but invited him back at his leisure to spend more time in the stacks.

An aluminum can clattered across the alley behind him. Rakkim turned, but no one was there. He listened, but there was only the faint hum of cars on the freeways. He waited for another minute, immobile, then started walking. He was being followed, but whoever it was, wasn't particularly adept. Accidents happened when shadowing someone. You were tempted to hurry so as not to be outdistanced, but in your haste you stumbled or knocked something over. It happened. The secret was not to go silent, but to make a great show of noise afterward, cursing to the moon, howling that you had hurt yourself. The one being followed would actually take comfort in the racket, consider you harmless, and go on his way. Silence was certain to rouse suspicion.

Rakkim could easily escape his pursuer; he knew every twist and turn of these alleys, every loose cobblestone and open manhole, but he waited. Knife in hand. A Fedayeen knife was a technological wonder, a carbon-polymer alloy infused with the DNA of its owner. At a half-inch thick, it was unbreakable, sharper than surgical steel, invisible to metallic and biological scans. Literally part of the fighter.

Two thugs in black trench coats scurried around the corner behind him, stopped when they saw him.

Rakkim beckoned them closer, then turned, hearing motion in the alley *ahead* of him.

Anthony Jr. and another kid, also in trench coats, slid down a fire escape, putting Rakkim between the four of them. Anthony Jr. wore a headset. He must have been following Rakkim from the roofs, where the light was better, coordinating the movements of the other two. Not bad.

"You shouldn't have taken my goods at the Super Bowl." Anthony Jr. slipped off the headset. "That ain't kosher."

Rakkim smiled. The kid was a lousy thief, but he had his father's sense of humor.

All four of them took baseball bats from the slings inside their trench coats.

"Nice choreography," said Rakkim. "I like the matching coats too. Whose idea was that?"

"That was Anthony," said the one beside Anthony Jr. "Not bad, huh?"

"Shut up," said Anthony Jr.

The first two closed in. They looked like brothers, overgrown hyenas with stringy blond hair and narrow, protruding foreheads. They tapped their bats on the stones as they approached. The tapping was probably supposed to scare Rakkim, but they looked like blind men testing the terrain with their canes.

Anthony Jr. assumed a batter's stance about ten feet away and took a few practice swings. Rakkim felt the breeze on his face.

"You sure you want to do this, Anthony?" said Rakkim.

"*Fuck* yes," said Anthony Jr.

Rakkim stood relaxed, watching them close in. If there had been only two of them, he might have kept a wall at his back, but in this kind of situation, he preferred mobility.

"He got a blade," said the first hyena.

"You got us really terrified, mister," snickered the one beside Anthony Jr., a bandy-legged punk missing a couple of front teeth.

He blew balls of spit when he talked. "We took down some soldier boys last month. They had knives too. Lot bigger than that little bitty thing of yours."

"Careful of this guy," warned Anthony Jr. "He's not like the other ones."

"I hit a home run on one of them soldier boys," said the first hyena. "Blew out his kneecap and he practically begged us to take his gear." He held up his left wrist. "This here's his watch. What time *you* got, mister?"

"You can keep your watch, Rakkim," said Anthony Jr. "My father thinks you're hot shit and that counts for something. You want to hand over your wallet, we'll call it even."

"Good to see a son who respects his father," said Rakkim.

"You going to give us the wallet?" said Anthony Jr.

Rakkim looked from one to the other, shook his head. "I'm carrying three or four thousand dollars. I'd hate to lose that."

"Fucking *jackpot*," said the punk next to Anthony Jr., lunging forward, eager now.

"I said be *careful*," said Anthony Jr. "He's Fedayeen."

"He's Fedayeen," the first hyena mimicked in a high falsetto. He tossed his blond curls, pretended to yawn, then attacked, the bat raised high.

Rakkim stepped into the charge, dodged the bat, and jabbed him in the shoulder with his knife, just a little stick, turned, and poked the other hyena in the chest, felt Anthony Jr.'s bat whistle past his head, and stuck him in the belly, then slid the tip of the knife across the chin of the toothless punk as he swung and missed with the bat. It had been one smooth, continuous movement on Rakkim's part, a dance move where he was the only one who could hear the music. A Fedayeen training game, one they played every day in boot camp, parry and thrust, feint and jab, using only the very tip of the knife, just enough to draw blood, not enough to do lasting damage. By the end of boot camp, most of the recruits had at least a hundred scars. Rakkim had barely a dozen.

The four of them came at him again and he stuck each of them in turn, dodging and twisting, always someplace where they didn't expect him, the tip of the knife nipping their arms and legs, their back and sides, hands and face. They came at him again and again, howling with pain and frustration, cursing as he slipped out of reach, but still coming after him, blood flying, their trench coats in ribbons.

Rakkim slowed slightly, as though tired, and Anthony Jr. unwound, swinging for the fences. Rakkim backed away at the last moment, and the bat caught the first hyena square in the chest. It sounded like a tree limb cracking. The hyena made a small sound, more of a moist gasp, then collapsed onto the alley. His bat rolled across the cobblestones.

"What did you *do*, Anthony?" squealed the other hyena, rushing over to help. Rakkim had sliced his right ear, cartilage flapping as he ran. "What did you *do*?"

"I . . . can't . . . breathe," hissed the first hyena, as his brother bent beside him.

"You're okay." Anthony Jr. was bleeding too, but he still circled Rakkim, the bat cocked.

"Can't . . . can't . . . breathe," repeated the first hyena. A bubble of blood inflated from one nostril. Popped.

"I'm getting him to a hospital," said the other hyena. He slid an arm under his brother.

The first hyena screamed as he was lifted.

"We got a job to finish," said Anthony Jr.

"*We're* finished," muttered the other hyena, carrying his brother down the alley.

"This ain't right, Anthony," said the punk with the missing teeth. His trench coat was spattered with blood, his face opened up. "This guy's a buzz saw."

"Okay, he's got some moves," admitted Anthony Jr. "So do we."

The punk shook his head and trotted down the alley after the others.

Anthony Jr. stared at Rakkim. "I'm not afraid of you."

"They don't give medals for that. They should, but they don't."

Anthony Jr. hefted the bat, his knuckles slick with blood. "We still got to settle up for what you did to me at the Super Bowl. I stole that wallet fair and square."

Rakkim held up a hand. "Take a breath."

In spite of himself, Anthony Jr. did what he was told.

"Tell your father, I'm going to recommend you for the Fedayeen."

"*Right.*"

"I'm serious." The Fedayeen had a high fatality rate, but the way Anthony Jr. was going, he had better odds in uniform than on the street.

Anthony Jr. peered at him. "Don't fuck with me. I won't tolerate that."

"I'm not fucking with you."

Anthony Jr. slowly nodded. "Thank you." He slipped the bat back into his trench coat, hands trembling. "I mean . . . I'd like that."

"You won't be thanking me once you hit boot camp, but maybe you will when you get through it. *If* you get through it."

"I'll get through it." Anthony Jr. glanced around. "Is it true what they say? You know. Fedayeen . . . you're amped up, aren't you?"

"No, it's not true."

"Come on. Look what you just did to me and my boyos. They do something to you when you become Fedayeen, don't they? New and improved, that's what I want."

"Fedayeen aren't supermen."

"No way you're normal."

Rakkim laughed. "Well, *that's* true. The thing about Fedayeen . . . after the first month of basic, the docs take the ones who survive, the ones who haven't dropped dead or quit, and they give them the cocktail."

"What's that, some magic potion?"

"Gene therapy. It's a series of injections—"

"I *knew* it."

"It's not magic. Ninety-eight percent of what makes Fedayeen so dangerous is training. Training and . . . attitude. All the gene juice in the world isn't going to help if you don't have the right attitude, and all the attitude won't do you any good without the training. In fact, attitude without the training is guaranteed to get you killed. What the cocktail does is allow you to train at a level no one else could physically or mentally tolerate. Fedayeen basic lasts for a whole year, a year of ten-mile swims and fifty-mile runs, of improvised weaponry and hand-to-hand combat in heat and cold, and in that whole time you're lucky if you get three hours of sleep a night. The cocktail makes it possible. Fedayeen have quick reflexes. They have a high pain threshold, a perfect sense of direction, and their wounds heal faster, but it's the *training* that makes a Fedayeen. Are you ready for that?"

"This cocktail . . . you still got it inside you?"

Rakkim nodded. "It's permanent."

"Once Fedayeen, always Fedayeen, that's what they say."

"That's what they say."

"I want it."

"Tell me if you still believe that when you get through your first year."

Anthony Jr. grinned. "You said *when*, not if."

"You should go home and take care of those cuts. You want me to tell your father?"

"I can handle it." Anthony Jr. stared at him, plucked at his lip. "Rakkim . . . sir, how could you leave the Fedayeen? Why would you want to?"

Rakkim smiled. There was hope for the kid yet.

CHAPTER 14

After late-evening prayers

Sarah awoke from a nightmare—Rakkim on his knees, a hand clasped to his side, blood leaking through his fingers. She awoke from that nightmare and found herself in another. This one real.

Sounds of bubble wrap popping woke her up. A scrap of packing material left in the shadow of the alley where the security light didn't reach. A scrap she had placed in the funnel point where anyone coming in the back way would have to step. The nearby trash can overflowed with cardboard boxes, Styrofoam, and packing material. Anyone walking on the piece of plastic might think it just an unlucky break . . . a bit of sloppiness from the tenants, but the footsteps outside were hurrying now. Whoever was coming for her was not fooled.

She rolled off the couch, fully dressed, everything she needed in the loose pants and zippered jacket she slept in. The apartment was on the third floor, the window open to the alley below—she didn't have time to get away, but she had time to unlock the door to the hallway and leave it ajar, as though she had fled in haste. She had time to remove the piece of wood paneling behind the radiator. It was an old building, pretransition, with thick outer walls to keep the heat in. Gas and oil had been expensive then. There was room in the wall for her to hide, a tiny space she had lined with insulation. Footsteps pounded up the stairwell as she squeezed into the tiny hiding spot. She locked the panel back into place and prayed that the seam in the dark pine was aligned with the others. She lay flattened in the dark, the radiator hissing. Waiting. Just as she had rehearsed so many times, except that in rehearsal she hadn't already been drenched with sweat. She thought of Rakkim and wondered if he was still angry at her for standing him up at the Super Bowl. Probably. He held a grudge. Footsteps in the hallway. Creak of the front door being pushed open. Her heart was beating so loudly it sounded like thunder.

Sarah closed her eyes, fought off the fear and the claustrophobia. With her eyes closed she could imagine that she stood in an auditorium, gathering her thoughts before giving a lecture. There were voices in the room now, and the sound of furniture being knocked over. She opened her eyes. There was a crack in the paneling from the radiator's heat, a crack that allowed a glimpse of the men ransacking the apartment. There were two . . . no, three of them. She didn't think they were Redbeard's men . . . they were too loud, too clumsy. Most of them. One of them though . . . her eye was pressed against the crack, eyelashes brushing against the rough wood. While the others darted around, a bald man moved to the couch and placed a hand on the cushion, felt the heat from her body still lingering. She shuddered as though he had touched *her*.

"Go check the roof," ordered the bald man.

Sarah saw a man in a long leather coat rush out the door, heard his footsteps beating up the stairs, not even trying to be quiet. It was the middle of the night, but the neighbors knew well enough not to investigate sudden noises.

"The bitch is *gone*," grumbled a tall, freckled scarecrow.

The bald man picked up a container of half-eaten Chinese food on the coffee table, remnants of her dinner. Sniffed it. "Thermal this shithole. I'll decide if she's gone." He put his feet up on the coffee table, dug in with the chopsticks. A glop of chicken and bean sprouts fell into his lap on the way to his mouth. He went back for more.

Scarecrow circled the living room, using a handheld thermal imager to look for her. He scanned the stuffed chair, the hutch, walked out the ceiling and the floor. He hit the walls too, the unit beeping as he passed the radiator.

Sarah bit her finger to stop her teeth from chattering, sweat pouring down her face.

Scarecrow kept walking. When he finished, he started toward the bedroom.

"Don't forget to get around the closet," said the bald man. "And behind the shitter!" He started on the leftover sweet-and-sour pork, chewing with his mouth open.

Leather coat came back. "Nobody on the roof. It's a jump to the next building, but she could do it." He laughed. "If she was motivated."

The bald man licked the chopsticks clean, stood up from the couch. "Toss the place. I'll hit the bedroom and check her personals."

Leather coat tore a mass-produced picture of the Great Mosque in Jerusalem off the wall, examined the back, then threw it onto the floor. He moved around the room. The desk was emptied, drawers overturned. Bent the TV screen in half.

Sarah turned away from the crack in the paneling, listening to the sounds of destruction, breathing through her mouth. Roasting. She had rented the apartment months ago, hoping she would never need it. Hoped she would never need the hiding spot either. She couldn't believe they had found her. She had been so careful. These weren't Redbeard's men . . . it had to be the Old One who had sent them. She peeked out again through the crack.

"Little missy travels light," scarecrow said to the bald man, as they walked back into the living room. "Just a toothbrush in the bathroom, no purse, no notepad, no papers."

The bald man sat on the couch with a quart of milk in his hand, drinking straight from the carton, and the idea of him raiding her refrigerator enraged her out of all proportion.

"I don't know about Ibn Azziz taking over from Oxley," said

scarecrow. "They say he don't smoke, don't drink, don't pump whores. How can you trust somebody like that?"

"That's what a grand mullah is *supposed* to be like, you heathen prick." The bald man shook his head. "All that matters is if he pays the bounty."

"I'll take Oxley any day," said leather coat. "Man knew how to throw a party—"

The bald man chucked the empty milk carton onto the floor, wiped his lips with the back of his hand. "This Ibn Azziz, he's in a hurry. We're going to work steady with this one."

Sarah shifted slightly in the hiding spot and a raised nail scraped her arm. The Old One *hadn't* sent these three men—they were bounty hunters. The Black Robes had a small army of mercenaries under contract for their dirty work, ex army, ex-police, ex-cons. Even so, the Black Robes had never dared to challenge Redbeard directly. Now they were actually going after his niece?

"We got here five minutes sooner, we would have caught the bitch," said scarecrow. "I could have bought a new car with my share." He booted an antique mahogany bookstand, shattered the thin wood. "If asshole hadn't stopped to take a piss . . ."

"I got a weak bladder," said leather coat.

"Yeah, and if you *didn't* have a weak bladder, I'd be riding in style tomorrow." Scarecrow played with one of those Filipino flip knives that went *snickity-snick*. "Now maybe one of the other teams is going to collect the reward."

Other teams? Sarah tasted dust in her mouth.

"We'll find her," said the bald man. "Little girl can't hide forever."

Scarecrow jabbed the couch with his knife, drove the blade in and out without passion. "What do the Black Robes want with her anyway?"

The bald man sat on the couch watching scarecrow play with the knife. "Don't know. Don't care, either."

Sarah heard liquid splash on the floor, and leather coat saying, "Ahhhhhhhh. That's better."

"You're disgusting," said scarecrow. Stuffing from the couch drifted across the floor.

The bald man stood up. "Let's call it a night. She's on the run now, scared and not thinking straight. We'll catch little miss high and mighty another day."

Sarah listened to them shuffle out, slamming the door behind them. She didn't move. She stayed where she was, in the cramped darkness. She hated the dark. She had slept for years with a night-light on. Redbeard had tried to break her of the habit, but even he had been forced to give up. Rakkim . . . Rakkim had slept on the floor next to her bed when she had nightmares. It had been the only thing that helped.

The living room was quiet. She was half dozing from the heat. How had they found her? What mistake had she made? She changed outfits every time she left the apartment. Sometimes she dressed as a good fundamentalist. Sometimes as a modern. Sometimes as a Catholic. She never took a direct route to the apartment, never went to the same grocery store twice. Still, they had found her. Her eyes burned and she didn't have room to wipe them. She was going to have to move again. The bald man had said she was going to be scared and not thinking straight. He was more right than she wanted to admit.

She craned her neck. Squinted at the luminous dial of her watch. It had been over twenty minutes since the bounty hunters had left. Her legs ached, and her lungs were heavy from the heat, but she stayed where she was. If you can't be smart, be patient, that's what Redbeard used to say, his insult the price of his wisdom.

She wished Rakkim were here. He would know what to do. She had wanted to tell him what she was up to, she had argued that he could be trusted, but the answer had always been the same. *Trust no one*. Sarah should have told him.

Her leg was cramping and her nose itched. A few nights ago she had walked within a block of Rakkim's club, close enough to hear the music from the Blue Moon, close enough to imagine walking in and having a drink with him, her hand on his knee under the table. Instead she had turned away, angry with herself for getting too close. The Blue Moon would be the first place anyone would look for her. In spite of everything she knew, these last few days she had acted as though it were another game between her and Redbeard, just another round of hide-and-seek. The appearance of the bounty hunters tonight had put that lie to rest. Redbeard was the least of her worries.

Sarah checked her watch again. Over an hour since the men had left. She peered through the crack, then popped out the panel. Winced as it clattered to the floor. No sound from the hallway. She eased herself out from behind the radiator, joints popping, so stiff she could hardly bend. It was five minutes before she could breathe freely.

The apartment was trashed, drawers emptied, her few items of clothing on the floor. It didn't matter; she wasn't taking anything with her. She walked over to the small kitchen, picked up a knife. It was cheap and had a thin blade, but it made her feel better. She walked to the blinds, peeked out the corner. The alley was dark and empty. She crossed to the door, slowly turned the handle, and opened—

The bald man leaned against the opposite wall, big and blocky, arms crossed. "Jesus, lady, I was wondering if you were *ever* going to come out from wherever you were hiding."

Sarah slammed the door, but he kicked it open, and when she came at him with the knife, he slapped it away, sent it flying. Then he smacked her, almost knocked her out. He was inside the apartment now, carrying her forward, his hand on her throat. When she tried to bite him, he hit her again.

"Hope you don't mind that I sent the boys home," said the bald man. "I just hate to share the reward . . . or anything else, for that matter." He laughed, threw her onto the couch.

Sarah struggled as he lay on top of her, and she smelled the Chinese food on his breath and milk . . . the milk from her refrigerator, sour now, warm and rank. His eyes were gray and terribly calm, as though a woman squirming under him happened every day.

"The Black Robes want you alive and kicking," he said, his knee pressed between her legs. "So you don't have to worry about me doing any permanent damage. I'm not about to hurt you." He kneed her harder, made her gasp. "See, that didn't hurt, did it?"

"—off me," Sarah gasped, slapping at his face. "Get *off*."

"That's it," said the bald man, one hand unbuttoning his pants. "I like a fighter."

Sarah spit in his face. "My uncle . . . I'm Redbeard's niece, damn you."

The bald man pulled back for an instant, then grabbed her hair and twisted. "I almost believed you for a second there, sweetheart. Nice try."

Sarah jerked free. "It's *true*."

The bald man pinned her down with one elbow, unzipped her pants. "Pleased to make your acquaintance, Redbeard's niece. I'm Mister Dave Thompson." His eyes were like stagnant water. "You feel better now?"

Sarah screamed.

"*Louder*," he said, grunting as he slid his hand into her panties. "I can't hear you."

Sarah arched her back, tore at his face.

"This is what I do," he said, panting. "This is old Dave's job. I find little runaways and I bring them back, and sometimes, *sometimes*"—he slipped a finger inside her—"sometimes I get the okay to ruin them a little. To make sure no one wants them back." He wriggled his fat finger. "That's *nice*," he whispered as she kicked at him. "You're tight as a new glove."

Sarah thrashed around on the sofa as his finger slid deeper inside her. She tried to bite him, but he kept out of reach.

The bald man tried to pull down her pants with his free hand. "You know the more you fight, the better it's going to be for me, don't you? I like educating runaways about the real world, the world outside of their daddy's house. I'm going to give you a grade-A schooling, little miss."

Sarah knocked over the empty container of food, chopsticks clattering on the coffee table, and she reached out, feeling around.

"Most runaways . . ." The bald man was groaning now, his eyes eager. "Most of them just blubber and say their prayers the whole time, but you . . . I can tell you're going to be fighting the whole time." Sweat rolled off his sideburns. "Come on, fight me. Come *on.*"

Sarah fumbled around on the coffee table, fingernails skittering on the glass.

"I'm not such a bad guy. You'll see. Old Dave is going to give you a fun time, whether you appreciate it or not." He laughed, nuzzled her breasts, came up for air. "I'm gonna split you wide—" He blinked. His mouth worked but no sounds came out. He stayed in position on top of her, frozen, one hand still in her panties. His lips quivered, showed his uneven, yellow teeth.

Sarah looked right at him. The wooden chopstick was stuck in his left eye, only the end protruding from the ruined socket. Driven deep into his brain. Red Chinese ideograms were on the end of the chopstick. Probably *Good luck* or something. She didn't move, didn't hurry. She watched as a single spot of blood appeared in the white of his other eye. A tiny rose blooming in his gray eyes, and then he was limp on top of her. She rolled him off her. His dead hand flopped out of her panties as he banged his head on the coffee table and landed on the floor in a heap. She raced for the bathroom and washed her face, washed her hands. Tore off her panties, washed herself, washed herself again. She could still feel him inside her. She wasn't nauseous. Her hands didn't shake. What was even more surprising was how happy she was.

When she came back to the living room, the bald man lay there, a trickle of some viscous liquid running down his cheek. He might have grandchildren somewhere, fat, ruddy kids he played ball with, little girls he brought sweets to and read to sleep at night. She kicked him in the head as hard as she could. The hollow thud was music. No more sweets, no more stories.

CHAPTER 15

Before sundown prayers

Rakkim sat at the table on the inside wall of the downtown restaurant, just as the message on his cell had suggested. The early-dinner crowd of beardless moderns had returned to their jobs in the high-rises, the conservatives had left for sunset prayers, but the restaurant was still busy, voices bouncing off the raw brick interior. If he and Sarah could be seen in public together, they might have gone to this kind of place, relaxed and fun and with a good mix of people. His phone beeped. Another call from Colarusso, the third since Rakkim had run into Anthony Jr. last night. Colarusso was either calling to berate him for recommending Anthony Jr. to the Fedayeen, or inviting him to Sunday dinner. Either way, Rakkim thought it was best not to respond.

A waitress approached, and Rakkim was grateful for the distraction. She was tricked out in a knee-length, blue velvet dress and plaid stockings, her hair piled into a tight beehive. She bent down, rested her elbows on the table. "You'll want to pick up your menu and point to things, handsome." Her nametag read *Carla*.

Rakkim had never seen her before. The only one of Spider's children he ever had contact with was Elroy. Carla looked to be around seventeen or eighteen, a big-boned girl with a soft face and a button nose that didn't suit her. She had her father's eyes. All the kids did. Hard and dark and alert—she might carry around a touch pad to write customers' orders, but it was just for show. She probably kept an encyclopedia in her frontal lobes and could call up any page you wanted. Rakkim studied the menu.

"He's still working on the memory cores you gave him," said Carla, her hand on the back of his chair, "but he pulled up the mail from the Mecca Café that you wanted."

"Great. I'm not expecting much from the memory cores anyway."

"Shows how much you know." Carla put a hand on his shoulder, flirting, a trademark of any establishment geared to moderns—it brought in tips and it kept the fundamentalists away. "Spider said the one from the university computer is wiped clean, but the core from her home unit is interesting."

Rakkim pointed at one of the options on the menu. "*Interesting* how?"

Carla swayed to music only she could hear. "I don't know . . . he's still working on it. I haven't seen him this excited in a long time."

Rakkim stared at the menu. "Tell me about the mail from the café."

Carla moved closer, one finger sliding across the menu. She smelled of sweet onions and french fries. "Last Friday, seven twenty-two a.m. Short exchange. No formalities. LEAVE NOW, that was the first thing. All capital letters, which is kind of old-fashioned, if you ask me." Carla acted as if he had made a joke, tugged playfully at his goatee. She kept her mouth down while she spoke, no line of sight to the rest of the room. "Then Sarah said, I can't. The first person responded, NOW. RIGHT AFTER CLASS. DANGER. Still with the all-caps. Then Sarah said, I'm meeting *him* Sunday. I have to see him." Carla looked at him, smiled, and it wasn't because she thought someone might be watching. "That's you, isn't it? You're the *him* she was talking about. This Sarah was tough, wanting to keep her appointment with you, even after being warned to leave. She must have thought you were worth something." She swayed to the music again. "Then the first person said, LEAVE NOW, and there was a long interval, maybe twenty seconds, and then Sarah said, okay." Carla pointed at the list of specials on the wall. "That's it, over and out."

"Does Spider have any idea who mailed her . . . or where it came from?"

Carla shook her head. "Whoever it was, they used a series of unregistered servers. They bounced him all over the globe, but he thinks the point of origination is someplace in the Islamic Republic." She squeezed his shoulder. "I turn eighteen in three months. Ripe as a plum and never been plucked." The tip of her tongue slid across her teeth. "Spider's open to marriage proposals, but I've got the final say, so that puts you ahead of the game."

Rakkim looked up at her. "What game is that?"

"Just keep it in mind. Sounds like your girlfriend isn't coming back." Carla scrawled something on her pad and sauntered off. Her hips drew plenty of attention from the foursome at a nearby table.

Rakkim swirled the ice in his water glass before taking a drink. Carla might be right about Sarah not coming back. He crunched through an ice cube. Why didn't she go to Redbeard if she felt threatened? Why didn't she go to *him*?

A young couple walked down the sidewalk, moderns in blue unisex suits, zippers everywhere, hair cropped an inch from their scalps. Probably in advertising or marketing, judging from the black plastic portfolio cases they swung, chatting away. A Black Robe watched them from the far side of the street, speaking into a cell phone as they passed.

Rakkim turned at the sound of laughter from a nearby table, and when he looked back outside, the Black Robe was gone. He played with the silverware, thinking about Sarah's mail conversation, and wondering who had the power to order her to leave so abruptly. Even more, who had the authority to make her comply?

Carla came back with his cheeseburger, fries, and vanilla Jihad Cola. "There was one other exchange two weeks before the one on Friday. Very brief. The first person said, BE CAREFUL. BE READY. Then Sarah said, Can I tell *him*? NO. Please? said Sarah, but the answer was the same."

"Sarah said *please*? You're sure of that?"

"Don't insult me." Carla slapped the check onto the table. "Spider will let you know when he finds out more. Remember what I told you before— three months and counting. I come with a dowry, but, trust me, after our wedding night you won't even care."

Rakkim watched her walk away as he dredged a french fry through a pool of ketchup. Sarah had a hard time listening to anybody, but she had obeyed the person on the other end of the mail, even begging for the chance to see Rakkim again. There was no way to tell if the person she was in contact with was male or female, but Rakkim found himself burning with jealousy. Sarah asking for permission to see him . . . it was as if she were talking to a father, or a husband. He started in on the burger, barely tasting it.

Carla hustled back to the table, refilled his water. She was chewing gum now, really working it. "You have to leave."

"What's wrong?"

"I don't know." There was no trace of her prior flirtatiousness.

"Get up after I leave and head toward the bathroom. Elroy's there. Spider needs to talk with you."

"I'm meeting Spider?"

She champed away at her gum. "Smile, nod your head."

Rakkim did as he was told, holding up the burger for emphasis. "I didn't think Spider allowed direct contact with clients."

"This is a first."

"What's going on, Carla?"

She blew a big pink bubble, popped it with a fingernail. "Spider pulled something off that memory core. It must have been something really special." She strolled off, started bantering with the two moderns at the next table.

CHAPTER 16

Sundown prayers

"Do *you* know what this is about?" Rakkim followed Elroy through the alley. "I heard Spider lives under the bus tunnel. Is that where we're going?"

Elroy took an abrupt right turn, squeezed through a narrow space in the wire fencing, and kept going, not looking back.

Rakkim tore his jacket getting through the opening, hurrying to keep up as they rushed through the twilight. It was past sunset now and this part of downtown was poorly lit, lined with flophouses and abandoned buildings. Rakkim had lived in this general area after his father had died, lived here until Redbeard had brought him home. The maze of alleys gave way to gravel footpaths, then a succession of worn stone steps. At one point they scuttled through a long, corrugated-metal pipe strewn with garbage, broken eggs crunching underfoot, and he knew by the growing stink of rotting vegetables that they were getting closer to the waterfront under the Public Market. At the last minute, they veered away from the market and toward Pioneer Square, the oldest part of the city.

Elroy quickly ran a microwave scanner across Rakkim. "You're clean," he said, putting it back into his sweatshirt. He pressed a hand against a seemingly solid brick wall and a section swung aside. He waited until Rakkim squeezed through, then closed it behind them. A latch snapped into place. They were in total darkness, the air cold and damp.

Rakkim waited a few seconds for his eyes to adjust, but it was still pitch-black.

"This way," said Elroy.

Rakkim walked toward the sound of his voice, hands out.

"Keep coming," said Elroy, ahead of him. "There's a turn coming up."

Rakkim stumbled, heard Elroy snicker. "Elroy?" His voice echoed. "Put a light on."

"I don't need a light," sniffed Elroy, his voice farther away. "I know where I am."

Rakkim moved quickly, hands waving. He snagged Elroy's shirt, but the kid pulled away.

"Touch me again and I'll leave you here. A few days of banging into things and the cats and rats will be fighting over you."

"Take me to Spider. That's what you were told to do." No answer. Rakkim stepped toward where his voice had been, hit his head on something, cursing now.

"You're not getting scared, are you?" said Elroy.

Rakkim didn't move. He had excellent night vision, but there was no light anywhere, and he couldn't be sure the direction he had come from. The darkness smelled mossy.

Elroy's laughter echoed.

Rakkim stayed where he was. He heard Elroy moving closer,

the kid barely making a sound. He waited, trying not to breathe, then reached out and grabbed something, a skinny arm. He hung on as the kid slapped at him, tried to twist away, but there was no way Rakkim would let go, and Elroy finally stopped struggling.

"Good for you," gasped Elroy. "I bet you're proud of yourself."

"Take me to Spider," said Rakkim, still hanging on to him.

"If I wanted to ditch you, I would have already done it. Wouldn't be the first time." Elroy wriggled but couldn't pull free. "Hands off, okay? I don't like being touched. *Please?*"

Rakkim let him go, then waited for him to leave him alone in the dark.

"I bet you thought I was going to run off," said Elroy.

"Not at all."

"Liar." Elroy sniffed. "Stick your right hand out until you find the wall. Did you do it? Okay, keep your hand on the wall as we walk. I'll tell you when to turn."

They made good progress, maintained a slow but steady pace for the next half hour. Rakkim kept count of his steps and turns, making a mental map. Forty-seven steps, right turn, two hundred and eighteen steps, left . . . They seemed to be on a slight downward spiral, and he was sure that Elroy was doubling back from time to time, trying to confuse him. Sometimes Rakkim heard the rumble of a subway in the distance, felt the vibration through the stone floor. Twice they splashed through pools of cold water. Rakkim bumped his head three or four times, tripped once. He almost lost his count when he fell, but he repeated the numbers and turns in his head, reestablishing the pattern. He heard things run past on the floor, claws skittering. Never a glimmer of light.

"We're here," said Elroy.

Rakkim hadn't realized how loudly his heart was beating until they stopped. He blinked as Elroy opened a door, the boy standing there in the light. Rakkim followed him inside.

They were in a storage room of some kind, a small space with a sink and towels. Elroy was already washing up, soaping his hands and face, splashing water everywhere. He quickly put on a pair of oversize clean coveralls from a hook on the wall, tossed a pair to Rakkim, and removed his shoes. The water from the tap was icy, but Rakkim was grateful for the chance to wash the grime off. Blood was on the towel when he dried his face, and the mirror showed a gash in his forehead.

"I'm Spider," said the man waiting for them, a barefoot gnome with a dark, luxuriant beard and a black skullcap. He shifted from one foot to the other. "Pleasure to finally meet you." Rakkim offered his hand, but Spider turned away and started walking. Elroy hurried beside his father, the two of them talking as Rakkim followed.

The interior room was softly lit, and the size of a small warehouse. Thick carpets covered the floor, museum-quality Persians in reds and blues, and silk ornamentals in subtle shades of pink and yellow, so delicate that he didn't want to walk on them. The room was warm and clean, the air fresh, smelling faintly of garlic and roasted chicken. Not a hint of the dampness of the stone corridor that had brought them there. The walls were hung with rich tapestries, dozens and dozens of them. He had been in wealthy households with Redbeard, homes of senators and business leaders—just *one* of these tapestries would have occupied a place of honor. Rakkim was looking around so often that he fell behind and had to hurry to catch up. At last, Spider pushed aside some embroidered curtains and stepped into a small office. He waited for Rakkim to sit on a pile of purple cushions, then sat across from him. Elroy stayed outside.

Spider was an intense ball of tics, his skin white as a pearl. He wore black silk pajamas, his hands and feet knobby. His beard was long, his graying hair plaited into a single braid that fell past his shoulders, and, just as Rakkim had heard, his nose was an imperial beak. It was hard to gauge his age as he had been out of the sun for so long, but he didn't look older than forty. "My son said you did well on the trip through the tunnels."

Rakkim glanced around. The office was bare, except for shelves along the back wall containing rows and rows of glass snow globes. Pretransition tourist items. He saw the Golden Gate Bridge, the Hollywood sign, the Space Needle, Santa Claus and his sleigh . . . even the Twin Towers. From another part of the warehouse, he could hear women's voices, and the sound of a baby crying. "How far underground are we?"

Spider didn't respond. Another baby was crying now, a regular howling chorus, but Spider didn't seem to notice, intent on Rakkim. The pupils of his eyes were hugely dilated. Given the whiteness of his skin, the only spots of color on his face were his black pupils tracking Rakkim. "I've wanted to meet you for a long time. Did you know that the Blue Moon is the only club in the Zone that doesn't pay protection?"

"That's fascinating, but why am I here? What did you find on the—"

"You don't even pay off the police. You give *gifts* to the officers. Birthday presents for their wives and sweethearts, graduation gifts for their children. Generous gifts, but no bribes." Spider blinked. "They must appreciate not being treated as thieves in uniform."

"What did you find on the computer cores?"

"When you first started the club, I was curious to see what would happen when the local goons showed up." Spider twisted his neck from side to side. "The Hammer Trio were the first to call . . . and the last. Vicious bastards. Those three left a trail of cripples all over the Zone. Not anymore though, right?" His smile jerked. "Two former army special forces and a retired Fedayeen—"

"He wasn't Fedayeen. He washed out the first month."

"Really? Everyone said . . ." Spider nodded. "Not that it matters anymore. The three of them came around . . . and then they were gone." He blinked at Rakkim. "Is it true you left their hammers on the bar for a week afterwards? Three ball-peen hammers?" Rakkim shrugged. "I deplore violence, but no one tried to collect from you again, did they?"

A couple of Spider's children, twin girls about eight years old, burst through the curtains, giggling. They pointed at Rakkim, whispered to each other, laughing now.

Rakkim waited until the children had darted away. "How many kids do you have?"

"Not enough," said Spider, completely serious.

"What am I doing here, Spider?"

"Yes. Of course." Spider blinked. "The core from the university computer had nothing of interest on it, but the one from Sarah's home unit contained a very ingenious security system." He folded his arms around himself. "I'd love to know where she got it."

"I'll ask her when I find her."

Spider's fingers twitched. "There was a dual memory on her personal core. One was readable to anyone able to crack her access code, which was no great difficulty, but behind that primary memory was a second, a *ghost* memory much more difficult to penetrate. Even more interesting, the ghost memory had an autodestruct timer. If a code word wasn't typed in every seventy-two hours, a virus would tear through the files, but leave the primary memory intact. So, someone examining the core would find it filled with nothing but the usual academic clutter. No one would even know that there had been anything to delete. Impressive. I have no idea who created it, but it's not Russian, or Chinese, or Swiss. None of the usual suspects for top-flight code. It was an individual. An individual using backwater code . . . but with a very high-level intelligence. Just like me." His fingers fluttered. "Maybe that's why I was able to crack it."

"You cracked the ghost memory?"

Spider's smile jerked.

"Could you tell if anyone else had read the files?"

"Like Redbeard?" Spider snorted. "No, I was the first to pop them." He pulled at his lip, flashed nubs of white teeth. "If you had been able to get the core to me *sooner*, I could tell you a lot more. The virus wiped out most of the files, but there was enough left for me to reconstruct certain parts. I saved the prologue of a book she was working on. It must have been one of the last things she entered. First in, first wiped, that's the way the virus worked." A tic started under his right eye, lifting his cheek several times before subsiding. He leaned forward, stared at Rakkim as he recited:

"'The Zionist Betrayal was the pivot point of modern history, the axis on which the world shifted. The story is taught to every schoolchild, marked by a moment of silence at noon on the anniversary of the attack. We all know that on that terrible day, renegade elements of the Israeli government struck targets in the United States, and the holy city of Mecca, attempting to blame the actions on radical jihadis and discredit all of Islam. We all know that their plan was discovered, Israel itself overrun, while the forces of Islam spread their beneficence across the globe. And yet . . . what if all that we know of these attacks was wrong? What if the Zionists were not behind the Zionist Betrayal?'"

Rakkim shrugged. "I've heard dozens of conspiracy theories about the Zionist attack. Did she have any evidence?"

"The book's unfinished, and I was just able to retrieve bits of it, but her conclusion is obvious. The Zionist Betrayal was another blood libel against the Jews. The worst yet."

"Obvious to you. No evidence, but the Jews are innocent. How convenient." Rakkim saw he had hurt the man's feelings. "Who did Sarah think was really behind the attacks?"

"Her r-r-research," Spider stuttered, "her research wasn't definitive. She mentions an unnamed Saudi or a Yemeni . . . maybe a Pakistani. He's referred to usually as the Old One. She doesn't even know if he's still alive. He was evidently in his sixties at the time of the attack, which would make him in his nineties today, but—"

"The terrorists *confessed*. They were born and raised and trained in Israel, and they confessed on live TV. You've seen it. The whole world has seen it."

"The man works on an incredibly long-range time frame. He must have spent twenty or thirty years putting the operation into place." Spider's hands flapped from the sleeves of his pajamas. "According to Sarah, he seeded his operatives into Israel as Jewish immigrants. It was the children of these deep sleepers, raised and educated in Israel, who rose within the political and military establishment—"

"The terrorists were *executed*. You think their parents raised them, loved them, knowing the whole time they were going to be sacrificed? And the children agreed?"

"I know, I know, but the Old One occupied some sort of cultural and religious sweet spot. The devotion he inspired . . ." Spider's fingers wriggled. "He's taken on the mantle of a Muslim figure of antiquity, the old man of the mountains, an eleventh-century mystic—"

"Yeah, Hassan-i-Sabah. I've read the story. He supposedly inspired such loyalty that his followers willingly threw themselves off cliffs if he merely beckoned."

"The stories are true. Hassan-i-Sabah believed that God had anointed him to unite all Muslims, and he acted on that belief. His acolytes assassinated dozens of Muslim monarchs in his day, including the caliph of Baghdad."

Rakkim remained skeptical. "So the Jews are blamed for the attacks, and Damon Kingsley becomes president-for-life of the new

Islamic Republic. You think *he* was part of the deception? Sorry, but Kingsley is no extremist."

"Yes, Kingsley is a moderate, a grave sin to a true believer. In fact, if the Old One is anything like the original old man of the mountains, he's as hostile to other Muslims as he is to Jews. Kingsley's election means that the Old One didn't completely achieve his goal." Spider twitched. "But that doesn't mean the plan isn't still going forward, whether or not the Old One is still alive."

"Why didn't Sarah tell Redbeard about this?"

"Maybe she didn't trust him to help her . . . or maybe she knew he didn't have the power to do anything about it." Spider blinked. "I cracked the congressional budget code eight years ago. Follow the money, and you'll find the truth." He blinked faster. "In the last three years, Redbeard's budget has been cut forty percent. Recruitment and training have been crippled. The money is going to the army and the religious authorities . . . Fedayeen, of course. No one outside the Select Committee knows. I thought it was the Black Robes outmaneuvering him with Congress. Now I wonder."

"You see a lot from bits and pieces."

"That's what I do. That's what you do too, Fedayeen." Spider watched Rakkim trying to process the new information. "Hard work to reimagine the world, isn't it? It's kept me busy too." He handed Rakkim a flash-memory wafer. "This is everything I pulled off the core so far."

Rakkim slid the wafer into the port of his watch. "Who contacted Sarah at the Mecca Café? Did you find out who she's working with?"

Spider shook his head. "It was sent through a feed in Las Vegas, but that doesn't help. Vegas is a hub. There are so many satellite uplinks over that city that the sender could be anywhere in the world." A baby was crying again. "So many of us killed.

Homes burned. Businesses looted. Civil war . . . and it was all a lie." His tics were like mild electric shocks. "You were lucky, Rakkim. Being an orphan allows for certain . . . opportunities."

"What's that supposed to mean?"

"All those records lost during the transition. Databases infected . . . I couldn't find you anywhere. Just another displaced person. Who could blame you for rewriting your own history?"

"I'm a Muslim."

"A Muslim who risks his life to save Jews? I've never met such a creature."

"Jews and homosexuals, apostates and witches too—I've led them all to the promised land. Does that make me Moses?"

"It makes you too good to be true."

Rakkim ignored it. "Any mention of China on the core? Or the Three Gorges Dam?"

"No, why?"

"How much do I owe you?"

"We'll settle when I'm done." Spider's expression smoothed out. Serene almost. "What did you think of my daughter?"

"Carla? She seemed . . ." Rakkim laughed. "I *wondered* why you didn't just have Elroy bring me here right off. I didn't need to go to the restaurant. You could have told me everything she did. I'm flattered, Spider, but you didn't need to run your daughter past for my approval—"

"*Your* approval?" Spider's face crinkled with restrained laughter. "I sent you to the restaurant to see if you met with *her* approval."

"She can do better." Rakkim stood up. "Ask Elroy to take me back." He didn't need help, but there was no need to advertise it. "Keep working on the core."

"Shalom, Rakkim."

"Salaam alaikum."

CHAPTER 17

Dawn prayers

Rakkim used the call to prayer to hurry past the *No Admittance* sign to the upper level of the House of Martyrs War Museum. The uniformed army sergeant at the top of the stairs was busy with his prayer mat—Rakkim stayed at the edges of the guard's peripheral vision, silently mirroring the man's posture as he slipped past. Fedayeen training, shadow warrior training, the closest thing to invisibility. Rakkim could walk through a crowd of devout women, barely grazing their chadors, and if questioned afterward, none of them would remember him, they would merely have a fleeting impression of someone urging them forward, a nagging sense that they were late to mosque. He could trudge along with a flood of coal miners in the Bible Belt, part of the conversation and the weariness, until a grimy peckerwood looked around and the man he had been talking to about the price of hogs would be gone. Shadow warrior training.

"In the name of Allah." The collective whisper . . . "In the name of Allah." From the balcony, Rakkim could see the early-morning visitors lined up on their mats below, beginning their ablutions. The air in the museum was purified; according to the grand mufti, believers were not required to perform ritual cleansing with water. Most still followed the proper forms, rubbing their hands, then mouth, nose, face, ears, forehead, head, and feet in the sanctified atmosphere. Finished, they stood in neat rows, hands raised to the level of the face. Men in front. Women behind them. Modesty and subordination, moderns and moderates and fundamentalists, wheels within wheels before Allah. Rakkim watched, calmed by the rhythmic movements of their devotions. Bowing forward from the waist, hands resting on their knees. Prostrate, hands flat, foreheads grazing the mat. Returning to the upright position, to start the process again and again, to finally end seated on their heels.

Unlike the rote prayers at the Super Bowl, the cycles of the believers here were graceful, hands and feet perfectly positioned. Something about the majesty of the War Museum, the somber minimalism of the interior, the wreckage of the shattered Space Needle visible through the windows, made even the moderns cleave to their faith. He listened to the believers reaffirm the power and protection of Allah, their voices echoing in the great hall— "Glory be to our Lord the Most High."

Rakkim moved on. Redbeard was here already. Rakkim had spotted his advance team about twenty minutes ago—four men dressed as tourists, gawkers with nametags. He had watched them split up, ambling toward the choke points, the narrow areas of the museum where an ambush would be most effective.

Rakkim had barely slept after seeing Spider last night, but Redbeard had insisted on meeting this morning, eager to discuss Rakkim's progress. *You have made progress, haven't you, Rakkim?*

Of course, I have, Uncle, it just depends on what you mean by progress. Rakkim wandered over to the Devil's Chamber, stepped aside as a mother quickly led her children out. The little boy was weeping. The chamber seemed five or ten degrees colder than the rest of the museum, a darkened room where a wall screen played an endless loop of Richard Aaron Goldberg's confession. This year would be the twenty-seventh anniversary of his public confession to the Zionist attack. The newspapers and television would run round-the-clock coverage as they did every year on this date, billboards and cell phones flashing *5-19-2015 NEVER FORGET.*

Rakkim watched Goldberg on-screen, the man thin and frightened as he sat facing the cameras. The sound was nearly off, but it didn't matter. Everyone in the country could repeat his confession verbatim.

My name is Richard Aaron Goldberg. Eleven days ago my team simultaneously detonated three nuclear weapons. One destroyed New York City. Another destroyed Washington, D.C., and the third left the city of Mecca a radioactive death trap. Our intention . . . Goldberg placed a hand on his shaking knee. *The plan was for radical Islamists to be blamed. To drive a wedge between the West and Muslims, and to create chaos within the Muslim world itself. I think . . . I believe we would have succeeded had it not been for some bad luck.* He lifted his chin. *My name is Richard Aaron Goldberg. My team and I are part of a secret unit of the Mossad.*

Rakkim watched the confession again. Then he walked back into the main hall. Spider might believe the bits and pieces he had pulled off Sarah's flash-memory. *Sarah* might even believe what she had written. Rakkim didn't. For Sarah to be right about the Zionist Betrayal meant that Richard Aaron Goldberg and the other confessed Mossad agents were lying their way to a date with the executioner. It meant Richard Aaron Goldberg and the others, born and raised in Israel, had turned against their country and their religion. Nothing was impossible, but Rakkim had just watched the confession the second time ignoring everything being said. Concentrating instead on Goldberg's posture, his involuntary muscular movements, the look in his eye . . . the bastard was telling the truth. Sarah was wrong.

There might still be an Old One, some Arab eager to assume the mantle of Mahdi, some sworn enemy of Redbeard. Fine, get in line, Redbeard had plenty of enemies, but the Israelis were solely responsible for nuking New York and D.C. and Mecca. Sarah's alternative history was wrong, but it didn't matter. She was still in danger. If Redbeard was losing influence, though, as Spider said, then his ability to protect Sarah was compromised, and the Old One, or some other enemy, was in ascendance. An ominous power shift. Maybe that was the real reason Redbeard had asked for his help.

Rakkim kept walking.

The War Museum was a modest, understated dome built beside the crumpled Space Needle, the old monument lying on its side, rusting in the weather. The exterior of the museum was surfaced with small tiles made by schoolchildren, each one inscribed with the name of a martyred soldier. The interior was sparsely decorated and dimly lit, the walls lined with blue-veined lapis lazuli. Visitors, even the young, found themselves walking slowly, adding to the somber elegance of the site. At the center of the museum rested a simple, Arabic edition of the Qur'an. No bulletproof plastic or nitrogen-rich bubble was necessary to protect it. The book had been recovered from the ruins of Washington, D.C., found surrounded by broken glass and twisted girders. The Qur'an was untouched by the atomic blast, the cover pristine, its pages shiny and white.

Taking photographs inside the museum was not permitted, nor were reproductions available. This was sacred ground. Open to all, regardless of religion. The Black Robes had long sought to restrict the site to devout Muslims, but by presidential decree, the federal government maintained sole responsibility for the museum, with army personnel in charge of operations, and army imams responsible for prayers.

After the civil war, both sides had claimed Washington, D.C., fighting over the dead streets, hoping to recapture the glory of the former capital. The D.C. Qur'an had been the great prize for the Islamic Republic, while the Bible Belt carted off the statue of Thomas Jefferson from its memorial, installing the scorched marble in their new capital of Atlanta. Rakkim had actually seen the statue, waiting in line for hours to file past, silent, staring at the president's solemn face through lead glass. New York City had remained largely untouched, its crumpled skyscrapers mute, the dingy Hudson lapping through Manhattan, the waters rising as the ice caps slowly melted.

Rakkim had been to New York only once, part of a recon team of Fedayeen dropped in to search for financial records rumored to be under the Stock Exchange. Three days in full containment gear and he never saw a bird. Or a rat. Or any other living thing. Except cockroaches. The roaches carpeted the basements, shimmering in the flashlight beams, wings aflutter, and he didn't want to think about what they fed on. Three days . . . if there was anything under the Stock Exchange it remained safe and secure from the living. He was never so happy to leave a place.

Rakkim strolled toward the wall maps showing the great battles of the war. Chicago, reduced to cinders. Detroit's auto works gutted by terrorist bombs. Santa Fe. Denver. The St. Louis arch collapsed. Newark, the deepest penetration into the Islamic states by the Christian armies. Newark fought block by block, a city given up to the flames. Newark, where Islamic reinforcements, most still in high school, had finally stopped the Christian advance. Bloody Newark. The photos of the dead went on for fifty yards. Rakkim had visited the museum hundreds of times, and the photos of the war's leftovers always affected him the most. A single shoe, a black lace-up dress shoe, still so shiny you could see the photographer reflected. A crushed bicycle. An upended mailbox, letters spilling out onto the mud: phone bills and love letters and birthday cards.

The official death toll of the second civil war was 9 million, but Redbeard said the true figure was three or four times higher, much of that from outbreaks of plague and typhus and other dark diseases that had sprung up in the aftermath. The worst were the man-made toxins, lab-grown fever brews that twisted the infected into screaming knots or left them vomiting gouts of blood. Even now, whole cities were still quarantined — Phoenix and Dallas and Pittsburgh, hot zones where no one dared enter.

Rakkim watched a robed pilgrim moving slowly along the far wall, head tilted in prayer. His face was hidden within the folds of a hood, but something about his gait was familiar. Faces could be disguised, height and weight altered, but something as elemental as walking was almost impossible to shift. The pilgrim was Stevens, the pockmarked dandy Redbeard had sent to arrest him that night at the Blue Moon. Rakkim started toward the staircase. He wondered if the agent's face was still swollen, if he liked the look of his broken nose, flaunting it as an injury in the line of duty.

Redbeard rolled his electric wheelchair through the crowd of schoolchildren visiting the War Museum, their voices hushed, glancing around as though they were in an unfamiliar mosque. He wore opaque glasses, his beard powdered white and extended, hanging over his belly. He rolled silently across the granite floor, his left arm twitching, useless. A single medal was pinned to his voluminous jellaba, a combat infantrymen's badge. An honest medal, devoid of fame or favor, marking him as a wounded veteran of the war of independence. A businessman approached, bowed, and placed a $20 bill into Redbeard's lap, joining the other bills that he had been given. Redbeard murmured a blessing, head lolling, and the businessman backed away, thanking him for his service.

Still no sign of Rakkim.

Redbeard liked the museum, particularly at dawn. The House of Martyrs was never closed and never empty. The people honored the dead, those who had paid the greatest price for their faith. He still remembered the old days, before the transition. Graveyards for the nation's war dead had been overgrown, the graves untended. There had not even been enough buglers to play taps; the army had been forced to use recorded music to honor the martyrs. Military parades had played to empty streets, or worse, the color guard had faced catcalls from those whose freedom to jeer had been paid for with others' blood. A terrible time for heroes. A world without glory, a people with their eyes on the mud instead of the heavens. No wonder the wisdom of the Prophet, may his name be blessed, had swept across the land like a wildfire, cleansing all before it. After all that had happened since the transition, after all he knew about the Old One, there was never a moment that Redbeard regretted the passing of the former regime.

Another man in a wheelchair glided past, nodding at Redbeard. A young man, wearing an army uniform, his legs removed above the knee.

Along the far wall, a woman in a bright blue chador led a young girl by the hand, led her along by the fingers as though they were on an excursion in the woods to pick wildflowers. The girl was young, five or six perhaps, but it was the woman who drew Redbeard's attention. She looked like Katherine. Sarah's mother. His brother's wife.

Redbeard trailed along after them, heedless of who was in his way. People stepped aside, apologizing, as though they were in the wrong, but he kept his eyes on the woman. It was impossible of course, Katherine wouldn't dare be here. He wasn't even sure she was alive. She had fled after his brother's murder, fled leaving Sarah in the hospital, run for her life. He had thought at the time she was afraid of the Old One. The early reports were that both he and his brother had been assassinated, reports that Redbeard himself had planted, hoping to draw out the conspirators. The ruse had worked. Even though he had been wounded, Redbeard had worked almost nonstop for weeks interrogating those arrested. He had rolled up the Old One's network, most of them anyway, but the nation had paid a terrible price. James was a charismatic figure, loved and admired by the citizens and the politicians alike. Redbeard was merely feared. A few weeks after Katherine had fled, he realized she had been afraid of *him*. She had thought he had murdered his own brother. For power . . . and perhaps, for her. He had searched for her for two years, put all the men and resources he could spare into finding her. He had failed.

The woman in the blue chador and the child were swinging their arms gently as they walked. Redbeard had not seen Sarah smile like that until he'd brought Rakkim home. The street thief who had melted her heart. Melted Angelina's heart too. Redbeard had been more careful with his emotions, but the boy had finally won him over too. It had taken years, but he had come to love the boy. The urchin with the eyes of a wolf. His only solace was that he had never revealed his feelings. Redbeard was experienced at such deception. He had never revealed his feelings for Katherine either.

Redbeard slowly wheeled across the great hall, getting closer to the woman and the girl. It couldn't be Katherine. It had been over twenty years . . . surely she didn't look the same. It couldn't be her, yet he couldn't stop himself from finding out.

The woman turned as he approached. His wheels were silent, but she turned anyway, sensing his presence, and his heart leaped at the connection between them . . . and just as quickly sank. The woman was beautiful, her mouth tender, but she wasn't Katherine. The woman bowed to him. Her little girl scurried over, kissed Redbeard's hand, and retreated. He blessed them and rolled on. Head high, his jaw clamped shut.

Rakkim closed in on Stevens, matching his footsteps to the pockmarked dandy's. While Stevens hid his form and features within the hood of the burnoose, Rakkim had on a plain, gray suit and thin, knitted skullcap, as befitted the well-dressed modern. He had narrowed his goatee, his beard extending in a thin line from his sideburns down his jawline. His walk was poised, shoulders back, eyes sweeping the room—the best camouflage was to move as though unafraid of being observed, of inviting observation.

A man with a baby carriage cut across his path and Stevens went to cuff him aside, but stopped himself, allowed the man to pass.

Rakkim moved as Stevens moved, closing in. A tug on the man's right earlobe . . . yes, that would be the perfect greeting. Turn him around by that clump of cartilage. Lead him like a lamb. Eye to eye. No permanent damage. Just a bruised ego. Keep hate alive.

Rakkim didn't know why he had taken such an immediate dislike to the man. His preening at the Blue Moon had been part of it, but it was more than that. Their hostility had an instinctive, almost a cellular component, a mutual *recognition*. Rakkim had shared the last of his water with dying men who had tried to kill him minutes earlier, had held their hand and told them they were going to be fine. Stevens was different.

Rakkim was only two steps behind Stevens now, close enough to smell his aftershave. Stevens had enjoyed using the stun gun on Rakkim. Given the opportunity, Stevens would veer across three lanes of traffic to run him down, and Rakkim would welcome the attempt. Which was, of course, the reason that Redbeard had Stevens accompany him here today. Why Redbeard had sent Stevens to fetch Rakkim at the Blue Moon. Rakkim had thought it was just an accident that first time, but he should have known better—Redbeard didn't have accidents. He had wanted to stir Rakkim up. To gain a faint advantage then . . . and *now*. Rakkim stopped, let Stevens walk on. It was too late though.

"Shall I slice your femoral artery or deball you, boy?"

Rakkim didn't turn around. He could feel the tip of the knife pressed against his thigh, the tip poking through the fabric of his trousers. "Good morning, Uncle."

Redbeard slipped the knife back into his sleeve, sat back in his wheelchair.

Rakkim slowly turned. A *wheelchair*. No gait to give him away. He bowed.

"Don't just stand there, push me." Redbeard waved Stevens back, the security agent sullen now, retreating. "You've embarrassed him again," he said, as Rakkim got behind him. "I would have thought you had made enough enemies."

"You should talk."

"What have you found out about Sarah?"

"Do you want to talk here?" Rakkim slowly pushed the chair. "There's a man with a briefcase eyeing the aerial photos of Indianapolis. He's supposed to be a businessman, but he has faint stains at the corners of his mouth. Betel nut juice. A Black Robe—"

"I've got a blocking device in effect. You can say anything you want."

"You're certain?"

"It's *Russian*. Sonic, subsonic, microwave, and ultrahigh frequencies." Redbeard shook his head. "I remember when the best gear was made in this country."

"I don't."

"That is your loss." Redbeard waved to an annex. "What have you learned?"

"I talked to one of her colleagues . . . one of her friends. A sociology professor named Marian Warriq. They used to have tea, but she hasn't spoken with Sarah for weeks."

Rakkim slowed as they passed the D.C. Qur'an. The clicking of prayer beads from a hundred hands echoed off the gently sloping dome.

"I *said*, is that all you've accomplished?" said Redbeard. "I would have thought you had some method of contacting Sarah." He stood up as they entered the annex, left the wheelchair behind.

"We had a method. I've used it. No response."

"So much for the power of love." Redbeard stretched, seemed to expand to twice his former size. "You must be disappointed."

"I'll find her."

"We haven't much time." Redbeard took Rakkim's hand, the

two of them strolling the perimeter of the museum. "Do you know who Ibn Azziz is? No? He's the new grand mullah of the Black Robes."

"So what? He can't be any worse than Oxley."

"Don't be a fool. Oxley was predictable, content to bide his time, gathering power slowly. He would never have gone after Sarah. Ibn Azziz is a zealot, angry and impatient. *He's* the one who sent the bounty hunters after Sarah. He acted in secrecy before, fearing Oxley's displeasure. Now . . . there is no one to stop him."

"I'll stop him."

"Tempting, but, you're needed to find Sarah. I'll take care of Ibn Azziz."

"I discovered that Sarah didn't run away from an unwanted engagement. That's something useful, isn't it?" Rakkim leaned closer. "Did you say something? Or was that the sound of your story collapsing." He locked eyes with Redbeard. "She was working on a book. She seemed to think it was dangerous."

"If this book was dangerous, she should have stayed where I could protect her."

"Maybe she didn't think you *could* protect her." Rakkim patted Redbeard on the back and he stiffened. "You should have told me the truth, Uncle. You wasted our time, and as you said, we don't have much of it." Rakkim gave a perfect bow. "Go with God."

CHAPTER 18

After noon prayers

Rakkim sensed something wrong as soon as he pulled up to the security gate at Marian's hillside community and saw the guard shack empty. He waited in his car, engine idling as he looked around. He hadn't called Marian before driving over, certain that Redbeard already had her phone bugged. No reason to let him think that Marian was more than a colleague of Sarah's, a good Muslim intellectual she shared only tea with. A follow-up call from Rakkim would tell Redbeard that she merited closer scrutiny. Better to show up unannounced. Marian had told him he could come by anytime.

He wasn't sure how China and the Three Gorges Dam figured into Sarah's research, but Sarah had been looking for something in Warriq's journals. Besides, he wanted to talk more with Marian, she might have remembered something. Something that Sarah said. Something she didn't say. First contact was always awkward. Trust took time. Distrust was immediate. For an instant at the War Museum this morning he had actually considered telling Redbeard about the journals. The impulse had passed. He tapped his fingers on the steering wheel, watched another car drive into the residents' lane and flash an entry code. The gate flew up, then back down as the car zipped past.

Rakkim backed up and parked in the visitors' lot, then slipped into the guard shack and buzzed Marian's house. No answer. Marian and her staff might have gone into the city, or shopping, or left for afternoon prayers at the mosque, but he took off toward her house, walking at first, then faster, until he was running flat out up the steep, winding streets.

He was out of breath when he got to Marian's front door, chest aching. He rang the bell, then beat on the door before anyone inside would have had a chance to answer it. The door was locked. A good lock too, and he didn't have any tools. He trotted around to the back, peeked through the windows but couldn't see inside. The back door was ajar, an invitation. The knife was in his hand.

He slowly opened the door, moved inside on the balls of his feet, taking a few steps, listening, then taking a few steps more. A fly hovered around his ear. He swatted it away, but it returned, a sluggish, fat green fly humming an ugly tune as Rakkim silently worked his way across the kitchen. No sound other than the ticking of the antique grandfather clock in the foyer. And the buzzing of the flies.

Rakkim put the knife away. Even before he caught the smell, he knew that whoever had been here had left hours ago. He took a deep breath, walked out of the hallway and into the living room. A few moments later he was back in the kitchen, hands on his knees and grateful that he hadn't had breakfast. He had seen men blown apart by land mines and bullets, guts and glory flung to the winds, some dying with a surprised how-the-fuck-did-*that*-happen expression, some dying quietly, dead before they were even aware of it. He had seen all that and more, but one glance into the living room and he could barely contain his anger and revulsion. The other dead had been outside of him somehow, killed in *action*, part of some greater process that anesthetized guilt and left Rakkim a bystander, albeit not an innocent one. This was different. The living room was an atrocity exhibition arranged for his private benefit. He washed his face in the kitchen sink, but the cold water did nothing to numb his rage. Then he walked back into the living room. He didn't bother holding his breath. It wasn't the smell that tore at him.

The flies stirred at his entrance, rising up in a buzzing, dark cloud, then settled back down on the heads of the bodyguard and his wife. Terry and his wife sat beside each other on the purple, floral-print sofa as though sitting for a formal wedding portrait. Terry cradled his wife's severed head in his lap. She did the same for his head. Their hair was matted with blood, their eyes staring straight ahead. Blackened blood crusted their gray clothes like a rusty carapace. Flies moved across the soaked sofa, the carpet shimmering with their metallic green brightness. Green, the color of Islam, green the color of the Prophet's banner, green the color of the robe of Ali, the fourth caliph. Rakkim remembered his lessons well. The flies squirmed, green the color of obscenity.

Rakkim moved closer, wanting to see, *needing* to see, not to turn away. This tableau was a challenge someone had laid down, a moral and visual dislocation. Closer now. Marian's bodyguard was a seasoned warrior, but someone had killed him easily, killed him and his wife while they sat there waiting to die, then left them with their heads exchanged as a greeting specifically meant for Rakkim. On the wall behind them, scrawled in blood, was written, *R U Having Fun Yet?* The same slogan Mardi had in neon on the wall of the Blue Moon. In spite of his efforts to hide his tracks, Rakkim must have led the killer here . . . and the killer had left a calling card that could not be ignored.

Rakkim wasn't sure how he knew that it had been a lone individual who had done this . . . perhaps it was the singularity of the aesthetic. The killing had a grotesque artistry; the mocking phrase from the club, the switching of heads, all spoke to a unique point of view. A joker who didn't want or need assistance.

He waved away the flies, bent down, and looked into the bodyguard's dead eyes. It had been a long time since Rakkim had prayed, but he said a prayer now. A prayer that Terry forgive him for bringing death to the house, and a prayer that Terry be welcomed into Paradise, that he spend eternity in the company of the faithful. *Those who have fear of God will have gardens wherein streams flow and wherein they will live forever with their purified spouses and with the consent of God.* Then he closed Terry's eyes and did the same for his wife. Rakkim didn't even know her name.

Marian wasn't in the living room, but Rakkim just had to follow the bloody footprints. It was like the diagrams of dance steps he had seen in old books, fox-trot and waltz and tango and rumba, party dances for good times that weren't coming back. He followed the footsteps up the stairs, the blackened imprints getting fainter with every step. There were no clouds of flies in this part of the house, no flies at all. He found Marian in the master bedroom, found her submerged in the soaking tub, her hands and feet bound with electrical wire, her black hair drifting like seaweed. She was nude. Of course.

Marian's chador was thrown into a corner of the bathroom, slashed apart, but there were no wounds on her body. Another indication of the killer's skill with a blade. Rakkim sat on the edge of the tub, looking down at her. The tub was filled almost to the top, and water had sloshed across the floor from her struggles. Her face was underwater, turned shyly to one side, away from Rakkim. Her breasts and pubic bone broke the surface, an archipelago of sad flesh.

He stared at her profile, saw the bruises on her neck from when she had been clasped and held under, two small bruises on either side of her windpipe . . . he had a delicate touch, this killer, using just enough force to hold her down, not to strangle her. Marian had not been carved up like Terry and his wife, not posed in some horror show diorama, but her death had been even more cruel. Marian, who had loved only one man in her life, who had allowed only one man to see her nakedness, had been drowned slowly, thrashing and screaming and coughing up water, fully aware that she was to be left exposed for all the world to see. No wonder she had fought so hard, even tied hand and foot.

Rakkim should have told her the truth on the balcony. She had asked him if he believed that there was one love for each of us, one love and one love only, and he had told her he didn't know. She had known he was lying, but he had stayed with the lie. Maybe the lie wasn't meant for her, but meant to convince himself. He hadn't fooled either of them.

He was going to have to contact Colarusso. This area of Seattle was out of the detective's jurisdiction, but Redbeard could take care of that with a call to the police chief. Redbeard would have plenty of questions, but that was the price of getting him to make the call. Otherwise, it wouldn't be long before the neighbors started wondering what had happened to the guard at the front gate, or the next security shift came to work, and then the local cops would be brought in to comb the area. Better to send in Colarusso; he would listen to Rakkim and would do what he was asked. A true investigation was out of the question. The forensic techs would tell him the approximate size and weight of the killer based on the bloody footsteps, and there might even be fingerprints and skin samples from under Marian's fingernails, all sorts of DNA possibilities, but it didn't matter. The man who had done this was outside the jurisdiction of the police. He was beyond the law. That's where Rakkim would find him. That's where Rakkim lived too.

Colarusso would have questions, of course, but he would accept the answers Rakkim gave him. The detective might even be able to help. First though, Rakkim had something more important to do. He walked out of the bathroom and over to the closet. He was going to find Marian a clean chador. He was going to lift her out of the tub, carry her over to her bed, and get her dressed. Then he would pray for her too.

CHAPTER 19

Midafternoon prayers

Sarah felt an ache in the pit of her stomach. "Keep going."

The taxi driver shrugged and drove on.

Sarah covered a groan as they approached Marian's house, the yard circled with yellow tape. Far too festive a look for such an overcast and dreary day. She was too far away to read the words rippling in the wind, but she knew what they would say: *Police Line Do Not Cross.* A couple of patrol cars were parked in front, along with a crime scene van, the officers leaning against their cruisers and talking to each other. Neighbors dotted the sidewalk, bundled up against the cold. "You can pull over here." Her voice sounded hollow to her, bled of emotion. Rakkim wouldn't even recognize the sound as coming from her.

The driver parked the cab against the curb. He turned around, peered at her through the clear plastic partition that separated them. "Do you want to get out here, sister?"

"No." Though the windows of the cab were smoked for privacy, Sarah still adjusted her veil as the neighbors glanced at the cab. They quickly turned back to the house. There was no sound in the cab except the rumble of the engine. Something terrible had happened to Marian. Sarah was certain of that. She hadn't called before getting into the cab. She had only decided to visit at the last minute, hoping to surprise Marian, to prevail on her to let Sarah borrow her father's notebooks. Now she didn't know what to do.

The driver rolled down his window. "What's going on?" he barked at an older couple on the sidewalk.

"Woman was murdered," said the elderly man, elegant in a blue suit with a yellow handkerchief matching his yellow necktie. He pointed at the house. "Professor Warriq. Taught at the university. A devout woman, may the mercy of Allah be upon her."

"You don't *know* that she's dead," said the woman, a prim, fine-boned lady in a cashmere coat. "You're just showing off."

"You don't see an ambulance, do you?" said the elderly gentleman. "She got *murdered*. Her and the help. A regular slaughterhouse inside, that's what the policeman said. Terrible thing. Probably a gang of Catholics hopped up on something, that's my guess."

"You and your Catholics," sneered the woman.

"They *drowned* her in her own bathtub," said the old man. "Probably told her they were baptizing her, laughing about it while she begged them to stop."

The couple wandered away, still arguing.

Sarah took small, shallow breaths as she watched the house. Marian had been murdered, but she didn't believe it was Catholics who had killed her. Redbeard had always said it was fine to believe in coincidences, but to always act as if there were no such thing. No, someone had targeted Marian because of her connection with Sarah. She should be scared, should tell the driver to take her out of here, but she didn't want to leave. Not yet. She stared at the house. Strangest thing . . . she thought of Marian's hands. She had lovely hands, strong and capable, but Marian said they were too big. Unfeminine. She kept her nails cut short, kept her hands clasped in company so as to not draw attention to them. Now she was dead and when Sarah thought of her . . . she thought of her lovely hands and wished someone had been able to convince her how beautiful she was.

The soft, sobbing sounds must be coming from her, because the driver half turned. "You mind if I turn on the radio, sister?" When Sarah didn't answer, he switched it on. Out of deference to what he assumed were her traditional sensibilities, he put on a popular call-in show for pious Muslims, *What Should I Do, Imam?*

"Hello, Imam. I know that as a good Muslim I am not supposed to listen to music, but I was wondering if there are certain kinds of music that would be okay. And would it matter if I listened by myself?"

"Good question, my daughter. The Holy Qur'an is quite clear that music is forbidden. One of the messengers of Allah said. 'There will be a nation who will make music their lot, and one day, while enjoying their music and alcohol, they will awake with their faces transformed into swine.' In fact, this messenger said he was sent to destroy all musical instruments. And, no, my daughter, the sin is as great whether you listen to music in solitude or with another. Instead of music rather listen to the Holy Qur'an."

Sarah watched the cabdriver as he idly scratched the back of his head. She was supposed to have had lunch with Marian last Friday, but that was before she'd gotten the e-mail. Even so, she had considered contacting Marian, just to let her know she would be away for a while. Then the bounty hunters had come . . . Sarah winced, remembering the bald man's breath . . . his foul *touch*. She should have called Marian after that, *cautioned* her . . . Sarah shook off the thought. Refused to give in to despair. It was too late for recriminations. Marian was dead, Terry and his wife too, if the elderly neighbors were to be believed, and regrets weren't going to bring any of them back.

She checked the sidewalks, looking for someone who didn't seem to belong. The gawkers were mostly couples, middle-aged or older, a few mothers with children. No single men, but a couple of businessmen in suits were walking slowly past the house on the opposite side of the street. She wasn't sure if the businessmen had been there when she'd arrived. She wasn't sure if anyone in the crowd had just walked over. All the years of Redbeard's teachings and she had failed his first rule. *Observation is the key to survival, Sarah. Take in the big picture first, burn that snapshot into your brain, then focus on individuals. A few minutes later, take in the big picture again and notice what is out of place—what's been added, what's been taken away.* She had let her grief distract her. Rule number two: *Emotions are assassins of survival.* Another failure on her part.

Redbeard had raised her and Rakkim the same way, making no excuses or allowances for her being female. *Life is dangerous, Sarah. Complacency is for the innocent, the foolish, or the dead, and we are neither. Think, Sarah.* She had allowed her attention to falter. Rakkim would not have made that mistake. She straightened, took a careful scan of the whole area, using the driver's rearview mirror to see behind her.

Two of the policemen shared a joke and a smoke while they stood around, handsome lunks with their hands in their pockets and their hats pushed back. Sarah wanted to bolt out of the taxi and knock the cigarettes from their mouths, order them to show some respect. To at least *act* as if they were interested in what had happened inside the house, rather than just going through the motions. She stayed where she was. She had made enough mistakes today.

"Blessings upon you, Imam. Please settle a debate I'm having with my girlfriend. According to Islam, are women lacking in intellect compared to men?"

"Blessings upon you, my son. The teachings assure us that women have less intelligence than men; therefore it is the husband and not the wife who heads the family. The wife may be consulted, but final authority lies with the husband."

Sarah winced behind her veil, infuriated by the imam's smug certainty. The radio was another distraction to be avoided. Better to watch the house. Marian's front yard was filled with her prize rosebushes. They were dormant now, all thorns, but come spring they would be bursting with blooms. Marian wouldn't be there to smell their fragrance, or to keep them pruned, wouldn't be there to prevent the rust and the mites and the root rot. The ones who had killed Marian had killed everything she cared for too, and the ones who had killed her had not acted on their own—Sarah had helped them.

Marian had died because of her connection with Sarah, there was no other explanation. Sarah had tried to downplay their friendship, particularly after starting the new book, but too many people at the university had seen them together. It would have only taken one person to talk, to mention seeing them having tea together. One person, that's all the Old One would have needed.

It had to be the Old One who had sent the killing team. The government or the Black Robes would easily commit murder to stop her from writing the new book, but she doubted they had any idea what she was up to. If they knew, Redbeard would know—he had spies everywhere—and Redbeard had given no indication that he was aware of her efforts. It *had* to be the Old One's hand at work, but why kill Marian? Why not just put her under surveillance and wait to see if Sarah showed up. Why not question her? Marian wasn't worth anything to the Old One. Unless she had already talked.

Sarah fought back a sudden rush of fear, forced herself to examine the situation dispassionately. No, Marian had been killed because the killers had erroneously determined that she had nothing to offer. Sarah *knew* Marian. She was a woman of courage and loyalty. Even if she could have bartered her life by giving up Sarah, giving up what information she had, she would gladly have died first. Marian had faith, and her faith gave her strength. Sarah had no such illusions. She adjusted the veil again, annoyed; she would never get used to it.

Nothing was to be gained by staying here, but she couldn't take her eyes off the house, hoping that somehow Marian would come walking out, and it would all have been a mistake. A miscommunication. That wasn't going to happen though. Sarah had known that since she'd seen the crime scene van speed past their cab on the access road to the gated community. A premonition, perhaps. Or a guilty conscience. She set her jaw.

Time enough for guilt later; now she had to find out if the killing team had taken the journals. Did the Old One know the reason for Sarah's regular visits? No way to find out now, but she *would* have to find out, and if the journals were still inside the house, Sarah was going to have to come back and get them. She felt the ache in her stomach again, the feeling of falling. It was fear. It didn't matter though; regardless of her fear, Sarah was going to have to come back for the journals. The journals were the key . . . one of the keys. The only one she had been told of.

The wind kicked up, bent the surrounding evergreens, and

Sarah shivered in the warmth of the cab. She needed to get some rest. Lying in a strange bed for the last week, tossing and turning . . . everything kept her awake; the wind, the rustle of branches on the window, her own thoughts most of all. She had money. She had bought clothes and a toothbrush, and in two more days she would go online and find out what she was supposed to do next. All she had to do was stay calm for the next two days. Stay calm and stay safe.

"Hello, Imam, I'm fourteen and, well . . . I know the Holy Qur'an says we can't pluck facial hair, but my older sister has really, really bushy eyebrows and . . . and I wanted to know if it would be all right anyway so she can look prettier. Thank you."

"Thanks be to you, my daughter. Is your sister married?"

"Yes, Imam."

"Then you may tell her that though the Holy Qur'an forbids such practices, if the eyebrows have become so dense that her husband is repulsed, she may then trim them to a more appropriate and normal size."

Sarah stared out the window. Last night she had almost called Rakkim. She had been dozing and heard running footsteps and woke up in tears. A false alarm. This time. She had picked up her phone, desperate to hear his voice . . . then put aside the cell. Too late for such weakness now. Too many lives were in the balance. She started to tell the driver that they could leave now, then Marian's front door swung open. For an instant she actually thought Marian was going to walk out, then she saw Rakkim coming down the steps with that police detective friend of his . . . Anthony Colarusso.

"Is there a problem, sister?" asked the driver.

Sarah shook her head, so startled she couldn't speak. It was Redbeard, of course. He must have called in Rakkim to help find her. She wasn't surprised that Rakkim had been enlisted; she was surprised he had found Marian so quickly.

Rakkim was talking to the policemen. The uniforms must not have known who he was, because they kept glancing at Colarusso, who was busy rummaging in his ear with a forefinger.

She hadn't seen Rakkim in six months. He looked handsome as ever, but exhausted and worried. His shirt had damp spots on it and she wondered what he had seen inside Marian's house. A regular slaughterhouse, the white-haired neighbor had said. A tear ran down her cheek and was captured by the veil, but she kept her eyes on Rakkim, hungry for the sight of him.

She still wondered if she should have told him what she was working on, maybe even asked for his help. She trusted Rakkim with her life, why couldn't she trust him with the truth? He was talking to the technicians from the crime scene van now, and she noticed how he nodded when they spoke, how he patted their shoulders. He was intruding on their turf, and he knew he could get better cooperation if they were on his side. Redbeard would have been demanding, more forceful, but he wouldn't have gotten any more out of them than Rakkim. He might even have gotten less.

She should go. It was dangerous to stay here. The cab would draw attention after a while—a curious policeman, a bored policeman, and things could unravel. Redbeard used to say it was the minor details that invariably tripped people up, because they had only prepared for major confrontations. No, better to leave now. She could come back for the journals later, when it was safe. Even if it wasn't safe, she would have to retrieve them, more certain than ever that *somewhere* within their pages was what she sought.

Sarah stayed. She stayed and watched the wind ripple through Rakkim's short, dark hair . . . he had such soft hair, even his goatee, and she blushed at the memory of it tickling her most intimate places. Rakkim ran a hand through his hair, as though feeling her gaze. She rapped on the plastic partition, rapped harder than she meant to. "We can go now." She kept her eyes on Rakkim as the cab turned around. If she stayed here much longer, there was no way she could stop herself from going to him.

CHAPTER 20

Midafternoon prayers

"You don't call me," said the Wise Old One, "I call you."

"Shall I hang up?" Darwin said brightly. "Then you can call me back and I'll pretend to be thrilled by the attention." He listened. "Hello?"

"Go ahead."

"You're sure?" said Darwin. "I'd be happy to oblige."

The Old One stayed silent, refusing to engage.

Darwin stood with his hands in his pockets, the privacy cell adhered to the inside of his ear canal, the receiver the size of a bloated tick. The mouthpiece was even smaller, a birthmark affixed just above his lip. You could stand beside him and not know he was in the middle of a conversation. The cell was the latest model from Japan, a real breakthrough. "I just wanted to update you. I've been playing cat and mousie with Rakkim, but along the way I paid a social call with Sarah's girlfriend from the university. Rakkim had done the same thing the day before. Great minds and all that."

Darwin had stood on Marian's doorstep yesterday, pretending to be a religious census taker, papers spilling from his briefcase, a nervous pencil pusher with a scraggly goatee and a suit that was too big for him. Marian's bodyguard had ordered him away, a swarthy, barrel-chested sluggo barring the door, but Marian had invited Darwin in. He had apologized for disturbing her, then shuffled into the living room and smelled Rakkim, caught the faint scent of the man and known he was at the right place.

"Give me your update," said the Old One.

"The girlfriend's name is Marian Warriq," said Darwin, freshly shaven and wearing a $3,000 suit. "Midfifties. Sociology professor at the university. Devout but no fundamentalist. That ring a bell?"

"No."

"Makes no never mind. Lady Marian is in the past tense now."

"You *killed* her?"

Darwin watched the police tape fluttering around Marian Warriq's house and the people standing around on the sidewalks, staring at the windows and the policemen. He felt like an impresario putting on a spectacular production for an audience who didn't really appreciate what they were seeing.

"Why would you do that? It's only going to alert Rakkim that he's being followed."

"How about you don't tell me how to do my business, and I won't tell you how to take over the world?" Darwin heard the Wise Old One's fine dry laugh, like the rustle of old newspapers. He loved that laugh. "Alerting Rakkim isn't going to make a difference. Rakkim's got a hair trigger. I'm still learning his pattern, but so far I can't quite keep up with him. I thought finding Marian all gift-wrapped might spark him a little, might force him to make a mistake."

"How do you know he's going to find her?"

"I can see him," said Darwin as Rakkim stepped out onto the porch with some fat cop. "From the expression on his face, I'd say he's unwrapped the meat."

"He's there *now*?"

"Roger-dodger." Darwin beamed in the chilly air; he had sparked Rakkim all right, sparked him good. He'd be off stride now.

"Does he see you?"

"Wouldn't matter if he did. I'm nobody." An elderly couple walked past Darwin, the two of them arguing with each other. Darwin nodded at them, wished them a good afternoon, and the gentleman nodded back. Darwin had gotten word of the bodies being found by monitoring the police lasercom—he hadn't anticipated Rakkim already being here. The possibility that Rakkim had been the one who'd discovered the bodies was almost too much to hope for, but there he was, live and in person, looking as if his lunch hadn't agreed with him. It made Darwin all tingly.

Darwin watched Rakkim talk to the fat cop, the fat cop's face getting redder and redder. Any man who could piss off a cop that badly had Darwin's respect. He could hardly wait to find Sarah and get all this business settled. Then he could kill Rakkim in peace. At his own pace too.

"Did this Marian Warriq tell you anything about Sarah before you . . . gift-wrapped her?"

"Not much."

"All the more reason for you to keep her alive until she talked."

"It wouldn't matter—she had a strong faith, and you know what that's like," Darwin said, remembering the woman's initial quiet protestations, her increasingly frantic quoting from the Qur'an. The things people came up with when they knew they were going to die . . . it never ceased to amaze him.

"Faith can be broken. *That's* what I know."

"She wasn't going to talk, she was just going to waste my time." Darwin waved cheerfully at a young mother pushing a baby stroller down the sidewalk. Cootchie-cootchie coo. The mother ignored him but the kid in the stroller waved back. Ugly brat, a smear of dried milk crusted on one cheek.

"You acted in *baste*," insisted the Old One. "You got the killing urge and you lost all perspective."

"My *perspective?*" Darwin chuckled. "You have no idea of my perspective."

"I'll make some inquiries about this sociology professor. Perhaps something will emerge. Just restrain your impulses. I need Rakkim alive."

Darwin stared at the taxi parked far down the block. A checkered Saladin cab, smoke bubbling from the exhaust pipe. Condensation dappled the windshield.

"Darwin?"

"I'm here." The taxi had been sitting there for five minutes, at least. Plenty of time for the fare to get out. "Talk to you later." Darwin broke the connection, started toward the taxi, eager now, but not hurrying.

"Sir?" The handsome young policeman held up his hand as though directing traffic. The other hand stayed on the butt of his pistol.

Darwin smiled, kept his eyes on the taxi. "I'm late for a business call, Officer."

"May I see some identification, sir?"

Darwin pulled his wallet out of his suit jacket, flipped it open. "Darwin Conklin, at your service." He showed his license, then handed the policeman a white business card. "I'm a real estate broker. Just got a call from the office. I really have to go."

The policeman stared at the business card as though it were written in Mayan hieroglyphs. The nametag on his chest said *Hanson.* "This is you?"

"That's right. Officer . . . please?"

The policeman flicked the card, handed it back. "We're supposed to check all the bystanders, Mr. Conklin. Standard procedure. My sergeant's a stickler, but it seems like a waste of time to me too." He was tall and pink and dim, his long, bony face covered with a sparse blond beard. His hand still rested on his pistol. Typical rookie. Handguns had strictly been prohibited under the new Bill of Rights, having one a capital offense for anyone other than police. Baby cops always took delight and comfort in their firepower, like religious pilgrims clutching chips from the thighbone of a saint, assuming they were protected from evil.

Darwin smiled.

"So you're in the neighborhood because you have a house to sell?"

"I make regular sweeps of these upscale neighborhoods for my clients."

"Terrible business in that two-story over there. The Warriq place. I bet you'd have a hard time selling that one. Not if what my sergeant told me is true."

"Yes . . . well, real estate can be a challenge."

"My sergeant was puking all over his shoes. I'd call that more than a challenge."

Darwin watched the cab pull away from the curb, then back into a driveway. "Are we done, Officer? I really *am* in a hurry."

"Do you handle condos?" asked the policeman. "I'm living with my folks and it's driving me crazy. My mom's a great cook and everything, but still . . ."

Darwin offered the card again. "Give me a call tomorrow and we'll talk."

The policeman ignored the card. "I'm just looking for a onebedroom. Catholic area is fine. I got no problem with fish-eaters." He grinned his big white teeth. "Their women can be a lot of fun too, if you know what I mean."

"I know exactly what you mean," said Darwin, watching the cab disappear down the street. He compacted his frustration into a tiny ball of ice and tucked it into his heart. It would be safe there. Home at absolute zero. He patted the policeman on the shoulder. A muscular boy. Probably took all kinds of extra self-defense courses and hit the gym like a metronome, sweating out the tension. "Officer Hanson, is it? We really should get together and go over my listings. Give me your address. I'm sure I've got something in your price range."

"Hey, I'd really like that." The policeman grinned again. "A healthy growing cop has no business living at home. How about tonight? My shift is over at four."

Darwin watched Rakkim and the fat cop walking around toward the back of the house, Rakkim striding along, leading the way. Mr. Take Charge. "Tomorrow would be better. I've got plans for this evening."

CHAPTER 21

After late-night prayers

"Thanks again for dragging me into your crime scene, buddy." Colarusso belted down his drink. "Man calls me away from a nice, clean burglary investigation to check out a couple of poor bastards with mix-and-match heads, I just feel a surge of gratitude. I didn't even know you were still talking with Redbeard. Chief of detectives himself gave me the word. I never seen him so impressed with me." He rapped his empty glass on the bar. "One more time, Padre."

The Catholic priest sidled over from the other end of the bar, refilled Colarusso's glass with fortified wine. He blessed the wine with two fingers, looked at Rakkim.

Rakkim shook his head. He waited until the priest had retreated down the bar, back to the argument over the greatest baseball team of all time with three retired cops who kept threatening each other with bodily harm. "I owe you, Anthony."

"Yeah, but not enough to tell me what this is really all about."

"I've told you as much as I can."

"As much as you *want*." Colarusso shook his head. "Forget it.

I only met Sarah a couple times, but I liked her. You say she's in trouble, that's good enough for me." He rubbed his bulbous nose. "Still, I see *R U Having Fun Yet?* written in blood on a crime scene wall, I got to think the killings were supposed to send you a sign. Am I wrong?"

"No, you're not wrong."

"Well, *that's* good news. Thought I was losing my finely honed cop instincts, and where would law enforcement be without them?" Colarusso belched, dug a big hand into the bowl of stale peanuts on the bar, the overflow bouncing across the polished hickory.

"I thought you were supposed to eat Communion wafers with wine," said Rakkim.

"Don't fuck with my religion, okay?" Colarusso tossed the peanuts into his mouth one at a time, rapid-fire. "No pork chops, no Scotch whiskey, no dogs, no rock and roll, no titty bars," he muttered, chewing noisily. "Ain't there anything you people are in favor of?"

"Don't blame me, I voted for all of the above."

"You're a lousy Muslim."

"That I am."

Colarusso nodded. "That's okay. I'm a lousy Catholic."

Rakkim took a swallow of wine. Terrible stuff. Colarusso had brought him to a Catholic church in Seattle whose basement doubled as an after-hours cop bar. Colarusso said after the crime scene he needed a drink, and he didn't want to go to the Zone for it, he wanted to be around his own kind. Rakkim needed a drink himself, and even though this Communion juice was swill, he liked the quiet and the company. Rakkim might not be the first Muslim allowed into the basement, but from the looks he got, he might as well have been. Colarusso had introduced him to the dozen or so cops standing at the bar, said he vouched for him, and anyone who had a problem with it could say so. The cops went back to their wine and the priest set them up.

"You sure the surveillance team swept the whole house?" said Rakkim.

"*Twice*. Just like I told you. If there was a bug there, they would have found it. I called in pest control too, made sure the story don't make the news, just like you wanted."

"Good. Have them sweep it again tomorrow."

Colarusso had been annoyed with Rakkim for disturbing the crime scene, but he knew Rakkim had his reasons. Seeing Marian laid out on her bed, discreetly dressed, the Qur'an in her hands . . . Colarusso had understood.

"This is one crazy case." Colarusso gestured with his drink. "I say, you want to kill somebody, go ahead and do it. That's your business and mine is catching your ass, but propping people up on the couch with their heads all jumbled? Who *does* something like that?" He shifted his bulk, his gray suit bagged out and stained with a week's worth of handheld lunches. "I'm not lightweight, you know me. I've seen things that would make your eyes pop out like Wile E. Coyote."

"Who's Wile E. Coyote?"

Colarusso shook his head. "I feel old." He grabbed some peanuts off the bar. "I put in a call to Major Crimes, asked if there was another thrill-kill gang in operation. You remember those huffers we had last year?"

"Glue sniffers, right?"

"Glue, gasoline, turpentine, you name it. They'd hit some nice neighborhood, kick in the back door, and butcher everyone inside. Fast and sloppy. We'd find ears in the refrigerator, bodies crammed up the chimney . . . but today seemed worse."

"There was intelligence at work today."

"There was *something* at work." Colarusso drank half his glass of wine, his face going slack. "I just want to find the crew who did it."

"It might not have been a crew. It might have been one man."

Colarusso snorted. "The bodyguard was a hard-core vet with a chestful of ribbons. It would have taken more than one man to bring him down."

Rakkim didn't argue, exhausted, as much from the crime scene as from lack of sleep. He hoisted his drink. After the second glass, the wine tasted better. He remembered Marian in the bathtub, her hair floating around her. He remembered the stiffness of her flesh and the effort it took to get her dressed and the feel of her wet hair as he carried her. Wrestling with the dead. "I killed her, Anthony. I killed all three of them."

"Well, that should make closing the case easier."

"I thought I covered my tracks, but somebody must have followed me to Marian's. I might as well have killed her myself."

"Quit your blubbering. You want me to forgive you? I can do it. I used to be a priest."

Rakkim stared at him.

"It's true. I was ordained in Woodinville when I was twenty-one. Left the priesthood after the transition. I could see which way the wind was blowing . . . and the celibacy thing was getting to me. You think you can handle it when you start seminary, but you get out in the world and your pecker has a mind of its own. Anyway, I'm not a priest anymore, but I still got the instincts. Still go to mass every week. Father Joe there, he hears my confession . . . then afterwards we retire down here and he sets 'em up. Can't ask for more than that from a man of God." Colarusso leaned closer to Rakkim. "You want me to hear your confession."

"Muslims only bare our souls to Allah."

"You sure?"

"Well, mostly I keep my sins to myself. Allah has enough on his mind." Rakkim was laughing . . . it sounded like laughter, but tears were rolling down his cheeks. "I must be drunk. I can't keep up with you Catholics."

"You're doing okay."

Rakkim finished his wine, rapped the glass on the bar for a refill. He nodded at the pool table off to one side, the green felt shiny, ripped in a couple of places, but still inviting. "I'm surprised nobody's playing."

"The table's off-limits," said Colarusso. "Last year a couple of knuckleheads got into it over a game of eight-ball, fists flying, just really tearing the place up. Father Joe had to break a cue stick over one of them."

"Did it leave a scar?"

Colarusso grinned, rubbed the back of his head. "No, but I still get headaches."

Rakkim watched the room in the mirror, took in the cops strung out along the bar, and was glad he had accepted Colarusso's offer. It was a plain, dark, low-ceilinged room filled with hard cases, tough and bitter men who didn't need the thrash and clatter of the Zone. The choirboys, that's what Colarusso had called the regulars, although most of them weren't practicing Catholics. Lutherans and Catholics, agnostics and atheists, it didn't matter— sergeants and detectives and a few patrolmen, but no brass. The choirboys may not have been religious, but they were too proud to convert just for the career advantage. Dust was on the floor and photos of boxers were on the walls and a painting of Jesus with his heart pierced with thorns. The basement bar was a place to get peacefully hammered on quasi-legal wine, to sand off the raw edges of the day, one glass at a time.

"You want to tell me about those books you took from the house?" asked Colarusso.

"They belonged to Marian Warriq's father. His private journals. There's something in them. Some information that I need. I just don't know what it is."

A huge detective staggered over, draped an arm around Colarusso. The well-dressed behemoth had satiny black skin, a shaved head, and a gold stud in his nose. He glanced at Rakkim.

"Didn't you hear about the dress code, Anthony? No towel heads." His booming laugh filled the immediate vicinity with the stink of fermenting grapes.

"Rakkim, this poor excuse for a lawman is Derrick Brummel," said Colarusso. "Derrick, this is Rakkim Epps."

They shook, Rakkim's hand lost in the detective's paw.

"I just wanted to say hello," Brummel said to Colarusso. He shifted his eyes.

"You can say anything in front of Rakkim," said Colarusso.

Brummel gazed at Rakkim. "Is that right?"

"Take a chance," said Rakkim.

Brummel turned to Colarusso. "You hear about my grab-and-scram? Punk snatched a ruby ring off the finger of some business-man, grabbed it right off the street and disappeared into rush hour I got the call, did my homework. Description matched a kid I busted a few times previous. Scooped him up the next day." He leaned closer and seemed to bring a heat with him. "This after-noon I find out the imam of the businessman is going to try the kid under sharia law." Brummel glanced at Rakkim. "Kid's *Catholic,* Anthony."

"That can't be right," said Colarusso.

"It's true," thundered Brummel. Heads turned along the bar. "You think I don't know the disposition of my own case?"

"Watch your pressure, Derrick," said Colarusso. "Sit down and have another drink."

"Am I a law-and-order cop?" demanded Brummel.

"You're a law-and-order cop."

"Am I a deepwater Baptist?"

"Deep as they come," said Colarusso.

"Then you know I'm not making excuses for this kid. He's a thief and a loser, but no way he deserves to have his hand chopped off."

"The Black Robes can't do that to a Catholic," insisted Colarusso. "No way."

"If the businessman said he intended to donate the ring to his mosque, he might have a case," Rakkim said quietly. "It's a stretch, but that's one interpretation of the statutes."

"If the Black Robes can haul a Catholic into religious court, they can haul in anybody." Brummel looked hard at Rakkim, the overheads reflecting off his skull. "Shit jobs, shit housing, shit treatment. Now *shit* law? Christians can take a lot of abuse, but at a certain point we're going to get fed up, and then you best watch what happens."

"I don't like it any more than you do," said Rakkim.

"He's telling you the truth," said Colarusso.

"If you say so, Anthony."

"He doesn't have to, *I* say so," said Rakkim.

Brummel pounded Rakkim on the back. "Okay, tough guy, we'll discuss it some other time." A glance at Colarusso. "I'm not drunk, but I'm close enough. Time to go home and take out my troubles on the little woman."

Colarusso and Rakkim watched Brummel leave, the bar silent, then suddenly louder as the door closed behind him.

"He's a good cop, but he dearly hates Muslims. Probably wished he had migrated to the Bible Belt when he had a chance. Most black folks did, but he stayed behind, figured he'd give the new government a chance. I was the same way." Colarusso sighed, exhaled the scent of overripe grapes. "You were too young to remember what the country was like before, but let me tell you, it was *grim*. Drugs and desperate people beating each other's heads in for reasons they couldn't even explain. Man against man, black against white, and God against all—that was the joke, but I sure never got a laugh out of it." Colarusso shrugged. "Then the Jews took out New York and D.C., and it made our troubles before seem like one of those tea parties where they serve watercress sandwiches with the crusts cut off. Taught us what hard times *really* were. Muslims were the only people with a clear plan and a helping hand, and everyone was equal in the eyes of Allah. That's what they said, anyway." He was bleary-eyed. "Besides, your people are big on the punishment part of crime and punishment, and they don't take to blasphemy. I like that. The old government actually paid a man to drop a crucifix into a jar of piss and take a picture of it. Don't give me that look, I'm *serious*. He got paid money to take the picture, and people lined up around the block to look at it. So, I'm not exactly pining for the good old days, but now we got Black Robes walking into police stations like they own the place." He shook his head. "That ain't right."

"No, it's not right."

"I got a look at Anthony Jr. yesterday when he got out of bed. Must have had twenty or thirty cuts on him. None of them deep. They were already scabbed over. Sprayed himself with Heal-Qwik. Amazing stuff. He wouldn't tell me who cut him. Said it was *private*." Colarusso rooted around in his mouth with a forefinger, dislodged a bit of peanut from his back teeth, and flicked it onto the floor. "You sure you don't want to go to confession?"

"Just help me find Sarah."

"Anything you want. You know—" Colarusso reached into his jacket for his cell. Listened, nodding. "You're *sure*?" He slipped the cell back, squinted, bothered by something.

"What?"

"That was the ME." Colarusso plucked at his lower lip. "There was hardly any blood spatter in the living room, just what soaked the couch, so I thought for sure those two folks were killed someplace else and then posed, but the ME said they were killed right where you found them. It was the arterial . . . something that threw me off."

"Arterial spray."

"You know about these things?" Colarusso gave up waiting for an answer. "Cause of death was a knife thrust to the base of the throat, but according to the ME, the reason there was so little spatter was because they weren't excited when they died. Minimal arterial spray because their heart rate wasn't elevated at all. It was as if they were just calmly sitting there waiting to die." He shook his head. "Doesn't make sense. There were strangers in the house . . . strangers forcing their way in, those two people *had* to be scared. They should have sprayed the walls when they were cut."

"It was one man and they didn't see it coming."

"I told you, the chauffeur was hard-core," said Colarusso, exasperated. "I checked his sheet—he was *trained*. Hard to imagine him being so surprised he didn't even move. Even if he was killed first, don't you think his wife would have time to react? She just kept sitting there. I mean . . . who kills that fast?"

"Fedayeen," said Rakkim. "A Fedayeen assassin could kill you so fast that you'd be dead before you tasted the blood in your mouth."

"Fedayeen? Like you?"

"No, not like me."

Colarusso stared at him, suddenly sober. "You're scaring me, troop."

Rakkim could see Terry and his wife posed on the couch, sheeted with blood, their heads in their laps. "The assassins specialty is a small unit within the Fedayeen. A thousand recruits, the best of the best . . . you might find one selected for assassins, and he might not even make it through. I had the speed, but I wasn't right psychologically. It takes a certain . . . disconnect."

"You had a heart."

"Don't bother dusting the place for prints, this guy isn't going to be in any of the data banks, but when the uniforms finish their canvass, I'd like to see the report. On the off chance that one of the neighbors noticed someone suspicious, it would be nice to get a description."

"This assassin . . . you think you could take him?"

"No."

"You said you had the speed."

Rakkim didn't answer.

"Okay, I'll drop the subject." Colarusso dug into the bowl of peanuts, shook them in his fist. "Let's talk about Anthony Jr. At the Super Bowl you told me you wouldn't recommend him for Fedayeen, now you're signing off on it. What changed your mind?"

"He's got an aptitude . . . and what he's doing now is more likely to get him killed than being Fedayeen. Even if he washes out, he'll still be better off."

"I know he's hanging out with some roughnecks—"

"He's *leading* the roughnecks. He's directing them."

Colarusso kept shaking the peanuts.

"I did what I thought was best for him. You know that."

Colarusso avoided eye contact. "You should have seen his face when he told us that you were going to recommend him. I haven't seen him so happy in years."

"He's a little wild, but he's a good kid."

"You were a good kid once too." Colarusso tossed the peanuts onto the bar, sent them tumbling. "Look what happened to you."

CHAPTER 22

After late-night prayers

"Jesus, mister, this is some kind of record." The Catholic teenager behind the counter had bright red pimples with white centers. "You must really like strawberry malts."

Darwin stuck a straw in the malt. "Food of the gods."

"What's that mean?" The teenager's face was shiny with

grease, the neon lights turning his confusion incandescent. He rested his elbows on the counter, a pumped-up hunk with tiny blue eyes and an idle curiosity. "You got a pregnant wife at home, is that it? We get that sometimes, little mama goes on a milk-shake binge and hubby sprints out the door."

Darwin took the strawberry malt. "There's no mama at home, just me and my appetite, but thanks for asking." He slid a $5 bill to the kid and told him to keep the change. Darwin was a generous tipper, unfailingly polite, and he never littered. A perfect citizen. He walked away from the counter of Dick's Drive-In whistling a happy tune.

It was almost midnight and not a star in the sky as he strolled down the street to where his car was parked. He had been waiting across from the church parking lot for almost three hours, leaving only to walk to Dick's. Three hours and four large strawberry malts. He sucked at the straw, siphoning up the sweetness. Dick's made a great malt, with real ice cream and real fruit. Their burgers and fries were supposed to be good, but Darwin avoided meat and fried foods. He sucked at the straw, imagining himself as a giant wasp with gauzy wings and flat eyes, a giant wasp with a curved black stinger, living on sweetness.

One block over, Aurora Boulevard was still busy, but this residential street was quieter, the houses dark. An old working-class Catholic neighborhood with small, spotty lawns and beat-up cars in the driveways. He slid into the front seat of his own gray sedan, still sucking on his strawberry malt, his palate deliciously numb from the cold.

From the shadows under a magnolia tree, he had a clear view of the church parking lot, Rakkim's car next to a dozen other vehicles, unmarked cars and patrol units. A cop watering hole with stained-glass windows—a man had to take comfort where he found it. Darwin smacked his lips. Amen. The lot was surrounded by a ten-foot chain-link fence topped with razor wire, a video camera keeping watch. Darwin didn't care. Rakkim would have to come out eventually, and Dick's was open twenty-four hours a day. The blond kid behind the counter had no idea what a record really was. He picked a strawberry seed from between his teeth with the nail of his pinkie.

It had been easy to follow Rakkim and the fat cop from the crime scene, the fat cop leading the way in his government-issue ride, Rakkim right behind him on the freeway. Darwin stayed well back, using a tractor-trailer to shield his own nondescript, dark blue sedan from view. He had caught Rakkim checking his rearview a few times, but he was certain he hadn't been spotted. Just as he'd told the Old One, Rakkim had been knocked off stride by the cheerful little scene back at the house. The old man should mind his own business. Darwin had left the Fedayeen almost fifteen years ago and had taken assignments from the old man almost ever since. You'd think he would have learned to trust Darwin's judgment. Good thing for him that Darwin didn't take such slights personally. Another pull of the strawberry malt. Darwin hadn't been there beside Rakkim when he'd walked into the master bathroom, but he had been close enough. He had seen his face. Guys like Rakkim could shrug off what Darwin had left on the sofa, but it was the subtle touches, the love taps like Marian in the tub with her eyes bulging out of their sockets . . . *That* got the tough guys every time.

And Rakkim *was* a tough guy. About an hour ago Darwin had gotten a call from one of his contacts in government records, a senior-level tech able to cut through various security clearances. Rakkim Epps had been an outstanding Fedayeen recruit, top of his class, quickly given charge of small-unit ops in the Mormon territories. Dangerous duty with hit-and-run raids here, there, and everywhere. Training time, part of the blooding essential to the elite force. Two years later he had been rated exceptional in all categories—with his contacts he should have been shifted into command and control, but instead he had volunteered for long-range reconnaissance, become a shadow warrior. Darwin had raised an eyebrow at the news, asked his contact if he was sure of the information.

Shadow warriors infiltrated enemy territory for months at a time, becoming part of the population, solitary, deep-cover operators who avoided killing. It was the most dangerous designation in Fedayeen, even more dangerous than assassins. Shadow warriors faced not only the risk of being caught behind enemy lines, but a more insidious danger of going native, of internalizing the habits and traits of the enemy, an internalization required to function in-country, but one that eventually made them unable to fit back into the Fedayeen. Too dangerous to cut loose, too dangerous to keep close, they were sent back again and again until they were killed in action. Shadow warriors averaged just over two and a half years from the time of their first mission to their death, but Rakkim had survived for almost six years, done it all, then walked away when his tour was over. Amazing. Darwin was glad he didn't have to kill the man, not yet anyway, glad that he would get a chance to know him better first.

Darwin swirled the strawberry malt, took another long drink, eyes half-closed. Delicious. Shadow warriors and assassins were the two most extreme Fedayeen specialties, lone wolves set loose on their covert assignments. Shadow warriors were sent into the Bible Belt or the Mormon territories to assess the capability of the enemy, and to help plan future attacks. Assassins were used strictly for overseas missions, taking out business and political leaders, creating turmoil while maintaining an inner peace. Assassins were limited by statute to foreign operations, it was clearly specified in the federal guidelines. Darwin smiled. At least that's the way it was supposed to work.

He reached into his jacket, took out the Cyclops. It was a receiver-playback unit designed to mimic a cigarette case, its outer shell sterling silver. Russian-made, of course. The screen was the thickness of a human hair, the surveillance cameras that came with the unit sized like a pinhead. He flipped open the Cyclops, speed-forwarding. He had marked his favorite parts. There was Rakkim walking into the Warriq living room, then leaving, then coming back, like the brave little toaster. He slowed the playback, zoomed in on Rakkim's face, impressed by the way the man managed to put aside his disgust quickly, bending close to the meat, getting right to business. Fedayeen forever.

Darwin had put four cameras in the house: inside front door, inside back, one in the living room, and one in the master bathroom. The cameras gathered and stored the information continuously, then transmitted it in one brief burst on command. Almost undetectable. It was a good system, but it had its limitations. He watched Rakkim and the fat cop each carrying a cardboard box out of the house. The front-door camera had caught them leaving, but he had no idea what was *inside* the boxes. Other systems could scan through clothing or cardboard, could read if a woman was pregnant, but they were bulkier and had a louder electronic signature. Darwin preferred a quiet approach. He backed up the footage, watched it again. From the way the fat cop was grunting, whatever was in the boxes was heavy. Whatever it was, it was something Marian must have known about, something she had withheld from him. Well, good for her. He meant it too.

The old man was really spooked. All the work Darwin had done for him, this was the first time he'd sensed that the old man was worried. Four years ago, the old man had had Darwin kill an army intelligence officer, a three-star general on the fast track after a stint reorganizing the state archives. It had been a difficult assignment. The general was a martinet who never left the military compound and surrounded himself with his own personal security detail. The old man had been concerned about the general, but nothing like this. Darwin was never told why the old man wanted the general dead, or why he wanted Sarah kept alive. Wanted her found and followed. The old man must expect her to lead him to something, some kind of treasure . . . but, the old man already was richer than anyone needed to be, so it must not be valuable in the normal sense of the word. Maybe it wasn't something, but *someone* that the girl was supposed to lead him to? Darwin didn't really care; it was only the job that mattered, the challenge. Still, for this *girl* to make the old man repeat himself—*I don't want her harmed, Darwin. Not her, or Rakkim. Not yet*—well, you couldn't really expect him not to be curious.

Darwin had slid down in his seat before becoming consciously aware of footsteps approaching. Using the car's side mirror, he watched a young couple amble down the sidewalk, holding hands. They stepped into a pool of light from a garage and he glimpsed the woman, a thick, pale redhead with a smear of lipstick, her boyfriend slump-shouldered. They stopped, kissing now, bodies pressed together. They finally untangled themselves, the girl slogging up the steps to her house, the boy heading back the way he had come. She waved from the porch, but he didn't see her, hurrying away with his hard-on. Darwin went back to his malt, almost to the bottom now, sucking air as much as sweetness, and he thought of Marian in those last moments, gasping for air, bubbles pouring from her nostrils.

In a fundamentalist neighborhood the young couple would be stoned to death for their debauchery, stoned by their fathers and uncles for disgracing their families. Even moderns avoided intimate physical contact in public. Catholics, though, seemed to revel in such provocation. Holding hands, kissing, displaying their skin for all the world to see. Such egregious behavior was an act of rebellion, a sedition of the flesh, as one of the ayatollahs had said in a famous sermon. Darwin finished the malt, tossed the empty plastic cup into the trash bag he kept in the car. He didn't care if Catholics fucked in the middle of the Grand Mosque at the height of Ramadan, or if fundamentalists burned homosexuals alive and toasted marshmallows on the embers. It didn't matter to him, and he was certain that if there was a God, *He* didn't give a shit either.

Fundamentalists always talked as if God were easily offended, but Darwin knew better. Any God who could create this raging shithole of a world had no fragile sensibilities. *Nothing* offended God. Anyone who kept his eyes open would have to conclude that all we knew about God, the only thing we could be absolutely certain of, was that He thought the screams of men were sweeter music than the singing of nightingales. Darwin smiled. He probably was partial to strawberry malts too.

Fedayeen recruits were ostensibly Muslim, either converts or born to it, and Darwin had been no different. Religious instruction was part of training, with prayers said five times a day and dietary laws scrupulously kept. It didn't help. Devotion might help those who lacked courage on their own, but to a man like Darwin, faith was a distraction, if not a hindrance. When he was accepted into the assassins, he no longer had to pretend. There were no laws, no restrictions, no prayers for assassins. They were free.

Darwin fiddled with the Cyclops, watched Rakkim in the master bathroom again. He liked the part where he lifted Marian out of the tub, cradling her against him. His clothes got wet, her dripping hair splashed his boots, but he carried her with a strange, tender respect, trying not to look at her. Darwin was going to use that very tenderness against him. That tenderness was going to get Rakkim killed.

A touch and the Cyclops downloaded the last hour of surveillance. Darwin zipped through the footage, the screen divided into quarters, one for each camera, filming in infrared now. The Warriq house was quiet and dark, the bodies removed. Too bad. He had hoped that whoever was in the taxi this afternoon might have come back for a look-see once the police had left. Whether or not it was Sarah, there was a connection. Darwin had an instinct for such things. He slipped the Cyclops back into his jacket, smiled. Maybe Sarah was waiting for a suitable period of mourning before returning to the house.

The door to the church basement swung open and Rakkim and the fat cop walked out, the two of them slightly unsteady.

Darwin was ready. He would follow Rakkim and find out where he was living these days. The old man's people had staked out the Blue Moon, but Rakkim had stayed away. Morons. Darwin had actually found Rakkim's apartment, but it hadn't been used in days. Rakkim had cleaned out anything that might have been useful, but Darwin had enjoyed being there, trying on the clothes in the closet, sitting on the bed, giving it a little bounce. Rakkim probably had hiding spots all over the city, rooms and studios and garage apartments rented under fake names. Rakkim was full of tricks, but none of them would help him tonight. Darwin just needed to know where his base was, the safe spot where Rakkim laid his head and dreamed his dreams. Once Darwin knew that, the rest would take care of itself.

Darwin saw Rakkim open his car door, take out one of the cardboard boxes, and load it into the fat cop's vehicle. He did the same thing with the second box, the fat cop not offering to help. Was there evidence in the boxes? Unlikely. If it were evidence, it would have been put into the fat detective's car from the start. Interesting. Rakkim's car was stolen, of course. Darwin had run the plate. So why were the fat cop and Rakkim standing around? What were they waiting for?

The door to the church opened again, and three cops staggered out, whooping it up, throwing pretend punches at each other. Rakkim called them over. The fat cop got into the act too, his voice so loud that Darwin could almost make out the words. The three cops separated, got into their patrol cars while the fat cop walked over and unlocked the security gate. The three cops drove slowly out of the parking lot, waited, engines idling, sweeping the street with their spotlights.

Oh, you *are* a clever boy. Darwin eased below the dashboard; the spotlight slid across the windshield. He could hear a car roll slowly past, then another, but he stayed put. The spotlight returned, a regular pattern. He heard cars accelerate, peeked up, and saw red taillights in the distance. The patrol cars were strung in a line behind the fat cop's car, peeling off at each corner, trolling for anyone who might be following, making sure he made it to the freeway without company.

Darwin started his car, but didn't bother trying to give chase. He had to hand it to him—Rakkim always acted as if he were being followed. A tough guy who knew how easily even the toughest could be brought down. The power of humility, a real shadow warrior move. Darwin had only known two or three of the breed; they were all easygoing until circumstances changed, then watch out. Like assassins. Drop them anywhere in the world and within ten minutes they would fit right in, become part of the human landscape. It took an effort to be invisible, though, and the slightest slip could be fatal. Eventually even the best shadow warriors were found out and killed. Except for Rakkim. The survivor.

For some reason, he thought of the young cop at the crime scene this afternoon, bright and shiny as a new penny, eager to find an apartment and move out on his own. Ah, to be young again. Darwin pulled away from the curb. He felt like another strawberry malt.

CHAPTER 23

Before dawn prayers

Rakkim slipped out the side door of the half-empty office tower, stepped out into the cool night air. Jeans and a dark blue sweat-shirt, the hood pulled low on his forehead. *R U Having Fun Yet?* That's what the assassin had asked him. A message in blood on Marian's living room wall. Let me find you, motherfucker, and we'll see who has fun. Rakkim had told Colarusso he didn't have a chance against the assassin, but nothing was certain. He just needed to get lucky. Luckier than a man could hope to be.

Broken glass crunched underfoot, the sidewalk cracked and crumbling. Four a.m. and alone in Bellytown, what the locals called the rundown neighborhood surrounding the vast open-air market that kept the city fed. Four a.m. and hungover from church wine, his stomach knotted with anger and fatigue, but he didn't want to sleep—every time he closed his eyes, he saw Marian's face in the bathtub, her hair floating around her. A dead mermaid far from the sea. He wondered where Sarah was, and if she was safe. Most of all, he wondered if she knew what she had started.

A yellowed newspaper tumbled down the street, carried by the wind. Bellytown was poorly lit, the building lobbies barred and boarded up, home to squatters and busted retirees and immi-grants from the hinterlands come to find fortune in the capital. The government had been talking about tearing it down for years, tearing it down and starting over, but talking was all that had been done.

Colarusso had dropped off Rakkim an hour ago in the alley behind the office tower, helped him load the boxes into a service elevator before driving home. Rakkim had been sleeping in a vacant office suite since Redbeard had called him in. He wouldn't stay there more than another day or two now, just long enough to skim through the journals, then take them to his next hideout. First though, he was going to talk to Harriet.

The assassin was out there and he wanted Rakkim to know it. He was either hoping Rakkim would panic or he was just too arrogant to contain himself. Arrogance and self-indulgence were occupational hazards for assassins. Snatching lives did that to you. Such godlike power hollowed out even a strong man eventually, and assassins were weak by nature, weak men with a special gift. By announcing himself, the assassin was counting on Rakkim to lose his focus and make a mistake. It was the assassin who had made a mistake, though, and if the assassin didn't realize it, that was another mistake.

Music came from the apartment building across the street . . . old music from the war before the *last* war, music from when people touched and held each other in public. Some ancient pensioner must be having trouble sleeping or had got up to pee and thought of better times. The music stopped, then the same song started again, and Rakkim imagined the old man or old woman playing it over and over, summoning up who knows what memories. He kept walking.

The sidewalks were filling with workers headed toward the main market, men dressed as he was, hands in their pockets, cigarettes in their mouths. Trucks full of produce rumbled through the streets, horns blaring, the air thickening with the smell of ripe fruit and vegetables. He stepped into a Starbucks, its windows grimy, the interior crowded and loud. He ordered a double espresso and a cinnamon roll. A few moments later, the barista set down his order and he handed her $6, told her to keep the change.

The money was pretty, you had to say that much for the new regime. He barely remembered the old money, but he knew it was green and showed the faces of dead men. The new bills were brightly colored, a mix of blues and pinks and yellows, larger than the old money. No dead presidents. The five-dollar bill showed the mosaics of the Detroit armory, the ten showed the fallen Space Needle, the twenty pictured the crescent moon over the ruins of New York City, the fifty showed the capital's Grand Mosque, and the hundred showed the holy Kaaba, the great black cube in Mecca, radioactive for the next ten thousand years.

He belted down the espresso, started on the cinnamon roll as he walked out the door. He hadn't realized how hungry he was. He finished the pastry, carefully licked his fingers clean. After everything that had happened, he still had the habits of a good Muslim at least. Christians looked askance at Muslims for licking their fingers after eating, considering it unhygienic and a mark of poor manners, but Muslims knew better. Food was a gift from Allah, and who knew which morsel contained the blessing of God?

He saw Harriet up ahead, pushing through the crowd, forcing people to make way for her enormous girth. She was a bully in a long fur coat; a blubbery matron in her sixties with bright orange hair and a staircase of chins jiggling with every step. She leaned over one of the fruit stands and picked up a peach, brought it to her nose for a quick appraisal, then tossed it back down and barreled on. The fruit vendor glared, but didn't complain.

Rakkim followed her. Harriet was a creature of habit, making her regular rounds of the market, always among the first customers of the day, so she could select the best for her discriminating palate. Predictability was no danger to her. She needed to be available to potential clients, and besides, she was protected. Rakkim saw a man on the opposite side of the street eating from a bag of hot chestnuts as he kept pace with her, a stocky brute in a blue peacoat with the collar turned up, a watch cap pulled low. Home is the sailor . . . but he was no sailor. He didn't have the saltwater squint. Another bodyguard was just a few steps behind Harriet, a tall fellow using a cane, but he was no cripple; the sole of his right shoe didn't have the proper wear pattern for the dragging he was putting on, and he wasn't rotating his hips enough. People thought all it took to play the part was a heavy walking stick, but a whole set of subtle markers had to be learned, and the man hadn't put in the time.

Harriet checked out another vendor's peaches. Picked one up, ran a thumb over the skin, sniffed. She nodded, then handed over a succession of peaches to the proprietor. After paying, she tucked the paper bag of fruit into a shopping bag, then crossed the street to the Muslim butchers' stalls. Rakkim strolled after her. He saw one of her bodyguards shift position, the one in the peacoat sensing his interest. Good catch.

The butchers were in full tilt over the cutting tables, sharpening their knives as they bent forward, the sound like giant insects clicking their mandibles. Their white aprons blotchy with blood, the butchers muttered as they worked, endlessly repeating the name of God. It wasn't strictly necessary; Muslim law only required that the name of God be pronounced at the time of slaughter, but the Black Robes had deemed the name of God could not be invoked too often, and the butchers were eager to comply. The Christian butchers were on the far side of the market, near the main garbage dump. The Christians sold meats slaughtered improperly, animals killed by stunning, and their stalls were next to the fishmongers that sold seafood devout Muslims wouldn't touch: crabs, lobsters, oysters, mussels, and octopuses.

"Hello, Rakkim." Harriet eyed the perfect T-bones as the butcher behind the counter waited patiently for her decision. She was a devout atheist, contemptuous of all believers, but she knew the best of everything was reserved for the faithful. She pointed at one large, well-formed cut of meat, then turned, gave Rakkim an awkward embrace, her fur coat warm and steamy in the damp. She smelled like $300-an-ounce French perfume. "You look like shit."

Rakkim fingered the rich brown fur. "Muskrat?"

"Russian sable." Harriet flicked his hand away, then checked to see that her strand of black pearls was still around her neck. She paid the butcher for the steak. A few moments later she and Rakkim were walking down the sidewalk while her two bodyguards kept their distance. "Are you finally ready to take me up on my offer?"

"That's not why I'm here."

"Don't play hard to get." Harriet's bright orange curls were gray at the roots, her cheeks crusted with rouge, but her gray eyes were intense. "I've got a CEO for an oil-drilling firm who's involved in a messy patent dispute with one of his competitors. Very messy. He's got an armored limo and twenty-four-hour bodyguard protection, but he still pisses his pants every time he goes to mosque. A two-year personal security contract with him and you could buy a villa in Hawaii and stock it with dancing girls. Assuming he survives, of course. Just name your price."

"I don't have a price." Rakkim reached into her shopping bag. He passed up the peaches, snagged an apricot instead. Bit. It was incredibly sweet, perfectly ripe. Her bodyguards were closer now, the one in the peacoat pretending to examine a rack of lamb.

Harriet gave a hand signal, and her bodyguards moved back. "So, why are you here?"

Rakkim took another bite. "I've got a little problem."

"You want a little gun to take care of your little problem?" Harriet said, chins bouncing. "I don't handle such things, of course, but I have sources."

"Guns are overrated." Rakkim finished the apricot, tossed the pit into the gutter, scattering the seagulls who picked at the trash. "I need your help finding an assassin."

"That's easy enough. I work both sides of the street, you know that."

Rakkim stepped closer. "A *Fedayeen* assassin."

Harriet cackled. It sounded like a crow being torn to pieces. Other early shoppers glanced over, then away. She kept walking, her fur coat swirling around her knees.

"There's not many of them on the open market, I understand that," said Rakkim.

"There's *none* on the open market. Twenty years in the business, and I've never met a real one. Oh, there's been plenty tried to pass themselves off as the real thing, but they all turn out to be fakes." She patted his arm, suddenly squeezed him with her thick fingers. "The real ones don't draw attention to themselves, do they?"

Rakkim didn't respond.

"I've got plenty of ex-military in my little black book, plenty of ex-police too, and even a couple former presidential bodyguards, but Fedayeen . . . you're hard to come by. Like I said, you could write your own ticket just based on that." Harriet's eyes narrowed. "You're more than Fedayeen though. I know that much."

"I was no assassin."

"Whatever you are, you're grade-A top quality, I saw that the first time I met you. Smart and quiet and you have that three-hundred-and-sixty-degree vision without being obvious, and it all just *clicks*, doesn't it?" Harriet licked her crenellated, orange-painted lips. "I took one look at you and thought, this one could dodge his way through a rainstorm and not get wet."

"This assassin I'm looking for, he may not have offered his services after he left the Fedayeen. Even if you haven't met him directly, I'm hoping you might have run into his work. Maybe you had a high-profile client, one very well covered who turned up dead one morning and your people never saw it coming. Sound familiar?"

Harriet stopped beside a fishmonger's stall, peered at the rows of silvery salmon and red-speckled trout lined up for inspection.

"Harriet? Has that scenario with a high-profile client happened to you before?"

"Occasional lapses in security are part of the business. When it happens, I pay the failure penalty to the family or whoever and move on."

"This wouldn't be a lapse in security. No one would have made a mistake. The man I'm looking for has flair. Everything would be fine one minute . . . your people might have even been in voice contact with the client's security when suddenly things would go silent. When reinforcements showed up, everyone would be dead. Security, the client, everyone. They might be *interestingly* dead, or maybe you still haven't figured out how they got surprised. Do you remember anything like that? Or something like that happened to your competitors?"

Harriet peered at him. "If you weren't an assassin, what *was* your Fedayeen specialty? I know you weren't standard-issue."

"I was a laundry clerk. I never met a stain I couldn't get out."

Harriet smiled, moved along to a display of butchered meat, bright, shiny slabs of beef and sheep and goat. "Yes, that's one way to look at it." She checked out an arrangement of goat heads, tapping her chins with a forefinger. "Lovely, aren't they?"

Rakkim glanced at the heads, all eyes and snout. Pink rivulets ran through the bed of ice they were nestled in. "I don't like food that looks back at me."

"Well, aren't you the delicate flower."

Rakkim saw the brute in the peacoat reflected in the stainless-steel basket of the butcher's scale, the man's image distorted as he shifted from one foot to the other. The one with the cane limped toward them from the other side of the street. "I think your boys are getting restless."

"You spotted them." Harriet shook her head. "I'm still evaluating these two. They may not be much good for surveillance, but they both have high combat ratings. Tipps, the tall one with the cane, was a street-fighting instructor with the Congressional Police. Grozzet, in the peacoat, is ex–Special Forces. Led a Black Robes kill squad for five or six years. A real Jew hunter from what I hear, passionate as a pig going after truffles. I guess I pay better or maybe he didn't like the idea of working for the new mullah, Ibn Azziz."

"Maybe Grozzet just ran out of Jews."

"They say Oxley had a heart attack. That's the official version, anyway." Harriet made another hand sign. "What do you hear? Did Redbeard have anything to do with it?"

Rakkim kept his eyes on the scale. "Call off your boy."

She turned, saw Grozzet closing in. "I don't think I can. He's a little twitchy."

"I'm in a bad mood, Harriet."

Harriet stepped away from him, settled into the soft pleasures of her sable coat. "Let the games begin." Her eyes were girlish.

The other one . . . Tipps, was on the far side of the street. He pulled a rapier from his cane, circling. Grozzet was closer, fist flashing with something sharp, making no attempt to hide his intentions. *Definitely* twitchy. Probably on one of the heavy-duty amphetamine variants. The kill squads functioned best on lab courage . . . anything to amp them up and diminish any moral overrides for the dirty work.

"You sure you want to do this, Harriet? They're not going to be any use to you dead."

"They're no use to me now. Not yet."

The early-morning shoppers scattered, but not too far, taking cover behind the nearby counters. They wanted to watch, and so did the security guards, and the butchers and fishmongers, all of them leaning forward, murmuring to each other. A couple of Black Robes stood on the corner with their prayer beads, expressionless, silently counting out the ninety-nine names of God.

Rakkim greeted Grozzet. "Good morning."

Grozzet slowed, a big man with a bull neck and a scraggly black beard. His eyes were pinwheeling. "This kike bothering you?" he said to Harriet.

"Do you require *verbal* confirmation of my distress signal?" snapped Harriet. "I'll have to mention that to any prospective clients."

"I was just leaving," said Rakkim.

"No, you were just dying." Grozzet crouched, clasping a Special Forces dagger.

"I never liked that fighting stance," said Rakkim. "That position is fine for slash-and-dash Black Robes ops, but you lose mobility." He yawned, clocked Tipps at the edge of his peripheral vision. "You're holding it too tight, but maybe you don't care."

Grozzet smiled. He had beautiful teeth, even and white. Everything else about him was coarse and well-worn, but his teeth looked as if they'd come right out of the box. He kept his eyes on Rakkim as he adjusted his grip on the dagger. "You watch this, Harriet. When you see what I do to this monkey, you're going to double my minimum rate."

"You're hurting my feelings." Rakkim watched Grozzet, his attention not on the man's eyes, but the *corners* of his eyes. That's where his attack would be launched. "I feel like I should sit down and have a good cry—"

Grozzet charged, gave a little stutter step that was actually a pretty good move. A change of pace threw plenty of fighters off-balance. A good move, but Rakkim was fast enough not to need to watch Grozzet's hand . . . he just watched his eyes.

When the stutter step didn't force Rakkim off-balance, Grozzet came in hard. Rakkim timed it perfectly, grabbing a goat head and swinging it into Grozzet's face. The goat head, all bone and horn, broke Grozzet's nose, shattered his front teeth. Grozzet staggered, dropped the dagger, then collapsed onto the pavement.

Rakkim swung the goat head by one stubby horn as Tipps

slowly approached. Tipps had the rapier out, but Rakkim just kept spinning the goat head round and round. Blood dripped off his fingers.

Grozzet lay curled on the sidewalk, blood gushing over the stumps of his teeth and sluicing through his beard.

"It's hard to know what to do, isn't it?" Rakkim said to Tipps. "Maybe I got lucky . . . or, maybe Grozzet wasn't as good as everybody thought. I bet you're a *lot* better."

Tipps hesitated, then raised the rapier to his forehead in salute and backed away. When he got to the other side of the street, he started running.

Rakkim tossed the goat head back onto the bed of ice.

Harriet watched Tipps dodge between the stalls across the street, knocking people aside in his haste. "You can always tell a college man—they're smart enough to know when they're overmatched." She patted her hair. "Ah, well, look around, Rakkim. There are thirty or forty people who watched your little show. Ten times that number will have heard all about it by lunch. How many do you think will decide they *have* to have a bodyguard? It's a dangerous world, you proved that to them." She watched Grozzet crawling away, touched her pearls. "I thought he would give you more trouble. He was *very* highly recommended."

The crowd stirred, the shoppers started on their way, eager to get on with the day. To tell their friends. Just as Harriet said. A butcher called out the special of the day, chicken breasts, $3.99 a pound, and a huge laborer trudged past with a half side of beef on one shoulder. A truck horn blared at the end of the street, sending the people scurrying. The two Black Robes stayed where they were.

Rakkim washed his hands with a hose the fishmongers used, rubbing hard, the water so cold he felt numb. "This man I'm looking for, this assassin . . . people might not know him, but they wouldn't be able to forget his work. I want you to ask around."

"You make it sound like an order."

"Consider it the cost of doing business." Rakkim wiped his hands on his jeans.

Harriet stroked her throat. "You know I'm always happy to help you." Grozzet had made it to the gutter before collapsing. She watched the blood streaming down the cobblestones, eddying around a curled lettuce leaf. "I don't know if this qualifies as *interesting* dead, as you put it, but last Thursday a bounty hunter was found in a Ballard apartment with a chopstick shoved through his eye. Is that the kind of style your Fedayeen assassin might display?"

"No . . ." Rakkim cocked his head. "Were they working for you?"

"Of course not. You know I don't deal with that element."

"Who were they looking for?"

"Some runaway bride." Harriet selected a ripe peach from her bag. "All very hush-hush, as usual, but I heard they were paying top dollar and they didn't mind if the goods were a little damaged during retrieval."

"*Was* there a retrieval?"

"No." Harriet took a big bite out of the peach. Juice ran out the side of her mouth and she caught the dripping with a crooked finger. "But, as they say, tomorrow is another day."

There was blood on Rakkim's boots, but it would wash off too. He looked at Harriet. "*Where* in Ballard did they find the body?"

CHAPTER 24

After midafternoon prayers

Rakkim circled the apartment building where Harriet said the bodyguard had been found, looking for vehicles that looked as if they didn't belong in the neighborhood. Harriet's information was usually reliable, but that didn't mean she was. Rakkim had no idea if there was a price on his head, but Harriet would, and though she might buy flowers for his funeral and weep real tears, business was business. Rakkim parked behind the building. Trash cans overflowed, flies floating around rotting food and soggy pizza boxes. A cool wind stirred the flies, but they returned. It was going to rain soon.

Ballard was an older, run-down section of the city, a blue-collar mix of Catholics and lapsed Muslims. The mosques themselves seemed sad and neglected, their outer walls cracked and dusty, and the call to prayer just completed had been a recording and not a good one at that, the muezzin's voice weak and distorted. The people on the street were mostly burned-out moderns and give-a-shits, collars turned up against the damp.

The monorail zipped on the trestles over the main street, its gleaming cars heading toward downtown. The monorail system was the pride of the capital, a multibillion-dollar project initiated by President Kingsley in the first years of his administration, designed to show the world that the Muslim state was capable of grand technological projects. Twenty years later, while usually packed, the monorail remained clean, quiet, safe, cheap, and dependable. No graffiti. Not since a few taggers were executed its first year of operation. The monorail operated at a huge loss, but the exact cost to the city was a state secret. The buses were dirty and sluggish, the freeways decaying, but the monorail remained true to the president's proud vision. It didn't impress Rakkim. He had been in South American dictatorships where the streets flowed with raw sewage, but the movie theaters were digital palaces, free to everyone, with buttery leather seats and symphonic sound.

The bounty hunter's body had been found in apartment 302. Rakkim took the stairs two at a time, keeping to the sides to minimize noise. He climbed to the fourth floor, walked the corridor to the opposite stairwell, listening. Television sounds from the apartments, commercials and laugh tracks and news bulletins. Always a breaking news bulletin.

Cooking smells in the hallway, a heady mix of onions and mint tea. Someone was roasting a chicken in 409, a child singing off-key—Rakkim imagined a man coming home from work soon, climbing the steps, clothes sticking to him, wondering if they were ever going to be able to afford a home of their own. He imagined the man walking down this very hall, the smell of dinner getting stronger, stopping outside the door to listen to the child singing. The man would straighten himself, smooth his clothes before he opened the door, the child launching himself or herself into his arms. His wife would ask how his day was, and the man would lie, say it was fine, just fine. He would kiss her, smell her sweat and the hint of perfume behind her ear, the small bottle he had bought for her birthday. Last night's perfume still lingering. Rakkim stood outside the door, listening to the child sing, and the song was different now, and he had no idea how long he had been standing there. He took the steps to the third floor slowly, checking up and down the stairwell, shaken by his lapse, his momentary inattentiveness.

Different smells on the third floor. Someone was cooking cabbage, and it covered anything tasty that anyone else was making. Apartment 302 was down almost at the end of the hall, just past a boarded-up broom closet. As he passed 300, he heard a creaking behind the door. Rakkim stopped. He stayed where he was, watching the peephole, and saw the shadow under the door shift as someone moved back into the room. Rakkim moved on to 302, and there was another smell now. Worse than cabbage. The door was locked, but one of the hinges had been twisted, and Rakkim did what the last visitor had done. He gave it a push, and the bolt, which barely made contact with the frame, gave way. He stepped into the room. The windows were wide-open. It helped, but not much.

Sarah *had* been here. Her clothes were strewn around the

floor, a sunflower-yellow dress she had worn to one of their assignations. A spring dress, though spring was over a month away. A sign of her confidence then. He took pleasure in the destruction in the room, furniture overturned, cabinets kicked in, the refrigerator pushed over. Good to see the wreckage, the rage of the search—it meant that they hadn't found her. A search of the room would give him nothing, but he searched it anyway. She had left nothing of value behind, nothing that would point to where she had gone. More of Redbeard's lessons.

Back in the hall, he closed the front door and started for the stairs. Another creak from 300. He knocked. No answer. Knocked again. "Open up or I'll knock the door down."

A muffled voice. "Who are you, the big bad wolf?"

Rakkim laughed. "Just open the door."

The door opened slightly. An old man in a striped bathrobe peered through the gap between the door and the jamb allowed by the security chain. He had three days' growth of gray stubble.

"The woman who lived next door was a friend of mine."

"Lucky you."

"She had to walk past your door to reach the stairs. I think you saw her every time she left. Every time she came back too. I don't think you miss much."

"I don't want trouble, mister."

"My name is Rakkim."

"Hennesy."

"Could you let me in, Mr. Hennesy? I don't mean you any harm."

"I heard that before." Hennesy wiped his nose with the sleeve of his striped bathrobe. "Might as well come in, you're going to do what you want to anyway." He opened the door, the security chain falling onto the floor. "The other bastards didn't bother introducing themselves, so I guess that makes you the polite one."

Rakkim closed the door behind him. The carpet was worn in

front of the door where the old man had been keeping his vigil on the hallway for a couple hundred years. The wall screen in front of the sofa had been torn down, the screen shattered.

Hennesy walked to a small table next to the window and sat. He folded his hands, waited until Rakkim had seated himself across from him. A cup of cold coffee on the table, cream curdled. A plate with toast remnants next to an open jar of boysenberry jam. "I told you I don't know anything."

Rakkim saw the shell of Hennesy's right ear was evenly notched all around. The edges raw. Crusted over. Whoever had done it had stopped halfway around the left one. Grown bored, probably. "You should put some antibiotic ointment on that."

Hennesy gingerly touched his ear. "My own fault for keeping a pair of pinking shears lying around. They were my wife's . . ."

"They would have found something else to use. Something worse. People like that . . . they always reach for the first thing at hand."

Hennesy screwed the lid on the jam, brushed crumbs onto the floor. "They said she was a wanted criminal. A runaway who killed a man trying to bring her home. I didn't have anything to tell them. Don't have anything to tell you either."

"I don't believe you, Mr. Hennesy."

Hennesy sipped at the cold coffee. "I squint my eyes . . . I squint and I see death all around you, mister. Are you here to kill me? I'd just like to know."

"I *love* her, Mr. Hennesy. The men who took pinking shears to you . . . what do you think they'll do to Sarah if they find her?"

"That ain't none of my business."

Rakkim shook his head. "It may not be your business, but you took it on. That's the kind of man you are. You're not the only one who can see things about people."

Hennesy toyed with an unopened bag of pistachio nuts on the table. "*She* gave me these. Told me her name was Rachel, but I knew better. She was a runaway. She just had that look. *Fierce.* My granddaughter left her husband a few years ago. Took her two kids and ran." He sipped the coffee. "I can't eat nuts . . . they play holy hell with my digestion, but I appreciated her kindness."

Rakkim let him talk.

"I played dumb with the other ones. Told them my hearing was shot, but I got good ears." Hennesy touched the ragged cartilage again. "I know the footsteps of everybody in this building. I can close my eyes and tell if they belong here. Sometimes I wish I didn't hear so good." His voice cracked. "I heard them come up the stairs a couple of nights ago . . . three of them. Two of them left a while later, but one stayed, hiding out in the hall. After that . . ." He shook his head. "After that, I heard things I'd like to forget." He glared at Rakkim. "She killed that man, that bounty hunter, but he deserved it. I had my ear pressed against the wall and I heard every word." His eyes shimmered. "That could have been my granddaughter, and I just stood there listening."

"Was she hurt?"

"I heard her fighting back. I heard her, and I didn't do a thing."

"Was she *injured*, Mr. Hennesy?"

"I didn't see any blood on her." Hennesy looked at his hands. "I didn't used to be such a coward. I was wounded at the Battle of Chicago. Supposed to be the turning point of the war, but don't ask me. All I know is I played dead for two days on Illinois Avenue with a bullet in my guts. Peckerwoods walking all over, shooting the wounded. I was young then, it was easy to be brave. Now, I ain't worth shit."

Rakkim covered the man's hand with his own. Hennesy's skin was like wax paper. "How did you *know* she wasn't hurt?"

"I saw her walk past my door. She was in a hurry too. Who could blame her?"

"Yes, but how could you see that there was no blood on her? Walking past your peephole . . . *hurrying?*"

Hennesy kept silent.

"Maybe *this* is your time to be brave. Maybe you're getting a second chance."

"I followed her," Hennesy said at last. "I followed her when she left. I can be quiet when I want to. You get old, nobody notices you anyway."

"Where did she go?"

"Monorail," Hennesy said quickly, eager to get it out before he could second-guess himself. Redbeard always said the hardest bit of information to extract was the first piece. "She was traveling light. Walking like she was going somewhere too. Never looked behind her once. As if she didn't care anymore or maybe she was afraid to look. I almost lost her in the crowd at the monorail station. I got into the next car just as the door closed. Always been lucky that way. I know how that sounds, but it's the truth. There was one time—"

"What stop did she get off at?"

"Yeah, just the facts, right?"

Rakkim met his gaze. "Right."

"That's okay. I'm glad you're not trying to bullshit me." Hennesy pulled at his nose. "She got off at Orion Street, and I got off too. Edge of the Zone. Funny place to run to."

"Where did she go in the Zone?" Rakkim already knew the answer, but he had to ask.

"Some nightclub. Bright lights and loud music . . . I used to be quite a dancer when I was young. Trying to remember the name. Blue Moon, that's it. There used to be a song called that. My father sang it to my mother when I was a boy. Long time . . . what's the matter with you?"

"Did you follow her inside?"

"She didn't stay long. I saw her get into a cab and that was that."

"Where did she catch the cab? In front of the club?"

"Down the block. Right in front of the arcade where they show those old movies. *Star Wars* was playing. I love that movie. You ever see that one?"

"What time was that?"

"About ten forty-five. You just keep asking questions, don't you? Rat-a-tat-tat."

"You're sure about the time?"

"The next show of *Star Wars* was at eleven so I had time to get a hot dog. Like I said, I've always been lucky about little things." Hennesy leaned over the table. "She was *different* when she came out of that club. After all that happened that night, she was steady before then. I followed her, I know. She looked like just another modern girl out for fun . . . but when she came out of that club, she looked like she was about to cry. Like the whole awful night finally caught up with her." He peered at Rakkim. "You okay?"

"What kind of cab did she get into? Yellow cab? Saladin Transit?"

"No, it was one of those unlicensed rigs . . . gypsy cabs we used to call them. It was a maroon Ford, but I didn't get a license plate or anything, so don't bother asking."

Rakkim stood up. "Thanks."

"The ones who came knocking on my door after they found their buddy dead . . ." Hennesy stared straight ahead. "Those two bounty hunters, they sat me down, and this ugly one in a leather jacket picked up the pinking shears and my teeth started chattering before they even touched me. They laughed. You heard that laugh, you'd never think anything was funny again. I told myself then, I *promised* myself that I wasn't going to tell them squat."

"You kept Sarah's secret, Mr. Hennesy. You don't have anything to be ashamed of."

"I listened to that girl being attacked and I didn't do a thing." Hennesy stared straight ahead. "I didn't bang on the wall or pull the fire alarm. I just *listened*."

"You didn't give her up. You let them burn you, but you didn't give her up."

Hennesy fingered the bag of pistachio nuts. "When you find her . . . tell her I'm sorry."

CHAPTER 25

After sunset prayers

"This seems a little out of my price range, Mr. Conklin," said the handsome young police officer, looking around the living room of the condo. "I'm sure you're a fine real estate agent and all, but you probably don't know what a patrol officer brings home."

"Nonsense, Officer Hanson," said Darwin. "Where there's a will . . ."

"Where there's a will . . . what?"

"A *way*. Where there's a will, there's a way."

Hanson scratched his sparse blond beard. "That's a new one on me. Live and learn, I guess."

Darwin nodded. "I couldn't have said it better."

Hanson paced off the empty living room with his big, shiny black shoes. Hitched up his belt, adjusting his sidearm. He had just finished his shift, his long face tired, but excited at the possibility of moving out of his parents' basement. He ran a finger across the mantel of the gas fireplace, noted the small silver sconce on the wall that indicated the direction of Mecca.

"There's a mosque within walking distance, and a grocery story two blocks over," said Darwin. "Quiet neighborhood, recently remodeled kitchen. Nine hundred square feet. It's not a mansion, but it should be plenty big enough for you . . . and those Catholic girls you indicated a preference for."

Hanson squared his shoulders. His eyes were eager as a puppy's. Filthy beasts.

"As I said, you've got a mosque close at hand, but you're only a fifteen-minute drive from the Zone. I'm sure you're familiar with the temptations of the Christian Quarter."

"Yeah . . . well, not in uniform." Hanson grinned, squatted down, and felt the blue shag carpet. Turned his long, horse face up at Darwin. "This is really nice. The rug in my room now has got cracker crumbs that are older than me." He stood up, wiped his hands on his trousers. "Hard to believe the price though."

"Motivated seller. That means the owner is eager to sell it. He wants to retire to Palm Springs. Says he's tired of the rain."

"I like the rain."

"Me too. Cleans things up, doesn't it?"

"You got that right. After yesterday . . . after what I saw inside that house, we could use all the cleanup Allah can deliver." Hanson looked queasy. "The bathroom . . . tub or shower?"

"Both."

Hanson shook his head. "This is Paradise."

"You'll have to supply your own virgins, but that shouldn't be a problem with a handsome young man like yourself."

Hanson gave him a look. "I do okay."

"And the uniform . . . one can't overestimate the power of the uniform over the female of the species." Darwin smiled. "How soon would you like to move in?"

"Soon as possible." Hanson hitched up his pistol again, then walked over to the window and checked out the view. The Grand Mosque was dimly visible through a gap in the surrounding buildings, floodlights gleaming off its azure sides. "My dad might be able to help me with the down payment. And I can tap the police credit union."

"There you go."

"Where there's a will, right?"

Darwin winked at him. "You're a quick learner."

Hanson checked his watch. "Evening prayers are in eighteen minutes." He nodded at the sconce. "You want to join me, Mr. Conklin?"

"I'd be honored. We can wash in the bathroom."

Hanson sat down on the carpet. Unlaced his shoes and removed them. Peeled off his socks, tucked them neatly inside. Placed the shoes against one wall. He took off his patrol jacket, hung it on a doorknob. His blue shirt sweat-stained. Hanson didn't seem to mind that Darwin still had on his suit jacket and shoes, standing there with his hands in his pockets. They had time.

"Bathroom's this way." Darwin started down the hallway, hearing Hanson padding along behind him. He stopped outside the bathroom door, gestured inside. "Here you go. Be my guest. I'll finish up after you."

Hanson carefully washed his feet in the bathtub with the chip of soap left from the previous tenant. Washed them again, water splashing, then looked around for a towel. Nothing.

Darwin took a handkerchief from his suit jacket, unfolded it.

"I couldn't do that to your fancy handkerchief, Mr. Conklin."

"Nonsense." Darwin handed it to him. "Please. We can't be expected to offer our prayers to God in a state of filth, now can we?"

Hanson dabbed at his feet with the handkerchief, draped it over the bare towel rack. The bathroom was small, the shower stall tiled in pink, the floor a checkerboard of black and white. He rolled the sleeves of his blue shirt past the elbow, started lathering his hands and forearms in the oversize sink. It would have been easier to take off the shirt, but he was modest . . . or uncomfortable with Darwin standing in the doorway watching.

"What exactly *did* you see in that poor woman's house yesterday?"

Hanson rinsed off his thick forearms, water sluicing down his wrists. "Trust me, mister, you don't want to know."

"Actually, I do."

Hanson glanced over at him. "I don't want to talk about it." He grabbed the handkerchief off the rack, wiped himself damp, and refolded it. Held it out.

"No, thanks."

"You're not going to wash?"

"I can assure you, my handsome young police officer, it wouldn't do any good."

Hanson squared himself up, jaw forward, on guard now. "What's going on?"

Darwin applauded. "You've just posed the ultimate philosophical question. Although, as usual, the question is asked too late for the answer to do any good."

Hanson looked Darwin over, saw an owlish, slightly built Realtor in the tailored gray suit. Give the young policeman credit, he didn't smile. Not exactly. His right hand rested on the butt of his pistol, but it was more reflex than genuine concern. "Get out of my way, Mr. Conklin."

Darwin didn't move. "No need to be so formal."

Hanson stepped forward. "I asked you to get out of my way, buddy."

"My name is Darwin. I'll be your killer tonight."

Hanson had barely tightened his grip on his pistol when Darwin hit him. Hanson was 195 pounds of grade-A muscle, but the punch emptied the air from him, knocked him backward. Hanson clung to the shower curtain rod with his fingertips, all of his tender parts open to the world. Darwin stepped into him, hit him full force just above the solar plexus, sent him tumbling into the bathtub. Hanson's head smacked the inside of the tub.

Darwin sat on the edge of the tub. Hanson's legs hung over the rim, dangled above the checkerboard floor. Darwin tugged at the young policeman's little toe. "This little piggy . . ." There was just a minimal autonomic response. He looked into Hanson's face. "Take your time. Shallow breaths. Pretend you're sucking in air through a straw. The second punch broke the two lower ribs on your left side. Shattered them, actually. Your insides are filled with splinters of bone. Shrapnel to the vital organs. You're filling up with blood. So, as I said . . . shallow breaths. Look at me. Stay with me. Do you have a foul taste in your mouth? A rotting-meat taste? Do you?"

Hanson gurgled a response.

"See there? Your liver's been shredded. Amazing how quickly the bile backs up when the ducts have exploded. The human body . . . what a playground."

"W-w-why?" whispered Hanson.

"Always the why with us, isn't there? We always have to know *why*. A steer waiting in line to be slaughtered sees the steer in front of it getting its throat slit . . . do you think either of those dumb beasts wonders why?" Darwin smiled at the handsome young policeman. "It's a heavy burden being human, isn't it?"

Hanson tried to speak, groaned, his face twisted on the bottom of the tub.

"I know eighty-seven ways to kill a man with one punch. Eighty-seven kill spots on the human body if the blow is perfectly placed and struck with sufficient force. I don't mean to brag; I just thought you'd be interested. You'll be dead in a couple hours, but I wanted us to have some time together first. I so very rarely get to discuss my handiwork. That's why I asked you about the Warriq crime scene." Darwin played with Hanson's toes again. The policeman needed to trim his nails. "I was trying to get your impressions."

Hanson's eyes widened.

"I don't mean to be a poor sport, but there wasn't a word about the killings in the papers, no footage on television. It was as if it hadn't really happened." Darwin stuck his forefinger in the young policeman's open mouth, hooked him behind the front teeth, and repositioned his head to help him breathe more easily. He wiped his finger on Hanson's shirt. "Vanity is a weakness, but a man deserves to take pride in his work. At the end of the day, family and friends are nothing—all we have is our work. Every one of my kills is *seared* in my memory. Every one. I could describe in detail how I killed them, and the look on their face at the moment of death. I could tell you about the way they fought, and what they were wearing and the sounds they made or didn't make. I could prove it to you. I could run through the complete list"—Darwin smiled, smoothed the young policeman's eyebrow—"but you don't have that much time."

CHAPTER 26

After sundown prayers

Jill Stanton buzzed open the gate to her ranch and Rakkim drove through, the car bouncing over the dirt road. A drizzle started and he hit the wipers, the stiff rubber leaving a smeared, muddy trail on the windshield. The guy he'd stolen the car from should keep up on the maintenance. Probably didn't change his oil at the recommended intervals either. Lightning in the distance. Early evening and the clouds blocked the stars, made it darker. He kept his foot heavy on the accelerator.

It had taken him a day to find the gypsy cabdriver who had picked up Sarah in the Zone late Wednesday night. Her neighbor Hennesy had been right, it had been a Ford that had picked her up, but it had been dark green, not maroon.

The cabdriver had recognized the photo of Sarah—his eyes

gave him away—but, he just said, what's it worth to you, brother? Silvery protective medallions picturing Osama and Zarqawi dangled from his rearview, faces turning as the Ford roughly idled. "How much, brother?"

The lights in the ranch house came on as Rakkim navigated the road. He had only been here once before, five years ago when he'd been home on leave, jangled, unable to sleep. *Nothing* had seemed familiar. Except for Sarah. She had brought him to the ranch, not even telling him where she was taking him, wanting to surprise him. It had worked. Jill Stanton was easy and unaffected, quick to laugh, a woman who had willingly left the glamour of Hollywood behind fifteen years earlier and never looked back. The three of them had ridden horses all morning, then picnicked beside a river, lazing with cheese and fresh peaches and cold cider in the sun.

Sarah had interviewed Jill for *How the West Was Really Won: The Creation of the Islamic States of America through the Conquest of Popular Culture*. Lousy title, Rakkim had thought, but he wasn't complaining if it got him the chance to meet Jill Stanton. "The Face" herself, the woman considered the most beautiful and talented actress of her generation.

Jill Stanton's proclamation of faith while accepting her second Academy Award would have been enough to interest tens of millions of Americans in the truth of Islam, but she had also chosen that moment in the international spotlight to announce her betrothal to Assan Rachman, power forward and MVP of the world champion Los Angeles Lakers. Celebrity conversions cascaded in the weeks after that Oscars night, and according to Sarah's research, the newly married couple were feted on fifty-seven magazine covers over the next two years. Jill and Rachman had been divorced for eighteen years now, and it had been more than that long since Jill had been in a film, but she remained a revered, if reclusive, personality. Her interview with Sarah was one of the few she had given since retirement, and Sarah had taken pains to safeguard her privacy.

Jill stepped out onto the porch as Rakkim's car approached. She waved as he pulled up, walking down the steps to meet him.

"Where is she?" said Rakkim.

Jill put her hands on her hips. She was almost sixty years old, still lean and beautiful, radiantly healthy, her long, braided hair salted with gray. She wore boots and jeans and a chamois shirt the color of butterscotch. "You've lost your manners, Rakkim. A pity."

Rakkim stepped up onto the porch and threw open the door. "Sarah!"

Jill was beside him. She smelled like horses. "She's not here."

Maybe it was the movie star voice, or the face, but Rakkim knew that she was telling the truth. He had no idea what it would take to make her lie. Jill had turned down multimillion-dollar offers to write a tell-all book about her marriage. She had never advertised a product or endorsed a political candidate. He had only met her that one other time, but if Jill Stanton said that a great white whale was swimming up her driveway, Rakkim would look for a harpoon. "Where is she?"

"I don't know. Come on in." Jill took his hand in her rough grip, led him into the living room. Knotty-pine interior, thick antique carpets, plush sofas and easy chairs. Clean and comfortable. "She left a half hour ago. I'm worried about her too."

"Call her."

"She always keeps her phone turned off. She says a cell phone can be used to pinpoint your position. Is that true?"

Rakkim nodded. "Call her anyway."

Jill didn't like being told what to do, but she did it. A guest, even a boorish one, had certain privileges. She was right though. Sarah's phone was off.

"How much has she told you?" said Rakkim.

"She said she's working on something dangerous. She wanted

to make sure I understood there was a risk to taking her in." Jill's gaze was cool and clear. "I told her I haven't been afraid since I found my faith. What about you, Rakkim? Are *you* afraid?"

"Only when I breathe."

"Yet, you're here." Jill smiled. "You can wait here for her."

Rakkim wanted to put some distance between them. It was hard to get a read on things with her so close. Redbeard used his bulk and physical presence to intimidate, but Jill used her femininity the same way. He walked over to the spot on the wall marking the direction of Mecca. A large photograph of the Great Mosque hung at the precise proper direction on the wall. The photo was taken at sunrise during the hajj, a sea of believers spread out from the square, black Kaaba, the prostrate multitudes touched by golden light.

"I made my journey three years ago," Jill said, coming over beside him. "There was a peace I can't describe, Rakkim. In a way, the lingering radiation makes the passage even more precious. A few months ago my doctor found a lump in my right breast . . . a tiny lump, no bigger than a poppy seed. I had it removed. Some pilgrims, older ones mostly, choose to do nothing. They think it's a sign of their devotion, but I—"

"Anybody else living here with you?"

Jill's eyes flashed, that old diva power, and he felt it like a slap. "A few ranch hands and their families live in the outbuildings, but they've been with me for years. They have no idea who Sarah is, and no interest in asking. They're good Muslims. You can meet them at midnight prayers, if you like."

"I don't think so."

"I see." Jill lowered her eyes. Hard to see a beautiful woman who felt sorry for him. She patted his arm and made the hair stand up. "Perhaps Sarah will be back before then."

Rakkim checked the driveway. "Do you have *any* idea where she went? She must have said *something* to you when she left."

"She said she would be back in a few hours, that's all. I'm going to make some tea."

Rakkim followed her into the kitchen. "Did she take a cab?"

"Sarah borrowed a car from one of the hands." Jill ran water into a copper teapot, set it on the stove. "Carl is a mechanic. He builds Frankenstein cars from wrecks he drags back from the junkyard. Mostly he drives them around the property—they're not licensed. Sarah insisted on taking one of his creations."

"She didn't want to bring any trouble on you . . . in case something happened to her."

"She's a friend. Her troubles are my troubles."

It was an easy thing to say, but hard to live with the consequences. Rakkim kept silent. No point in trying to communicate the possibilities to Jill. A small photo was above the sink, a picture of two teenage boys each with an Academy Award balanced on his head. They had her smile.

"My boys," said Jill. "Ahmed and Nick. Ahmed is an executive with Puget Shipping, Nick is Fedayeen." She looked at Rakkim. "Sarah says you're not Fedayeen anymore."

"I'm *retired*. Once Fedayeen, always Fedayeen." Rakkim watched as she poured water into a couple of ceramic mugs, then dropped a bag of black tea in each.

"Sugar?"

Rakkim shook his head, took the mug. The kitchen was as comfortable and unassuming as the living room, spacious and clean and practical, with pots and pans dangling from hooks and a large, freestanding butcher block. A plain white-pine table was in a breakfast nook. He imagined Jill and Sarah having scrambled eggs with cheese early in the morning, watching the sun rise over the mountains. Then clearing the plates and tending to the animals, shoveling out the barn and dredging the duck pond. "Do you miss it?"

"Hollywood?" Jill knew immediately what he was talking about.

She was probably weary of the question. One more reason to stay on the ranch, raise horses, go to the small mosque in town, and let the rest of the world go by. "Sometimes." She sipped her tea. "What about you? Do you sometimes wish *you* weren't retired?"

Rakkim smiled. "Sometimes."

"I've got one more performance in me, although I have to admit I'm not thrilled with the role." Jill watched him through the steam in her tea. "In a few weeks I'm being given a lifetime achievement award at the Oscars. So, I think we can conclude that I'm officially certified as a living fossil."

"Lady, you don't need to fish for compliments."

Jill laughed. "I see why Sarah is crazy about you. You're like a rough kiss." She toyed with one of her braids. "Sarah told me so much about you. I feel like I know you."

"That would be a mistake."

"You make her feel safe. You and Redbeard both do, but with him there was always an agenda. Maybe that's why Sarah and I became friends—we both know what it's like to be in the public eye. To be judged. To be *used*. I can remember all those photo ops of her visiting shrines, the televised meetings with the president. Sarah Dougan, the child of the nation's first great martyr—"

"Redbeard put a stop to that when she was six. No more photos. No nightly news segments. He was worried about her safety—"

Jill snorted. "Redbeard stopped it because he didn't need her in the spotlight anymore. She had served her purpose." Jill wandered over to the photo of her sons. "Nick is my youngest. His father was so proud when he became Fedayeen, but I'm a mother. I was worried."

"He's all right?"

Jill nodded, still looking at the photo, the boys young and silly with the Oscars balanced on their heads, eyes crossed for the camera. "Sixteen years since Nick took the oath. A few scars and scratches, that's all. He's posted to Chicago. Three wives. Ten children. A Fedayeen colonel . . ." She carefully replaced the photo above the sink, ran a finger lightly across the frame. "I'm proud of my son. He serves Allah and the nation . . . but when he visits, I don't recognize him." She looked at Rakkim. "Is it a sin for a mother not to recognize the fruit of her womb?"

The guard checked Sarah's identification, his mouth moving as he read. "You're collecting money?"

"For the United Islamic Benevolence Society, just as it says."

The wind and rain battered the guard as he stood beside her open window. His green uniform looked brand-new, but the collar was wilting in the damp. He looked over the battered car she was driving. "You got permission to go door-to-door, sister?"

"*Asking* for donations is as much of a responsibility for good Muslims as *making* donations," Sarah said piously. The chador she had borrowed from Jill was a deep plum color that set off her eyes. "I'm sure you know that."

The guard scratched his puffy face with the card, the sound like sandpaper. He was a big, strapping fellow with slow eyes and a half-eaten sandwich waiting for him on the desk in the guard shack. "We had a problem here earlier this week. A . . . situation. Woman got killed. Two of her servants were butchered along with her."

"I'm certain the neighborhood is safe now, Officer. After all . . . you're on duty."

The guard chewed his lip. "I got to be careful who I let in. I could get in trouble."

"Do I look like trouble, Officer?"

The guard peered at her, taking the question seriously.

"This is a devout neighborhood," said Sarah. "It's after dinner. The brothers and sisters will be happy to have the opportunity to satisfy their obligations from the comfort of their own homes. What could be wrong with that?"

"I . . . I don't know, sister."

Sarah inclined her head, blessed him. "Then lift the gate, Officer."

The guard backed up, stumbling, muttering a blessing in return.

Sarah drove on through.

"When Sarah arrived at the ranch . . . how did she seem?"

"I got a call from her at three a.m. We hadn't talked for over a year, but I recognized her voice immediately. I'm a light sleeper . . . even if it hadn't been the middle of the night, I could tell she was upset. She said she was at a gas station about five miles away. Protecting me again. So the man who dropped her off wouldn't know where she was going." Jill listened to the rain on the roof. "We stayed up until dawn, talking. She was very upset."

"Was she injured?"

"She said she had killed a man a few hours earlier. Does that count?"

"No."

Jill shook her head. Once Fedayeen, always Fedayeen. She didn't even have to say it. "Sarah went to bed after dawn prayers, slept until late. We went riding the next morning, not talking, just enjoying the day. She seemed better. Then she left for a few hours and when she came back . . . she was worse than she was the first night she showed up. Sarah is strong, but when she came back, she couldn't stop crying. She wanted to leave. She said everyone she was close to was at risk—"

"Where did she go Friday?" Rakkim's voice was so soft that she wouldn't have heard him except that he had moved closer, close enough to smell horses on her again.

"I don't know. She said an old friend . . . a dear friend had been murdered and she blamed herself—" Jill pulled back as he jumped up, knocking the chair over. "Rakkim! Where are you going?"

CHAPTER 27

Before late-night prayers

"Excuse me, Officer Hanson . . ." Darwin carefully reached under the handsome young policeman, slipped his badge-wallet out of his pants. Flipped it open. "William Hanson. I like that. William. A good, steak-and-taters American name. Pleasure to meet you. I bet they call you Bill, don't they? How about Willy? I prefer that. *Willy.* Sounds friendly. Innocent. Do you think of yourself as innocent, Willy? Most people do." Darwin laughed, the sound echoing off the bathroom tile as he tucked the badge and ID into his own jacket. "A man like me . . . I have no illusions."

Hanson's right hand inched toward his sidearm, hanging half out of its holster.

"Well, look at *you.* Aren't you the tenacious lawman." Darwin reached down, pulled the gun free, checked it out. Standard police-issue 9mm semiautomatic, with a personal-ID grip. The weapon couldn't be fired unless the registered owner's thumbprint was pressed into position. The 9mm was useless to anyone other than Hanson. Darwin expelled a round, looked down the barrel, then jacked a fresh bullet into the chamber. "You keep a well-maintained weapon, Officer. You like those expansion slugs, I see. Give you a sense of security, do they? I wager you never fired your weapon in the line of duty, though. Am I right? That changes things, trust me."

Hanson groaned.

"Let me help." Darwin bent forward, placed the pistol in the man's hand. "There you go."

Hanson's fingers curled around the grip, made contact. He tried to raise the 9mm, but it was too heavy for him.

"Take your time. Get your strength back. Just keep breathing. Terrible calculus—each inhalation tears you up a little more inside, cuts into the soft pink parts, but a man has to breathe."

Hanson's forehead beaded. A ball of sweat ran down into his eyes, sent him blinking.

Darwin daubed at the man's face with his handkerchief, his movements strangely tender as Hanson's eyes tracked him. "Don't worry, I don't have anything embarrassing planned for you. Homosexuals, heterosexuals . . . you each make your choices, the wheel of love and desire." He stroked Hanson's cheek. "Me . . . well, truth be told, men and women, they're all the same to me. Flesh buckets. You can have them." Laughed. "Take a note, Willy. You can have my share."

Hanson shifted, cried out. Blood poured out of his mouth.

"Stay put. *Down*, boy. You're going to die soon enough; you don't need to be in a hurry. Let's chat a bit. I so rarely get the chance to talk with someone who knows me . . . the real me. Inauthenticity devours the soul, Willy, but what can I do?"

Hanson bit his lip, trying to stay conscious.

"That's the spirit." Darwin watched the policeman's blood trickle toward the drain. "I didn't do this for your badge, if that's what you're thinking. It's just that in my present job . . . there's a high frustration level. Having to hold back, hold myself in check . . . it gives me a headache. I'm a man with appetites, Willy. Vast appetites. *Terrible* appetites. And I'm not allowed to satisfy them." Darwin smiled. "You'll just have to do for now. You don't mind, do you?"

Hanson gripped the 9mm. His blue eyes were going muddy, but he held on to the pistol.

"I'm a Fedayeen assassin. You should be honored to die at my hands. You could have been run over by a bus or had an artery burst in your brain. You could have choked on a piece of tough steak or had an allergic reaction to peanut butter. Instead . . . here you are." Darwin tapped the man's front teeth as though he were playing a xylophone. "If you can get outside yourself for just a moment, get beyond the pain, I think you'll realize that a certain amount of gratitude is in order."

Hanson tried to focus.

"Perhaps that's too much to ask." Darwin watched the young policeman struggle to raise the 9mm. Blood ran down the drain faster now, curls and eddies. "That's it . . . there you go. Just a little higher. Come on, you can do it. Pull the trigger, Willy. Pull it. *Pull* it."

The gun wobbled. Clattered into the tub. Hanson took short, little breaths.

"Disappointing, isn't it?" clucked Darwin. "Welcome to my world." The wireless Cyclops inside his jacket vibrated. Still balanced on the edge of the bathtub, he slipped out the silver case, flipped it open. "Well, will you look at this?" He grinned, turned the plasma screen to Hanson. "This is the inside of the Warriq house. Real-time. It's a night-vision image so there's a green cast, but you can see her quite clearly. That's Sarah Dougan standing inside the front door. Wearing a very elegant chador, I might add. The hajib flatters her features, wouldn't you say? Hi, Sarah! Say hi to Sarah, Willy. No?"

Hanson's eyes glazed over.

"What did you come back for, Sarah? It must be something very important." Darwin pointed at the screen. "Look. She's wrinkling her nose at the stink. They may have removed the bodies, but the fragrance lingers." He watched Sarah start up the stairs and out of range of the camera in the foyer. He flicked to the living room camera. The sofa crusted with dried blood, empty now—sad somehow, like party candles guttered down. He looked at the handsome young policeman.

Hanson was drifting.

"Nothing on TV, nothing in the papers. What would I do if I kept a scrapbook?" complained Darwin. "Collecting clippings is gauche, of course, but still, don't you think the news blackout is rather petty? I blame that fat detective who was with Rakkim. Someone should teach Detective Colarusso that it's only fair to give credit where credit is due. I have to admit, Willy, I'm a happy guy right now. I thought she might come back to the house, and here she is. Nothing like being right. Best feeling in the world. Willy? You're no fun. See, there's something at the house that she wants. Pay attention, Willy. Find the focus of desire, that's the secret. Remember that. I've just given you some wisdom."

Hanson's fingers twitched, but the 9mm was an inch away. It might as well be miles.

Darwin snapped the Cyclops case shut. "Time to go. I need to find out what sweet Sarah is so interested in." He stood up, looked down at Hanson. The young policeman's hand moved ever so slightly toward the pistol. Impressive. Darwin wished he had more time to spend with the handsome policeman, but he was already late. He carefully placed his foot on the man's abdomen, right on the third button of his blue shirt. "Can I have your blessing? Yes? No?" Darwin stamped down. Just hard enough, the pressure precisely calibrated. Hanson's scream was still echoing as Darwin headed for the door.

CHAPTER 28

Before late-night prayers

Sarah slumped on the worn leather chair in Marian's library, her head in her hands. Too tired to cry, but more than enough anger to hurl every book on the shelves across the room. She didn't do it, though. She loved books . . . and she loved Marian. *Had* loved her. Loved her clarity, her intelligence, her shy laugh. Loved the way she laughed when she poured tea, as though the two of them were children playing grown-up. Marian was gone now and so were her father's journals. Sarah sat in the dark, the room lit only by moonlight. The loss of Marian was a stone in her heart . . . but the theft of the journals was even more devastating.

It had taken her a year to focus on Richard Warriq, a year of fruitless contacts with other China experts, engineers and seismologists and architects, men who had worked on the Three Rivers Gorge project, most of them retired now or, like Warriq, long dead. She had cultivated these sources or their survivors, cross-checked their information before discarding them and moving on to the next name on her list.

An owl hooted nearby and Sarah crossed to the library window, looked outside. Owls were a bad omen, but the security lights from the house next door revealed nothing. She paced the room, restless, the empty shelf on the bookcase mocking her.

Compiling the list of names had been relatively easy. She had run a computer model to track American Muslims who had worked on the dam, supposedly as part of a research paper to highlight scientific talent among the faithful. The Chinese had kept most of the work among their own citizens, but many of the engineering requirements were specialized, and the Chinese had been forced to use several American firms. Marian's father had been a fractal engineer, a devout Muslim who had returned again and again to the project and who seemed to travel widely. Sarah had almost decided to move on to the next name until Marian mentioned that her father had made a pilgrimage to Mecca after finishing business in Asia, had gone to pray at the holy city less than a month before it was devastated by a dirty nuke. Marian had thought his timing a blessing, but Sarah saw a darker coincidence, convinced now that Warriq's meticulously detailed journals were the key to unlocking the truth behind the Zionist attack.

Sarah stared at the empty bookcase, not knowing what to do. The Old One's killers must have taken them after murdering Marian and Terry and Terry's wife. No other books had been removed, just the journals. So the Old One *knew*. Which had to mean that Sarah's theory was correct . . . didn't it? That was something, wasn't it? Sarah took no pleasure in being right. She wished that Rakkim had been at the Blue Moon club Wednesday night. She was sworn to secrecy, but Rakkim . . . their hearts were joined. She was ready to tell him the truth now.

The clock ticked away in the corner. Another couple of hours until midnight prayers, but she would be long gone by then. No reason to make the security guard suspicious. First though . . . she started up the stairs to Marian's bedroom. The neighbors had told the cabdriver that she was found dead in the bathtub. Sarah wanted to see the spot where Marian had died, to pray for her there. Sarah owed her that much.

The stairs were dark, the rain beating against the windows as though someone were trying to get in. Her legs felt weak, and in spite of all her good intentions, her brave intentions, she slowed as she neared Marian's bedroom. A stone the size of a fist was in her throat, and she had a sudden, overpowering fear that Marian's body had not been removed, that unlike the bodies of the butchered servants, the police had kept Marian where they had found her, part of some complex forensic necessity. It was a ridiculous thought . . . but she could barely breathe as she stood outside the closed door to Marian's room.

Her hand trembled as she opened the door, but she quickly stepped inside, leaving it ajar. Redbeard said that at the moment of greatest fear, the best solution was to go boldly and without hesitation. Sarah stood in the center of the bedroom, heart pounding, and knew it was good advice. If she had waited another moment with her hand on the knob, she would have turned around and raced down the stairs, her chador floating behind her.

She opened the curtains. The wind blew leaves against the glass, and she stepped back, frightened. Smiled at herself. God hates a scaredy-cat, that's what she and Rakkim had told each other as children, egging the other on to mischief and disobedience. He was five years older than she was, an eternity at that age, but she had never felt the gap between them. If she did, she knew it would be breached soon enough.

Through the open bathroom door she could see the edge of the tub. Too many shadows. She walked into the bathroom, checked the tub. Nothing there. Just a bit of water in the drain, black water in the dim light. The towels were uneven on the racks. Small details that would have bothered Marian. Sarah walked over and straightened them. She didn't have the courage to turn on the light. Back into the bedroom, her stomach doing flips. The dresser drawers were half pulled out, the tiny Chinese figurines on top knocked over. The police had been in a hurry . . . or someone else had. She shivered. Yes, it had been a bad idea to come up here.

She heard a tiny click as the front door closed downstairs. It might as well have been a thunderclap. She was frozen now, afraid any step might be heard downstairs. Listening, knowing she had heard something. The rain seemed to stop for a moment, and in that moment she heard footsteps across the hardwood floor of the entryway, a whisper of sound. She had parked on the street, but it wasn't the security guard come to see what she was up to. There was no way *he* moved so lightly.

The rain was back, carried on gusts of wind. She slipped out of her chador, tossed aside her head scarf. Underneath the chador she wore the slacks and thin sweater of a modern. Just in case. Another of Redbeard's lessons. Never let a description of you be accurate for too long. Reversible jackets. Hats and no hats. Sunglasses and no glasses. Umbrellas that shielded the face. When leaving her tiny apartment in Ballard, she had always left as a modern, then changed into a chador at the first opportunity. Changing back on the return. It had worked. Until the night the bounty hunters had come for her.

She moved in tandem with the steps from below, heart pounding. She crossed across a bar of moonlight, blinking now as she flattened herself beside the door.

Someone was coming upstairs.

Sarah looked around for something to use as a weapon. *There*. A heavy granite clock on the nightstand. She hefted it. Heavy enough to brain someone. She was barely breathing, all of her energy focused on *listening*, filtering away the outside sounds, the wind and rain, focusing on the sounds of the approaching steps. She could isolate the sound of a flute from a performance of the philharmonic, could pick out the individual violinists with her eyes closed. This was no different. That's what she told herself.

Someone was outside the half-open door.

She pressed herself against the wall, tightened her grip on the clock. Better to attack him as he entered, or wait until he was inside, his back to her?

The door creaked open. "It's me, Sarah."

Rakkim! She threw herself into his arms, kissing him, sobbing, lost in the feel of him, the strength of him, the smell of his skin. She hung on to him, digging in, as though to reassure herself that he was really here, that it wasn't a dream, some desperate trick her mind was playing on her. She felt him squeeze her back, lift her off her feet, and cover her face with kisses, and she knew . . . it was Rikki. She went with the sensation, eyes closed, the two of them swaying in each other's arms . . . no idea how long they stayed there like that, alone in the big, dark house. It could have been seconds . . . minutes . . . hours, she didn't know. She bit him, nipped at his neck, more playful than angry. "You *scared* me."

Rakkim laughed. "You can take care of yourself."

Sarah wasn't laughing. "Did you . . . did you hear about the bounty hunter?"

Rakkim must have seen the look on her face, holding her now. "Killing a man like that is a good deed in my book." He held her close. "Don't second-guess yourself. *Don't.* It will only slow you down the next time."

"I don't want there to be a next time." She felt Rakkim stroke her hair and she wished they were someplace else, someplace quiet and safe and with a fireplace. The rain beat against the roof, louder now.

"We should go."

"How did you find me?"

"I was at Jill's ranch. She said you knew Marian had been murdered. I figured you had come back for the journals."

Sarah looked up at him, dizzy. "You *know* about the journals?"

"I have them. They're in boxes beside my bed—"

Sarah kissed him hard. "Let's get out of here."

Rakkim smiled. "Definitive as ever."

"Did you expect me to go all gooey once I left Redbeard's protection?"

They walked downstairs together, Rakkim slightly in front, head cocked. He stopped in front of the door, checked outside through the side windows. Sarah waited. He knew what he was doing, that was one thing she was sure of. He rested a hand on the back of her neck as he watched the street, his hand light. The familiarity of his touch, the intimacy . . . not possessive, not a bit of that, it was a connection that ran both ways.

"Does your car run all right?" asked Rakkim.

"It's beat up, but it's a smooth ride."

"Beat up is good, it will fit in with half the other cars on the road. I'd rather take yours than mine. We leave your car, one way or the other, it's going to be traced back to Jill."

Sarah opened the door, they stepped outside, then she closed it behind him. Locked it. She stared at Marian's key. Marian had given it to her the last time she had visited. The wind lifted her hair, the night air cool against her scalp—a relief after the confinement of the head scarf. She tucked away the house key, stopped. Rakkim had taken the journals, not the Old One's killers. The Old One didn't know their value . . . if the journals even had any value. Her theory about the Zionist Betrayal was still just a theory.

"Is there a problem?" asked Rakkim.

"No . . . no problem."

They walked through the rain to the car, refusing to hurry, waiting for the other one to break and run. Neither of them did. Sarah handed him the car key, then got inside, while Rakkim did a last survey of the area. "That's odd," she said as Rakkim got in.

"What?"

Sarah reset her wristwatch. Same result.

"What's *wrong*?"

"I'm not sure." Sarah checked her watch again. Same result. "Redbeard gave me this watch after my book came out. It detects a full range of tracking devices. Microwave, ultrasonics . . . everything. He was worried that I would be targeted—"

"The car is bugged?"

"I don't see how. It wasn't bugged when I got here. Anyone who wanted to harm me would have to know I was in Marian's house."

"Maybe they don't want to hurt you. Maybe they just want to know where you are."

Sarah opened her door. "We should take your car."

Rakkim switched off the interior light. "Close the door."

"We have to—"

Rakkim started the car.

Sarah closed the door. "We have to find the bug, don't we?"

"No." Rakkim switched on the wipers, watched them flick back and forth across the cracked windshield. "This is perfect."

Darwin rested the side of his face in the palm of his hand as the headlights approached the guard shack. Beep-beep-beep went the tiny scanner on the counter. The rainstorm beat against the shack, sheets of water streaming down the glass sides, distorting the view. A blur looking out. A blur looking in. Bitter with the sweet.

He had waved Rakkim through about fifteen minutes ago, face down, pretending to read a newspaper. Sarah's car drove past, not stopping. All Darwin got was a glimpse of the red taillights shimmering through the rain. They were both inside the car. Darwin had seen that much. He had watched them on the Cyclops. Watched them nuzzling in the front hallway, the two lovebirds finally reunited. Darwin had actually applauded at the tender moment, his clapping echoing off the walls of the guard shack. Sarah had discarded her chador, was garbed as a modern, a modern woman with all the modern desires. They would be inseparable now. Until Darwin decided to separate them.

Darwin *still* didn't know if she had found what she had come back for, which was annoying. Very annoying. Sarah had been off-camera for ten or fifteen minutes in Marian's bedroom, but she wasn't carrying anything when she left. Neither was Rakkim.

There *were* those two boxes Rakkim and the fat detective had removed from the house a few days ago. That might be what she had come back for. Hard to know. Darwin could ask the Wise Old One about it, but the old man treasured his secrets. Ah, the mystery of it all . . . Darwin could hardly wait to find out what the old man was really up to. It would be interesting, that was for certain. In the early days he had done a few jobs for the Black Robes, but quickly grew tired of their narrow intentions, their joyless theological bickering. The thing about fundamentalists was, they had no curiosity. All they cared about was deciding where the line should be drawn, determining which side of the line was black, and which side was white. Right and wrong, good and bad . . . Darwin transcended all such categories. In spite of all the old man's God talk, he was the same way. The two of them were unique.

Darwin whistled a happy tune as he peeled off the security guard's lime green jacket. An ugly color for an ugly man. He tossed the jacket onto the floor, right next to where the guard lay curled beside the wastebasket, neck broken. Two guards killed in this same shack within a week. The homeowners' association was going to have to pass a special levy to cover the increased cost of protection. An amusing thought. Death always brought so many surprises. So many unexpected consequences. A butterfly splatted against the windshield of a speeding car, and there went all hope of that typhoon in Japan that the philosophers were always prattling on about.

Some would call the killing tonight unnecessary. He had intended to talk his way past the guard, show his insurance-company ID, but then . . . then, instinct took over. A predator who takes no prey is no longer a predator. God had created Darwin to take pleasure in killing, and Darwin would not deny the wisdom of God. Darwin smiled at the blasphemy.

He slipped the scanner into his pocket, waved good-bye to the dead. It was a short walk to his car, the scanner beeping away. The microwave transmitter attached to Sarah's car was working properly. Good timing on Darwin's part. He had placed the device and gotten back to the shack just before Rakkim had driven up. Darwin slid behind the wheel, started his car. All things considered, things were working out perfectly.

CHAPTER 29

After late-night prayers

Sarah turned around, looked back into the dark.

"He's there. The bug's range would have to be at least four or five miles to make it effective." Rakkim kept his eyes on the road, the headlights cutting a corridor through the night. He could sense her concern. "The bug gives *us* an advantage. We know he's back there. He'll follow us anywhere now . . . anywhere we take him."

"This man who killed Marian . . . you're sure that's him behind us?"

Rakkim shrugged. "The Black Robes don't go in for such sophisticated technology, and bounty hunters wouldn't bother with a bug—they would have grabbed you back at the house. No . . . this guy is more interested in what you're up to than killing you. Not yet, anyway. He doesn't care about bringing you in. He wants to know where you're going, who you're meeting. That's why he killed Marian and the others the way he did. He wanted you to know. To scare you. To make you do something stupid."

"It worked, didn't it? Going back to Marian's *was* stupid."

They drove on through the rain and into the badlands at the foot of the Cascade Mountains, a nest of narrow roads cut through the forest. A route for smugglers and illegal timber cutters, a dangerous detour for out-of-staters who took a wrong turn. He had taken this same road through the foothills when he'd left Redbeard's last week, but he was headed deeper into the badlands now. Outlaw country. The last refuge for crazies and losers and malcontents with a million grudges. The abandoned ones. Only forty miles from downtown Seattle and the seat of government, the badlands were off the map, beyond the reach of God or man.

"There's just one man following us? One man who did all those things?"

"He's a Fedayeen assassin. They always work alone."

"Like you."

Rakkim glanced over at her, then back at the road.

"I'm just saying, there's only one of him and one of you. So why are we running away?"

"I'm not going to go hand to hand with him, if that's what you're thinking."

"Okay."

"I'm going to outsmart him."

"I said, okay."

"Are you disappointed? The flower of Islam refusing combat? It must shake your faith. I could call Redbeard, if you want. Ask him to send reinforcements."

Sarah moved next to him, her face so close he could feel her warm breath. "Just kill him."

"Assassinate the assassin?" Rakkim smiled. "What would that make me?" He couldn't leave well enough alone. "You should have contacted me. You should have told me you needed to disappear."

"I made a promise." The only sound in the car was the beating of the rain and the slap of the wipers. "Did Redbeard tell you about the Old One? Is that how you knew what I was working on?"

"Redbeard would sooner share his left ventricle than share information. I didn't need him." Rakkim edged the car over, pines and cedar crowding the road, their roots cracking the pavement. "Once you open up a secret, it starts leaking out all over. There's no way to stop it . . . unless you kill everybody even remotely connected to it."

"Are you blaming me for Marian's death? You don't have to, I've already done it."

"There's enough blame to go around."

The road took a hairpin turn, headlights flashing across a skeletal, burned-out truck at the bottom of the ravine. Rakkim relaxed his grip on the wheel, steering with his fingertips. The shocks on the car were lousy, the suspension mushy—it was all he could do to keep them on the road.

Sarah turned on the heater. Still broken. So was the defroster. Rakkim wiped condensation off the inside of the windshield with the edge of his hand. Checked the rearview. "I'm surprised Redbeard didn't put one of his own tracking devices in the watch he gave you."

"He *did*. I had an electronics tech in the Zone remove it. Said it was Russian. Paid me a thousand dollars for it. Redbeard had to know what I had done, but he never mentioned it."

"I brought the computer memory to a contact of mine. He pulled pieces of your book off it before the destruct program was fully actualized."

Sarah looked out the window.

"I know you want to believe the Zionist Betrayal was some monstrous historical fraud, but I think you're wrong."

"Then why is this assassin following us?"

"For the same reasons the Black Robes sent the bounty hunters after you. Redbeard has enemies and you're a bargaining chip. The Old One is just another player."

"You may be right." Sarah stared straight ahead. "I just need to read through the journals. I'm only partway through the relevant volumes. With your help—"

"I could get us to Canada." Rakkim watched the road. "We can switch cars and shake the assassin. Four or five days, depending on the weather and the patrols—"

"Don't be ridiculous."

Rakkim glanced over at her, then back at the road. "You haven't changed from the first day I met you. Five years old and you were already a troublemaker."

Sarah laid her hand on his leg. "Let's go get the journals. You know I like to read in bed."

Rakkim gasped at the boldness of her touch. He checked the rearview mirror again to cover his arousal. "First things first." Brave words from Sarah, but he could see her face by the dashboard lights, the strain showing as she stared out into the rain. She had never been out here before. Most city people hadn't. Even the police avoided the badlands.

It had only been six months since Rakkim had seen her, but she looked older. It wasn't just fatigue circling her eyes, it was recognition of the monsters that lurked out beyond the lights of home. For someone like Sarah, who prided herself on her logic and intellectual toughness, it had to be a shock to find out how insulated and privileged her previous life had been. Finding a friend murdered did that to you. Killing a man, and *knowing* you would do it again and it would be easier that second time . . . that was the ultimate wake-up. Sarah was learning. If they survived, she would be the better for it.

"Why are you slowing down?" Sarah asked.

Rakkim turned off the lights, but kept the car idling in the middle of the road. "If we're not going to Canada, we'll have to kill the assassin."

A small mound of concrete was all that remained of a sign that had once announced Green Briar Estates, one of many outlying subdivisions built to house workers for Seattle. *Affordable Muslim living in an unspoiled Muslim place.* It hadn't worked out at Green Briar, or any of the other remote housing developments. The moderns had fled the long commute, frightened by the surrounding forests and the growing lawlessness. The subdivisions had gone to rot and ruin, picture windows broken, chimneys crumbling, moss so thick on the walls you could stuff a pillow. Squatters had moved in, not caring that the power had been turned off. In fact, they would have cut the power lines and dynamited the water mains had they been working. The access road into the subdivision was blocked by dozens of felled trees. Green Briar existed now only in blueprints long since filed away.

"I don't like this place," said Sarah.

Rakkim flashed his headlights twice. Waited. Flashed them once again.

"We should go." Sarah looked around. "The assassin . . . he's going to catch up."

"No, he stopped when we did. He doesn't want to catch up. He doesn't want us to know he's back there. He wants to stay right where he is, lurking in the background. He enjoys being close, but choosing to stay back, holding our lives in his hand. It's intoxicating for him. Better than sex. Our stopping here doesn't make him think we're onto him—he thinks we're just exercising caution. He respects that. He'd become suspicious if we acted too trusting. It's going to make killing us later all the sweeter for him."

"You talk like you're inside his head."

Rakkim stroked her shoulder, felt her fear under the thin sweater. He didn't blame her. The assassin's head was filled with broken glass and tortured animals. Rakkim watched the woods on either side of the road. "That was *him* in the guard shack when we left. I was hoping to get a look at him, but he—"

"I *talked* to the guard. He didn't seem—"

"The guard you talked to is dead. The assassin waved me through when I drove up, his face behind a newspaper. I was in a hurry . . . I didn't think anything of it, but when you told me the car had picked up a bug at Marian's, I knew it had to be him at the gate. I would have rammed the guard shack on the way out, but it had a concrete barrier."

"Why would the assassin kill the guard? What would be the point?"

Rakkim smiled. After all that had happened to her in the last week, she still didn't understand what they were up against. "I'll be right back." He opened his door, but remained in darkness. He had unscrewed the interior lightbulb. "They're here."

"*Who?*" Sarah saw them now. Three men had appeared out of the rain, stepped out of the night like ghosts. Phantoms in soggy wool clothes, their hair and beards long and matted. Phantoms armed with axes and machetes.

Rakkim showed the men his hands and got out of the car.

CHAPTER 30

After late-night prayers

"I should be going with you," said Redbeard.

"I need you here, Thomas," said his brother. James tucked the latest progress reports into his gym bag, trying not to hurry. "I need you to look after Katherine and Sarah."

"The best way to protect them is to keep *you* safe," protested Redbeard, wanting to shake him, to make him understand. "Chicago is dangerous—"

"Every place is dangerous." James added a wireless handheld, allergy pills, and his well-worn copy of the Holy Qur'an. The sun was bright through the bulletproof windows of Redbeard's second-floor study, the villa's undulating expanse of lawn impossibly green. James zipped the gym bag.

In the blue, nylon athletic suit, James looked just as he had at the Beijing Olympics, the gold medal around his neck as he declared his new faith to the cameras. One of the first of the high-profile converts, James's hair was a mane of reddish blond, his goatee still downy as a youth's. He was so handsome Redbeard had a hard time believing they were brothers. Redbeard was bulkier and more heavily muscled, a college wrestler, his full beard coarse. An ugly duckling, but James had never treated him that way, and Redbeard loved him all the more for it.

Redbeard stood with one hand in his pocket, fingering his prayer beads, the clicking of the amber beads muted. There was something he needed to remember, something nagging at him. He fingered the beads faster, trying to recall what it was.

"Don't look so sad, little brother," said James. "It makes you look like one of the pinch-faces in the Bible Belt." James smiled. "You haven't gotten that old-time religion, have you, Thomas?"

Redbeard grimaced. He didn't have his brother's sense of humor. Or his charm either. Few did. James Dougan was director of State Security, but he was as much of a politician as an intelligence chief, a moderate Muslim, devout, yet practical. In the chaos following the Zionist attacks, James had been the new Islamic president's choice to head the agency. The fundamentalists had been opposed, but James had disarmed them with his wit, his popularity, and his adroit handling of the media. When those failed, Redbeard, his second-in-command, had been eager to step in. Redbeard had an eye for detail, the ferocity of a Kodiak bear, and was willing to lie to God himself if necessary.

Now, two years after the cease-fire that had ended the civil war, they should have been celebrating their success. State Security had stymied major terrorist attacks and forced the remnants of the Christian underground to flee to the Bible Belt. Civil liberties had been curtailed, but after the chaos that had marked the transition from the former regime, complaints were few. Except from the fundamentalists. The right-wing clerics had called for James's ouster for his refusal to stone unbelievers, denouncing the brothers as converts in name only, soft on doctrine, soft on sin.

Redbeard wanted to strike back, but James said the government might not survive such internal dissension. Besides, it was better to save their ammunition for when the hour was truly perilous. *Timing, Thomas,* he had said, *this is the lesson you must learn,* then turned away any resentment Redbeard might have felt in being so schooled by taking off the watch around his wrist, their father's watch, and giving it to him. Redbeard had protested, but James had kissed him on both cheeks and told him that no man had been so blessed as he, to be given such a loyal brother.

"You're staring at your watch, Thomas. We still have a few minutes, don't we?"

Redbeard nodded, unable to speak. The numbers on the clockface were familiar . . . the hands in position, but try as he might, he couldn't tell the time.

"Senator Simpson assures me he has the votes to defeat the hard-liners' latest amendment," said James. "Fine work. You've kept the Black Robes so busy fighting among themselves that they haven't been able to rally support."

"We've got other problems. One of my operatives in San Francisco has gone silent. One of my best men." Redbeard hesitated. "He's noticed some . . . disturbing activity in his sector. What with Ramadan approaching, I'm concerned."

James moved closer, moved so quickly that he seemed to cross the office instantaneously, an old Sufi trick that Redbeard had never mastered. "Mormons? Or dead-enders?"

Redbeard shook his head "That's what bothers me. The activity doesn't seem connected to any group we've dealt with before. It's a totally unfamiliar signature. My man said he had to dig in, and I haven't heard from him since. It's been three days. He was worried when last we spoke. He was *frightened,* and this is not someone who frightens easily."

"Operatives are always worried, and the good ones are always frightened." James was smiling again, but Redbeard knew him too well to believe it. James plucked at his mustache, serious now. "Do you have a name? A *target*?"

Redbeard shook his head. "My man wasn't even sure there is

a threat. He just said he felt there were too many coincidences. Accidental deaths and disappearances, people suddenly deciding to retire or relocate, and *none* of the traditional players seem to benefit from these events. It's as unsettling as an empty chair at a dinner party—not what's seen, but what's *not* seen that gives one pause. I wish I had more to tell you."

James nodded, distracted.

Redbeard stared at his brother. "What's going on?"

The intercom on the desk crackled. "Director? We're finishing the check on your car."

James crossed to the window. Through the one-way glass he noted the armored limousine parked out front. One of his security men slid along the undercarriage, his uniform streaked with road grime. Another slowly walked a German shepherd around the vehicle.

Redbeard joined his brother. "You *knew* we had a new player in the game."

James rested his hands on the windowsill. "He's not new, he's been in the game a long time. A *very* long time."

"Why didn't you tell me? Look at me, James."

James turned to him. "I only had suspicions, but I have proof now, Thomas, proof *enough*, but I can't act. Not yet. This is a time for caution. When I come back from Chicago, we can move against him then."

"Director, your car is ready," crackled the intercom.

"Check it again," Redbeard barked at the intercom, not taking his eyes off his brother. They stood side by side at the window, as the dog handler made another slow circuit. A buzzing was in Redbeard's head, as though his skull were filled with wasps. If he could only remember . . . "Who is our enemy, James?"

"We'll talk when I get back. Trust me, I'll tell you everything I know."

Redbeard bit his lips shut. "As you wish, Director."

"I had to keep my own counsel on this, even from you. I just . . . I thought we had more time." James squeezed Redbeard's massive shoulder. "You'll understand my reticence when I show you the information I've gathered. We'll have to tread lightly."

"Stay here, then. We can get started—"

James shook his head. "I'm meeting the president in Chicago. I have to talk to him in person." He looked in pain. "I'm sorry, Thomas."

"I'll ride with you to the airport."

James picked up his gym bag. "I need you to go to the hospital and wait with Katherine."

"I thought Sarah was being released today."

"Damn pneumonia's resistant . . . she's had a relapse. The doctors want to keep her a few more days. The hospital is secure, but Katherine could use a friendly face."

Redbeard smiled awkwardly. "Since when does Katherine consider me good company?"

"Take care of them for me, Thomas." James touched the intercom. "I'm leaving now." He keyed a number on his cell. "Go." Through the window, he watched as his double strode out the front door of the villa and into the limo, his face half hidden in a burnoose.

The brothers stood beside each other, watching the limo accelerate down the winding driveway. Watched the gate swing up as it approached. Even after the limo was lost in the distance, the two of them stood at the window, half-expecting to see a flash of orange light, and the rumble of an explosion.

"The delivery van is waiting at the loading dock," Redbeard said at last. "My bodyguard, Miller, will drive you to the airport."

James slung the gym bag over his shoulder, eager now.

There was a light rap on the door, then two more.

Redbeard checked the peephole before unlocking the door.

Miller stepped inside rather than waiting in the doorway, and

Redbeard *knew*. Miller brushed past him. "Let me help you, Director," he said, his right arm reaching for something in his spotless white deliveryman's jacket.

James rummaged around the couch. "I left my reading glasses somewhere."

Redbeard tried to move, but his body was filled with concrete.

The room echoed with gunshots, and the sound seemed to break Redbeard free of his immobility. He grappled with the bodyguard. More gunshots, the sound muffled now, the gun pressed against him. Miller, who had been with them from the beginning, sneered up at him. Redbeard could see that the man's eyes had been snipped out, replaced by images of James's body lying in state under the Capitol dome. Sarah was holding on to the casket, but where was Katherine?

"My master sends greetings to you both," said Miller. Another gunshot, but Redbeard had a grip on the man's wrist and the bullet went wide, hit the wall. Miller tried to wrench free, fired again, and Redbeard felt the heat, his clothes smoldering from the muzzle blast. Redbeard broke the man's wrist. Heard the gun hit the carpet.

Redbeard had his hands around Miller's throat now. Redbeard had weak knees, it had cost him a national wrestling championship, but he had strong hands. Miller kicked and struggled, but Redbeard ignored the pain, ignored the blood oozing from his wounds as he slowly crushed the man's windpipe.

"Thomas," James called. "Don't kill him. You will need what he can tell you."

Redbeard watched the photos fade in the bodyguard's eyes. The man's arms were at his sides now, twitching, but Redbeard kept squeezing.

"*Thomas*," James gasped.

Redbeard threw Miller to the floor.

Someone was beating on the door to the office.

Redbeard cradled James in his arms. His brother's running suit smelled of smoke, and the blue nylon was singed smooth where the bullets had entered. No blood, though. Not a drop. "Don't move," said Redbeard. "You're going to be all right."

James patted Redbeard's cheek. "Ah, Thomas . . . who would have ever suspected *you* of being an optimist?"

Redbeard was slumped over his desk, weeping, when Angelina finally shook him awake. He clung to her, pressed his face into her flesh while she stroked his hair. "I couldn't save him. I couldn't save my own brother."

"Let me help you to bed," said Angelina. "You have fever."

"I'm afraid to sleep."

"Shhhh." Angelina helped him up.

"If I couldn't even save my brother, how can I save my country?"

Angelina braced herself against him as they walked. He was like this more and more lately, delirious, racked with nightmares and riven by doubt.

"If James were here, *he* would have known what to do. James had allies . . . James had friends. You . . . you're the only one I can trust." He staggered against her and Angelina almost fell. "Rakkim . . . I was counting on him and he joins the Fedayeen."

"You drove him away," said Angelina.

"I should have died that day, not James."

"Are you God? Then do not question that which He has brought about."

Redbeard broke free of her. Was she his *wife* to speak like that to him? He shuffled forward, head bowed, so weary his very bones ached. He had barely slept these last weeks, and when he did, he found no peace. It was too much for one man. Angelina was right, he had driven Rakkim away. Had driven Sarah away too. His brother's only child and the son he had never had. Gone. Angelina was right. She was always right.

He staggered down the hallway and into his bedroom. Left the lights off. The darkness cool on his smoldering skin. He shrugged off his robe and left it in a heap on the floor. The mattress groaned under him like the beams of a sailing ship. Just a chance to close his eyes, that's all he wanted. No sleep. No dreams. Just to close his eyes for a moment.

It was so hard to maintain the impression of strength. To appear resolute and confident at all times. Redbeard kicked off the sheets, sweating. The world seized on the first hint of weakness. His so-called allies would turn on him in an instant. The Old One was waiting. Always he was waiting. Where did such patience come from? It wasn't faith that kept the Old One in the shadows, it was devilry. Yet . . . such devilry was succeeding. The president was sick. Redbeard had seen the private medical records. When the president died . . .

The bedroom door opened. Angelina sat on the bed, laid a cool cloth across his forehead.

Redbeard covered his nakedness with the sheet. "I don't need babying—"

Angelina slapped his hand away as he tried to remove the cloth. "If the fever isn't broken by noon prayers, I'm calling your doctor."

Redbeard waved her away. He waited until the door closed behind her, started to toss aside the damp cloth, then thought better of it. The coolness of it felt good. He would rest his eyes. He would give himself time to recover his strength. Sleep was the answer. Sleep the balm to the thoughts boiling in his brain. If only James were here. Twenty-five years dead and gone. Redbeard's head lolled against the pillow, pulled the darkness closer. The Old One preoccupied his waking moments, but at times like this, drifting deeper, he thought of James . . . and Katherine. *Both* gone.

Katherine . . . the name he never spoke aloud. The face he

saw when he closed his eyes. Forgive me, Brother, for the thoughts I had. The desires I harbored. He had hidden such thoughts from his brother, but Katherine had sensed them. Must have sensed them. To abandon her daughter . . . to flee without a word after hearing of James's death. She was a rare woman to hold her husband's honor so dear. Forgive me, James.

CHAPTER 31

Before dawn prayers

Rakkim got back into the car, soaked, water dripping off his goatee. "You have a choice."

Sarah looked out through the windows. The men surrounded the car, axes and clubs resting on their shoulders.

"You can stay here with the squatters—"

"No."

Rakkim held up a hand. "They owe me a debt. You'll be *safe*. If my plan for the assassin works out, I'll come back for you. If it doesn't . . . they'll get you back to the city."

"Why not have them help you kill him?"

"It's my responsibility."

Sarah's eyes glinted in the red lights of the instrument panel. "Mine too."

Rakkim started the car. Switched on the lights. The men had disappeared back into the darkness.

"What have you got planned?"

Rakkim kept his eyes on the road. It was raining harder now, and he had to keep his speed to thirty-five. He took an abrupt right turn onto a single-lane cutoff, one of the many unmarked roads. Lightning flashed at the base of the nearby mountains, a photo flash of the bad road. "You ever heard of the term *werewolves*?"

"Horror movies from before the transition. Full moon, hair and fangs—"

"Not that kind. Those werewolves are made up. The ones I'm talking about are real." The headlights barely illuminated the darkness, the wipers making little headway. "Werewolves . . . that's what the squatters call the ultraviolent predators who live out here. Packs of drug maniacs, rapists, and thrill killers—"

"Why haven't I ever heard of them?"

"There's plenty you haven't heard of. A week ago I thought the Zionist Betrayal was a historical fact."

"Why doesn't the government send the army in to wipe them out? The squatters aren't a danger to the public, but these werewolves sound—"

"The government *uses* the werewolves. Look around. You think any good Muslims are on this road? Any good Catholics? This is a free-fire zone. The only people passing through are smugglers on their way into the capital, and Jews and apostates on their way out. The werewolves intercept them and loot the vehicles. They ransom the survivors or turn them over to the Black Robes." His fingers tightened on the wheel. "Sometimes they don't bother."

"So what are we doing here?"

"The werewolves move around so their presence doesn't become well-known. The squatters told me there's a nest of them about ten miles down this road."

The wind whipped tree branches overhead, scraping the roof and sides of the car. "You expect the werewolves to kill the assassin?"

"Something like that."

"They won't kill us? You can talk to them?"

Rakkim laughed. "No, I can't talk to them. I know how to use them though." His hair was still dripping. He wiped his face with his forearm. "Last year I was doing a run. Family needed to flee to Canada. Muslim family, two kids, an eight-year-old daughter and a fifteen-year-old boy. The son was gay. Nobody's business, but they had a neighbor . . . Maybe they didn't cut the grass short enough, or maybe the daughter listened to music. For whatever reason, the neighbor went to the local imam. The family didn't wait for the edict." Rakkim steered to the left, one tire bouncing in a pothole, jarring his teeth. He slowed. A flat tire now . . . He felt Sarah watching him. "I drove their car. It was fall, the roads not snowed in. Three nights should have done it. Three nights to get us down through Washington and then up into Canada. There's a border crossing where the guards go home for dinner every evening. Weather was perfect when we left. Clear night, quarter moon. I didn't even need to use my headlights most of the time. There was an accident on a logging road I usually use, police cars and ambulances with lights flashing, and I got worried. The police sometimes set up a fake accident to catch smugglers . . . so I took another route." He wiped his face again. "We hit a werewolf trap."

"You never told me."

"Werewolves had dug out the roadbed. Covered it with a thin sheet of plastic and sprinkled gravel over the top. I was driving faster than I should have . . . carried away by the moonlight, trying to make up the time we had lost." Rakkim checked the odometer. The squatters had given him an estimate of where the werewolves were camped, but he didn't know how accurate it was. "The car hit the trap going about forty-five, snapped an axle, and started rolling. Ended upside down in a ditch. Everyone screaming. We were all hurt . . . the eight-year-old daughter was unconscious. By the time I got everyone out, the werewolves were all over us."

Sarah caressed his neck. "What happened?"

Rakkim cleared the condensation on the windshield with a sweep of his hand. "Hard to talk about."

"Try."

"I had hit my head when the car rolled over, and my knee was banged up, but I had my knife." Rakkim could barely hear his own voice. "They had torches, and bats wrapped in barbed wire, and crowbars, and this one guy, this big, fat, hairy bastard, he had a golf club. What do they call those ones . . . ? A *driver*. He had a titanium driver. Expensive club. Must have taken it off some rich tourist who got lost, taken it off him and beaten him to death with it probably. He swung at my head, grinning, just missed me. Had to be at least twenty of them, screaming and singing, so *happy*, like they had been waiting for us and now the party could begin." He swept the windshield again. It didn't need it, but he did it anyway. "I killed a couple of them fast, slashed their throats so they'd make a mess and maybe make the others back off." He shook his head "It only excited them more. I kept backing the family into the woods, trying to protect our flanks, but the father was carrying the eight-year-old, and he kept tripping in the underbrush. It was dark in the woods, and he had city eyes. Every time the werewolves made a rush at us, I would kill a few more, but there were so *many* of them. They didn't have training, but they knew the terrain, and they were maniacs, painted up and howling. I half expected them to lope on all fours. I was scared. I had it under control, but I could taste it."

Sarah rested her hand on his neck, kneading out the knots.

Rakkim smiled, but there was no joy in it. "You should have seen the mother, this good Muslim woman who prayed five times a day and had been putting aside quarters for her hajj since she was five. This good mother killed one of the werewolves, a skinny little psycho with his hair in braids—she split his head open with a rock and she never even blinked. Allah be praised, right?"

"Without the assistance of Allah, we cannot save ourselves from any evil," Sarah recited.

Rakkim shook his head. "I found an animal path, a path so faint even I could barely see it, but it was all we had. I told the father to take his family and not look back. Said I'd stay behind and pick them off as they followed. I told him to *run*, but he was gasping, and there was blood running from his nose and into his little girl's hair. The blood was black as oil in the moonlight." He could feel Sarah's touch. It felt as if she were inside him. "I kept telling him to go, but he handed me his little girl and darted off into the brush. Deliberately making noise, crashing and thrashing, and the werewolves . . . they went after him. He saved us. Nervous man with a potbelly and glasses, he lured them away. I took his little girl, and I carried her against my chest, and I led her mother and brother down the path, all of us running, and when we heard the father screaming in the distance . . . we *kept* running." He looked at Sarah. "That's what happened."

Sarah kissed his cheek. "I love you."

"I told them I would get them to Canada. I said I would protect them."

"Where are they now?"

"The little girl . . . she died in my arms. I took the mother and son to Green Briar and left her with the squatters. I came back a week later, but they didn't want to leave. The squatters had accepted them. Made them welcome. Both of them, and the daughter was buried there . . ."

They must have driven another mile before Sarah spoke. "You're going to snare the assassin in one of the werewolves' traps. You thought of it back at Marian's house. *That's* why you didn't get rid of the tracking device."

Rakkim nodded. He loved a smart woman.

"How are you going to work it so he gets trapped and not *us*?"

Rakkim slowed, let the car come to a complete stop. Turned off the lights. Wind whipped the trees, sent dead leaves skittering. The road was a slight downhill, running straight through the trees.

Perfect place for a trap, the traveler eager to get past the dense forest, accelerating, taking advantage of the terrain.

"Oh." Sarah sounded sick. "I see."

Rakkim got out. "Get behind the wheel. If something happens . . . if this doesn't work—"

"It'll work."

Rain streamed down his face. "If I get ambushed, drive on the shoulder and keep going. Don't stop for me, or anything else. Go back to Jill's. I'll find you."

"I'm not scared." It was a lie, but he was glad she made the attempt. She slid behind the wheel. "Bombing the Holy City, blaming the Jews . . . the Old One is cursed. That's why his plan has been frustrated. We're instruments of God, Rakkim. Allah has power over everything. He won't allow us to fail."

Rakkim kissed her on the lips, savoring her warmth. "If you say so."

Sarah reached for him, but he was already gone, trotting down the road. The wind gusted, made his clothes flap, but it felt good to be outside, good to be cold, battered by the storm. A few minutes later, he heard gravel crunching far behind him. Sarah slowly followed him, engine off, coasting, lights out. He would have preferred she stayed put, but he didn't think it likely that the werewolves kept patrols out all night. The squatters had to be alert to attack, but no one was going to go after the werewolves. He kept his eyes open anyway, staying to the edge of the road, and when a tree limb cracked in the darkness, he crouched for an attack.

It was another mile before he saw the spike strip laid across the road. Painted flat black, nearly invisible, so well hidden that he nearly stumbled on it. He dragged it into the underbrush, listening. No one was there. He closed his eyes, waited, then opened them. No one other than Fedayeen would have spotted it, but there, through the trees . . . a light flickered. A candle lantern probably. Rakkim ran a couple of hundred yards past where he had found the spike strip. There were no other traps. The werewolves figured rightly that the spike strip would be enough to blow out the tires of cars going in either direction, send them careening into the ravine or crashing into a tree.

He ran back to Sarah, had her drive forward, then pulled the spike strip back into place behind the car. He tried to get into the driver's seat, but she waved him around to the other side and started the engine. He kept expecting the werewolves to break from the underbrush, howling, face paint dripping in the storm.

"I want you to drive very slowly away—"

Sarah floored it. The tires spun, churning up gravel as they roared down the road. She hit the high beams.

"What are you *doing*?"

"You said the assassin would stop when we stopped and drive on when we did," said Sarah, still accelerating. "I'd rather he was speeding when he hits those spikes."

Rakkim looked behind him. It was a good plan. "Just stay on the road." Far behind them, at the turnoff from the logging road, Rakkim thought he saw a glimmer of headlights through the rain, but it was just lightning flashing. He kept watch anyway.

CHAPTER 32

Before dawn prayers

Darwin sat in the car, headlights off, listening to the patter of rain on the roof and thinking of the handsome young police officer. He remembered the way the man had washed his feet in the bathtub prior to prayers, his long toes, and the care with which he had prepared himself for his devotions. They said that a good Muslim was always ready for death. So, in this case, Darwin had been an instrument of divine instruction, a reiteration of the need for—

The tracking receiver suddenly started beeping, startling Darwin out of his metaphysical musings. With his night-vision goggles the flashing diodes of the receiver seemed bright as shooting stars, the beeping a high-pitched keening now. What's your hurry, love-birds? Darwin tromped on the accelerator, wheels spinning for a moment on the wet road, leaving tire patches as he raced after them.

Smart move on Rakkim's part, speeding off after another fif-teen-minute stop, a near surefire way to shake anyone tailing them. Anyone without a receiver. Darwin doubted that they knew he was following them, but it was a clever tactic. Just what he would have expected from Rakkim. That was the unique thing about this assignment . . . the challenge.

Not that his previous jobs had been without risk or difficulty. That was to be expected. That's why the Old One used him. Dar-win had once assassinated a powerful, liberal ayatollah within his own mosque, killed him as he was getting ready for dawn prayers. The ayatollah's bodyguards and acolytes were just outside the door of his office when Darwin struck, the killing perfectly timed, the call of the muezzin drowning out the cleric's dying groans. Dar-win smiled, remembering how he had carved a Star of David on the ayatollah's chest, the man still alive, struggling silently, his screams blocked by the head of a fetal pig Darwin had shoved into his mouth. It was those kinds of creative touches that Darwin took the most pride in. Oh, planning the operations was interesting, and the killings themselves were often done under perilous cir-cumstances . . . but it was those jazzy little riffs that he remem-bered so fondly afterward.

Yes, when the time came to kill Rakkim, Darwin was going to make sure the method of his dying was worthy of the man. The girl . . . Sarah, she would have to figure in somehow. Was it turtle doves that mated for life? When one died, so did the other? Or was that just a story? Darwin accelerated, tires squealing around the curves, his hands loose on the wheel, steering with his fingertips. Most people thought that love was as close to immortality as we got in this corrupt and material world, but Darwin knew better. Love was the first tentative step into death, the toe-touch into the cold, infinite night. Darwin drove the curves, thinking of the way Rakkim and Sarah had clutched each other in the foyer of Marian Warriq's house, one last touch before braving the dark. Rakkim and Sarah sitting in a tree . . . k-i-s-s-i-n-g. They could keep their love, sweet love. Darwin was going to live forever.

Darwin accelerated through the storm, heedless of the bad road, his goggles turning the darkness gold and glowing. The road dipped down into a series of switchbacks, and he was forced to slow, the beeping from the tracking device still faster now— Rakkim had obviously found a straightaway. Must have chosen that particular stretch of road to make his run. Should have known he had driven it before. Rain and leaves pelted the windshield, but the wipers swept it clear. He was tempted to discard the goggles and turn on his headlights, but Rakkim and Sarah would be looking back, looking to see if lights were following them. No, better to keep them guessing. The tracking device had a ten-mile range. They weren't going to get away.

Darwin was driving a modified black Cadillac, a roomy, luxury sedan appropriate for his role as a real estate salesman, but the car had four-wheel drive and advanced steering and suspension. It handled like a race car. Darwin punched it down the slick road, exhilarated, tiny beads of sweat rimming the back of his ears. The car hit a pothole, but the heavy shocks absorbed the impact with barely a bump. Faster now, the road beginning to flatten out. The beeping from the receiver slowed slightly. He was gaining now. No danger of them outrunning the range of the unit. He intended to get close enough to see their red tail-lights and then back off.

Darwin raced through the night, lights off, thinking again of the handsome young policeman and the way he kept trying to raise the pistol, even at the very end. The persistence of the common man, the ones who knew they were overmatched and yet still kept fighting . . . it was a source of wonder and delight, as inspiring as the aurora borealis or an ancient Al Green gospel song. When this business was all over, when the dead were buried and the Old One was satisfied, Darwin was going to visit the handsome young policeman's grave. He would return the policeman's badge to him. Leave it resting against his headstone with a bouquet of red roses. It was the least he could do.

The car was doing sixty-five down the straightaway when Darwin caught a gleam of light on the road. A mere shimmer, but he knew what it was. Knew too late what Rakkim had done. He didn't even try to brake. Not at that speed. Not on the wet road.

The spike strip blew out all four tires, the sound like distant fireworks within the thick-insulated interior of the Cadillac. *Pow-pow-pow-pow*. Rakkim was having a regular celebration. Darwin gripped the wheel, trying to maintain control as the car fishtailed. The tires had a solid core, a secondary tire able to be driven on . . . just not in these conditions. Not at this speed. The Cadillac veered to the right, caught the soft, rain-soaked shoulder, and flipped. Darwin relaxed, settled back in the seat cushion as the car landed on its roof, sending pain shooting through his neck.

The air bags deployed as the car rolled again and again, Darwin bouncing from side to side, over and over as the car tore through the tree line and down the embankment. Branches snapped against the frame, glass shattering, and with each bone-jarring impact, he drifted farther away. His last idle thought before the car came to a halt was whether the gas bladder would leak. It was designed like the fuel tank of a high-performance aircraft.

Sheathed in a spark-resistant titanium alloy . . . but, still, one had to question. Technology was always prone to human error and the optimism of the engineers who had designed it. That's why the Fedayeen always said the most reliable technology, the ultimate weapon, was a trained warrior left naked in the snow.

Darwin awoke to shouting. Men with flashlights and torches were outside the car. Lots of men. Beating on the sides of the car. Drumming on the dented metal. Men with painted faces. Teeth filed to points in the torchlight. Did he *really* see that? He pulled off his night goggles. The car was on its side, tilted downhill. The air bags deflated, sagging across the interior of the car like jellyfish. His right eye was swollen. His neck hurt. His knee too. The tracking receiver beeped steadily. So Rakkim and Sarah had stopped again. Were probably watching him from some vantage point. A picnic in the rain. Enjoy yourself, Fedayeen. In the rearview mirror he saw men popping open the trunk with crowbars, hooting and hollering, *howling*. Darwin tasted blood in his mouth. How nice to be the life of the party.

A shirtless fat man waved a golf club outside his window. Hairy teats like a sow. Taking a full windup.

Darwin covered his eyes with his arm as the golf club blasted through the window. He cupped his knife as they dragged him out the window, a shard of glass cutting a swath across his torso. A ribbon of flesh. Darwin gently eased the knife into the fat man with the golf club, slipped the blade into his belly button, slipped it in and out, with just the right twist at the deepest penetration.

The men around him didn't even notice the sound the fat man made, too intent on kicking at Darwin, shouting in his face, tearing at his suit and patting his pockets for money. A boy swatted Darwin across the ear with a flashlight, and Darwin's hand flew out, greeting him. A bulbous fellow in a soggy army jacket kneed Darwin, and Darwin thanked him with the edge of his blade. More men arrived, torches high, sliding down the steep slope. They didn't even notice when man after man fell in a gush of blood, torches guttering on the wet ground. They just assumed the men had lost their footing and were eager to take their place, already arguing over how much ransom Darwin would bring.

Some people thought Fedayeen assassins moved outside of time, either too quickly or too slowly for the laws of the universe to apply. Of course, it wasn't true. Assassins knew the *moment* to strike, the instant of vulnerability, the minute interval between attention and inattention.

Darwin let the men pass him around, his head ringing from their blows, his knife dancing among them as though looking for a partner. When they finally realized what was happening, when the mud was thick with them, Darwin threw back his head, rain beating against his face, and *laughed* at the little trick that Rakkim had played on him. It had been a long time since he had been fooled so badly.

The men stopped for an instant, looking at each other. Filthy men. Bleeding. Hair matted. Beards full of dirt and leaves. Dead men. They raised their weapons, hefted their bats and chains and clubs and knives. They screamed and cursed, and they charged.

"That's *him*, isn't it?" Sarah shielded her eyes from the rain with her hand. Pointed at the lights flickering in the distance. "The werewolves got him." She sounded giddy.

Rakkim hefted the tracking device he had removed from the undercarriage of the car, sailed it into the night. "Maybe."

Sarah looked at him. "You said the crash alone would probably kill him."

"The car didn't explode. The gas tank should have gone up. Even in the rain, there should have been a fireball . . . something big enough to set the trees ablaze." Rakkim watched the torches bob in the night. Torches up and down the ravine. If Rakkim were alone, he would drive back and see for himself if the assassin had survived the crash. And if he *had* survived, see if he had survived the werewolves. Rakkim wasn't alone though.

"Let's go back and make sure," said Sarah. "What's so funny?"

"I love you, that's—"

There was a blast of light brighter than all the torches as the gas tank exploded.

Rakkim counted the seconds until the echo reached them. About four miles away. In that instant when the gas tank blew, Rakkim thought he had seen bodies flying through the air. The fire was shrinking, going out in the downpour. There were still torches, but they were fewer and scattered now. Two or three pine trees around the site crackled, their lower branches going up.

Sarah stood beside him, the two of them holding hands as though they were watching fireworks at their wedding. "You did it, Rikki. You killed him."

Rakkim watched the trees burning in the rain.

"Can we go now?" said Sarah. "He's dead, isn't he?"

Rakkim kissed her, felt the warmth of her lips. "We can go now."

CHAPTER 33

After dawn prayers

Watching Sarah sleep in the morning light . . . a pleasure he had thought he had lost. Her face was half covered by her dark hair, tangled ringlets damp with sweat. Even with the curtains pulled, he could see her skin glowing from their groaning lovemaking, beyond words. Locked together afterward, eyes closed, still seeing the fireball as the assassin's car exploded in the rain. Candy and flowers were fine, but fear was the ultimate aphrodisiac. Rakkim watched her breathe, fascinated by the way her lips parted, the shape of her mouth—the gate to heaven and hell. Ripe with promise.

For all their talk of fire and brimstone, the Christian vision of Hades was a pale reflection of the Muslims' hell. Those who rejected Allah were burned alive throughout eternity, their skin instantly replaced so they could be incinerated again and again. If the Christian hell offered half-measures of pain, their heaven offered equally dilute joys—an afterlife of wings and clouds and harps. Muslims expected the full measure of ecstasy in Paradise, virgin lovers and perfect mates, the joys of the flesh in rapturous and infinite varieties, a suitable reward for devotion in this life.

Rakkim ran the tip of his tongue across Sarah's lower lip. Paradise might not await him in death, but he was grateful for the glimpse that Sarah offered him. Her heat, the curve of her lips . . . he was never closer to God than when he was inside her. At moments like this, Rakkim could almost forgive himself his sins. He thought of Colarusso in the basement of his church, asking Rakkim if he wanted Father Joe to hear his confession. Catholics. Their God forgave *everything*. What a pushover.

Sarah watched him, her eyes silky.

"I thought you were sleeping."

Sarah reached down between his legs, drew the hardness from him, squeezed him harder still, her fingers gently working. "My sweet assassin."

"Don't call me that."

Sarah kissed him. "You're too modest."

Afterward, Sarah lay on top of him, dozing. He rested his hand on the downy patch at the base of her spine. A moist patch. He had licked every inch of her in the last couple of hours. Salty and sweet . . . warm as summer . . . Sarah.

She raised herself up. Braced on her elbows, looking down at him, still sleepy-eyed. Her small breasts brushed his bare chest. "I missed you, Rikki."

He felt her nipples thicken against him. "I can tell." She rested her face against him as he cupped her ass, pulling himself deeper inside her.

They were entwined on the pullout sofa in the half-empty office building, their clothes abandoned. Dropped beside the cardboard boxes filled with Warriq's journals. The snapshot of Sarah as an infant in her father's arms lay on the coffee table. Traffic sounds filtered from below. Horns and engines, faint conversation from the street. A perfect moment. Too perfect to last.

"Do you think he's still alive?"

"Assassins are hard to kill." He stroked her flanks, raised goosebumps. "All I know is that he's not here. There's just us."

Sarah rolled off him, rested on her side, one leg across his thigh, and he stiffened yet again. "I keep thinking about Marian. I didn't even tell her what I was looking for in her father's journals."

"You haven't told me either."

Sarah yawned. "Lose the tone. We're not married yet."

"Yeah, that'll change everything. You'll be a good wife who never contradicts me, and I'll be bored out of my skull." He got a smile out of her, and she put her hand on his chest. "What *are* we looking for in the journals?"

Sarah's hand on his chest trembled. "A fourth bomb."

Rakkim sat up.

"New York City, Washington, D.C., Mecca . . ." Sarah winced. "The fourth bomb was supposed to detonate in China."

"You *know* this?"

"If the fourth bomb had gone off, China wouldn't have stayed neutral. They were never going to become an Islamic state, but a billion and a half Chinese would have shared our grief and anger. Russia would never have dared offer the Zionists sanctuary. The whole world dynamic would have shifted. From a strictly academic view, the Old One's plan was really . . . quite brilliant."

"Is the bomb supposed to be under the Three Gorges Dam?"

She covered her surprise. "Maybe."

"*Maybe?* What, you stuck a pin in a map and figured it was a good place to start?"

Sarah stared at him. "You were in my bedroom? You *noticed* that?" She shook her head, seemed to consider whether she should keep talking. "My father learned of the existence of a fourth bomb shortly before he was murdered. It was somewhere in China, that's what he told my mother. She still thinks it's in Shanghai, but I'm convinced the Three Gorges Dam—"

"Your *mother*?" Rakkim stared. "You've met her?"

Sarah shook her head. "Katherine contacted me a couple years ago, right after my book came out—"

"You haven't seen her since you were a child—"

"It was her. The first e-mail . . . she called me *ciccia*. It's Italian. It means little fatty. I was chubby as a baby." Sarah was crying, embarrassed, laughing too. "My mother was the only one who ever called me that. It's one of the few things I remember about her."

Rakkim held her, felt her sobbing against him. Sarah had never talked about her mother, even when they were children. Redbeard had forbidden any mention of her, but that wasn't it. Sarah did what she wanted. No, it was her way of pretending her mother's absence didn't matter. If Sarah believed she was in contact with her mother, he trusted her instincts. It made sense. Katherine Dougan had fled after her husband's assassination. If anyone would have delved deeper into the Zionist attack, it would have been the first head of State Security. The Old One had him murdered, but James Dougan had talked to his wife first. Pillow talk, the oldest means of communication.

Sarah wiped away a tear. "I promised I wouldn't tell anyone. Not Redbeard. Not you."

"Redbeard probably already knows." All those men Redbeard had interrogated after his brother's murder . . . even if they didn't know about the fourth bomb, some of them would have talked about the Old One before they died. No telling the extent of Redbeard's knowledge. "Where is she?"

"I have no idea. I'd go there if I did."

"Why involve you after all this time? She had to know it could get you killed."

"She didn't have a choice. She's been searching for the bomb for twenty years in Beijing and Shanghai, the political and financial centers, just like D.C. and New York. She had people she could trust, but they couldn't find anything because they were looking in the wrong place. She wanted me to use my research skills to help her pinpoint the location in Shanghai, but I told her she had made a mistake."

"Just like that, you knew she was wrong?"

"Not *just like that*." Sarah yawned again. It was as though sharing her secrets had drained the last of her energy. "My specialty . . . my research specialty is aberrant data collection and interpretation. Do you even know what that means?"

"It means you use comic books and country music to write history."

Sarah smiled. "It means you find treasure in places most people don't dig." She nestled against his chest. "Katherine's basic premise was suspect. The Old One nuked New York and D.C. because he wanted to bring the country to its knees, but he couldn't hope to take over China. Besides . . . wiping out Shanghai would have brought down the global financial community and crippled China for a generation. Destroying the dam and blaming the Jews would have been wiser. The dam is a source of national pride as well as a vast industrial engine. Its destruction would have made the Chinese part of the Old One's new world axis and set them back twenty years economically."

"Sarah . . . this is an interesting academic exercise—"

"In 2012, fissionable fuel rods from a new Tajik reactor were stolen. The reactor's technology was risky," Sarah muttered into his chest, "the rods made from a rare isotope, supposedly much more powerful than plutonium. Highly unstable. Half the workers at the plant died of radiation poisoning within a year. The theft of the rods was never publicized. My father only found out . . . a few months before his murder. That's why . . . why he suspected there was another bomb."

"The material used in the other bombs was standard plutonium," said Rakkim.

"The dam was designed to survive a 9.5 earthquake. Chinese military provided security, so no way would the Old One's men be able to get close. Bringing down the dam required a *big* bang, five megatons at least. That's why the Tajik fuel rods were needed."

"Okay."

"Don't humor me." Sarah's eyes fluttered. "I went through so many people before I found Marian. A Chinese folk dance expert in Los Angeles . . . geologist in Chicago . . . this retired politician from the former regime who attended the dedication of the dam in 1995. The old letch smacked his lips describing the pickled fruits they ate at the celebration afterward, but *he* was the one who told me about Marian's father. Called him an 'odd duck, always writing everything down.' Marian was on campus, and I had to go to a trailer park outside of Barstow to find out about her."

"I've skimmed a couple of the journals. Richard Warriq was a nut."

"The journals gave me my first real clue." Sarah breathed heavily. "Three years *after* the nuke strikes, Warriq was in a tavern near the main reservoir. He wrote about some travelers complaining about the poor fishing in one of their favorite lakes. Not that the fish weren't biting, but that the shore was littered with dead carp."

Rakkim stroked her hair. "What was the name of the lake?"

"Warriq was more interested in describing their foul odor." Sarah yawned. "I know what you're thinking."

"No . . . not at all."

"I track little things . . . small details that add up. Radiation detector at the airport in northern Laos went off a month *before* the attack. Town was a known smuggling center. The staff logged it in, but didn't follow up." Sarah dozed off for a few seconds, suddenly spoke. "See . . . the fourth bomb was leaking before it even got to China."

"Go back to sleep, I'll—"

"Article in a ten-year-old *Journal of Aviary Science Online*. There's a species of arctic tern that rests in the wetlands around the Yangtze on their annual migration south. The broods have declined every year since the nuke strikes, and many of the chicks that did hatch were deformed. That's interesting . . . don't you think?"

"Where are the wetlands this flock used? Did the article name a specific spot?"

Sarah closed her eyes again. "There are wetlands for a hundred miles along the river. No one even studies arctic terns anymore. Virtually extinct. Pollution and global warming." She yawned. "I'm so tired, Rikki. I'm tired, but I'm right."

Rakkim kissed her. "You're onto *something*. You scared the Old One, Sarah. That's why he sent the assassin to dog you. He's hoping you'll lead him to Katherine."

"Katherine said she missed me. I know I missed her. You miss your parents, don't you?"

"It's been a long time."

"I know you, Rikki, you can't fool me." Sarah clung to him. "Let's go to sleep. Let's lie down and wake up in each other's arms."

"You sleep. I'm not tired."

"Don't leave me."

"I won't. No telling the kind of trouble you'd get yourself into without me."

Sarah smiled . . . drifting now. "I haven't had a good night's sleep since I left home."

"You're home now."

"We're safe here, aren't we?"

"We're safe."

Rakkim waited until her breathing evened out, then stepped into the privacy room off the main office, and closed the door behind him. It had been a state-of-the-art facility ten years ago, the builders dreaming of redevelopment profits, but the economy had remained stagnant. The office complex was largely vacant, but the privacy units were still working, signal diffusers built into the walls and windows. Even under the best conditions, no one could pinpoint their location.

Redbeard fumbled the phone before answering, his voice hoarse. He sounded half-asleep.

"It's me."

"Have you found her yet?" barked Redbeard, gruff as ever now.

"I want you to check on a werewolf encampment. I assume you still have contacts—"

"Do *they* have Sarah?"

"No. It's approximately eight miles east of Green Briar Estates. Do you know it?"

"The werewolves are bad business, Rakkim, even for you. If you're asking them for help in finding Sarah, I'd be very careful—"

"The encampment is located on a lane logging road that jogs off from Green Briar. From the air, you should be able to spot a burned-out car at the site. *Recently* burned-out. I want to know what else you find there."

"You think Sarah was in that car?"

"A Fedayeen assassin was tracking me through the badlands last night. A rogue Fedayeen—"

"So you sicced the werewolves on him?" Redbeard's chuckle was warm. They could have been discussing a practical joke played on a member of an opposing team.

"Contact the werewolves. I need to know if the assassin is dead."

"Is he working for Ibn Azziz?"

"You know who he's working for."

Silence from Redbeard.

"I'll call you in a day or so."

"Do you know where Sarah is?"

"She's in the next room. I found her, just like I promised." Rakkim broke the connection.

Sarah was still sleeping, one arm cocked under her head. He could see the pulse beating in her throat and wondered if she was dreaming about her mother.

At times, walking through a crowd, Rakkim would hear a woman laugh, and it was his mother's laugh. He would find himself wondering if she wasn't *really* in New York when the bomb went off. Wondering if maybe she was outside the city that day. He imagined her adrift after the attack, the communications grid crashed, lost on the opposite side of the country. Better to be lost than to be dead. She could still laugh if she was lost.

Sarah stirred. He wanted to curl into bed beside her. Instead he went over to the box of journals and started reading.

CHAPTER 34

Before noon prayers

Angelina answered her phone on the first ring. A throwaway phone, bought an hour ago. Untraceable. Hopefully. Her heart fluttered in her chest like a white dove. "Y-yes?"

"What's wrong? Is Sarah all right?"

Angelina forced herself to catch her breath. Katherine had responded to her posting quickly—she must have been monitoring the message site they used to make contact. Or she had set up some automatic alert. Angelina never asked. The less she knew . . . Sometimes weeks would pass before Katherine responded. Months. Years.

"Angelina?" There was the familiar echo in Katherine's voice, the signal routed back and forth to disguise its point of origin. "Has something happened to Sarah?"

"No, there's no word yet."

"Don't scare me like that."

It would have been easier if Katherine had given Sarah the means to contact her directly, but Katherine limited such access to Angelina alone. Compartmentalization of information. No exceptions. There were moments, and she always felt guilty afterward, when Angelina thought that if only James Dougan had been as disciplined and cautious as his wife, he would not have been assassinated.

"There was a new imam at dawn prayers this morning . . . Imam Masiq. One of the disciples of Mullah Ibn Azziz, sent round to the major mosques to deliver their foul sermon. Barely old enough to grow a beard and he lectures us as though we were children." Angelina ground her teeth. "You should have seen Imam Jenk's face." She drew her chador around her as the wind kicked up. "This new imam told us that we have been too tolerant of the Catholics, said they are a viper in our midst and we must be on guard against their apostasy. We were all looking around . . . I was, at any rate. Most of the faithful were too stunned. Or too fearful."

"The Black Robes trot out the Catholics whenever the need arises," said Katherine. "Oxley did the same thing when it suited him. It will pass. We have greater concerns—"

"A monastery outside of Portland was burned to the ground two days ago. A dozen monks were trapped inside while the fire department stood around and watched."

"Portland has always been a backwater—"

"Yesterday, three churches in Seattle were vandalized. Stained-glass windows broken, altars overturned. This was *Seattle*, not some fundamentalist backwater."

Angelina sat on a bench across from a large building site. A skeleton of steel, six stories high and rising. Jackhammers blasted the air. Trucks and concrete mixers rumbled past. Workmen shouted to each other. The noise from the site insured that Angelina and Katherine's conversation would not be monitored. A tall man on the second floor took off his hard hat, wiped his forehead. Showed off his beautiful red hair. He went back to work with a vengeance, beating on a beam with a large hammer, the muscles of his arms clearly defined as he pounded away. Dust floated in the air, gray and white specks settling on her black chador, but she made no move to brush herself clean.

"Does Redbeard suspect why Sarah left?" asked Katherine.

"I don't know."

"What do you *think*? You've been sharing his home for twenty-five years, woman."

"Redbeard doesn't reveal himself to me or anyone else," said Angelina, annoyed at Katherine's tone. After all these years Katherine still thought of herself as the lady of the house. A place for everyone, and everyone in her place.

"Forgive me, Angelina. I . . . I get frustrated being so far away. Having to ask you to be my eyes and ears. It's unfair of me. I'm sorry."

Angelina let her wait a few seconds before responding. "All I know is that Redbeard is preoccupied. Last night he scraped his spoon on an empty bowl five times before realizing that there was no more soup. He is worried about Sarah, of course, but it's more than that. He is not well, Katherine. I don't know what's wrong with him."

"What's wrong with him is what's wrong with all of us. We're getting old."

Angelina clicked her prayer beads. "I still think you should have gone to Redbeard with your suspicions, not Sarah."

"They are *more* than suspicions."

"All the more reason for you to have gone to Redbeard. Sarah is just a girl."

"You raised her, Angelina. You will always see her as a girl. I didn't get that privilege." No hint of reproach was in Katherine's voice. "Sarah is the daughter of James Dougan. She may be young, but she will do what is required."

"Redbeard has resources. If you had gone to him, he would have already found out the truth. That's all I'm saying."

"Redbeard would have buried the truth and told himself he was only doing his duty. He still believes in the dream of a pure Muslim state."

"So do I."

There was a long silence. "You didn't have to help me, Angelina."

Angelina worked her prayer beads faster and faster. Click-click-click-click. "How could I not?"

Katherine sighed, and it was so clear that Angelina looked around, expecting to see Katherine standing beside her.

"Be careful, Katherine. Ibn Azziz, he is not of God. The monastery in Portland . . . it will not be the last to be fed to the flames. We are in for dangerous times."

"The times have always been dangerous."

"Not like this."

"Well, then . . . we'll have to pray for each other," said Katherine, flirty as a debutante. "With two strong and passionate women like us bending his ear, God is going to *have* to pay attention."

Dry leaves whipped across the sidewalk, pirouetting in the eddy. In memory, Angelina could still see Katherine moving gracefully through the parties thrown for the new head of State Security and his lovely wife. The republic was still new, fresh with hope, promising peace and tolerance. Katherine had danced with the president, charming him with her lithe femininity, her openness and wit. Much of the political class had been outraged at her lack of deference, suspicious of her conversion, but the president had been smitten by her. Smitten by her husband as well. James Dougan was handsome and forthright, a defender of the nation, ruthless when he needed to be, charitable even when the cameras weren't on him. They were the golden couple. The hope of a Muslim future.

It had been a glorious time. Angelina had been hired to help care for the new baby. Sarah had been a sickly child, not a rarity in those early days, not even for the powerful. The baby had blossomed under Angelina's care, grown fat, with a squall to match. Redbeard had been a constant guest at the villa, the gruff but doting uncle, a fierce, driven man. Angelina had to fight to keep her eyes off him. At times she felt his eyes on her too, but his eyes never lingered on her when Katherine was in the room. Who could blame him? Bright days filled with promise. Ended suddenly. James Dougan murdered. Redbeard wounded. Katherine fleeing after a hasty call to Angelina. Katherine barely controlling her hysteria and grief, begging Angelina to stay with Sarah. Begging her to tell her how much she loved her. Katherine immune from Angelina's pleadings. Insisting that she had to go. She had a responsibility to her husband. *Greater than your responsibility to your child?* Angelina had demanded. *Yes.* The pain in Katherine's voice . . . Angelina had never heard anything like it. *Yes, greater even than that.*

"Maybe when this is over . . . when the truth is known, I can come home," said Katherine.

"You could have come home *years* ago," said Angelina.

"We've been over that many times. It wasn't worth the risk."

The *risk*. Angelina would have risked anything to be reunited with her child, but not Katherine. She had greater priorities. As a good Muslim, Angelina understood the need for sacrifice, but Katherine was no longer a Muslim, and such a sacrifice was only justified for the greater glory of God.

"If you hear any news about Sarah, contact me."

"I'll send word immed—" Angelina heard the line go dead. She never knew when their brief conversations would end. Just that they would end abruptly. Katherine had her own timetable and no one was privy to it.

The redheaded workman on the second floor tucked his hammer into his tool belt, stood with his hands on his hips, surveying the site. The morning sun was behind him, set his hair aglow. Three young women passed by below, and he watched them. Once, the girls would have drawn whistles and catcalls from the men on the scaffolding, but now their passing was observed, but not commented on. The tall redhead pushed back his hard hat, following the girls' progress until they turned the corner. He looked at Angelina, noticed her watching, and grinned. She could almost see him blush.

There was a time before the takeover . . . a time when Angelina had been a young girl, barely eighteen with slender ankles and high breasts. The men had worked shirtless in the heat, sweating in the summer sun, their bodies gleaming as though anointed with oil. In those days so long ago, she had hurried past such work sites, eyes downcast, and the whistles had rung in her ears . . . and she had not been totally displeased. Angelina clicked away on her prayer beads, silently counting off the ninety-nine names of God as she watched the tall redhead back at work.

CHAPTER 35

After noon prayers

Rakkim reread the passage from Richard Warriq's journal. He looked over at Sarah snoring softly in the afternoon light slanting through the blinds. For a moment he considered letting her sleep. For a moment he considered putting the journal back in the stack. Sleeping dogs. He walked over to the sofa bed, gently shook her awake.

Sarah opened her eyes.

"I think I found what we're looking for."

"What do you mean *we*, kemo sabe?"

"What?"

"Old joke." Sarah stopped in the middle of a yawn. "Are you talking about the journals?"

Rakkim handed her the journal. "The journals are organized according to location. It made sense for you to look in the *China* selections for entries suggesting the location of the fourth bomb. Since you didn't find anything, I thought I might as well start on the other ones." He tapped the page. "This is from a business trip he made to Indonesia in the spring of 2015. The entry is dated eleven days before the Zionist attack."

Indonesia, May 8, 2015

Flew in for last week to check seismic activity on the Sukarno bridge. Usual vulgarities of the Indonesian character. Found dead cockroach between bedsheets at my hotel. (Jakarta Ramada, Room 451, mini-suite, breakfast included.) Have sent e-mail complaint regarding cockroach to front desk and CCed home office in hope that future accommodations will be upgraded. Bought lunch of supposed halal meat from street vendor. Tossed skewer in gutter after one bite and rinsed mouth. Must avoid ground meat no matter the hunger. Can't trust the Christians. Temperature 81 degrees F. for late-night prayers. Water in the ablution room of the local mosque tepid and lacking in cleanliness. Complained to imam without effect. Bad teeth on the man, chipped right incisor. Did extensive tests on suspension bridge. Had to recalibrate instruments three times due to high humidity. Local assistants dismissive of my efforts. Eye rolling. Formally certified that bridge. Advised home office to recheck every three years as prolonged shift in weather pattern and attendant heavy rains may alter necessary soil compaction. Also made point that bridge should have been constructed further downstream where deep rock anchoring more feasible. Typical pattern of taking cheapest route. Wanted to get in the record that I had better placement in worst-case scenario.

Odd encounter at the Jakarta airport while waiting for flight to Mecca. (Air Indonesia, seat 37D, economy class.) Saw former colleague Safar Abdullah, waiting in the Islamic lounge. Safar seemed to be in some distress. Sweating profusely, face flushed, trembling. I thought at first that he had food poisoning. No surprise, considering the abysmal hygienic standards in the archipelago, but, from the ticket clutched in his hand, I saw that he was in transit from Hong Kong to San Francisco. Since there are numerous direct flights from Hong Kong to San Francisco, I can only surmise that this is yet another instance of corporate parsimony. We field engineers, in spite of our advanced education and experience, are always at the mercy of bean counters at the home office, from substandard hotel accommodations, to unrealistic per diems. I sat down beside poor Safar, expressed my concern for his health, and commiserated with him on his inability to get a direct flight home. The poor man was so surprised, he did not recognize me, looking about as though to find someplace to flee. As it was approaching midday, I offered to pray with him, but he declined, saying his recent travels had left him unclean. Indeed he was in terrible shape, with burst capillaries in his eyes, blistered skin, his beard and hair patchy. Two of his teeth had actually fallen out, although he had always taken pride in maintaining a proper appearance. He rightly seemed embarrassed to be seen in such a foul state, so I bought him a cup of sweetened tea—for which he was quite grateful. When I told him I was on my way to the Holy City, he started to cry, tears of blood running down his face as he begged me to pray for him. I made the promise and excused myself.

An hour later I boarded my flight (#349), grateful to be on my way. Alas, even though I had specifically requested to be seated with Muslims on the connecting flight to Delhi, I was informed that such seating is only guaranteed in business class. Instead, I was placed beside a fat Indian from Bombay who proceeded to gorge himself on satay and rice balls the whole flight. Actually offered me a taste of his fried shrimp, a deliberate insult I'm certain. May he roast in hell.

Sarah looked up at him, nodded. "You did it."

Rakkim shrugged. "Hair loss, blisters . . . I thought radiation poisoning was a possibility."

"More than a possibility." Sarah smiled, shook her head. "It wasn't Marian's father who was part of the Old One's network, it was this . . . Safar Abdullah. The bomb *was* leaking. I wonder if he was the only one who escaped alive from the mission."

"From Warriq's description, it seems unlikely he lasted for very long."

"Maybe he didn't expect to survive," said Sarah. "It wouldn't be the first suicide mission done at the bidding of the Old One." She stood up, the sheet sliding down, and she was slim and golden, thighs slightly parted, hairless as a peach. "Does the journal name the engineering firm Safar Abdullah worked for?"

"Not that I could find. There are so many volumes—"

"It doesn't matter. If it was radiation sickness, he's long dead, but we can find his family, or his friends." Sarah was pacing, now. "Warriq wrote that they used to be colleagues. We should check Warriq's employment history, then contact every company he worked for and see if Safar Abdullah is listed on their pension plan. Even if he's dead, we'll at least get a last address and a beneficiary."

Rakkim watched her stride around the room, clicking through her plan of attack. "Are you sure you want to do this?"

"You want to run away?"

"It's not a dirty word. Your mother did it." Rakkim thought Sarah was going to slap him. "Redbeard and the Old One have been playing against each other for twenty years. Maybe we should stay out of their game."

"Could *you* run away?"

"With you? Sure."

"I don't believe you."

"Even if you find this fourth nuke, that doesn't prove the Old One is responsible. Maybe Safar Abdullah was working for the Israelis."

"Tell that to Marian. You think the Israelis murdered her?"

"What happened to Marian is just the beginning," said

Rakkim. "You need to be ready for that. You have to decide if it's worth it."

"I'm not some ivory-tower intellectual. Not anymore." Sarah stalked over. "I *killed* a man last week. I drove a chopstick through his eye. It made this moist popping sound that I'm going to remember the rest of my life. I look in the mirror and I hardly recognize myself."

Rakkim watched her slip into one of his clean white shirts, her legs bare. "I just want you to realize you may not get the result you're expecting. History books get written *after* the war, after the dying. I'm on the outside, Sarah. I don't care about the president or Martyrs Day or any of the rest of it."

"If I knew things wouldn't get worse, I might be tempted," Sarah said quietly, "but history is never static, there's always a rise and fall. The fundamentalists are getting bolder, and the moderates just want it to all go away. Four professors at the university have been dismissed this year. *Insufficiently Islamic.*" She chewed on her pinkie, forced herself to stop. "Last week I had an encounter with a Black Robe . . ." She shook her head. "You can run away. I won't."

"I don't like Canada anyway." Rakkim took a couple of cans of coffee out of the cabinet. Shook them. Popped and poured them each a hot cup. He sat in the window seat, placed her coffee on the sill. She sat beside him. "I know a hack who can run down Safar Abdullah's work history." He smiled. "I might have to marry one of his daughters though."

"I don't share, you know that. I'm Redbeard's niece." Sarah sipped her coffee, one leg tucked against her chest, content to drowse in the late-afternoon sun.

Rakkim peeked through a gap in the curtains. He had chosen this office suite, chosen this window seat. The perfect vantage spot. The glass front of the building opposite allowing him to see both sides of the street. The market must be shutting down for the day. Housewives trudged down the sidewalks, string bags bulging with produce. Two workmen argued with each other as they walked, hands waving, the collars of their jackets turned up. A kid on a blue bicycle dodged through traffic. The trick in active observation wasn't to look for someone dangerous, but to sense things that were out of place. A parked car with the engine idling. The wrong shoes. The wrong gloves. An old woman who squared her shoulders. A man reading a newspaper who never turned the page. If you wait to see the knife, you'll be dead, his Fedayeen instructor had taught him—better to notice the empty scabbard and live.

This morning Rakkim had seen a long-haired modern hanging around the entrance to his building, sheltered under an overhang, shifting from one foot to the other. Probably thought himself invisible. Rakkim had been about to wake Sarah, tell her to get dressed, when a young woman had shown up, kissed the modern, the two of them clutching each other in the shadows before hurrying away.

"Did you call Redbeard?" asked Sarah. "I hate worrying him."

Rakkim watched the street. "I told him." A line of cars idled at the corner, waiting for the light to change. Blue exhaust drifted on the wind. New cars, old cars, it didn't seem to matter—they were all rusting, paint peeling, mufflers rumbling with corrosion. "Do you want to go out and get something to eat?"

"Don't you have anything here?"

"Canned tuna . . . bottled water . . . beer, artichoke hearts, apples and oranges." A man with a gray beard crossed against the light and a horn blared. "I think I have some crackers."

She put her foot on his leg, squeezed him with her toes. "Let's stay here. I'm tired. I just want to eat and read and make love." Her eyes were playful. "I'd like to take a shower first. If you're good, I'll let you wash my back."

"What do I get to wash if I'm bad?"

Sarah started unbuttoning the white shirt, taking her time.

"Your prospective father-in-law . . . he won't mind me coming with you?"

"He won't. You might, though."

"What do you mean?"

"Are you still afraid of the dark?"

CHAPTER 36

After noon prayers

"Refrain from gawking, Omar," Ibn Azziz said to his Yemeni body-guard as they were led down the corridor by the two Fedayeen. "It makes you seem like a kaffir at mosque."

Stung, Omar straightened to his full height, throwing his broad shoulders back as he kept pace with the Fedayeen.

Ibn Azziz maintained his slow, steady walk, and Omar fell back beside him. Omar's swagger was a sign of weakness, as was the way he rested his hand on his dagger. The dagger had been in Omar's family for three hundred years, a double-edged blade, ten inches long, made of the finest Damascus steel. Ibn Azziz had expected the unarmed Fedayeen officer who had greeted them outside the academy to ask Omar to disarm, but he had merely glanced at the weapon, smirking as he bowed to Ibn Azziz. Pig.

His advisers had warned against visiting General Kidd at the Fedayeen training academy, the seat of his power, but Ibn Azziz had dismissed their concerns. He needed to make it clear to General Kidd that in spite of Ibn Azziz's youth, Kidd was dealing with an equal, a spiritual warrior and master tactician. In the week since Ibn Azziz had seized power, he had disappeared dozens of Oxley's loyalists, used his contacts in the media to sugarcoat his ascension to power, and begun a campaign against the Catholics. On this twelfth day of fasting, his breath was foul, but his heart was pure as a blowtorch.

Two Fedayeen escorts proceeded ahead, almost ignoring Ibn Azziz. They walked with the long gait typical of Fedayeen, a pantherlike glide that was nothing like the crisp cadence of army personnel. Even their uniforms were somehow . . . unmilitary. Plain, light blue uniforms with dull brass buttons. No epaulets, no medals, no insignia. The Fedayeen stopped at the end of the corridor, knocked once, and threw open the door, flanking the doorway.

Omar started through first, as was proper, but one of the Fedayeen placed a hand on his chest.

"Just the mullah," said the Fedayeen.

Omar slapped his hand aside, started to draw his dagger . . . and then he was on the floor. He bolted up to his feet, but Ibn Azziz waved a hand.

"Wait outside, Omar, and keep our brother Fedayeen company," said Ibn Azziz, affecting boredom. "I will see General Kidd privately." He passed through the doorway, though not before noting the insolent gaze of the Fedayeen as he passed. Sooner, rather than later, General Kidd would see the wisdom of deepening the alliance with the Black Robes. He would see the value in treating Ibn Azziz as an honored ally. To seal the bargain, Ibn Azziz would ask only one thing . . . the eyes of these two Fedayeen.

General Maurice Kidd looked over as Ibn Azziz entered the balcony, then turned back. Tall and lean, Kidd stood casually beside a railing, middle-aged now, his face unlined and gleaming like obsidian. A devout Muslim, fiercely loyal, he had four wives and twenty-seven children, but lived simply. His rise to power began when, a mere Fedayeen captain, he had taken command of the decimated Islamic forces at the battle of Philadelphia, leading a counterattack that stopped the rebel advance. For the last twelve years he had commanded the Fedayeen, eager to send his troops abroad in furtherance of Islam or battling the Bible Belters on their common border. Today, as always, he wore the same unadorned uniform as the other Fedayeen, with only a tiny gold crescent on each shoulder denoting his rank. "Welcome, Mullah Ibn Azziz."

Ibn Azziz stood beside the general. His nose wrinkled at the scene below, the faint breeze carrying the stink. The balcony overlooked a hard-packed field filled with the dirtiest men Ibn Azziz had ever seen. He had visited hermits who were better groomed, observed gravediggers more sanitary.

"Do my men offend your delicate sensibilities, my young cleric?" asked General Kidd.

Ibn Azziz had not seen the general look over at him. "I find myself wondering how your men perform their devotions in such a state," he said evenly.

"These recruits have been in the field for three months. Three months of sleeping outside in the sun and rain and snow, and never for more than an hour or two at a time. Three months without a bath or a hot meal or a change of clothes. Three months of hand-to-hand combat and cat and mouse, of hiding under brush and brambles, three months of pain and fear. We started out with four hundred select recruits. One hundred twenty-seven made it through." General Kidd gazed at Ibn Azziz. "When my men have time to make their prayers, they do so with the assurance that Allah sees past their soiled exterior to the radiance within."

"Yes . . . well, I shall be happy to give them my blessing."

General Kidd stared at him with dark, liquid eyes.

Ibn Azziz offered his prayers to the men below, who ignored him. He watched as they sprawled on the ground, tearing into rations with their dirty hands, laughing and swearing. A raucous mob. "The reason I'm here—"

"My condolences on the death of Mullah Oxley," said General Kidd. "A most untimely event. He was a great friend of the Fedayeen."

"The Black Robes continue to support the Fedayeen, the most faithful of warriors. You are truly the thorny rose of Islam."

"A sudden heart attack . . . did Oxley truly get no warning?"

"It was as if Allah swept him up to Paradise."

"Oxley had a prodigious appetite. Perhaps there is a lesson there." The general smiled at Ibn Azziz, and his teeth were stark white. "You are thin as a wire, Ibn Azziz. Evidently Paradise is going to have to wait for you."

"My passion is not for food, dear general," said Ibn Azziz, annoyed. "My passion is for Allah, and for the purity of our nation. That's what I wanted to talk with you about." He moved closer. "We are under attack from all sides. Jews, gypsies, atheists, Bible Belters . . . and most dangerous of all, the moderns and Catholics who live among us, the moral rot within."

General Kidd watched his men. He seemed barely aware of Ibn Azziz.

"I have taken steps against the Catholics—"

"I know. Monasteries burned, houses of worship vandalized . . . some say you are overreaching. A particularly *risky* course from one so recently elevated to leadership."

"Moral offenses are within the purview of the Black Robes," said Ibn Azziz, unable to take the rough edge from his tone. "Catholics eat swine. They drown themselves in alcohol. They keep dogs in their homes so when they walk among us we must brush against the hairs of the beasts." Spit flew from his mouth as he warmed to the subject. "Catholics don't shave under their arms, or their pubic regions like good Muslims, so their sweat collects in these places with the most revolting stench. The nation would be better off without them."

"The Black Robes have jurisdiction over fundamentalist Muslims—"

"*True* Muslims," hissed Ibn Azziz.

"The nation can ill afford further dividing its people." General Kidd adjusted his immaculate blue uniform. "Come with me, you'll learn something." He started down the stairs that led from the balcony, and Ibn Azziz was compelled to accompany him. The exhausted Fedayeen got hastily to their feet, brushing off their filthy rags. They were scrawny as ravening wolves, sunburned, scratched and bloody, eyes swollen, their beards matted. "Look around you, Mullah Ibn Azziz, before you start burning churches. Many of those men were Catholics before converting."

"False conversions, as you well know," said Ibn Azziz, tagging along beside him as the general waded into the crowd. Ibn Azziz did his best not to touch any of them. "Conversions made only to be accepted in the Fedayeen."

General Kidd embraced one of the Fedayeen, the man wild-eyed, lips cracked, ferocious in his gratitude. The general's spotless uniform was dirty when they separated. He kissed another man on the cheek, had his hand kissed by others as they clustered around him, looking for his approval, his acknowledgment, croaking out his name. He moved deeper into the mass of recruits, nodding, patting them on the back—his uniform was filthy now, smeared with mud and blood, studded with burrs.

"We must be on guard against such falsifiers of faith," insisted Ibn Azziz.

"I do not have the ability to look within their souls. Nor do I *care* to look." General Kidd lightly tugged at the torn earlobe of one of his Fedayeen, turned to Ibn Azziz. "Besides, is it not Redbeard's job to keep the nation safe from its own citizens? That is a matter for State Security, not Fedayeen."

"Indeed." Ibn Azziz bowed his head, clutched his robe tightly around himself. Not a hint of his joy was revealed. The general had fallen into his trap. "The question I pose to you, General, is whether Redbeard is *doing* his job."

The general took a morsel of food from the crusted hands of one of the recruits, thanked him for it, and put it in his mouth. "We have had no major terrorist attacks in three years." He smacked his lips, smiled broadly at his men. "Terrorist cells are regularly broken up, and the guilty executed. It would seem State Security is functioning admirably."

"Redbeard's niece is a whore and an apostate. Bad enough she wrote a book that minimized the will of Allah in the founding of our nation, now she has run away from her home. She lives free from the restraints of faith and tradition, a mockery to the ideals of pious womanhood. How can we trust Redbeard to guard our nation, when he can't even guard his niece from sin?"

General Kidd saluted his troops. The recruits returned the salute, shouting his name, their voices cracking, a deafening, horrible sound. You would have thought it was the chanting of angels by the look on General Kidd's face.

"I need your help to find the slut," said Ibn Azziz. "You have men skilled in the shadow arts. It will be no great effort for them—"

"I don't send my men to chase women." The general beamed at his recruits. "Tell your Black Robes to get off their flabby asses if you want to find her so badly."

Ibn Azziz wanted to grab him, wanted to shake him until he realized the opportunity they had been given . . . but, the general was too soiled to touch. "General? Please, General? We must talk privately."

General Kidd led them out of the crowd and back up the steps. Ibn Azziz was going to have to spend hours in the baths. He was going to have to burn his robe. The filth would never be cleansed.

General Kidd waved to the recruits from the balcony, his face streaked with dirt. Their shouts were even louder now.

"You may not see the connection between Redbeard's private and his official failings, but others will," promised Ibn Azziz. "I have friends at the state television networks who would be only too glad to help. Do not be fooled by my youth, General. As you did in Philadelphia, I too know how to seize the initiative. This is an opportunity for both the Fedayeen and the Black Robes. *Surely* you can see that?"

General Kidd finally looked at him and Ibn Azziz shivered.

Ibn Azziz piously folded his hands in front of him, angry with himself for showing weakness. The body was treacherous. The body was an open door to the devil. "We have a mutuality of interest, that is all that I am saying. I have been told that there was a certain . . . understanding between the Black Robes and Fedayeen high command. A recognition that Redbeard has outlived his usefulness."

General Kidd turned back to his cheering recruits. "Any understanding that existed was between me and Oxley. If you can bring him back from the dead, we will have something to talk about."

Ibn Azziz turned on his heel, fuming. Omar, his bodyguard, was beside him again.

The Fedayeen stayed beside the door to the balcony, leaving them unescorted. Another insult. Their voices echoed down the corridor, garrulous as Jews'.

Let them laugh. Ibn Azziz had been mocked before, but the dead no longer laughed. His head pounded, though from the effects of his fast or his anger he could not tell. Regardless of the general's lack of cooperation, Redbeard's niece would be found. No matter what it took. No matter what it cost. The whore would be brought in, shown in all her debased squalor on television, perhaps even made to confess her uncle's role in her fall into sin. *Yes*. Help from the Fedayeen would have been a blessing, but Ibn Azziz had learned not to rely on anyone but himself . . . and Allah.

Ibn Azziz felt excitement course through him. The niece was said to be obstinate, but there were men in his employ skilled in the arts of persuasion. Given enough time, they could get the niece to confess to anything.

At great cost, Ibn Azziz had purchased a photograph of the niece and distributed it to every Black Robe in the country. The photo was several years old, taken on campus while she hurried to class, but her features were clear, as was the supple harlotry of her limbs. Word had come that Redbeard had enlisted his orphan to help him find his niece . . . Rakkim Epps. Another Fedayeen renegade. The photo of him was equally out-of-date, but his face showed the serene insolence that marked so many of the Fedayeen. Perhaps when Ibn Azziz was finished with Redbeard, he would start working on the transformation of the warrior elite.

He pushed past Omar, threw wide the doors to the outside. The wind buffeted them, sent his robes flapping. There had been good news this morning. A nest of Zionist vipers discovered. He had intended to invite General Kidd to the festivities. *His* loss. Ibn Azziz held his head high, barely aware of the cold. Last night he had dreamed for the third time of the city transformed. The streets of the capital like sheets of beaten copper, the gutters running red with blood. White doves flew overhead, a vast flock of doves, their wings beating like thunder. Ibn Azziz had awakened, weeping with joy.

CHAPTER 37

After noon prayers

"What was that comic book you used to talk about?" Rakkim's hand ached from Sarah's gripping him so tightly. He kept talking, anything to keep her mind off where they were. "The man who was half bat. He'd be right at home here."

"He wasn't half bat."

Rakkim felt her stumble in the utter darkness, kept her from falling. She had almost refused when he'd told her they were going to have to enter the tunnel without any kind of light. He had formed a mental map of the path to Spider's underground lair, a map formed in darkness. Light would only confuse him. Sarah had taken a few steps inside, but when he'd closed the door to the outside, she had clawed at him. He had sat down with her on the stone floor, let her get used to the darkness, the cool air of the tunnels, the *sounds*. It hadn't worked. She was still terrified of the dark, just as when she was a kid, but she didn't let it stop her. "This man-bat, he could see in the dark, though, right?"

"His name was Batman." Sarah's voice trembled, her nails digging into him. "And, no, he couldn't see in the dark. He just wore a costume so he looked like a bat."

"Why would he do that?"

"I don't know."

"Could he fly?"

"No, he just had the costume." Sarah stifled a cry as something skittered away in the distance. "There . . . there was another one, though. Superman. *He* could fly."

Rakkim felt for the wall, found the intersection, and took the right-hand tunnel. "They had a lot of gods in the old regime."

"They weren't gods. Not exactly. Movie stars were more like their gods."

"You want to go *back* to that?"

"No," snapped Sarah, voice echoing, and Rakkim was glad that she couldn't see his smile. "I want to go back to freedom to travel, to study and explore, to share information, to improve on what we have. I want to go back to making mistakes and trying again. Islam has nothing to fear from new ideas."

"Don't say that in the Grand Ali Mosque, you might get your tongue cut out."

"Ayatollah al-Hamrabi is an ass who doesn't know his Qur'an."

"*Definitely* going to get your tongue cut out."

Sarah laughed, swinging hands as if they were children on a walk in the park. They splashed through a puddle where water had seeped in. "Marian and I . . ."

"What?"

"Marian and I used to discuss the fact that the nation is coasting on the intellectual capital amassed by the previous regime, and we're running low on reserves. Islam dominated western intellectual thought for three hundred years, a period when Muslims were most open to the contributions of other faiths. *This* is the caliphate that should be restored, not some military-political autocracy like the Old One envisions."

The floor of the tunnel gradually sloped downward. Another 312 paces and they would turn left into another, even more narrow tunnel. Sarah was squeezing his hand again.

"Once the power of the fundamentalists is broken, once the Old One has retreated back to wherever he's hiding, then maybe we can build a nation that reveres innovation and intellectual inquiry. *Faith-driven* inquiry, but intellectually rigorous."

"I'd settle for loud music, cold beer, and coed beaches."

Sarah's laugh bounced off the stone walls of the tunnel. "I'll make sure we include that in the new constitution."

Rakkim made another turn, pulling her along. "It's not much further."

"You sure Spider won't mind me showing up unannounced?"

"No more than he's going to mind *me* showing up unannounced." Rakkim had tried to give Spider warning. He had gone by the restaurant where Spider's daughter Carla worked, but the manager said she had called in sick.

"Why have we stopped?"

"I'm feeling for something." Rakkim ran his hands around the doorframe set into the tunnel, trying to find a latch. There was a click and the door swung open. It was just as dark. He led Sarah into the storage room that served as a transition area. "Spider! It's Rakkim!" No response. He fumbled along the wall, found a light switch. The two of them blinked in the sudden glare.

"Thank God," said Sarah, basking in the light.

Rakkim hugged her. "You did good."

"I've been fighting back a scream the whole way."

Rakkim washed his hands in the sink, took off his shoes. He waited while she did the same, then opened the door to the main room. "Spi—" He clipped off his greeting, walked inside, looking around.

The room was empty. Worse than empty. It was a mess. Tables were overturned, carpets half-rolled, museum-quality tapestries hanging unevenly, as though someone had thought of taking them and decided at the last minute against it. The bank of computers had been stripped, memory cores removed and the sides hammered in. Cardboard boxes had been filled to overflowing with clothes and then abandoned. Beds had been overturned, drawers hung out of dressers. Toys were scattered about—a stuffed rhinoceros, a baseball, a single chess piece . . . a black knight. The two refrigerators were wide-open, discarded food lying in a puddle of spilled milk. No blood, though. No *blood*. Spider and his family had left in haste, but they had gotten away unharmed.

"What happened to him?" said Sarah, right beside Rakkim. She bent down, picked up the stuffed rhinoceros. "There's a . . . bootprint on this. We took off our shoes. Spider must have followed the same procedure. So who stepped on this?"

Rakkim took the rhino. Without speaking, they both put their shoes back on.

"The assassin wouldn't have done this, would he?"

"No. This isn't his style." Rakkim looked around, not rushing, trying to see something that whoever had trashed the place might have missed.

"All these beds and cribs . . . how many people lived here?" asked Sarah.

"He had a lot of kids. I saw five or six the time I was here. Heard more. There were others too, older ones. Spider didn't like to go out, but he liked company."

Sarah wrapped her arms around herself. It wasn't cold, but she was probably feeling the weight of earth and concrete around them. Imagining what it would be like to be trapped down here. "What are you looking for?"

"I don't know." Rakkim reached under a chair. One of Spider's antique snow globes lay shattered, New York City's Twin Towers crumpled among the shards of glass. Souvenir stands all over the capital sold similar versions, only with the towers in flames. This one was pretransition.

"We should go."

"We will."

"Are we going to have to use Redbeard to find Safar Abdullah now? Rakkim?"

Rakkim tossed the Twin Towers aside. "No, I've got . . ." He cocked his head, listened. Grabbed Sarah by the arm.

Sarah didn't resist, didn't protest. She couldn't hear them, but she knew Rakkim.

Rakkim led her into what had been the children's room, eased Sarah under a mattress that had been half pulled off the bed. Had her curl up out of sight. Checked it from several angles to make sure she couldn't be seen. A brightly colored mural of the periodic table of elements had been painted on the wall facing the beds. Voices echoed from the tunnel outside, loud enough for her to hear. She shrank deeper into the shadows. He bent down, kissed her. "I love you."

"Now, I *know* we're in trouble."

Rakkim moved away. The voices were louder now as he slipped behind a large, rolled carpet that leaned against a support wall. It wasn't the perfect hiding place, but he needed to see who was in the room and to put himself between them and Sarah. He needed to be able to move quickly, to spring out in a rush. His knife rested in his hand, and as always, it comforted him.

"Who left the light on?" A voice like sandpaper.

"Don't blame me."

Rakkim peered through a crack between the carpet and the wall, saw two beefy men in the doorway, hands on their hips. Two more were already inside the room, checking things out. Black nylon jackets, loose pants, daggers on their belts, neatly trimmed beards. Enforcers for the Black Robes.

The two in the doorway bowed as another man strode into the room, evidently a senior Black Robe. Two other bodyguards followed him. The Black Robe was younger than he expected, his beard scraggly, the skinniest man Rakkim had seen outside of prison. Dead white skin and red-rimmed eyes. He looked like a rabid dog Rakkim had killed in the Carolinas. A hollowed-out mongrel that had bitten two men, torn their legs open, and kept lunging at Rakkim even after he pinned it with a hay rake.

"My stars, this place stinks of *Jews*," said the Black Robe, his voice reedy. "Would that they were still here, Tarriq."

The largest enforcer hung his head.

"How many years have we been searching for this Jew?" said the Black Robe. "How long has this . . . Spider bedeviled us?"

"In all due respect, Mullah, we don't know for sure that Spider exists."

"We won't get a chance to find out now, will we?" The Black Robe kicked aside a browning head of lettuce, sent it rolling across the floor. "I had hoped to parade this Jew for the cameras. To show the people that we have succeeded where Redbeard had failed. To prove that he has allowed the enemies of Islam to burrow deep within our cities. Now we have nothing." He glared at the enforcer

as they circled the room. "Your informant failed us, Tarriq. All we
did was send the vermin scuttling off to another nest."

"We . . . we were close, my lord," rasped the enforcer.

"Ah, *close*," said the Black Robe. "That changes everything."
He threw wide his arms, his hands skeletal from the sleeves of his
robe. "See? My wrath has dissipated like dew in the glory of dawn."

Rakkim glanced at the bed, but there was no sign of Sarah. He
wondered if the mullah was Ibn Azziz. Redbeard said the new
leader of the Black Robes was a zealot, but this man seemed too
young to have achieved such power.

"The informant had been watching the waitress for weeks trying to find out where she disappeared to," said the enforcer. "He
didn't know if she was a Jew or if she just lived in one of the abandoned warehouses. There's plenty of that. It was his own good
instincts that kept him after her, and when he saw her duck into
the hidden tunnel, he notified us. He took a chance and he was
right, Mullah. We launched our raid an hour after his call, but
there was no way to know where she had gone, and she . . . she
must have sensed that she had been observed. By the time we
finally found this room, they were gone."

"What do we owe this informant?" said the Black Robe. "What
do we owe this man who allowed himself to be . . . *sensed* by a
female?"

"Twenty thousand dollars. Standard bounty for valid information. Plus, ten thousand apiece for every Jew we captured, but of
course, that doesn't apply here."

"Thank you for pointing that out to me."

"We'll find them, Mullah. They're on the run now."

Rakkim held the knife loosely as they got closer. And closer.
Six armed men and the Black Robe. It depended on how they
were bunched . . . and the level of their training. He had the element of surprise, but if he waited until he was spotted to attack,
he would lose that advantage. The biggest danger was that Sarah

would get involved—there was no way he could use his speed to full effect while defending her.

"Look at this filth," said the Black Robe. He sounded as if he was on the opposite side of the carpet. "See the scientific devilry these foul Jews use to teach their brood?" He walked right past Rakkim's hiding spot—were he to have turned his head, he would have seen him—walked right past and stood before the periodic table. He was close enough to where Sarah was hiding to kick her. The Black Robe reared back and spat on the center of the mural, a fat gob sliding down the wall.

The enforcers laughed.

Rakkim was motionless. The Black Robe would die first. Then the others.

The Black Robe turned on his heel, walked past Rakkim. "Pay your informant. Pay him in small bills and shove them down his throat. Fill his gullet. Make him choke on his money. Let him learn the price of failure."

Their footsteps faded. The lights went out. The door closed. Rakkim found Sarah in the dark.

CHAPTER 38

Before sunset prayers

"It's me," said Rakkim.

"Let me speak to Sarah," said Redbeard.

"What did the werewolves say about the assassin?"

"Let me speak to her. *Now.*"

Redbeard would be happy to go back and forth as long as Rakkim wanted to keep it up—the longer they talked, the better chance Redbeard had to pinpoint their position. Rakkim didn't take the bait. He passed the phone to Sarah. "He wants to talk to you."

"Hello, Uncle." Sarah looked past Rakkim, toward the ferry slowly crossing Baraka Bay, the water rusty in the setting sun. She was wearing a new, pink-camouflage hooded sweatshirt, and baggy, matching sweatpants. The anonymous retro-jock look that was all the rage among moderns. The two of them were sitting on a bench with a panoramic view of the waterfront. A relief to be out in the open air after the dark claustrophobia of the tunnels. "I'm fine . . . I *said*, I'm fine. I'm twenty-six years old; I'm capable of making my own decisions." She chewed her lower lip, listening. "Shame is not really an effective strategy at this point, Uncle." A glance at Rakkim. "That's not possible . . . No. I love you, but I'm not about to do that. Tell Angelina that I'm well. Tell her I'm saying my prayers." She stuck her tongue out at Rakkim, handed the phone back to him.

Rakkim watched the trolley roll along tracks paralleling the waterfront. A short run, back and forth, the trolley packed with tourists. "Your turn."

"There were no werewolves at the site," said Redbeard.

"Did you go to the right place?"

"I found the wreckage of the car, just as you described, but there were no werewolves. None to ask, anyway."

Rakkim was silent for a moment. "How many?"

"My men found seventeen bodies scattered around the site. All werewolves. If there were any survivors, they were gone by the time we got there. Fled into the woods, probably, because their cars and goods were still at the encampment. Boxes full of watches and eyeglasses and sporting equipment. I helicoptered in myself when I got the first report. A quick walk-through and I could see that one of their cars was missing. A four-by-four. There were tire tracks dug through the mud getting up the embankment. Quite a mess around the burned-out vehicle. Seventeen werewolves . . . even for a Fedayeen assassin, that's quite an accomplishment."

"Maybe the Old One will pin a medal on him." Silence from Redbeard. Rakkim watched the trolley start back on the return trip. Heard the faint clang of the bell.

"You should bring Sarah home. Leave the Old One to me," said Redbeard. "I've kept him at bay this long—"

"You can't stop him anymore."

Redbeard chuckled. "Don't tell me what I can do, boy."

"You don't have the men for the job, and the ones you do have, you can't trust. If you could stop the Old One, you wouldn't have needed me to find Sarah for you."

"Come *home*."

"I saw Ibn Azziz. At least I think I did. He's *young*." Rakkim watched three cars pull up alongside the trolley. A fourth car pulled onto the tracks ahead, forcing the trolley to a screeching stop. Men jumped out of the cars and into the trolley. Others covered the rear exit. One of them looked like the arrogant dandy who had fetched him the evening of the Super Bowl, but Rakkim was too far away to be sure. He *hoped* it was him. "You better watch yourself, Uncle. I think Ibn Azziz has already declared war on you."

"Better him than Oxley."

Rakkim had picked up a signature transmitter in the Zone, bought it an hour ago from the same electronics wizard who had bought Redbeard's tracking device from Sarah. A major felony for all concerned. The transmitter sent a cell signature to a small unit he had secreted in the trolley, the same signature as the cell he was using, only more powerful. He watched the tourists filing out of the trolley under the eyes of Redbeard's agents. "I'll get in touch with you again when I know more."

"You can't outwit the Old One. Not by yourself."

Rakkim could see the passengers being marched out of the

trolley. "Don't be so sure. *You're* smarter than the Old One and I just outwitted you." He broke the connection.

The setting sun glinted off the tips of Sarah's hair as the muezzin's call to pray undulated from the Grand Mosque, summoning the devout. They stayed where they were, watching Redbeard's men tearing through the trolley. Unnecessary roughness. A sign of weakness.

Rakkim stared up at the new Jihad Cola sign while Mardi's private number rang. Sarah was beside him, equally entranced.

There must have been five thousand people in Pioneer Square for the great unveiling, the crowd spilling over into the side streets. They were packed in so tightly that it had been no problem for Rakkim to lift the cell from the inside pocket of a young modern Zebraskin interactive, the latest model.

"It's me," said Rakkim as Mardi answered.

"What's wrong?"

Moderns in the crowd cheered, applauded, gasped as the sign lit up—a three-story-tall hologram that seemed deep as infinity. The fundamentalists swayed, lips moving as they prayed, ecstatic in their approval. Even Sarah was openmouthed with delight.

"What's that noise?" asked Mardi.

It wasn't the hologram that the crowd was cheering—holographic advertising had been common for twenty years. It was the ad itself. Islam didn't approve of representations of the human face or form, so signs in the new republic were forced to use a simple photo of the product, counting on vibrant colors and elaborate typefaces to get their message across. A poor substitute for image, and yet another reason for the economic doldrums.

"I can hardly hear you," said Mardi.

"You *need* to get out of the Blue Moon."

The new Jihad Cola sign portrayed a healthy young Muslim couple drinking a JC in the park, their chaperone discreetly in the background. What was unique about the ad was that it wasn't just holographic, but *mosaic*, the images formed from careful layering of Arabic text from the Holy Qur'an. Not only did the use of script circumvent the strictures against graven images, Arabic script itself, particularly script from the Holy Qur'an, was believed to possess a unique and mystical power. An added value to the brand. The computer program used to create the ad had taken three years to write, but the mosaic process was certain to revolutionize advertising. The launch was in the capital, but subsequent unveilings were planned in Los Angeles, Chicago, New Detroit, Denver, and other major cities. Mullah Oxley had given the technique the Black Robes' approval, but Rakkim wondered how Ibn Aziz felt about it.

"Where *are* you?" asked Mardi.

Rakkim turned away from the crowd, sheltering the phone from the worst of the noise. "You have to get out of the Blue Moon. You have to leave now. The liquor salesman you were so charmed by . . . he's a Fedayeen assassin."

"You don't know that."

"Take the money from the safe and *go*. Call Riggs from the airport and tell him he's going to manage the club for a month. He can handle it for a few weeks."

"He'll steal us blind."

"Consider it the cost of staying alive." Rakkim lowered his voice, trying to reach her. "Take a vacation, partner. You've already got more money than you can spend. Just leave. Don't even go home to pack. Just *leave*. Call the club in a month and ask to speak to me. If I'm not back yet, then stay gone for another month and call again."

"It's really that bad?"

"Worse."

CHAPTER 39

Before noon prayers

"I had to jump through hoops to get this for you." Colarusso straightened the collar on Rakkim's jacket, dropped the data chip into his pocket. "It's illegal what I done."

"Bet it was the first time you ever broke the law too," said Rakkim.

Colarusso stifled a smile as he leaned back against the railing of the roller rink. He watched Anthony Jr. and Sarah circle the rink, holding hands, Anthony Jr. clomping along, a little unsteady. "They make a nice couple, don't they?"

"Fuck you."

The indoor rink was filled with moderns and Catholics, plenty of moderates in posh hajibs too, the skating rink one of the few places where they could have physical contact with the opposite sex under the eye of their chaperone. "I just think if a man puts his career on the line for a friend, the friend should tell him what's going on, that's all."

"Sarah's working on a book that could bring her a lot of trouble. Safar Abdullah is part of her research. I'm along to make sure she eats right and gets a good night's sleep. That's pretty much it."

"Abdullah's been dead for twenty-five years, so you're not going to get much conversation out of him." Colarusso sucked his teeth. "Engineers must be the dullest people in the world. Who dies of natural causes at forty-three? Probably died of boredom." Colarusso hitched up his pants. "I've always been curious. If I hadn't gone into police work, I would have probably been a Peeping Thomas."

"I don't think Abdullah died of natural causes. Feel better now?"

"A little bit." Colarusso rocked on his heels. "Hope you're not planning to exhume the body, because somebody beat you to it. That's kind of odd, isn't it? Him being a devout Muslim and yet his family allows him to be dug up a week after burial. Dug him up and cremated him. The wife signed off on it, but the cemetery sure made a fuss. Martyrs of Fallujah Cemetery, Los Angeles. Best Muslim boneyard in the city from what I read. I got a copy of their angry letter to the wife in the file. You should read it. Another one from the poor woman's imam that's a real classic. Threatened her with the flames of hell. Her and her dead hubby. Leave it to a holy man to know how to twist the knife."

Rakkim watched the skaters in bright colors barrel past. In the old days the rinks supposedly played music too, but the rolling wheels made music of their own.

"Now, why would a good Muslim woman allow her husband to be backhoed up in the middle of the night?" said Colarusso. "I got the order from the mortuary that did the work. Two a.m. is when they did the deed. Mortuary had to pay their workmen double time." He leaned closer to Rakkim. "You can see why it got my attention."

Rakkim took in the spectators in the bleachers, the chaperones, and the skaters taking a time-out. All those faces, but none caught his attention. Sometimes the Black Robes would show up, just to cause trouble, but the rink donated to the local mosque. "Were you able to locate the wife?"

"She died a couple of years after the mister. Got planted in the al-Aqua Cemetery in Van Nuys. Not quite the pedigree of Martyrs of Fallujah."

"Children? Relatives?"

"One daughter. Fatima. It's all in the data chip. Let's just say it might be a good thing that her parents aren't alive to see what she turned out like."

Rakkim watched three middle-aged women nearby. Three chaperones in dark chadors talking rapidly to each other while focused on the three young women they were responsible for. "Thank you, Anthony."

"I don't care about being thanked," grumbled Colarusso. "You're chasing after dead people. I'd like to know why."

"This is probably a good time for you to step back and work another case."

"Don't tell me how to do my job. It makes me want to forget we're friends."

"Okay." Rakkim looked past Colarusso, keeping watch. "The assassin who drowned Marian Warriq . . . the one who swapped heads with her servants, he's following Sarah and me." He saw Colarusso resist the impulse to look around. "We gave him the slip a few nights ago, but he's not going to quit. When he gets desperate to find us, he's going to start tapping anyone we're connected to."

"You think he'd go after a police detective or his family?"

"I think he'd go after the president himself if he got the order."

"Who's giving him the orders?"

Rakkim had fallen into the trap. "How about this . . . how about when the time comes, I'll tell you everything. I won't hold anything back. For now though, I want to keep you out of the loop as much as possible. Out of harm's way. Then if I need you, you'll be alive and well and able to help me."

"How about *this* . . . how about you and I find this assassin and kill him? You said you couldn't beat him yourself. Let's do it together. I'll take care of the paperwork. Like you said, wouldn't be the first time."

"We'd just get in each other's way."

"You think I'd slow you down?" Colarusso lost his good nature. "I'm strapped with a full-auto Wesson and I score *expert* on the firing range. I've killed five men in the line of duty and never lost a minute's sleep over it. You think I'm worried about your assassin?"

Rakkim watched a father holding his daughter up on the rink, teaching her how to skate as the other skaters streamed around them. "Three nights ago the assassin got ambushed in the badlands by werewolves. He killed seventeen of them, then drove away in one of their vehicles."

"That . . . that's some serious shooting."

"He used a blade."

"Seventeen werewolves with a *knife*? You got bad information there."

"Fedayeen assassins don't even need a knife. They just enjoy using it." Rakkim watched the father and daughter. She was starting to get it, lengthening her stride, but the father hovered over her, ready to catch her. "I thought the car crash would kill him. Or mess him up so bad that the werewolves would be fighting over the pieces."

"*Seventeen?*"

They stood there, shoulder to shoulder, watching the skaters go round and round. Rakkim wished he could have seen the assassin's face when his tires blew. The assassin had fought himself clear, but falling into Rakkim's trap would have stung. Sometimes a love tap hurt a guy like that worse than a hammer.

"You need any help getting to Los Angeles? This assassin probably got eyes at the airport. I might be able to do something for you."

"I'd be happy to hear anything you've got."

Colarusso smiled. A few minutes later he nodded as his son whipped past. "Look at Anthony Jr. Ever since he got accepted in the Fedayeen, it's like he's grown a couple of inches. Seemed to happen overnight. Cleans up his room without being asked. Goes on five-mile runs every morning. Calls me *sir*, if you can believe that. More than that, though . . . it's like he's solid in a way he wasn't before. Like he's seeing things clearer. Like he finally knows where he's going." Colarusso shook his head. "I owed you before . . . now it's like I'm never going to catch up."

"You don't owe me anything."

Colarusso kept his eyes on the ice. "Anthony Jr. has a real case of hero worship when it comes to you. Everything out of his mouth is Rakkim-this and Rakkim-that."

"He'll get over it soon enough." Rakkim watched Sarah gliding along. She had separated from Anthony Jr., was doing spins in the center of the rink. Her skate caught and she almost fell, skated on, blushing. "When you ran down Abdullah's stats . . . you didn't do it directly, did you?"

"No data trail, just like you said."

"Did the cops at the crime scene know who I was?"

"I told them you were State Security. Said Redbeard himself sent you to take over the site. They knew better than to ask for your name. Don't worry. Nobody knows we're more than ships in the night. Reprobate like you. Word got out that we were pals, it could fuck up my climb to the top."

"What about the Super Bowl?"

Colarusso shrugged. "Half the detectives on the force got comped to that game."

"Okay." Rakkim waved back to Sarah. "How did you get the information on Abdullah?"

"I went through a girl in the personnel department. She's got access to databases all over the country so she can check out new applicants."

"She didn't ask why you wanted the information?"

"I told her it was a top secret project. I think she enjoyed the idea." Colarusso adjusted his poorly knotted necktie without noticeable improvement. "She's a moderate Muslim lady, a little overweight, past thirty and unmarried, so you know where she's headed." He scratched his belly. "She's kind of sweet on me. Laughs at all my jokes. Thinks I'm some kind of rough-and-tough character. I guess I'm the forbidden fruit." He grinned. "You know what they say about Catholics."

"What?"

"Come on, don't play dumb. You know what they say."

"What are you talking about?"

"Catholics are built larger," said Colarusso, whispering now. "Our equipment . . . it's bigger than Muslims'."

"I just never heard that about Catholics," Rakkim said innocently. "All I heard was the thing with the choirboys."

"We got rid of that problem a long time ago."

Rakkim watched Sarah and Anthony Jr. skate over to the refreshment stand. Anthony Jr. bought her a cup of hot cider. Glanced over at Rakkim, then quickly back.

"That's a fine-looking woman," said Colarusso.

"Yeah."

"You're a lucky man."

"What are you trying to say?"

"Marie's been puffed up like a partridge ever since Anthony Jr. got his papers. Every neighbor within a mile knows her boy's going to be Fedayeen. She's planning a big party next month, just before he leaves." Colarusso cracked his knuckles, taking his time. "I'm supposed to tell you . . . I'm supposed to let you know, if you want to marry one of our daughters, just say the word."

Rakkim stared at him. First Spider and now Colarusso.

"I know, I know, they're homely as an old boot, but Mary Ellen is a fine cook and has the hips for pounding out babies. She doesn't have to be your first wife. I figure Sarah's already hanging drapes in that spot. You can put Mary Ellen third or fourth in line."

"One wife is plenty."

"Tell me about it. Well, at least I asked."

Rakkim smiled. "You look relieved."

Colarusso started to answer, then Sarah and Anthony Jr. skated up. Anthony Jr. didn't make eye contact.

CHAPTER 40

Before sunset prayers

"Is it really true people used to swim here?"

"It's true."

Offshore oil rigs paralleled the coast, hundreds of them as far as Rakkim could see. Waves slapped the beach, the water foamy with black sludge. Huntington Beach was covered with balls of congealed petroleum, the sand clotted with gunk. "Did they have special soaps to wash off with afterward?"

"There didn't used to be so much oil on the beach." Sarah unwrapped another of the spiced-goat sandwiches they had bought at Bin Laden International. She took off the hot peppers, put them aside, and took a big bite. "They didn't drill for oil here."

"Why not?" Rakkim loved watching her eat. "Didn't they need gasoline?"

"They didn't care. They loved playing in the water more. They rode these boards . . . surfboards they were called. It was supposed to be fun. Tourists came from all over the world to swim and fish and spend money."

Rakkim looked around. The boardwalk along the beach was noisy and crowded—retirees strolling with arms linked, mothers and babies. Sarah had insisted that they spread a blanket among the young people picnicking on the grassy bluff taking in the sunset. Rakkim was only thirty, but he felt too old to be here among the moderns and wild-eyed Catholics, all of them long-legged and tan, couples tangled together in the afternoon. Even the Zone was never like this. Not in daylight. Not out in the open.

It had been forty-one degrees and overcast when they'd left

Seattle this morning. It was eighty-seven in Southern California. They had spent the day short-hopping from one small airport to another, finally landing at BLI an hour ago. The airport biometric scanners might have been off-line, but Rakkim had decided to puddle-jump their way south anyway. Colarusso had supplied fake IDs filched from the undercover unit, given Rakkim a list of airports with failed security procedures. A safe trip but tiring. They rented a car with their fake ID, programmed the GPS to take them to the beach with a minimum of traffic. Not much luck on that. When Sarah was ready, they were going to check into a motel. Tomorrow was soon enough to find Fatima Abdullah.

Rakkim hadn't spent much time in this part of the country, but the drive from the airport had been a wake-up. The freeways were congested, but twelve lanes wide and smooth as glass, with computerized on-ramps and ozone detectors. Seattle had political power, but Southern California seemed to have the money. Part of it was the oil wealth, but, according to Sarah, demographics were the crucial element. While the rest of the nation was heavily Muslim, Southern California's majority Latino population had remained Catholic. With their natural resources and hardscrabble work ethic, this part of the nation had flourished. You just had to look around to know things were different here. The buildings soared and the cars were better kept, many of them French and Japanese imports with fuel-cell technology and vector engines. There were still violent ghettos and decaying urban areas, but, unlike the capital, there was an excitement here, an eager rhythm, a sense that anything was possible. You just had to grab it.

Sarah had responded to the change at some deep emotional level, seeming to bloom in the heat. She had rolled up her trousers until they were above the knee, taken off her jacket. She dug her toes into the grass. "I've only been to L.A. for academic conferences. We hardly ever left the hotel and the convention center. Strictly formal attire." She looked around. "I could live here forever."

Rakkim smiled. "Colarusso once told me if I was Catholic on a Saturday night, I'd never want to be a Muslim again."

"I've seen movies from the old days," said Sarah. "There was a girl named Gidget. She and her friends practically lived at the beach. They were half-naked most of the time and nobody seemed to notice, which was strange, because she was a nun."

"That doesn't sound like any nun I ever saw."

"Gidget could fly too. Like Superman. Or an angel, I'm not sure." Sarah raised her shirt, bared her belly to the sky. "Ahhh. This must be what Paradise is like." Rakkim's gaze caressed the tight knot of her belly button. "Or hell."

Sarah grabbed the hot peppers she had put aside, plopped them into her mouth. She kept her eyes on him as she chewed. Reached over and kissed him, drove her tongue deep into him. Her kiss burned, but he didn't pull away.

Anthony Colarusso had a fine house in a Catholic neighborhood in the Madrona district. The lawns were neatly kept, the homes recently painted, the streets free from trash and dog shit. Darwin turned up the collar of his cashmere coat, his hands shoved into the pockets as he strolled along the sidewalk. Clean-shaven as a Baptist. He had parked a block away, made a slow circuit. A couple of kids raced past him on scooters, scrawny little brats in shorts and T-shirts, oblivious to the damp. A rheumy-eyed old man raking leaves in his front yard said hello to Darwin, asked him if he was looking for an address, offered that he had been living on this block for fifty-seven years. Darwin thanked him, but said he knew where he was going.

Darwin limped slightly, a twinge shooting up his spine with every step. Credit the accident last week. Accident. That wasn't really the proper term for what had happened. He had been stabbed a couple of times by the werewolves, but the wounds were almost completely closed up. The real damage was to his pride. Rakkim must have gotten a good laugh watching Darwin's car tumbling end over end that night. Rakkim and Sarah had gone underground, but someone had to know where they were. Darwin had remembered Rakkim and Colarusso walking around the Warriq crime scene the day after, the fat cop dogging Rakkim, passing on orders to the uniforms. One just had to look at the two of them to know it was more than a professional relationship. They were *buddies*.

It hadn't taken Darwin long to find Colarusso's home address. One of the Old One's little helpers in the police department had overridden the privacy safeguards that protected department personnel. Leaves swirled around his knees as Darwin crossed the street. He walked up the flagstones to Colarusso's front porch. Rang the bell. The opening notes of Beethoven's Fifth Symphony gonged inside. The epitome of prole chic.

Darwin brushed back his thinning brown hair with his fingers. Looked up as the door opened and saw Anthony Jr. staring at him from the other side of the security screen. Maximum quality. Half-inch Swedish-steel latticework. Expensive hardware, particularly on a detective's salary. The windows were probably equally reinforced. Colarusso must spend a lot of time away from his family. Such a good papa.

"Hi." Darwin smiled. "I haven't seen you since your parents' Christmas party seven or eight years ago. You've grown."

Anthony Jr. didn't react. He was a tall, muscular kid in a blue King Fahd High School sweat suit. Cropped hair. A thin beard ran along the edge of his jawline. "You going to open the door, or am I supposed to stand out here in the cold?" Anthony Jr. didn't move. "I guess I can't expect you to remember me." Darwin rooted in his jacket. "I compliment you on your caution."

He flashed the badge he had taken from the handsome young police officer. "Darwin Conklin. I'm police liaison with the mayor's office."

Anthony Jr. barely glanced at the badge. "Good for you."

"Is your father here? I need to speak with him."

"He hasn't come home yet."

Darwin made a point of checking his watch. "May I come in and wait?"

"Who is it, Anthony?"

Darwin saw a doughy woman in the kitchen doorway, drying her hands on a dish towel.

Anthony Jr. kept his eyes on Darwin. "I'm taking care of it, Mom."

Darwin pointed at the tiny silver crescent moon hanging above the door. "Have you been accepted in the Fedayeen?"

A wary nod from Anthony Jr.

"Congratulations." No response from Anthony Jr. "Can I *please* come inside?" Darwin grinned. "I caught a cold from the mayor last week, and I'm just getting over it."

Anthony Jr. slowly reached for the door lock. Stopped.

Darwin jiggled the handle. "What's wrong?"

"*You.* You're wrong."

"Anthony, you're not scared of me, are you?"

Anthony Jr. stared at him. Slowly nodded his head.

Darwin opened his coat. "I'm not even armed. I'm a liaison officer. We talk. We dialogue. That's all."

"Go dialogue with somebody else."

Darwin shook his head. "If you're the kind of young man the Fedayeen is reduced to accepting, I should sell my war bonds."

"I know who you are." Even protected by a half inch of steel, Anthony Jr. trembled.

Darwin smiled, sincere smile this time. He didn't remember the last time anyone had detected his true nature. Not before it was too late. Anthony might have the instincts of a born Fedayeen, but it was just as likely that Rakkim had warned him that someone like Darwin might be coming around. Him and his father, the fat cop. One big happy family, all looking out for one another. Telling one another all kinds of things. Darwin's little visit to the Colarusso homestead hadn't been wasted.

Anthony's mother reappeared in the kitchen doorway. "Anthony?"

"Call 911, Mom. Tell them to send a couple of cars."

Darwin waved to her. "Hello, Marie. You look lovely, as usual."

Anthony's mother touched her hair. "Don't play games, Anthony, let the man in."

"*Call* them, Mom."

"Good for you, Anthony," said Darwin. "I can't fool you."

"I don't like you saying my name."

"May I give you some advice?" asked Darwin. "You've probably been working out a lot since you got accepted. Taking all kinds of growth-hormone and cobra-venom hotshots." He smiled again. "You'd be better off training yourself to catnap. Set your alarm clock for one-hour intervals so you wake up every hour during the night. When you can wake up without the alarm clock, and wake up *alert*, fully alert, then set the intervals for a half hour. That's what you're going to need to make it through Fedayeen boot camp, because you're never going to get more than an hour's uninterrupted sleep that whole first year."

"I did it, Anthony," called his mother. "Close the door. Let the police handle it."

"I bet she's a fabulous cook," said Darwin.

"I'm already sleeping on a hardwood floor," said Anthony Jr. "I got the heat in my room turned off too. That thing with the catnaps, though . . . that's a pretty smart idea."

"I'm full of smart ideas." Darwin looked as if he were trying to decide something. "There's another thing . . ." He glanced around, the carbon-polymer knife slipping down his sleeve into his hand. "When the escape-and-evasion instructor asks for volunteers"—he lowered his voice and Anthony Jr. unconsciously leaned closer—"you should—" Darwin slammed his right hand into the screen, the blade plunging through the steel mesh. It should have driven into Anthony Jr.'s left eye, but he had pulled away at the last instant.

Anthony Jr. wiped blood off his cheek. He was breathing hard.

"Well *done*." Darwin put the knife away. "You just might make it through boot camp. We'll have to get together again sometime and discuss war stories." He gave Anthony Jr. a jaunty salute, turned on his heel. He was barely limping now, a new spring in his step.

Sarah pulled wide the curtains, let the last of the sunset into their beachfront motel room. She was nude and slick with sweat, all curves and hollows, and he hardened again just looking at her. She bent forward, hands on the sill, her ass canted toward him. The window was open, the curtains swirling.

"Are you *trying* to give me a heart attack?"

She looked back at him, laughed. "I've never been so happy."

He watched her as sounds drifted through the window. Bicycles. Seagulls keening. Steady pounding of the waves. The whir of jet helicopters passing overhead, almost silent. Airspace in the capital was restricted, but not here. Nothing seemed off-limits here. "Come back to bed."

"Say—"

"Please?"

The curtains boiled around her. "Look at us, Rikki, making love with the windows open. They *had* to hear us down below."

Her nipples were dark and hard. "Look at us, out in public, hold-ing hands, not counting the minutes until I have to be home. Not going over my excuses to Redbeard, rehearsing the answers for all the possible questions I might be asked. Colarusso is the only one who knows we're here. We're free." She walked toward him, the sunset outlining her in gold. "I don't want to look for Fatima tonight."

"Good."

"I don't want to look for her tomorrow either. I want to make love and sleep late. I want to eat breakfast in the café we saw. I want to run in the sun and drink Mexican iced coffee and listen to music. I want you to dance with me. Then I want to make love some more."

Rakkim watched her getting closer. She was at the edge of the bed now, and he could smell the sex on her. "I'd like that too. Except for the dancing part."

She slid across the bed, and he caressed the moistness between her legs. "Let's stay here as long as we can," she said, "because when we leave, when we find her, it's going to start up again. There won't be room for us anymore—"

"That's not true."

She slipped him inside her, slipped him inside so smoothly it was as if he had always been part of her. "It won't be like *this*." She gently rocked on him, and he fit himself into her motion, the heat of her radiating through him. "The clock will have started once we leave here. We'll be looking over our shoulders again." She tightened her grip on him, purring, squeezed him to the base, and he cried out as she rocked against him, driving him home.

Rakkim groaned, arched his back.

She shook her hair out as she rode him; dark curls flying in the twilight.

CHAPTER 41

Before noon prayers

"Ain't nobody going to answer their door, mister," said the kid as Rakkim pressed the call buttons. He was maybe ten, with feral eyes and dirty blond hair, skinny as rope. Sleeping in his clothes hadn't helped them. "Half them buttons don't work anyway."

Rakkim glanced around while Sarah rooted in her purse. They were on the landing of an apartment building, last known address of Fatima Abdullah, according to the information Colarusso had retrieved. A lousy neighborhood in Long Beach, Catholics mostly. Overturned garbage cans and stripped cars on the streets. If Fatima was still hooking, midmorning was the best time to catch her home. They had spent the last three days at the motel in Huntington Beach, taking it slow, pretending they were just two people in love and not wanting it to end. It was as close to a honeymoon as they might get.

Sarah handed the kid a $10 bill. "We're looking for Fatima Abdullah. Sometimes she calls herself Francine Archer. Or Felicity Anderson."

It was too soon to pay the kid. Too soon and too little.

The kid tucked the money into his sneaker. Carefully stubbed out the cigarette, wrapped it in a piece of gum wrapper. Ready to run. "Never heard of her."

"What's your name?" said Rakkim.

"Cameron." The kid held out his hand. "That's another ten dollars."

Rakkim knocked the hand aside. "I'll give you a hundred for useful information." He keyed up the most recent photograph of

Safar Abdullah's daughter on his cell. Taken from a five-year-old mug shot, it was the best that Colarusso's contact in personnel had been able to come up with.

Cameron gaped at the image, finally nodded. "Give me the money." He hesitated. "Make me a copy too."

Rakkim handed him five twenties. The cell spit out a print and he handed that over too.

Cameron handled the photo as if it were a snowflake. "She was beautiful. She . . . she don't look like this now."

"What apartment is she in?" Rakkim asked.

"She don't live here anymore. Her name ain't Francine or Felicity or Fatima, either. It's *Fancy*. Fancy Andrews."

"She's not in any trouble," said Sarah. "We just want to talk to her about her father."

"She ain't got no father. Ain't got no family at all."

"I'm Sarah, by the way." She shook his hand. "It's a pleasure to meet you, Cameron."

The kid looked at Rakkim. "What about you, mister? Is it a pleasure for you, too?"

"Where did Fancy move?" asked Sarah. "She wouldn't have left without telling you."

"I used to run errands for her sometimes." Cameron's eyes shifted between Sarah and Rakkim, settled on Sarah. "She gets migraines . . . and the muscleheads used to bother her. I tried to let her know when they were coming, but . . ."

"The muscleheads didn't bother you?" said Rakkim.

"I'm too fast." Cameron's face fell. "And I ain't got nothing they want."

"It was good she had you as a friend," said Rakkim.

"If I was bigger, I wouldn't have let them bother her," said Cameron, eyes flashing. "She said it was no big deal. Said she just hated to give it away for free. Like that was supposed to make me feel better."

Sarah put her hand on his shoulder, but he jerked away. "We need to find her."

"Get out of here, mister," said Cameron. "*Now.*"

Rakkim walked down to the sidewalk. He had already seen the muscleheads.

"Go *on*, mister. I don't give a shit about you, but I don't want them to get her."

"Rakkim?" said Sarah.

Three of the muscleheads loped toward him now, but one held back, taking his time. That would be the leader. The eager ones were big boys in their early twenties, clean-shaven and well-fed, but the leader was taut as a bowstring. They wore baggy silk pantaloons and tank tops that flaunted their biceps, combat boots buffed to a high shine, and army K-bar knives strapped to their belts. Their heads were shaved except for a floppy topknot. Ghetto esprit. The biggest one had a crudely drawn Virgin of Guadalupe tattooed on the side of his neck. They spread out around him. Too close. They should have given themselves more room.

The leader walked up, smiled at Sarah, and doffed a nonexistent hat. "Did you good Muslim folk take the wrong exit off the freeway?"

"They're just leaving, Zeke," said Cameron.

Zeke put a forefinger to his lips, shushed him. "Children should be seen and not heard. Haven't you learned nothing?" Zeke adjusted his nuts as he grinned at Sarah. "You folks probably forgot to pay the toll on your way in. Ignorance of the law, though . . ." He looked at Rakkim, pointed at the Ford parked at the curb. "That your car, Mohammad?"

"You like it?" Rakkim said brightly.

Zeke wiggled his fingers. "Keys. Wallet. You can walk. The bitch stays."

"Can I stay too?" said Rakkim. "You seem like a fun guy."

Zeke didn't like that answer. It didn't fit his experience, but before he could caution his mates, the other three muscleheads drew their K-bars, blades catching the light. Zeke took a truncheon out of his pocket, one of the three-pounders exclusive to police riot squads. Instant coma. Must be quite a story to how it ended up with him.

"Uh-uh," said Rakkim. "I'm in trouble now."

Zeke lightly tapped the truncheon into the palm of his hand. He started to warn the others, but it was too late.

The three muscleheads rushed Rakkim. It was better to stagger a group attack so as not to get in each other's way, but they had spent too long picking off easy prey.

Rakkim grabbed the knife hand of the one on his left, twisted hard. Drove the edge of his left hand full force into the windpipe of another one. Side-kicked the third's knee out as the man lunged at him. Without looking, Rakkim dodged the truncheon whizzing past his head. Zeke was backpedaling, but the miss had thrown him slightly off-balance, and Rakkim easily stepped into him, slammed the heel of his right hand into his nose, sent him sprawling. Within three seconds they were scattered across the sidewalk.

The one with the tattoo of the Virgin sat upright, cradling his broken wrist and cursing. The second man howled in pain, his leg bent at a wrong angle. The third was stretched out, arms and legs flailing as he gasped for breath. His windpipe was crushed, face bright red as his larynx swelled shut. Soon his face would be purple. Then black. Zeke was already on his feet, moving nimbly, ignoring the blood that gushed from his broken nose and onto his shirt. He picked up the truncheon from where it had fallen.

"Rakkim?" Sarah sounded stunned. "That man . . . that man can't breathe."

Rakkim was aware of Cameron coming down the steps and standing behind him.

Zeke spit blood, watched as the man's spasms slowly subsided. "You know, Mohammad, we was just joking with you."

Rakkim held out his hand. "I hope there's no hard feelings."

Zeke gripped the truncheon, but didn't take the offer.

The musclehead with the broken wrist used his good hand to help up the one with the ruined knee. They walked as though they were in a three-legged race, moaning with every step. They gave Rakkim plenty of room.

"Why don't you stick around?" said Zeke. "I got some more friends I'd like you to meet. We'll be coming back as soon as we organize a proper funeral for Benny."

Rakkim watched them go. Benny was quiet now, fingernails clawing at the pavement.

"Who *are* you, mister?" asked Cameron.

"You can't stay here," said Rakkim.

"I got a million hiding places. I'm not afraid."

"Do you have any idea where Fancy moved to?" said Sarah.

Rakkim glanced over at her. She had beaten him to it.

The kid stared at the dead musclehead. "Benny held me once when they made Fancy pay the toll. He held me by the hair and made me watch." He looked up at Rakkim. "I'd like to learn how you broke his throat. Could you teach me?"

"We haven't got that kind of time."

"Sure . . . I understand." Cameron turned to Sarah. "Last June, Fancy came by and brought me to her new place. She said it was for my birthday, but my birthday is sometime in May." He looked over at Rakkim. "I don't know exactly where she lives. It was night and she was driving all over the place picking up stuff. Said it was her girlfriend's car. Her girlfriend was nice. She gave me a pair of shoes one of her kids had outgrown."

"Give us a landmark," said Rakkim.

"You ever hear of Disneyland?"

"Old amusement park, right?" said Rakkim.

"Probably the most important *theme* park in history," said

Sarah. "There was a whole Disney empire. Films, television, cartoons, you name it."

"I couldn't find Fancy's apartment again if you paid me," said Cameron, "but you could see Disneyland from her back window. What's left of it, anyway. There's a mountain . . ."

"Space Mountain?" said Sarah.

"I don't know . . . it had snow on it. Not real snow, of course—"

"The Matterhorn," said Sarah. "Space Mountain was an inside ride. I always get them confused."

"Whatever you say," said Cameron. "That's all I know. Her apartment was on the second floor and I could see the snow."

Rakkim handed him another couple hundred dollars. "After we leave, you're going to be tempted to go through Benny's pockets. Resist that temptation. You'll tell yourself that if you don't take his money or his cell, somebody else will. Don't do it. *Let* somebody else steal from the dead. Not you."

The kid stared at him.

"When we find Fancy, do you want us to give her a message from you?" asked Sarah.

"Yeah." The kid blinked, looked away. "Tell her to come get me. Tell her to stand on the steps of Saint Xavier at noon, and I'll see her. Tell her I'll be watching for her every day."

CHAPTER 42

Before afternoon prayers

Breaking news. Terrorism by the bay.

Rakkim put down his lamb kebab as the video crawl flashed over the napkin dispenser. Images of shattered metal and whipping pylons. Rakkim slid across the red Naugahyde seat of his booth at

Pious Sam's Pious Eats, getting closer to the screen. A section of the General Masood Bridge across San Francisco Bay had collapsed at the height of afternoon rush hour. Hundreds dead. The camera zoomed in on bodies floating in the water, the current sending overturned cars bouncing against the support pillars. The mayor of the city came on camera, the wind whipping his robe and turban as he demanded that Redbeard answer for the failure of State Security to prevent the attack. Behind him, women in black burkas, impenetrable behind their eye slits, were beating large, flat stones together in the light rain, wailing in rage and sorrow.

Sarah had barely glanced at the screen.

Rakkim pointed at the video. "You see this?"

Sarah nodded. "Another bridge collapse blamed on terrorists. The usual excuse for years of official neglect."

"No, *this* time, instead of railing against the godless infidels for doing the deed, they're blaming State Security for allowing it to happen."

"That's Mayor Miyoki. He's always been an enemy of Redbeard."

"Has he ever criticized Redbeard *by name*?"

"Miyoki's up for reelection. It's San Francisco. Sharia City. They behead homosexuals at the Civic Center every week. Redbeard represents everything Miyoki hates."

Rakkim wasn't convinced. Miyoki's denunciation seemed like another manifestation of Redbeard's declining political power. "What's wrong? You haven't touched your food."

Sarah pushed aside her plate. "Did you have to kill him?"

"No. I could have let the musclehead debone me. Maybe Zeke would have given him seconds on you as a reward."

"I'm *grateful*, don't get me wrong. I knew what they would have done to us, but you didn't kill the other two. You just . . . broke their bones, so they couldn't hurt us."

Rakkim pretended to watch the video crawl. "It was easier."

"What does *that* mean?"

"It means things were happening fast. It means the training took over and I let it."

"But, if you had time . . . you wouldn't have killed him? Right?"

Rakkim knew where she was going. She had seen how fast he was an hour ago; she had seen the Fedayeen in him and it scared her. It scared him sometimes too. Something else was behind her questions. Anthony Jr. had talked to her at the skating rink. Probably told her how Rakkim had cut him and his boyos in the alley, how Rakkim had danced around them that night, stabbing them a hundred times, but never deep enough to do permanent damage. Anthony Jr. probably told her about his scars. Offered to show them to her sometime. Rakkim hoped Sarah had seen through the kid's bravado, that she understood what had really happened. Speed was easy. Self-control was the hard part.

Rakkim took her hand. "I'm not like the assassin, if that's what you're worried about."

"I just think . . . I think it must be hard not to enjoy something you're so good at."

Rakkim released her. "I'm not going to apologize."

"That's not what I'm asking." Sarah reached for him. "You sure you don't want to call Colarusso for help finding Fancy?"

"I've already put him at risk. I'm not going to make it worse."

"So we call Colarusso from a data farm. Totally anonymous—"

"A call from a data farm only means that someone is contacting Colarusso who wants to hide their identity. What do you think that tells anyone monitoring him?" Rakkim sat back in the booth. Lowered his voice. "Anthony is the only one who knows we're here. Any contact with him jeopardizes that. I've got someone down here we can use."

Sarah pulled her hand back.

Rakkim watched the traffic flow past on the freeway in the distance. They had driven inland after leaving Long Beach, sight-seeing, trying to decide what to do next. Sarah noted how many Catholic churches there were, many of them even with crosses on top, something strictly forbidden in the capital. The pollution was worse here than along the coast. Last summer over eighteen thousand people had died of acute respiratory distress during a three-week thermal inversion. The news had never been reported. Not in any of the local or national media. Colarusso had told Rakkim at the skating rink, said the cops all had oxygen units in their rigs. The bill for their lunch flashed on the video crawl. Rakkim fed money into the slot. Pressed *No change required.*

"We passed a mosque about a mile back," said Sarah. "I want to check the recipe site and see if my mother left a message for me. Their Internet kiosk will have the right filters."

"You didn't have any kind of a schedule worked out with her?"

Sarah shook her head. A truck drove past loaded with watermelons, big green ones with black stripes. "Contact was always at irregular intervals."

"She's careful. That's good."

Sarah stared out the window. "I want to meet her. I want to see her, talk to her . . . but, at the same time, I almost wish she had never contacted me." Sarah looked at Rakkim. "I wish we were back at the motel."

"Say the word."

Sarah shook her head. "Don't tempt me."

CHAPTER 43

After noon prayers

"You missed lunch, Sister," said Sister Elena, the novice, a little out of breath.

"I didn't want to be tempted by Sister Gloria's strawberry-rhubarb pie." Katherine had wanted to be alone. The lie was a venal sin, easily expiated.

"Mother Superior would like to see you."

Katherine stayed where she was. Sister Elena might be fooled by the lie, but Bernadette would not be denied Katherine's presence. The wind whipped her cassock, sent it billowing around her, but she made no attempt to push down her skirts. Angelina had been right about this new head of the Black Robes. Ibn Azziz was more than dangerous. He was toxic. "I had bad dreams last night," she said as tendrils of black smoke rose over the distant hills. "I awoke to find them true." She saw Sister Elena tremble, an earnest nun in her early twenties, soft and gentle as a white-breasted thrush. Katherine wondered what the girl would do when the conflagration reached her, wondered what Sarah would do in similar circumstances. They were about the same age. Elena had been left at the convent by her mother, a Muslim teenager who had taken refuge with the nuns during her pregnancy, then afterward slipped away to some city where she could get lost. Sarah . . . she had been barely five years old when Katherine had abandoned her.

"Is that a forest fire?" Sister Elena squinted at the smoke. "This isn't the season."

"It's Newcastle."

The convent was a former hunting lodge on the edge of a national forest in Central California. The closest town was Newcastle, a logging community fifty miles and a full-day journey over the winding, rutted roads. A town too busy for politics, with Muslims and Christians living together. The nuns had always been tolerated on their regular shopping excursions, but Katherine monitored the police band, knowing that trouble would come through Newcastle first. Katherine had noted a change last week, the national religious TV channels all rage and paranoia.

"Sister?" Sister Elena put her hand on Katherine. "We shouldn't keep Mother waiting."

The whole way back, Sister Elena kept glancing behind her at the wisps of smoke, trying not to look, stumbling once in her conflicting desires. She would probably confess her looking back as a weakness and receive her penance gratefully. After all, had not Lot's wife been turned into a pillar of salt for looking back at God's rain of fire and brimstone onto the cities of Sodom and Gomorrah?

A terrible story—Katherine had thought so the first time she'd heard it, to be punished for simple curiosity. She had been a Catholic then, and when she'd voiced her disapproval, the nun at Christ the King Elementary had said the destruction of Lot's wife was not because of her curiosity, but her *disobedience*, since God's angel had expressly forbidden such an action. Katherine responded that the angel was a fool to think someone would not want to see such a sight, and that Lot's wife was brave and Lot a coward. Katherine said *she* would have looked, even if she *was* turned into a stupid pillar of salt. It was the first of many beatings she'd endured at Christ the King. Now when she remembered the incident, she didn't think about the beatings, but rather the idea of a great city destroyed in an instant by a rain of fire, and she contemplated the possibility that all of human history was a dance in which God and the devil changed places back and forth.

Sister Elena was panting as they climbed the stairs to Mother Superior's office on the third floor of the nunnery. Too much time on the computer, not enough time outdoors. Katherine wasn't winded at all. She was fifty now, long-legged and fit. The nunnery was largely self-sufficient, and she put as much time in the fields and animal pens as any of them, and while the nuns prayed for hours every day, Katherine walked the surrounding paths and hills. Her hair was still dark, her slim breasts still high . . . high enough, and there were nights when she tossed in her hard bed, caught between sleep and waking, nights when she thought of her husband, nights, God forgive her, when she thought of his brother, Redbeard.

Sister Elena's knock on Mother's door was hesitant at first, then immediately harder, as though reproaching herself for her fear, and Katherine noticed the girl's red, raw knuckles. Elena was Mother Superior's favorite, and as such she was ordered to do twice as much as any of the other novices, scrubbing the stone steps daily, performing the most menial and laborious kitchen duties without complaint.

"Enter," barked Mother from inside.

"Thank you, dear," Katherine said to Sister Elena, letting herself in. She closed the door behind her. "You work that girl too damn hard, Bernadette."

"Good afternoon to you too, Kate." Mother was a grim, wizened nun with strands of white hair curling free of her headpiece, looking much older than her age.

For the last twenty years, ever since her husband had been assassinated, Katherine had been sheltered at the convent. If, at any time in those twenty years, the authorities had discovered her presence, everyone in the nunnery would have been executed, their bodies mutilated, and the nunnery itself burned to the dirt. Not once in that time, even on the two occasions when Redbeard's agents had searched the nunnery, had Katherine feared that she would be turned over. The last time—it was at least ten years ago—she had emerged from her hiding spot within the walls of the rectory with a shawl that she had knitted in the dark. Bernadette still wore it some winter evenings when they watched television together in the office, just the two of them. Bernadette, who ate almost nothing, enjoyed cooking shows, while Katherine cared only for news. They took turns.

"I just got word from Beijing," said Bernadette, coming out

from behind her desk and sitting carefully on a swaybacked sofa. Tufts of stuffing oozed out the sides in spite of the constant restitching. The office was small, the only ornamentation a large crucifix and a photograph of Pope John Paul II, the pope in office when Bernadette had entered the order. "The sisters finished their clinical work in the commuter district. Their dosimeters recorded nothing."

"Well, so much for Beijing, and so much for Shanghai. After all these years, I think we'll have to put our faith in Sarah now." Katherine smiled. "And God, of course."

Bernadette frowned. She had never enjoyed levity when it came to religion. They were cousins, and though Bernadette was twelve years older, they had always been close. When Katherine had converted to Islam and married James Dougan, all contact had ceased. Even so, when it came time to hide, Katherine had had no doubt where she would run. No doubt that she would be taken in.

"It's a heavy burden to lay on someone so young," said Bernadette.

"I waited twenty years to contact her," snapped Katherine. "Do you think I would have put her at risk if I had any other options?"

Bernadette's gaze hardened. "You should have thought of that before you converted to that barbarous faith. I never liked that husband of yours. Too handsome, if you ask me. Too ambitious."

"The faith is not the problem, Bernadette. The problem is the faithful."

Bernadette looked away. It was an old argument.

Twenty years. *Why did you leave me?* That was the first thing Sarah had tapped out, after she was convinced it really was her mother contacting her.

Sarah had been hospitalized when her father was assassinated, curled up in the ICU with acute pneumonia. Katherine was dozing in a chair beside her daughter's oxygen tent when

Redbeard called, his voice weak, called to tell her James was dead, saying a couple of his best men were on their way to the hospital.

Why did you leave me? A question without an answer. None that would satisfy Sarah. None that would satisfy Katherine either.

The night before his murder, James had held her close and whispered that if anything happened to him, *anything*, no matter how benign it seemed, she was to take Sarah and go into hiding. He had pressed a strand of prayer beads into her palm, said the plain wooden beads contained coded information, the keys to a secret more important than his life. The information had to be protected at all costs.

That morning in the hospital, Katherine had been forced to choose between an unknown secret and the daughter she loved. Still in shock from the news, and all too aware of her own adulterous fantasies, she had imagined that Redbeard was behind James's murder. That it was Redbeard that James was afraid of. With only minutes to decide, she had chosen to leave Sarah behind. The good wife. The bad mother.

"We missed you at lunch," said Bernadette. "There was lentil soup."

Katherine fingered her prayer beads. Even with her suspicions, she couldn't have left Sarah if Angelina hadn't promised to look after her until Katherine returned. Twenty years and she still hadn't returned. After the prayer beads had finally yielded their secrets, Katherine knew that Redbeard had been innocent . . . as innocent as she. The knowledge had come too late. Her flight had convinced the authorities that *she* had betrayed her husband and made her a marked woman.

"You heard about the difficulties in Newcastle?" said Bernadette.

"Early this morning I walked to the very top of the hill and I just knew something was wrong. All the stars in the sky and not one of them looked right to me." Katherine worked her prayer beads. She was no longer Muslim, but the beads comforted her. "Just before noon I heard calls to the Newcastle police. Accusations that the local truck dealer, a Catholic, had gotten his corneal transplants from the eyes of healthy Muslim children. A mob was forming outside the dealership, egged on by women from the most conservative mosque." Katherine looked at her cousin. "My instincts have always been acute, you know that. Not that it's done me much good. I warned James not to go to Chicago that morning. I begged him to stay with me in the hospital until Sarah was better, but he just kissed me and hurried off, as though he was impatient to die." She turned away, jaw firm. Even after all these years, she was still angry with him.

"The fire will burn itself out," said Bernadette. "The madness will pass."

Katherine took her cousin's hand, felt her cool, dry skin, light as a bird's wing. "I'm going away. With my glasses and dental appliance, I won't be recognized. I doubt if anyone is even looking for me anymore. I'm ancient history, now."

"I won't hear of it." Bernadette squeezed Katherine's hand. "You're safe here."

Katherine shook her head. "None of us are safe anywhere."

"'The Lord is my shepherd,'" recited Bernadette. "It's not just words, Kate. It's the word of God. It's His promise to us."

Katherine kissed her cousin on each cheek. "I love you, Bernadette."

Bernadette's eyes glistened. "The world is a dark wood full of wolves . . . every time you leave the convent, I light candles for your safe return."

Katherine had grown restless the last few years, taking ever more trips. Excursions to Sacramento and New Medina and Bakersfield. A secret visit to Tahoe in the Nevada Free State, where she had actually gone for a swim! Never to Seattle, though. She had been tempted to search out Sarah, observe her at a distance . . . but she never did. The risk was too great. Or her fear was. The best trip had been a glorious visit to Los Angeles three years ago with Bernadette. The sound of church bells had been everywhere.

"What's so funny?" said Bernadette.

"I was remembering our trip to Hollywood, and the way you put your hands into the imprints of movie stars. You kept choosing the most brazen starlets. Wanton women playing wanton roles. I kept wondering what sinful thoughts you were thinking."

Bernadette blushed. "Perhaps I was praying for their immortal souls."

"You were having *fun*, Bernadette. You were like a schoolgirl."

Bernadette looked away. The skin under her eyes was almost transparent. "It *was* fun."

Katherine patted Bernadette's hand. "I'm leaving tomorrow. There's work to be done, and I can't leave it all to Sarah."

A knock and the door was thrown open. Sister Elena stood there, without being invited in. "Men! There are two men at the gate." She was flustered. "They walked right in—"

Katherine and Bernadette were already on their feet.

"*Hide*," Bernadette said to Katherine.

"Too late for that." Katherine started for the door. "I'll make it clear that you had no idea who I was. I'll tell them I fooled you with my devilry. Perhaps . . . perhaps I can convince them." She embraced Bernadette.

Bernadette held her tightly while they heard footsteps coming up the stairs.

"Have no fear, Bernadette. Sarah will do what we haven't been able to." Katherine kissed her on the cheek, turned to face those who had finally found her.

There were not two men standing in the doorway. It was a man and a boy. A short, hairy man and a scrawny, sullen boy, both of them filthy with road dust.

"My name is Spider, and this is my son Elroy," said the man, smiling so broadly his face threatened to split. "You're Katherine Dougan and I'm a genius." He clasped his hands together with delight. "It's a pleasure to meet you. We're going to change the world."

CHAPTER 44

Before sunset prayers

Rakkim nodded at the *Welcome to Yorba Linda* sign as they drove past. "Isn't this where that old-time president was born?"

"I'm impressed," said Sarah. "Richard Milhous Nixon, thirty-seventh president of the United States. Born January ninth, 1913; Yorba Linda, California."

"Is he one of them carved into that mountain in South Dakota?"

"No. No."

He could tell from her expression that she didn't like being reminded of the mountain. *Mount Rushmore*, that was it. Blowing up the four faces on the mountain had been one of the first projects of the new Muslim republic. Redbeard had argued against it as a waste of time and money, but the Black Robes had insisted, calling it idolatry, and honoring kaffirs from a nation that no longer existed. In the end, Redbeard had deferred, doubtless using his acquiescence to extract concessions for his own goals. The destruction of the four faces had proven to be more trouble than anticipated, the sheer size of the monument daunting to even massive quantities of explosive. After six months of demolition, the faces still remained partially intact, grotesqueries in the wilderness.

There had been no message from Sarah's mother on the good-wife recipe site. Just advice from devout wives on preparing their favorite dishes. Sarah had been inside the mosque for an hour, had spent most of the time praying, while Rakkim waited in the car. In spite of her disappointment, she seemed . . . peaceful when she came out. Ready.

Sarah checked the GPS. "Have you ever been to Sergeant Pernell's house before?"

"Not since he moved down here. He was one of my hand-to-hand-combat instructors at the academy. We served briefly together when he rotated into one of the battle units a year later. The academy doesn't like to keep instructors out of the field too long, and the instructors get bored with classwork." Rakkim glanced up as a jet helicopter arced overhead, another one of the red corporate choppers. He was never going to get used to helicopters over the city. "We lost touch when I went into shadow warriors. Pernell's a good man. Bitter, but who can blame him?"

"What do you mean?"

"He was wounded on an op in New Guinea. Land mine. Lost his legs—"

"Fedayeen have never been sent to New Guinea."

"Tell that to Pernell. You'll probably learn a few new words." The GPS chirped, *Right turn at next intersection.* "His legs are gone and one of his arms was amputated above the elbow, but he got the best prosthetics available. Russian plastics. Chinese biochips. He can dress himself, run marathons, handle a knife better than any civilian. He's got four wives and he keeps them all busy. He just can't do field work anymore. Not by a long shot."

"That's why he's bitter?"

Rakkim shrugged. "Who wouldn't be?"

"Do *you* miss it?"

"Pernell tried teaching at the academy again," said Rakkim, not answering. "He lasted a year before he pissed off everyone in the chain of command. Pernell was never a very astute barracks politician, and his injuries just made it worse. He was awarded an honorable discharge and mustered out with full retirement pay. The day before he moved to Yorba Linda, he stopped by the Blue Moon. Knocked out two of my bouncers just on general principles before I could take him into the office. I'd never seen him drink anything stronger than khat infusion, but that night we finished off a bottle of Polish vodka while we solved the problems of the world. I haven't seen him since."

They passed a mosque, a grand one in the traditional style, the dome covered with tiny lapis lazuli chips. Yorba Linda was a bastion of devout Islam, a small city of scrubbed storefronts and one-acre housing lots, home to doctors and lawyers and successful businessmen. With the highest birth rate in California, its madrassas overflowed with serious students.

"What makes you think your friend is going to be able to help us find Fatima Abdullah?" said Sarah.

"I didn't say he was my friend." *Turn right at the stop sign.* "Pernell is connected with the local cops. He trains SWAT teams in advanced tactics, gives them a heads-up on any exotic weaponry. He'll be able to make inquiries about her where we can't."

"You trust him?"

"He's Fedayeen."

A few minutes later, after buzzing the house, they drove up and found Pernell waiting for them in the double doorway, his four wives behind him. One of the wives was burping a baby. All four were dressed in pale yellow hajibs and chadors, only the perfect ovals of their faces visible. Pernell was a tall, weathered man in his midforties, with short, dark hair, a full beard, and a cheek full of khat. Loose white slacks and a long-sleeved shirt on a warm day. He embraced Rakkim, kissed him on both cheeks, pounded him on the back with his good hand. "By the pope's saggy tits, I *missed* you."

"The only man in the world with a dozen kids who's lonely," said Rakkim.

"*Fourteen* kids. Two new sons hung like Arabians." Pernell eyed Sarah. "Who's this?"

"Sarah, may I present Jack Pernell. Jack this is Sarah, the woman I intend to marry."

Pernell sized Sarah up as though he were considering a bid. "Pleasure." He nodded, but did not touch her. "I'll let my wives show you the house." He grabbed Rakkim by the neck, steered him away. "Let's go out back. The last thing I want to hear is females jabbering on about episiotomies and migraines and the best way to cook a chicken."

Rakkim glanced over his shoulder at Sarah as Pernell led him away.

They walked around to the rear of the house, which was much larger than it appeared from the road. There were four wings, one for each of the wives and her children; the central structure was probably where Pernell held court. They crossed an expanse of manicured lawn and stood beside the Olympic-size swimming pool. A single white, inflatable swan floated across the surface in the sunlight. Sounds of children came from the house, shouts and cries, laughter too, but there was no sign of their presence on the grounds. No toys, no bicycles, no swing set. Just the swan. Pernell ran a tight crew. Children were the responsibility of the women. Or the madrassa. The older boys would receive specialized instruction from him, but it would be done far away from the house.

"You look good," said Rakkim.

"Sure, I do." Pernell led the way around the perimeter of his acre, double-timing it. "The knee servos in my legs are burning out and the replacement parts are back-ordered. I had a nasty infection that laid me up for a week. Just got out of the hospital. Other than that, I'm cocked and locked." He glanced at Rakkim. One of his eyes was milky and unhealthy looking. "What are you doing here? Come to ask old sarge to be your best man?"

"I need some help."

"I could have told you that years ago." Pernell spat khat juice into the grass. "You making major your first hitch shows just how fucked-up the Fedayeen is. You retiring after your first hitch, that shows just how fucked-up *you* are." Pernell shook his head. "Such a waste. The talent that Allah gave you . . . and you toss it away." He shrugged. "Inshallah."

"Nice place you got here. This consulting business of yours must be doing well."

Pernell grabbed an orange from one of his trees, tossed it over to Rakkim, barely breaking stride. "*Cops.* They think carrying a gun makes them a warrior, and the answer to every situation is a flash grenade. I do what I can. These SWAT hotshots think they know it all and I'm just a creaky has-been. It usually takes me ten whole minutes to straighten them out. Even faster if I have to break somebody's jaw, but the brass don't like me to do that. It's not real work, but it puts food on the table."

Rakkim peeled the orange, put the peels in his pocket.

Pernell glanced at him, kept walking. "You look fucked out. That little gal must be putting you through your paces."

Rakkim fed a slice of orange into his mouth.

A grasshopper jumped in front of Pernell, and he nailed it with a wad of khat juice. "You're a damn fool to wait until now to start settling down. You should have two or three wives at least by now. Don't go in for any of that one-wife foolishness. You been around Catholics too much, if you think that way."

The orange was sweet and juicy. "One at a time is plenty."

"That's a mistake. One wife thinks she owns you. You have two or three or four, they all know they can be replaced with a quick *I divorce thee.* Three times and it's back on the street. Good Muslim woman knows that, knows her only hope is to keep the man of the house pleased. Allah allowed us four wives for a reason."

"Thanks for the advice."

"Not that you'll take it. You were always a hardhead. That's okay, you'll find out. That little gal of yours looks fun, but she's got brains. I could see that just from the way she stood. Woman with brains, that's just *asking* for trouble."

Rakkim chewed the last of the orange, juice running down his chin. "I like trouble."

"Come talk to me in a few years and tell me if you still like it." Pernell raked a hand through his beard. They walked in silence until they made it back to the swimming pool. Pernell eased himself into a deck chair, the tiny scars across his face flaring. "I could use a partner in the consulting business. I'm making good money, but with the right partner I could expand. PDs fall all over themselves for ex-Fedayeen."

Rakkim sat beside him.

"Time for you to sell that den of iniquity of yours and go into an honest trade."

Rakkim watched the inflatable swan drift across the pool. "Where's the fun in that?"

"There's no fun in anything," Pernell said softly. He bucked up as two of his wives and Sarah came out of the back door carrying cups and tea and pastries. He waited as the wives set down the refreshments, poured tea for the both of them, then backed away, bowing. Sarah stayed. Pernell dropped five sugar cubes into his teacup. "I told Rakkim he should plan on marrying a quartet. He seems to think you're as much as he could handle."

"I *am* as much as he can handle."

Pernell banged the spoon against the cup as he stirred. "Don't be spreading that modern slop around my wives." His smile didn't even attempt to be convincing. "I'm serious."

"A husband like you makes women happy to be part of a quartet. It means they each only have to spend a fourth of their time pretending." Sarah smiled at Pernell. "*I'm* serious."

Pernell looked at Rakkim. "Yeah, you're going to have trouble with this one."

Rakkim watched Sarah as she walked back to the house. "I'm counting on it."

Pernell noisily sipped his tea. "What kind of help do you need?"

"I'm looking for a rent-wife. Short-termer—"

Pernell cackled.

"Not for *me*. Her name is Fatima Abdullah. Last aka was Fancy Andrews." Rakkim showed him her picture on his phone, printed out a copy for him. "This mug shot is five years old. She was busted in Little Vatican for stealing a customer's wallet. Had another bust the year before for heroin possession."

"Little Vatican is full of violators. What do you expect, though? *Catholics*."

"I was hoping one of your contacts in Vice could give me a lead on where to find her."

Pernell pushed a lip out at the photo. "Five *years* since her last bust? Five weeks is a long time living that life. She could be anywhere. She could be dead."

"I know." Rakkim leaned forward. "All charges were dropped on that last one. Administrative adjudication. Which means she paid the arresting officer off, one way or the other. I'm thinking she might have been picked up a few times since then and the paperwork never got filed."

"That's been known to happen from time to time." Pernell sipped his tea. "What do you want with her?"

"Her father is looking for her." The lie came easily. Smoothly. "He's dying and no longer cares about the shame she's brought to the family. I owe him a favor."

"So there's no money in it?"

"I'm happy to pay you for your time and expertise."

"Like you'd pay a rent-wife?"

"I don't want to fight, Jack. I just want to find the girl."

Pernell clapped him on the shoulder. Hard. "I haven't had a good fight in a long time. I'm probably outclassed trying to pick one with you."

"I know better. You're the man who taught me how to fight dirty."

"I'm the man who taught you there's no such thing as dirty fighting. There's just fighting."

They shared a smile in recognition of the truth. The only truth.

"You weren't the best recruit I had," said Pernell, staring at the swimming pool. "There were a couple better. Hector Cinque . . . *he* had the fastest hands I ever saw. He's dead now. Shot through the throat five years ago during an extraction outside of Mombasa."

"I heard the diplomat they pulled in didn't even have anything useful."

Pernell shook his head. "I didn't know that. Typical front-office op. Emir Zingarelli . . . you ever work with him? No? He was faster than you too. Not as fast as Cinque, but *fast*." A mosquito buzzed around Pernell, landed on his prosthetic hand. "Zingarelli's dead too. Helicopter went down off the coast of Texas. Might have been a peckerwood missile . . . might have been some asshole in maintenance didn't tighten the right bolt." The mosquito buzzed away and Rakkim pinched it between his thumb and forefinger. "Cinque and Zingarelli both dead, and here we sit, a couple of heroes baking our brains in the sun. Funny, isn't it?"

Rakkim watched him.

"There were times these last few years I hated all of you with your two good arms and two good legs. All of you who still had missions ahead of you. Sometimes . . . sometimes I wish I hadn't had body armor on when I stepped on that land mine. That titanium weave saved my life." Pernell wiped his milky eye. It wasn't a tear. Pernell had probably never cried in his life. He waited for Rakkim to say something, finally nodded. "Thanks for not telling me how lucky I am. Thanks for not telling me Allah must have a plan for me."

"If Allah has a plan, He's not sharing it with us."

CHAPTER 45

After sunset prayers

"They used to call this the happiest place on earth," said Sarah as they circled a fallen Ferris wheel. Half the girders had been stripped away.

Rakkim pointed to a man with his painter overalls around his ankles, smoking a cigarette while his rent-wife bobbed away. "He'd probably say it *still* is."

Disneyland had been abandoned twenty years ago, much of its infrastructure looted, but plenty of the original park was still left behind, either too heavy to move or not worth selling for scrap. They walked over to the remains of the Matterhorn. Most of the fake mountain had been destroyed, but the snowcapped peak remained, shining in the moonlight, the brightest spot in the darkness.

Last night Pernell had checked the local vice squads until he found a detective who knew Fancy; he said she had come down a few pegs since working Little Vatican. Last he heard, she was renting it out at Disneyland with the rest of the fifteen-minute skeeges. Detective said she still gave a mean no-hands, but it was better if you closed your eyes. Pernell had offered the hospitality of his home to Rakkim and Sarah—they had eaten dinner together, but declined to spend the night. It had been late when they'd left Pernell's, too late to go to Disneyland. They had slept until almost afternoon, then walked the boardwalk. Sarah insisting on feeding the gulls. When they got back to the motel, they made love, but were distracted, too conscious of time.

They started out on Main Street in Disneyland, asked a rent-wife who had set up shop in an overturned streetcar if she knew Fancy. It cost $5 to be told no. They had been told no a lot as they crisscrossed the park. Businessmen in twos and threes wandered the deserted streets, swinging their briefcases while women called to them. Muslims and Catholics, white-collar and blue-collar and everyone in between. Knots of young toughs leaned against the buildings, but in spite of its isolation and lack of police presence, the park was relatively crime-free. The rent-wives paid the toughs to keep the peace, and the toughs didn't want to scare away business.

A rent-wife working under a splintered Mickey Mouse said Fancy used to catch tricks near Cinderella's castle. The castle was a busy spot, men sitting around watching basketball on their phones while they waited their turns. No Fancy though.

"I didn't like Pernell when I thought he could help us," said Sarah. "I like him even less now that his information may be useless."

Rakkim walked over to three toughs sprawled across a beached gondola. "Evening."

The biggest tough was a pale anvilhead wearing only overalls to show off his tattoos. He looked at Sarah. "She's too fine for this rat's nest. You'll put every skeege here out of business. I got a number you can call in Newport. Mucho upscale. Tell them Jimmy Boy sent you."

"Thanks anyway," said Rakkim. "We're looking for a wife named Fancy."

Jimmy Boy snickered. "Fancy ain't so fancy. Nothing like what's on your arm."

Fifty dollars later, Rakkim and Sarah were on their way to what was left of the Finding Nemo undersea adventure. He had taken the money from a separate pocket so as not to flash the extent of their cash, but he kept watch for tagalongs anyway.

Sarah spotted the Finding Nemo adventure first, noticing a massive epoxy starfish that someone had taken a torch to. The ride itself was housed inside a large, concrete blue-white shark. Disneyland patrons had evidently once walked through a series of turnstiles and into the shark's wide-open mouth. Although most of the teeth had been broken off, the shark itself seemed mostly intact. Light flickered from inside its red plastic eyes. Sarah started toward the mouth, but Rakkim put a hand on her shoulder.

"Let's see if there's a back door."

Sarah smiled. The two of them made a circuit of the shark, found a ramp coming out of the shark's tail, an exit obscured by sheets of rotting plywood that someone had leaned over the opening. She scooted inside before he had a chance to stop her. Slipped through the canted plywood without touching anything. Rakkim was right behind her, moving slowly, giving his eyes a chance to adjust to the darkness. They heard voices ahead, a woman's laugh echoing. Sarah stopped and he edged beside her.

A woman was bent over a large red terra-cotta crab, her hands braced against its outstretched claws. She wore a frilly, white blouse and a short skirt hiked up around her hips. A trim businessman in a green suit was right behind her, grinding away, his pants still belted. Candles flickered in nesting spots dug out of the wall, and their movements sent crazy shadows across the room. The businessman orgasmed in a series of gasping curses, and he slumped away from her. Still panting, he tossed the condom onto the floor, wiped his penis on her skirt, and shoved his penis back into his pants. The woman turned around, threw back her long, dark hair. Smiled in the dancing candlelight. It was Fancy. "Wow. That was so good. You really got me started, my husband."

"Uh-huh." The businessman ran a comb through his hair.

"Don't go yet." Fancy stroked his face, but he pulled away. "Another fifteen minutes. I've got ways to bring a man back to life."

The businessman slipped his comb back into his jacket. "I divorce thee. I divorce thee. I divorce thee." He stalked out the shark's mouth, kicked something out of his path.

Fancy wiped herself with a cloth, arranged her skirt. Scooped up the bills the businessman had left. She jerked suddenly, sensing them. "I haven't got any money."

"It's all right." Sarah stepped into the light. "We're not interested in money."

Fancy flinched as she saw Rakkim, but her attention quickly returned to Sarah. "Two fine young Muslims out for a walk on the wild side. I can handle that."

"No, that's not it," said Sarah.

"Don't be shy." Fancy licked her lips. Cat eyes and high cheekbones, a grace to her movements. She must have been beautiful before all the businessmen. "Unless you enjoy that."

"We're here to talk to you about your father," said Rakkim. "We're willing to pay for the conversation," he hurried as she stepped back, afraid she was about to run.

Sarah took her hand. "It's important, Fatima."

Fancy turned her head away. The candle flames bobbed. Scented candles. Coconut. "Please . . . please, don't call me that."

Sarah held on to her. "I'm Sarah. This is Rakkim. We need to talk about your father."

Fancy looked from one to the other. "Why?"

"We talked to Cameron," said Rakkim. "He said to tell you hi."

"Is he all right?" said Fancy.

"He'd like to visit with you and your girlfriend again," said Rakkim. "He said it was the best birthday he ever had."

"Jeri Lynn liked him too." Fancy sat on the crab, her shoulders drooping. "I should have gone back for him. Cameron doesn't have anyone to look after him."

"Something we all have in common." Sarah sat beside her. "I lost my parents when I was five. Rakkim was orphaned when he was nine."

Fancy stared at her, making sure. "I . . . I was seven." This close, even by candlelight, the face under her makeup was visible. Fancy was hollowed-out, sick, wasting away. "You never get over it, do you?"

"No." Rakkim and Sarah said it at the same time.

"I'd like some money," Fancy said quietly. "You said you'd pay. I don't think it's wrong to ask for money if I'm helping you. That's what I'm doing, isn't it?"

Rakkim pressed a wad of bills into her hand. Her eyes widened and he almost expected her to tell him it was too much, but she just tucked it away in her brassiere. As she did, he saw a perfectly circular scar at the base of her throat. Sarah saw it too. Tracheotomy scar. The addict's badge of courage. She must have OD'd one time too many and been brought back to life. Against her will, probably. He had seen enough men dying, men who had fought against him as he'd struggled to save them, content to slip away from this world, ready to take their chances in the next.

"Your father died right after he came back from China," said Sarah.

Fancy shrugged. "My mother and I . . . we met him at the airport. He was angry with us. We weren't supposed to know that he was arriving home. We saw right away that he was sick. He said he had eaten some bad food on the plane, kaffir food, but I could tell he was lying. I could always tell." She looked at Sarah. "What do you care about all this for?"

"I'm doing historical research on that period. The years prior to the takeover. Prior to the Zionist attack."

"What does that have to do with my father? He was already dead by then."

"I'm just doing background. Your father—"

"It must be nice to be a history teacher." Fancy played with her hair. "I used to want to be a teacher. An elementary-school teacher. I always loved kids." She rolled her hair back and forth between her right thumb and forefinger. "I can't have 'em."

"I'm sorry," said Sarah.

"It's okay. I probably wouldn't have been a good mother anyway." Fancy looked at Rakkim. "*You're* no historian."

Rakkim smiled.

Fancy didn't return the smile. "I know men. I can tell things about them before they even open their mouth. Just from their shoes. Or their hands. Or their eyes. Their eyes most of all." She shook her head. "I can't tell anything about you, though." She glanced at Sarah. "Can *you?*"

"We grew up together," said Sarah. "I know him."

Fancy watched Rakkim. "I hope so."

"When your father came back from China, did he talk about his trip?" asked Sarah. "Places he had been, people he had met?"

"I just remember him throwing up a lot. And my mother crying."

"He was working on that big dam in China," said Sarah. "That must have been exciting for him."

"I haven't thought about those days in a long time. I was happy then. My father was strict, but he loved me very much." Fancy kept her eyes on Sarah. "He used to call me his jewel. He used to hold me in his arms and call me his jewel."

Rakkim let Sarah do the talking. Fancy had clearly had enough of men. The walls of the shark were covered with obscene graffiti, the floor littered with fast-food wrappers and worse. It smelled of urine and wet cardboard and dirty underwear. Fancy's scented candles were hopeless but endearing. Maybe she just thought it was good business.

"The house you used to live in was torn down many years ago," said Sarah. "I checked."

"No one would have lived in that house. It was bad luck. Every-one knew that when my father died. The *way* he died. So sick."

"You didn't take him to a doctor? We couldn't find any records."

"A doctor came to the house. One I had never seen before. He gave Father pills for the pain, told Mother to keep to the house. To tend him. A bad house. An unlucky house. Then Mother get-ting killed so soon afterwards . . ." Fancy shook her head.

Sarah looked at Rakkim. "Your mother died three years after your father. I'm sure it seemed too soon, but—"

"It was less than three months. I was there. Mother was driv-ing on the freeway and a tire blew and the car crashed. We were going to the desert to pray. She was driving fast. They said it was a miracle I survived. Mother went through the windshield, but I only had a tiny cut on my leg. They said it was God's will. They said He must have great plans for me." Her laugh echoed within the shark.

"What happened to you?" said Sarah. "Who took care of you?"

"A policeman took me home. I wanted to stay with Mother, but he said I had to get my things. It was very strange. Even now I wonder if I was dreaming." Fancy tugged at her blouse, and the scar at the base of her throat seemed filled with blood in the can-dlelight. "There were men at the house when we got there. They were loading all of our things into a moving van. The doctor who had taken care of my father was there. I don't know why, but he was there. The policeman let me put some clothes into a bag. The doctor seemed angry at him, but the policeman said he didn't care. Then he took me to my uncle's house. My uncle was a good Muslim. He was obligated to take me in, but I don't think he really wanted to." Fancy looked at Rakkim. "Talking about this is making me sad. I'd like some more money, please."

Rakkim paid her, watched as she tucked the bills away.

"Did Cameron look like he was getting enough to eat?" asked Fancy.

"You don't have *anything* from those days left?" said Sarah. "Not necessarily from your father. Maybe your mother kept a diary . . . or a calendar marking the days until he got home. His notebooks, his suitcases . . . something?"

Fancy shook her head. "The doctor had it taken all away. He emptied the house." Fancy's expression tightened. "Why are you *really* asking about my father? Don't give me that story about a history assignment either. I didn't believe that for a minute."

"We think your father was murdered," said Rakkim. "After what you told us about the car crash, I think your mother was probably murdered too."

"Are you a cop?" said Fancy. "I haven't had much luck with cops."

"When my father would go away, he would always bring me back something from his trip," said Sarah. "I treasured them—"

"Lucky you." The candles were bouncing, shadows racing around Fancy. "He didn't bring me anything."

"Not even a postcard?" said Sarah.

"What do you think you're going to do with all these questions, Miss History?" said Fancy. "You going to raise the dead? It doesn't matter how they died. All that matters is that they're dead and there's nothing you or anyone else can do about it."

"The doctor who treated your father, the one who emptied your house . . . did you ever see him again?" asked Rakkim.

"Listen to me. I don't *care*—" Fancy stopped as Rakkim held up a hand.

"Someone's outside." Rakkim was already blowing out the candles.

CHAPTER 46

Before late-night prayers

Jack-six. Eight-five. Ten-queen. Seeing the dealer had a six up, the Wise Old One stood pat on all three of his $1,000 bets.

The Texas soybean magnate in first position stared at his cards as though trying to read Egyptian hieroglyphs. His wife, a big blonde, jiggled her drink, the ice cubes rattling as she pondered her play. After careful consideration, the soybean magnate took a hit on thirteen, drew a face card and busted. The big blonde, with fifteen—*fifteen* with the dealer showing a six—demanded a card too, got a nine, and busted.

Anna, the dealer, turned up her hole card, a ten. Sixteen. Forced to take another card, she drew a five. For twenty-one. She raised an eyebrow at the Old One sympathetically as she swept the table of bets.

"What rotten luck," said the big blonde. She patted the Old One on the arm. "We'll get her this time, pappy."

The Old One fixed her with a cool stare. Touched by a Texan who called him pappy. A Texan with a diamond-crusted crucifix around her neck. A Texan who didn't know how to play twenty-one, taking the card that should have busted the dealer. How many ways was that an abomination? The only way it could be more of an insult would be if the woman were having her menstrual period.

Jack-nine. Jack-eight. Ten-ten. The dealer showed a four. The Old One split his tens, was given a queen for the first ten and a king for the second. Perfect. He now had two twenties, a nineteen, and an eighteen.

The big blonde took a hit on her five-eight, drew a jack, and busted.

The soybean magnate took a hit on his six-seven, drew a deuce for fifteen, and took another hit. The dealer actually made him repeat the request. "Hit me, damnit, you deaf?" said the pecker-wood.

Anna slid him a queen. Busted him. Turned over her hole card, a king, giving her fourteen. The next card was a seven, giving her twenty-one. Another sweep of the chips. Another slight smile for the Old One.

"Let's go, honey," said the soybean magnate. "This dealer's got it in for us."

Anna watched them leave. "I bet you hate to see *them* go."

The Old One laughed, put a $1,000 chip on all six spots on the table, cutting off any future players. Most of the time he enjoyed company at the table, enjoyed the mix of people who wafted through the casino. Different faces. Different histories. Catholics and moderate Muslims from Los Angeles and Chicago and Seattle, peckerwoods from Chattanooga and Atlanta and New Orleans. Businessmen from Tokyo and Beijing and Paris and London and Brazil. A buzz of languages and desires. The Old One was fluent in most of the languages. Most of the desires too. Today though, he preferred to play alone.

Anna dealt him six hands, dealt herself a ten upcard.

The Old One hit his seven-five. Hit his five-eight. Hit his six-five. Stuck his nine-jack. Stuck his ten-eight. Hit his nine-three.

Anna turned up a seven. She won two hands, paid him for his four winners. Her hands danced across the green felt, long and slim and perfectly manicured. Lovely hands. "You sure you don't want me to call the Texans back?" she murmured.

"We'll just have to carry on together," said the Old One.

A cocktail waitress came round, brought him his usual single-malt with one cube of ice.

The Old One tossed a $25 chip onto her tray, toasted Anna, and took a sip. Savored the sensation. He limited himself to one drink a day out of deference to his kidneys and liver. The transplants took more and more out of him, and his bouncebacks from his weekly transfusions were briefer and less intense as the years passed. He let a few drops of single-malt rest on his tongue. In spite of all the science in the world, there was an upper limit to human existence. Allah himself, the all-knowing and merciful, had decreed that all men must die. How else were they to enter Paradise?

Anna dealt another round of cards.

The Old One made his choices almost instinctively. Silently scratching his cards on the felt when he wanted a hit, placing his chip atop his cards when he was standing pat. After so many years he knew the most mathematically beneficial plays. He couldn't count cards with any certainty—the dealers used ten decks—but whether twenty-one was gambling or applied number theory was certainly debatable. Not that the Old One cared. The Holy Qur'an forbade gambling, but he was at peace with the game. At peace with his daily drink of alcohol. Even a pork chop crusted with garlic when the mood struck. Allah would excuse the occasional lapse. He smiled, thinking of what his first teacher would have said of such sophistry.

Anna smiled back at him, thinking his pleasure was directed at her. She paid off his blackjack, swept away the rest of his bets.

The Old One's disciples adhered to all aspects of the Qur'an, but the Old One did not feel so compelled. Had not Allah, the all-knowing, granted him a brain and appetite and free will? The

Old One followed the affirmations of the Book without fail. He had made his profession of faith, his shahada. He prayed five times a day. He abstained from food or drink during the daylight hours of the month of Ramadan. He gave away 10 percent of his wealth every year. He had made the hajj to Mecca, *and* Jerusalem.

Anna dealt another round. The cards swishing across the green felt like herons gliding across a lake.

The Old One took another sip of Scotch. The things the Qur'an *forbade* he chose to moderate. His dietary habits were not pristine. In his youth, he had often been clean-shaven. He had intellectual and business relations with unbelievers, had stayed in their homes, had dined with them. He gambled. He was embedded in the financial and banking industry, whose charging of interest was strictly forbidden. He lacked sobriety in the deepest sense, which is to say, he was often amused at the world and at himself.

Anna busted. Paid him off.

The Old One let his bets ride.

The cards slid across the table. Propelled by Anna's long fingers.

Perhaps the greatest difference between the Old One and traditional Muslims was his reliance on science and technology. Islam meant submission, but it was submission to *Allah*, the compassionate, that was required of the faithful. Not to submit one's intellect. Not to submit one's curiosity. The prohibitions of the Qur'an were because Allah, the all-knowing, was speaking to the prophet Muhammad, may his name be blessed, a man of the sixth century. The Qur'an was eternal truth, but the men who studied it were in a state of becoming. The prohibitions were designed to keep early Muslims focused on the day-to-day, but the Old One transcended history. Such beliefs would be viewed as apostasy by Ibn Azziz and the fundamentalists, but *they* were the ones driving the country into ruin. Satellites dropping from the sky. The power grid decaying. Twenty-five years after the civil war and partition, the former United States had been reduced to a third-world backwater whose principal exports were foodstuffs and minerals. The Old One intended to change that. The Islamic caliphate of a thousand years ago had conquered much of the known world, but it had also been a garden of science and learning, a flowering of all the arts. Those days would come again.

Anna busted. Paid him off. Her face was pink under the fluorescent lights. Last year, at the insistence of her boyfriend, she had had an abortion. A male child. She had no idea he knew. The Old One had sent flowers to her house the next morning. Dozens of white roses. No card. Just the flowers. Her boyfriend had been infuriated. Had struck her. Crushed the flowers underfoot. After Anna had left for work, the Old One had sent two men to the house. One man had packed up the boyfriend's clothes; the other had trussed the boyfriend up and put him in the trunk of his own car. Then they caravanned far out into the desert and buried him alive. Drove partway back and left his car beside the road with a hole in the radiator. Drove back to Las Vegas in their own car.

Anna smiled at him again.

He hadn't removed the boyfriend because he was romantically interested in Anna. The boyfriend had made her unhappy, and the Old One liked his dealers cheerful.

Ellis, the pit boss, watched him, expressionless. He had been a stockbroker at the London Board of Trade, a successful one too, but his wife had developed brain cancer, and in spite of all his efforts, she had died an excruciating death. Ellis had gone to Las Vegas to dilute his grief and never came back.

The cocktail waitress came by, picked up his empty Scotch. She wore a short skirt that showed off her fine legs. Seamed stockings. Wantonness in a long, straight line.

Her name was Teresa. Twenty-two years old, born in Biloxi, Mississippi. Moved here two years ago. She was working on a degree in hotel management at the local college. Had a 3.4 grade-point average. The Old One prided himself on knowing the people he came in contact with, and he came in contact with dozens of them every day, hundreds of them every month. It was one of the many things he loved about living in Las Vegas. There was always someone *new.*

The casinos and hotels were filled with Catholics, Muslims, and Bible Belters, none of them discussing religion or politics. You could have looked around and never thought that there had ever been a civil war. They came to relax, to sin, to be free. They came for business too. Salesmen and industrialists from China and Russia and Brazil cut multimillion-dollar deals while they floated in the pool, slathered on sunscreen. High-tech conventioneers flocked to the digitized amphitheaters, exchanging information while nibbling tiger prawns netted that very morning in the Philippines. The streets were awash with tourists from the booming economies of Brazil and France and Nigeria. Everyone came to Las Vegas. The Open City, that's what the sign at the airport announced.

Anna had two queens. Swept his bets.

The Old One glanced at his fresh cards. Still no word from Darwin. The assassin left messages. Demanded favors from the Old One, but was not available to update him on his progress. Or lack of same. Darwin knew his value, and so did the Old One.

He should have sent Darwin to kill Redbeard and his brother, James, instead of turning to Redbeard's personal bodyguard. Everything would have been different. With Redbeard dead along with his brother, the Old One's cat's-paw would have taken over State Security. Without Redbeard, the Old One could have used his influence to manipulate the president. To stoke his fears. A few more terrorist incidents and the country would have moved to a war footing. A diplomatic breakdown and an attack on the Bible Belt would have been launched, the army and Fedayeen committed, no matter what the cost. One nation, under Allah.

Anna swept his chips away again. Ellis turned away, watched the other tables.

Darwin wouldn't have failed to kill both brothers, but he was an unknown back then. The Old One had never used his services before, and what he had heard about the assassin he didn't believe. He *did* now.

The Old One checked his cards. It was rumored that Redbeard had survived the attempt on his life because he had a copy of the Qur'an in his clothing, the Holy Book blocking two shots to the chest. It sounded like the kind of disinformation that Redbeard would have spread afterward, holding up his survival as an act of divine providence.

The Old One reminded himself not to dwell on the past. One of the markers of senility. He remembered how he had laughed at old men who bound themselves with past mistakes, kings and princes lost in their own memories. There had been a time he had been able to see fifty or sixty years ahead . . . and act accordingly. Barely forty years old, already wealthy beyond measure, he had seen the fallacy in the European welfare state before any demographer. A cradle-to-the-grave system requires *children* to keep the wheels spinning, and the Europeans were godless libertines, fornicators without fatherhood. Starting in the early 1970s, he had begun making large donations to politicians and journalists. Men who shaped the debate on immigration. Hardworking Muslims were deemed the answer, and the floodgates opened wide. Young Muslims from North Africa and Turkey, fertile and faithful. The slow-motion conquest of Europe, the nearly bloodless transformation into an Islamic continent, had been perhaps his greatest victory. The fifty years had passed like an afternoon.

More playing cards slipping across the felt. He lifted a down-card. A one-eyed jack peeked back at him. The red betrayer. The Old One thought of the new pope. *His* new pope. Installed two years ago. Another crop come to its season. Forty years ago, he had seeded his men among the priesthood, a dozen of them, educated and well-connected, skilled in the ways of diplomacy. A dozen of them rising slowly up the church hierarchy. One had now become Pope Pius XIII. When the Old One gave the sign, the pope would make a public declaration of faith. His conversion to Islam would have a profound impact in the Catholic bastions of South America, and on the holdouts in Eastern Europe.

He took a hit on twelve and caught the other one-eyed jack. Busted by the jack of spades. The betrayer betrayed. A bad sign. In keeping with the bad news of these last weeks. Mullah Oxley, nurtured for years by the Old One, had been murdered by Ibn Azziz, a fiery ascetic barely old enough to sprout whiskers. Even now Ibn Azziz was stirring up trouble with the Catholics. Give him enough time and he would fracture the country.

More cards. Anna humming softly to herself. A lullaby to the son she would never have.

Meanwhile Redbeard's niece was creating her own mischief. Although . . . there was still a chance that the Old One could use her to his advantage. She and Rakkim might even become the pivotal pieces in the game. Rakkim was a shadow warrior, one of the invisible men. Darwin wanted to kill him, kill the both of them, but that was just another indication of Darwin's strategic limitations. The great challenge now was to reunite the country, to reclaim the old boundaries of the United States. In spite of its current malaise, the nation was still the best place for a truly vibrant Islam to take root, a transformational Islam. Rakkim's knowledge of the Bible Belt would be invaluable.

Anna swept away his chips with a clatter.

The Old One realized he had lost track of the cards played. So intent on his successes and failures that he had stopped paying attention. He stood up. Pressed a $1,000 chip into her hand and offered her his blessing.

A faint beep sounded in his ear as he walked through the casino. What did Darwin want *now*?

CHAPTER 47

Before late-night prayers

Rakkim flattened himself against the wall of the giant shark, listening. At least four or five of them were outside. The candles were out, the interior in darkness. Moonlight visible through the open mouth, jagged teeth hanging down. A figure darted across the opening. Rakkim loosened his grip on his knife. The figure that he had glimpsed had been wearing a shock helmet and body armor. Bulbous, old-style night-vision goggles. SWAT. No way they were here for Fancy. Oh, Pernell, what did you do? Figures moved past the opaque window toward the rear exit. Bad luck that they knew about the exit, but good luck in that they stumbled in their haste.

Sarah and Fancy were crouched where he had left them. "Who is it?" asked Sarah.

"Police. Is there another way out of here, Fancy?"

"Front and back door, that's it." Fancy primped herself. "What do the cops want scaring us like this? They know they just got to ask."

"It's SWAT. They don't ask." Even in the darkness, Rakkim could see that Sarah understood. "They're going to hit us from both sides. If you had to hide in here, where would you go?"

Fancy looked around. Pointed. "Under the sea tortoise. There's room for all of us."

"Go on then. Both of you," Rakkim said quietly. "When you get settled, I want you to keep your eyes closed and your fingers in your ears. It's going to get very loud and very bright in a few minutes. Stay low and take shallow breaths. Now, *go.*"

Sarah squeezed his hand as she and Fancy moved into deeper darkness.

Rakkim found a spot beside an octopus with only two unbroken tentacles. In an alcove off the main room, it offered good protection from both entry points.

"This is Anaheim SWAT. Come out with your hands raised."

Rakkim heard the plywood being torn away from the rear entrance. He slipped his fingers in his ears, but he kept his eyes open. He'd have time to close them.

"YOU HAVE FIVE SECONDS TO COME OUT."

Rakkim pushed his fingers deeper into his ears. A flash grenade bounced through the open mouth of the shark. Another came in from the back. He closed his eyes, opened his mouth to equalize the pressure when the—

BWAM. BWAM.

Two quick explosions, two bursts of light so bright he saw stars even through his clenched eyes. Opening his eyes wasn't much better. The room was filled with opaque white smoke. Just what he had hoped for. Pernell had said SWAT was in love with their flash grenades. They were used to detonating them in houses and apartments where the glass windows blew out, and the smoke quickly dissipated. The shark was poured concrete with a sloped roof and thick plastic windows. The smoke *stayed.* Rendering their night-vision goggles worse than useless.

The SWAT team entered quickly, took up positions on either side of the doorways, just as they had been taught. They clattered when they moved, their body armor unsecured. Sloppy. Rakkim stayed low, below the smoke, belly pressed against the filthy floor. They were carrying standard SWAT machine guns, short-barreled, folding stock. Forty-round clip. A lead man moved in from the front, another from the rear, but they were waving at the smoke, shouting to each other. Their voices echoed, disorienting them. The one in the rear took off his goggles, advanced farther into the room in a half crouch. The smart one.

Rakkim moved slowly toward the smart one, trying not to eddy the smoke.

"You see anything?" shouted the man in the front, standing on the shark's tongue.

"Shut up!" said the one in the rear. "Take off your—"

Rakkim drove his knife into the back of the man's neck, right into the gap between his armor and his helmet, drove the blade into the notch between the first cervical vertebra and the brain stem. A Fedayeen knife could punch through body armor in a single thrust, but it wasn't a guaranteed kill, and sometimes the blade hung up. A cervical strike was instant death and there was almost no blood. He dragged the SWAT down as quietly as he could. White smoke billowing around them.

"Do what?" called one of them.

"He said *shut up.*"

The smoke was at knee level. Rakkim squatted, watching them continue to advance into the room. He counted six . . . make that seven sets of boots. Not counting the dead man on the floor. Someone should have taught them how to make a tactical retreat. To wait until they had regained advantage of the terrain.

One of the team passed right by Rakkim, but he waited. The next man started coughing, and Rakkim stood up, cut his throat, kept coughing himself to cover it up. He quietly lowered the man to the floor, warm blood pouring across his hands.

"You sure they're in here, Cleese?"

Silence. Then the sound of coughing from all parts of the room. From behind the tortoise too, probably. At least Sarah and

Fancy had an excuse. SWAT had come on with flash grenades and no masks. Terminal stupidity or supply-officer high jinks.

"*Cleese?*"

"Fuck. Okay, everybody, stay where you are." More coughs. "Goggles off. Take 'em off! We'll wait for the smoke to clear."

Rakkim found a crushed soda can, tossed it toward the last voice. Machine-gun fire briefly illuminated the smoke. A man screamed, thrashed around on the floor, *below the smoke*, clutching at his legs. Rakkim moved, screened by a concrete puffer fish.

"Don't shoot unless you see what you're aiming at, *assholes*. We need to take the girl alive. That's where the money is. Kill the man. Don't think twice, don't let him talk, just kill him. He's Fedayeen."

"You didn't tell us that, Emerson."

"Yeah, what's with that shit?"

"Any man who doesn't want the reward is free to leave," said Emerson.

No one left.

Rakkim would have liked to make his way toward Emerson, but too many pairs of boots were between them. And the smoke was starting to thin out.

"Harris, you still in position?" said Emerson.

"Roger that."

"On my count we shoot out the windows. One, two, *three*."

Rakkim moved as they fired, used the sound and fury to cut down another of the team. And another. Smoke poured out the broken windows, pushed out by the cooler outside air.

"She's back here!" called Fancy, running through the thinning smoke, coughing, her hands raised above her. "Don't shoot!" She tripped over a starfish and landed at Rakkim's feet. "Don't—" She realized who he was, blinked at him through the haze. *I'm sorry*, she mouthed. She got up, started forward again.

Bullets hit the wall beside him, sent shards of hardened epoxy flying. Rakkim headed toward where Sarah had gone. He saw her rush out from behind the sea tortoise, saw her launch herself at one of the SWAT team.

SWAT swung his rifle, clipped her across the jaw, and sent her sprawling. The man turned, grinning, had time to see Rakkim's eyes before his neck was broken.

Rakkim was spun around. He thought he had been grabbed . . . until he heard the echo of gunfire. The sound so slow it was a funeral cadence. He was on the floor now. Flat on his back. He turned his head and saw Sarah. Tried to reach her, but he was so tired, and every breath made a gurgling sound. There was no air inside the shark. He was dying in a theme park. An abandoned theme park. It was funnier in the movies. He kept waiting for the rest of the SWAT team to come over and finish him off. They must have known he wasn't going anywhere. He reached around for his knife but gave up. Across the way . . . far across the floor he could see the SWAT who had gotten shot in the legs. The man was pointing at himself. Then at Rakkim. Then back to himself. Ah . . . *he* was the one who had shot him. Good to see a man who took pride in his work.

Someone leaned over the wounded SWAT. Where was the man's body armor? Where were his boots? *He* wasn't part of the team. The man grabbed SWAT by the hair, pushed his head forward, and slipped his knee into the back of his neck. Same spot Rakkim had used on the first one. The man looked over at Rakkim and winked.

The assassin. Rakkim rolled around, found his knife. It was heavy. Almost as heavy as his eyelids. He could see dead SWAT all over the floor. No boots in sight. None standing anyway.

Sarah was bent over him. Her lips were moving but there was such a long interval between when she spoke and when he heard the words that it was as if she were on the other side of the world, speaking with a satellite delay. He felt her tears fall onto his face.

He would like to take a long walk with her in the warm rain, but first he had to tell her about the assassin. He just needed to catch his breath. Sarah had torn a piece off her blouse and had put it on his chest, pressed down. He groaned and she eased up. That was a mistake. He wanted to tell her . . . but his mouth was filling up with blood.

Rakkim saw Fancy run up to the assassin. Saw her kiss his hand . . . both hands, the knife reversed, hidden along his forearm.

The assassin looked at Rakkim, maintained eye contact while he raised Fancy to her feet, comforting her.

Rakkim's grip on the knife kept slipping. Not too far to make the throw. Surprise the assassin. Fedayeen never threw their knives. The lesson drilled in from the first day. A thrown knife kills one. A knife kept close . . . a knife in the hand can kill hundreds. Wisdom there . . . but not now. Rakkim clung to the knife, fighting to stay awake.

A peckerwood in the Carolinas had taught him how to throw a blade. William Lee Barrows. Sergeant, First Carolina Volunteers. Fine man too. Not many of the old-timers left. He had been happy to teach Rakkim his tricks after work at the plant, the two of them staying up late drinking beer and tossing Barrows's pigstickers at an oak tree. Barrows amazed at how quickly Rakkim learned. *Wasting your time here, boy, you should enlist in the Knights of Jesus, kill ya some towel heads.* Rakkim taking another pull on the longneck. *Heckfire, Willy Lee, I couldn't hurt a soul if my life depended on it.* Rakkim opened his eyes.

The assassin looked back at him, still nuzzling Fancy. Waiting for something . . . waiting for Rakkim. The assassin nodded, then drove the knife into Fancy's ear. Drove it in to the hilt. Almost no blood that way. He must want to keep his nice suit clean. He laid Fancy down gently as a bridegroom. Then he started toward Rakkim and Sarah.

Rakkim thrashed harder, choking now.

The assassin turned Rakkim's head to the side, let the blood run out of his mouth. Then he took Sarah's hands, placed them back on Rakkim's chest, and pressed. "*That's* it. You had the right idea, but you have to keep the pressure on. Otherwise, he's going to drown in his own blood. Good. That's it." He had a soothing voice. A kind voice. He looked down at Rakkim. "Don't worry. We've got you."

"Who . . . who are you?" said Sarah, pressing down with both hands.

"Don't stop," said the assassin. "Put all your weight on it. Steady pressure." He flipped open his cell, hit a button. "Redbeard? It's me."

Liar, shouted Rakkim. No . . . he had only thought it.

"Thank God." Sarah smiled at Rakkim. "It's going to be okay, Rikki."

"We had some trouble, just like I thought." The assassin was a fit, middle-aged man with thinning brown hair, and a soft, clean-shaven face. A face you could trust. He could have been a loan officer in a bank. Or sold real estate. "You got the jet standing by? . . . Medical crew too? . . . Good. Rakkim has the classic sucking chest wound. Left lung is filling up with blood . . . I don't know, I'm not a doctor." He looked at Rakkim. "Redbeard wants to know if you're going to survive."

Rakkim struggled to sit up, but he couldn't even raise his head.

"He's going to be fine, Redbeard," said the assassin. "Can't kill a Fedayeen, you know that. Just have the jet ready to leave as soon as we get there . . . No, no time for a chopper . . . I don't know—ten minutes."

Rakkim tried to make eye contact with Sarah, to warn her, but she was intent on keeping pressure on the hole in his chest, and when she did look at him, she was too busy being brave to read his mind.

Still talking on the cell, the assassin strolled over to one of the dead SWAT. Started going through his pockets. "Yes, I know how far the airport is, but we're not taking a taxi." He held up a set of keys, jingled them for Rakkim's benefit. "Tell the medical crew we'll be there in ten minutes. I'll put the siren on so they can hear us coming."

CHAPTER 48

Before late-night prayers

"How is he?" said Sarah.

Darwin listened, a finger pressed against his earlobe. "How are *you* feeling?"

"My ears are still ringing from the gunshots, but I'm okay." Sarah walked to the bulkhead of the private jet, stood outside the door to the makeshift surgical unit. She couldn't hear a thing except for the faint throb of the engines. While the medical team operated on Rakkim in the main cabin, she and Darwin were crammed into the forward cabin. "Do they think he's going to live?"

"He's going to be fine."

"What do the *doctors* think?"

Darwin shrugged. "You know doctors . . . they never want to commit themselves."

Sarah slumped into the seat opposite him, put her face in her hands. She suddenly sat up, looked at her hands. They were smeared with blood. Her clothes . . . her hair . . . she was sprayed with blood. Rakkim's blood. The blood of the policemen. All of those dead bastards. Darwin said there was a huge bounty on her and Rakkim. The Black Robes were willing to pay almost anything for her capture. He said Redbeard had only found out the extent of Ibn Azziz's personal jihad in the last couple of days. Darwin had been sent to join them, to protect them with his life if need be. Sarah looked over at him, the cabin so cramped their knees brushed. "Have I thanked you yet?"

Darwin smiled. "Several times. It's really not necessary." His suit looked freshly pressed, with only a few small bloodstains. She didn't know how he had done it.

"You risked your life for us . . . and there were so many of them."

"It's my job. I enjoy it."

"Redbeard must trust you a great deal to have sent you." Sarah wiped her hands on her dress. It only made things worse.

"I'm sorry we don't have a shower on board, but you could wash up in the forward lavatory. I'll get you a clean scrub suit you can change into. Is that all right?"

Sarah stood up. "Oh, yes, that would be wonderful. I must look disgusting."

Darwin stood up, bowed. "You look lovely, Miss Dougan."

Sarah laughed. "You have a very interesting aesthetic." She slipped into the lavatory, closed the door behind her. Close quarters. She peeled off her dress and stuffed it in the trash. Soaped up her hands and lathered her arms, then her face. The soap smelled like lemons. She washed herself all over again. Splashing. Happily making a mess. Rakkim was going to be all right. Redbeard had sent the plane and the doctors. Redbeard had sent Darwin . . . and everyone knew that Fedayeen were hard to kill. Everyone. She wet a towel with warm water and cleaned her hair. A tiny bit of bone fell out, bounced in the sink, and she almost threw up. Sobbing now as she scrubbed herself. She jumped at the light knock on the door.

"Miss Dougan? I have the scrub suit."

Sarah opened the door a crack. Darwin stood there with his back toward her, hand extended, holding the blue scrubs. She took them, closed the door. "Thank you." When she came out five minutes later, she felt better. As long as she didn't breathe through her nose. "Can I use your cell? I've been trying to call my uncle, but it doesn't seem to be working."

"The plane has a damping mechanism. For security purposes."

"There must be some way to speak to him. Surely *you've* contacted him."

"I have. He told me to hold all further transmissions. Ibn Azziz has undoubtedly found out about what happened back there and will be taking steps."

"Yes . . . of course. Any change in Rakkim's condition?"

"The doctors said he was stable."

"That's good, isn't it? That's an improvement."

"They always say that." Darwin patted her arm. "Try not to worry. Why don't you sit back down." He indicated the seat. "I took the liberty of pouring you some sparkling water. We can talk. It will make the trip go faster."

Sarah sat across from him. "How soon should we be in Seattle?"

"Do you know, I've read your book? Twice."

Sarah relaxed slightly. "Were you trying to impress Redbeard? I have to warn you, he's no fan of the book."

"I enjoyed it very much." Darwin ran a hand through his wispy hair. "Your whole premise that the true gods of the old regime were movie stars and musicians . . . that converting them to Islam was a pivotal victory . . . well, it was quite brilliant."

Sarah nodded politely. "The doctors said you saved Rakkim's life."

"I couldn't have done it without you." Darwin had . . . quiet eyes. Light gray and translucent . . . familiar somehow. "You handled yourself very well at the amusement park, and on the drive to the airport. I hope you don't mind me saying so."

"No . . . not at all." Sarah looked at him and Darwin looked right back at her. So many men had trouble maintaining eye contact—they glanced away, afraid of appearing forward, or lowered their eyes, worried that they weren't sufficiently seductive. Darwin's gaze was neutral, cold even, but self-assured and steady. As though the world were just a passing parade. *Now* she remembered where she had seen eyes like his. The national zoo. Timber wolf. *Canis lupus.* She had spent hours watching the gray wolves when she was younger, fascinated by their predatory calm. No wonder Redbeard had sent him to protect them from Ibn Azziz. A good choice.

"What is it, Miss Dougan?"

"Please, call me Sarah. I think we're past the formalities."

Darwin smiled. "I appreciate that."

"Will we be landing at the airstrip behind Redbeard's villa or at the central hospital?"

"That decision hasn't been made yet."

Sarah looked at the door to the operating room. "It's hard to wait."

"One gets used to it. Waiting can even be pleasurable. Like anticipation."

"I suppose." Sarah crossed her legs, her foot scuffing his pants leg. "Sorry," she said, brushing the material. "How did you find us? Rakkim thought we covered our tracks."

"You should feel proud." Darwin folded his hands in his lap. "If I hadn't come into possession of the same information Detective Colarusso passed on to you, I wouldn't have known where to look. Once I did, it was relatively easy to—"

"*Anthony* told you?"

Darwin put his hands up. "Not at all. I simply used the same source he did. A most accommodating woman in the personnel department."

Sarah cocked her head as the plane banked. "What's happening?"

"Just a standard course correction. Everything is quite all

right." Darwin leaned forward slightly. "I'm something of a nostalgia collector myself. CDs, movie posters, comic books. Heroes and monsters. Perhaps that's why I was so attracted to your work."

Sarah drifted, lulled by the hum of the engines. She didn't like the conflation of old-regime popular culture with nostalgia, even though it was a common misperception. She closed her eyes. Still hearing gunshots. Still seeing the sad expression on Fancy's face. Fatima Abdullah. Lying on the bare concrete as they carried Rakkim out. Darwin said she was dead, said they had to hurry, and they *did* . . . but as Sarah passed by the body, she cursed the police who had killed her. Hoped that there was someone to give her a decent burial. Fancy had said a name . . . Jeri Lynn. Sarah hoped someone would call Jeri Lynn. Hoped Jeri Lynn would bury Fancy with the proper respect. The proper prayers.

"Have you ever researched late-twentieth-century pornography?"

Sarah blinked herself alert. "No . . . I never considered it."

"Oh, you *really* should. Very interesting stuff. The whole culture is there."

"I've never seen anything about it in the professional literature. I'm sure it would be restricted. Is there some sort of archive?"

"No, most of it's in private hands."

"So, how do you . . . ?" Sarah glanced again at the bulkhead door, a little uncomfortable with the conversation. "Of course. As you said, you're a collector."

"You can see a whole shift during the late nineties. Tattoos everywhere, women as well as the men. Piercings . . . piercings in places it's hard to imagine one volunteering for. Even their movie stars did it. Even their gods offered themselves up." Darwin steepled his fingertips. "Fascinating, isn't it? Return to the primitive, that's what their social scientists termed it. I see it more as a hunger for slavery. They were so free, so unencumbered by morality, that they craved chains. And the sexual practices themselves—"

"Were you . . ." Sarah's smile was forced. "Were you following us all the way from Seattle? I'm just . . . I'm just trying to find out if we made any mistakes."

"Laudable," said Darwin. "No, your mistakes were only human. I was waiting for you in Long Beach. Last known address of Fatima Abdullah. I thought I had missed you, then one of our roaming eyes called and said he had seen you two sitting in a coffee shop in Huntington Beach. You evidently weren't in as much of a hurry to find her as we thought."

Sarah felt her cheeks coloring.

"Something wild in the air in Southern California, don't you think?" Darwin flexed his fingertips. "You didn't even close your motel room windows. I was standing down below all night. Almost close enough to touch, and I could hear *everything*. Such sounds. The grunting and groaning. I wonder what your uncle would think if he heard them." Darwin's eyes hadn't changed in the slightest. They remained cool and gray and distant. "Something has been bothering me. Maybe you can help. That third time . . . where exactly was Rakkim putting it? I couldn't tell and it's been bothering me ever since."

Sarah stared . . . and . . . finally . . . saw him.

"I guess we'll have to mark that down on the list of eternal mysteries." Darwin seemed happier now. Satisfied, now that she knew. "It's a problem, isn't it? Deciding how you feel about me."

"No, it's not."

"I mean, in spite of those other things, I *did* save your life. Yours and Rakkim's."

"It's no problem." Sarah was surprised at her calm. It was as if she had taken something from Darwin and used it to anchor herself. To protect herself from her terror. "I feel the same way about you as I do about any other hired killer."

"I prefer the term *assassin*."

"I'm sure you do."

"Why don't you just call me Darwin and we'll let it go at that?"

"Darwin? Is that your real name?"

"I know, I know. Named after a blasphemer. Don't think *that* didn't cause a world of trouble growing up. Ah, well, we all carry the burden of history, don't we?"

The engines shifted tone, higher pitched now as the plane banked steeply.

"We won't be landing in Seattle. I'm afraid that's something else I lied to you about." Darwin smiled. "Do you appreciate irony?"

Sarah watched him.

"Rakkim is AB negative. A rare blood type. There were only two pints available on such short notice." Darwin leaned closer, and Sarah saw scuttling things in his eyes and wondered how she could have missed them. "*I'm* AB negative too. If the doctors needed more in-flight, they were going to give him a transfusion of my blood. Wouldn't that have been some-thing?"

Sarah fought to keep herself from trembling. She didn't suc-ceed.

"*My* blood." Darwin rocked with laughter. "I bet you would have thought about that every time he fucked you up the ass." He was howling now, head thrown back, teeth bared.

CHAPTER 49

Before noon prayers

"Thanks again for meeting me, Director," said Colarusso.

"I wanted to talk with you anyway." Redbeard didn't take his eyes off the metallic fuselage rising from the waters of Puget

Sound. The tail section of the downed 977 superjumbo jet jutted fifty feet into the air. The engines of the ferryboat throbbed, sending a vibration through the deck. The rest of the tourists were inside, watching the monument through the double-paned windows, but Redbeard and Colarusso stood outside in the elements, the cold wind whipping their clothes.

Salt stung Colarusso's nostrils. "My chief seems to think you and me are close because of you insisting I handle the murders at Marian Warriq's house," he said, uneasy hearing of Redbeard's interest in him. "That's how I drew this assignment."

"What was it the chief of police didn't want to ask me *himself*?"

"We've had all these dead bounty hunters turn up in the last few days," said Colarusso. "All of them affiliated with the Black Robes."

"And Chief Edson thinks State Security is responsible?"

"You got it."

"State Security *is* responsible."

"I see. Well . . . the chief is concerned things may escalate between you and Ibn Azziz, and it's the police who are going to look bad. I mean, we're supposed to keep the peace."

"Jerry Edson doesn't care about the peace, he only cares about keeping his job. Which he shall, as long as his father remains head of the Senate Appropriations Committee."

Colarusso rubbed his forehead. "I can't argue with you there, sir, but I have to work for the asshole. Could I maybe tell him that you deplore the violence and are going to do what you can to find out who is responsible?"

"Headache, Detective?"

"Off and on."

"I have them all the time. I wake up in the middle of the night lately . . . I think it's raining because I hear thunder, and it's my head. My housekeeper says I should go to a doctor, but once you start going to doctors, there's no end to the tests."

"Why don't we go inside?" said Colarusso, shivering. He had buttoned his topcoat unevenly and ignored it. "I'm freezing my ass off."

"I prefer it out here," said Redbeard, comfortable somehow in a plain woolen robe. He pointed to the downed jumbo jet. "Were you living in Seattle when the plane hit?"

"My wife and I were in Hawaii celebrating our fifth wedding anniversary. Seems like a long time ago."

"It was twenty-three years in March. Eleven hundred on board, most of them still right there." Redbeard's expression was unreadable. "We put out the story that it was hijacked by a Brazilian end-times cult, but, of course, that wasn't true."

"Hijackers weren't trying to ram the Capitol dome? Or that it wasn't an end-times cult?"

"I used to come out here all the time with Rakkim and Sarah," said Redbeard, eyeing the wreckage. The metal was still shiny, at least from a distance.

Colarusso didn't ask any more questions about the hijacking. Redbeard was using a bait-and-switch tactic to knock him off-balance, offering secret information, withholding it at the last moment.

"The first time Sarah saw the plane, she asked me why all the national monuments seemed to be celebrating death. Where were the monuments to scientific discoveries or poetry or medical break-throughs? That's what she wanted to know. She was seven at the time. Rakkim was twelve. You want to know what he said? He looked at the tail assembly jutting out of the water at almost a ninety-degree angle and told me the pilot had taken too steep a descent. He said it was impossible to maintain rudder control that way. Rakkim said the pilot should have come in low, almost horizontal, and *then* rammed the Capitol." Redbeard shook his head. "Twelve years old."

Colarusso wondered if he dared to go back inside and leave Redbeard out here.

"I hear your son has been accepted into the Fedayeen?" said Redbeard.

Colarusso nodded. Surprised.

"Stings a little, doesn't it?" said Redbeard. "I felt the same way when Rakkim was accepted. It's a great honor, of course, but I'm sure you had other plans for him. Following you into the force, perhaps."

"There's no future for a Catholic in the department. Catholic's lucky to make detective."

"Still, I'm sure you had your dreams for Anthony Jr." Redbeard looked past the tail assembly. "I had dreams for Rakkim. Dreams for Sarah too. Dreams for *myself*. Getting older . . . mostly it entails accepting the unacceptable."

"Ain't that the God's honest truth?" Colarusso caught himself. "Sorry. Didn't mean to be so familiar."

"No offense taken, Detective. We're just a couple of old men here, talking about things that might have been."

Colarusso kept quiet. He had been a cop too long to trust a powerful man going all soft and sentimental.

"Rakkim is fortunate to have a friend like you," said Redbeard. "It's been quite some time since he's confided in me."

Colarusso stifled a smile. When you think the worst of people, you're rarely disappointed.

"I sent Rakkim to find my niece. He succeeded. With all the men at my disposal, with all my experience and connections, he found her when I couldn't."

"You trained him well. Must give you comfort."

"To hell with comfort, I want my niece. Where are they?"

Colarusso leaned against the railing, watched the waves break against the fuselage of the jumbo jet. "I don't know."

"I could threaten you, Detective. I could tell you that with a nod of my head, drugs would be found in your house. Or evidence that you had been colluding with Jews. There's an infinite amount of ways to destroy a man's life, and I know them all." Redbeard stood with his feet wide. "I wouldn't do that though. I have too much respect for you. If Rakkim considers you a friend, it's because he knows you won't yield to threats. I just have to look at you and I can see that."

"You going to kiss me before you fuck me, Redbeard?"

Redbeard laughed, a hearty roar that ended with coughing. He bent forward until it stopped. Stood up, face flushed. "I wish I had a friend like you, Detective. A man in my position isn't allowed that kind of luxury. He is allowed family though. I never had children, but I thought I had family."

"You got one. I heard Rakkim talk often enough to know that. You were as close to a daddy as he could stand."

"Yes . . . thank you for that." Redbeard turned as the ferry finished its orbit of the downed jet, started back to port. "After Rakkim asked for you to lead the Warriq homicides, I've had you under surveillance. The only time you made an effort to elude a tail was last week. You ducked into the men's department of Kingdom of Heaven and slipped away when my man thought you were in the changing room."

"I can't afford that place on my salary anyway."

"Exactly what I told him. A lesson I'm certain he's learned." Redbeard smiled. "I didn't particularly mind your disappearance. I assumed you were meeting with Rakkim. It was confirmation that he and Sarah were still in the area, which was always my expectation. The capital is familiar turf for them, with all the attendant human networks and hidey-holes. Even so, I had my men monitor any curious developments around the country. Odd occurrences. Rumors. Disappearances. I've resisted putting their security profiles into the system for fear of alerting *others*. I'm sure you understand."

"Yeah." Colarusso pulled at his bulbous nose. It itched. "Once they're in the system, it's open season."

Redbeard wiped the edges of his mouth with a fingertip. "Late last night something odd came to my attention. Eight police officers were killed in the line of duty last night in Orange County, California. SWAT team members. Full gear. All dead. No arrests. The PD clamped down on the story. Then this morning, the official line is that it was an undercover drug sting gone bad."

"It happens."

"Eight geared-up SWAT officers down? How often does that happen? Last night there was no one but cops dead at the scene, and this morning there's a morgue full of the usual suspects." Redbeard raked a hand through his beard. "I haven't been able to get a look at autopsy reports on the officers, not *yet*, but when I do, I'll bet you dollars to doughnuts that they were killed with a knife, a well-trained knife." Redbeard looked at Colarusso. "I don't know where Rakkim and Sarah are, but *someone* does. Someone who means them harm."

Colarusso stared back at him.

Redbeard turned away. "When we get back to shore, feel free to check what I've told you. I wouldn't want you to feel foolish."

Colarusso watched Redbeard's robe flap in the wind. Good interrogators blindsided you. They came at you from a direction you didn't expect. Or they were polite when you were expecting bluster. The best ones didn't even ask the big question. They simply laid out a situation and let you decide if you wanted to help. Redbeard was the best Colarusso had ever encountered. "They're in Southern California. I don't know where exactly, but I worked out a bounce itinerary that ended up at Bin Laden. I don't know what they're after. Rakkim wouldn't tell me."

Redbeard kept his back to him. "I appreciate that, Anthony."

"I don't know about this SWAT team . . . but there's a Fedayeen assassin after him." Colarusso shifted. "I think . . . I think this assassin showed up at my place last week. Not more than a day after they left town. He talked to my boy."

Redbeard turned. Walked over. Right beside him now. Concerned.

"Nothing happened. Everyone's okay."

"Then it wasn't the assassin," said Redbeard.

"He showed up with some story about being from the mayor's office. Anthony Jr. wouldn't let him in. Said he got a bad feeling about the guy. Anthony Jr. said he practically pissed himself. You don't know my boy, but that's not the kind of thing he would normally admit to. I called the mayor's office. They didn't send anybody—"

"Call your family and tell them to pack their things. I'll send some men over—"

"Already shipped them out. Made Anthony Jr. go with the wife and girls. Told him he had to protect them. He didn't like it, but he went."

"What about you?"

"Let him knock on my door again," Colarusso growled, "I'll blow his brains out. I'll empty the fucking clip." He shivered in the cold wind. "Don't worry, Anthony Jr. didn't tell him anything. He didn't know anything to tell."

Redbeard shook his head. "He knows your boy was worried about visitors. A Fedayeen assassin can practically read minds."

Colarusso felt sick. "Rakkim needed some information and this woman in Personnel helped me. She hasn't been at work in a few days and I'm worried. The girls in the office say she's got all kind of sick days accrued, but she didn't give notice." He looked around. "I let myself into her apartment. Nothing out of place. Nothing that jumped out at me anyway." The engine of the ferry shuddered and he fought for his footing. "I tried calling Rakkim . . . but he has his cell switched off. He thinks people can track him just from accessing a message."

"They can."

Colarusso licked his lips. "I didn't know that."

"That headache of yours is back."

Colarusso rubbed his forehead. "Feels like a couple of guys cracking rocks inside me."

Redbeard had a sad smile. "I know just what you mean. Perhaps when you pass me the information you gave Rakkim, we can both get some relief."

CHAPTER 50

After morning prayers

The four men grabbed Angelina on the way out of the mosque. Big men who lifted her by the elbows and carried her quickly to a waiting black car. She cried out, her toes dragging across the parking lot. Others saw her. Heard her. Women she had prayed alongside of for twenty years, but they all pretended not to see or hear. Except for Delia Mubarak, who called her name. Delia, who looked around for support, but was smacked by her husband, led away by the hand like a naughty child. The men hustled Angelina into the backseat of the car, one on either side of her. The other two got in front. Doors slammed, heavy as the gates to hell.

"When Redbeard finds out what you've done, I wouldn't be you for all the gold in Switzerland," said Angelina.

The men remained silent. Stared straight ahead.

"So Ibn Azziz thought he needed four men to bring in a little old lady. You must be very proud to fetch for such a mighty lord."

The man to her right cursed her, but the driver ordered him quiet.

Angelina fingered her prayer beads. They could stay silent all they wanted now, she had learned what she wanted. It *had* been Ibn Azziz who'd ordered her capture. She listened to the clicking of her prayer beads, fingers flying, comforted by the names of God.

Rakkim slowly opened his eyes. It took an effort. Too much light coming in through the curtains. His eyes closed again, heavy-lidded. No. *No.*

"Good job." An old man sat beside the bed, legs crossed at the knee. Dapper old gent in a pale green three-piece suit. White hair. White beard, lightly perfumed. Light brown skin . . . the color of Rakkim's own face. "Don't doze off again. Stick around."

Rakkim struggled awake. The back of the bed moved silently to a more upright position.

"Better?" said the old man. "I was getting bored watching you sleep." He smiled. Such small teeth. "You looked like you were dreaming."

Rakkim licked his dry lips. Maybe *this* was a dream? He sipped cool water from the glass the old man held to his lips. "Where . . . am I?" His voice was as cracked as his lips.

"Las Vegas."

"Sarah?"

"She's quite all right."

Rakkim shifted in the hospital bed, winced. He and Sarah had been in California the last time he remembered. It had been night and . . .

"The thoracic surgeons are very impressed with the rapidity of your recuperation." Another smile from the old man. "Of course, they've had no experience with Fedayeen."

"How . . . long have I been here?"

"They wanted to medicate you for pain, but I told them you had an extremely high threshold, and beside, I'm sure you'd prefer clarity regardless."

"How *long*?"

"Two days. Your body has already absorbed most of the stitches. Amazing."

Rakkim took a deep breath. It hurt but he didn't show it this time. "Are you my doctor?"

"That's one way of looking at it." The old man's hands flopped. "My personal physicians are treating you. You couldn't get better care anywhere on the planet, although at this point it's just a matter of giving your body time to regain its strength."

Rakkim's head was pounding so loudly he could barely hear. The last thing he remembered was being frightened. Not for himself . . . but, for Sarah.

"What I wouldn't pay to have your constitution," said the old man.

"Sarah? Is she all right?"

"She didn't get a scratch. You were shot. Twice. Do you remember that?"

Rakkim shook his head. "I was inside a fish. How can that be?"

"Maybe you're Jonah. Or Pinocchio."

"No . . . I was inside a shark."

The old man patted his hand. "I shouldn't take advantage of your present condition. Will you forgive me? You were shot. One bullet just grazed your side, but the other tore a hole in your lung. You lost some blood. Don't you remember *anything*?"

Rakkim licked his dry lips. The old man had a faint British accent. "I'm in *Las Vegas*? How did I get here?"

The old man helped him to another drink. "You couldn't very well be taken to a local hospital. All those dead policemen . . ." The old man shook his head. "Rather hard to explain, don't you think?"

Dead police? Rakkim remembered now. SWAT pouring into the ride at Disneyland. Body armor. It was dark inside the shark . . . and there was all this smoke . . . and gunfire and blood splashing on his hands. "Where's Sarah?"

"She has a room in the visitors' wing, but she's spent most of the last two days sitting in this very chair. I suspect that now she's getting some rest herself." The old man plucked at the crease in his trousers. His socks had tiny clocks on them. Black silk socks with tiny orange clocks. "Or perhaps she's out shopping. Ah, the female of the species. What would we do without them?"

Rakkim stared at him. "Who *are* you?"

The door to his room opened and a nurse bustled in, a brusque woman with dark hair tucked back into a white cap. She bowed to the old man, then seemed startled to see Rakkim sitting up. "You're awake?" She walked over, took his wrist. "Hush." She glanced at her watch, waited, checked her watch again. "Good." She checked his eyes, shook her head. "I don't understand it . . . but, Allah be praised."

He remembered something else about being inside the big shark. Fancy. He and Sarah had found Fancy inside the shark . . . and then the assassin . . . the assassin had killed her.

"Where do you think you're going?" said the nurse, holding him back, surprised at his strength.

"I'd listen to her, Mr. Epps. We have to trust the professionals." The old man stood up. "I'll come back and visit at a better time. We have so very much to discuss."

Rakkim was dizzy. He clung to the nurse, not sure if his memory of the assassin was a dream. Another dream. No . . . it was real. He had seen the assassin kill Fancy. He had seen the assassin slide his knife into her ear as though he were whispering a deep, dark secret to her.

The nurse patted his shoulder.

The last thing Rakkim remembered was lying in Sarah's arms . . . lying in a sea of blood and seeing the assassin approach. Rakkim cried out and the nurse gently pressed him back into the cool white sheets.

*   *   *

"Welcome to the house of Allah," said Ibn Azziz.

Angelina looked around the windowless chamber. Took in the six Black Robes in attendance. "I do not see Allah here."

Ibn Azziz glared down at her from a high-back chair. "Do not mock me *or* God, woman. I am giving you a chance to atone for your sin. You have raised a whore. Perhaps it was not your doing. Perhaps you were merely following the instructions of Redbeard, but the fact is that Sarah Dougan is a whore and a blasphemer, and Allah demands that someone be held account-able."

Angelina adjusted her head covering, grateful that she had got-ten to pray this morning. "You're thin as a dried stick, Mullah Ibn Azziz. You need a woman to fatten you up, put some meat on those bones of yours."

Ibn Azziz glanced at his men to make certain that no one was smiling. "Your years serving Redbeard have spoiled your judg-ment. I need no woman for *anything*."

"Then, in the name of Allah, the lord of truth, why am I here, Mullah? Why else would you have me brought before you unless you were seeking a housekeeper? Surely you weren't seeking my counsel on matters of doctrine."

Ibn Azziz nodded. "It is good you behave thus. I am a man inclined towards mercy when it is merited. Your insolence makes the task at hand easier."

Angelina bowed. "It is my pleasure."

Ibn Azziz stood up, jabbed a bony hand at her. "You will tell me where I can find the whore. You were the only mother she had. She would not have run away without telling you where she was going."

"I love the girl as my own, but I don't know where she is."

"You love her, but she must not love you. To wallow in sin and leave you to explain her actions. She must think you a fool."

Angelina watched as he stroked his wispy beard. A pathetic

excuse for a beard. An even more pathetic excuse for an imam.

"I almost caught her in California a few days ago," said Ibn Azziz. "She was in my grasp but escaped. Allah must have his reasons—"

"What do you think Redbeard will do when he finds out that you have taken me? What do you think the people will do when they find out you have desecrated a mosque?"

"I'm not afraid of Redbeard or the people. I am only afraid of God."

"As you *should* be."

"Be silent, woman!" Ibn Azziz paced the room. Thinking. Nervous as static electricity.

In all her years with Redbeard, she had never seen him as unraveled as Ibn Azziz. What was he expecting, some frightened housewife begging for mercy? An intimidated moderate with knees of jelly before the leader of the Black Robes? Angelina had been beaten before. She feared only God, and she had nothing to fear from Him.

"You will tell me where to find the whore," said Ibn Azziz. He stood quietly now, watching her, and his nervousness was gone. "If you do not, or can not, then you will be brought before the religious court. We will charge Sarah Dougan with fornication and blasphemy in absentia. You shall be the primary witness against her."

Angelina started to speak. Held her tongue.

Ibn Azziz seemed almost disappointed. "Make no mistake, you *will* testify against her. It is only a matter of how much pain you wish to endure."

Angelina's eyes shimmered. The man was right. They both knew it, and the pleasure it gave him was obscene. She hung her head. Asked God for courage. Looked up at Ibn Azziz. Lips quivering. "I will tell you where she is."

Ibn Azziz sat back in his chair. He looked so young. "Speak."

"I . . . I can not bear to hear my own words." Angelina looked at the men around her. "I will not speak in front of *them*."

"I will not send my guards away."

Angelina took a deep breath. "She is . . . she is . . ." She lowered her voice, the words inaudible now.

"Speak up!"

"I love her, Mullah. The sound of my betrayal will burn my ears for eternity."

Ibn Aziz looked at his bodyguards. Saw them indicate that she had been searched. He beckoned to her.

Angelina took a halting step. She spoke again. The words even softer than before.

"Closer!"

Angelina was two feet away. Near enough to count his eyelashes.

"That's close enough. I can't bear the stink of a female."

Angelina lowered her head. Whispered.

Ibn Aziz smacked his hand against his leg, sent his black robe fluttering.

Angelina stepped forward muttering. They were close enough now that Ibn Aziz could hear the words. She was praying. Asking God to give her strength. Asking for God's blessing for what she was about to do.

Ibn Aziz started to shout but it was too late.

Angelina launched herself at him. Hooked one of his eyes with her forefinger, drove it deep behind the jelly and scooped it out. He screamed, struggled to escape her, but the chair held him in place, and fifty years of housework had made her hands strong. Fifty years of prayer had given her courage. The eye she had torn out flopped against her wrist as she clawed at his face, seeking the other one. The eye was like a grape. A muscat grape peeled for a pasha. Such things were done in the old days. She gasped as the knives entered her body, but the thought of Sarah made her hang on, raking his face with her nails. Such *screaming* from Ibn Azziz. Again and again the bodyguards stabbed her, and she felt her body shudder. She wished . . . she wished she had been granted the gift of seeing Sarah and Rakkim marry. To see them kiss. To hold their baby in her arms. The knives . . . the knives hurt, but not so badly as she feared. The pain was bearable. Above all else, Allah was merciful.

CHAPTER 51

After morning prayers

"Sorry, mister, I'm still not seeing anything."

Rakkim stood with his arms outstretched in front of the MRI screen. "Run it again. Maximum sensitivity."

The tech looked at Sarah. "It's already maxed."

"Just do it." Sarah watched over the tech's shoulder as the scan progressed. She turned to Rakkim, shook her head.

Rakkim let his arms drop. He should be happy. He had been certain the Old One would have implanted some sort of tracking device inside him during surgery, but the MRI body scan showed nothing. Nothing metallic. Nothing of a foreign or nonbiologic nature. Neither had Sarah's watch registered any electronic signature. They had run a full-spectrum check with it before going to the MRI lab of the hospital. He watched Sarah pay off the tech. It wouldn't have been hard for the Old One. Fedayeen tracking devices were as small as a poppy seed, and his wounds offered easy access for implantation. He had plenty of old scars that could have hidden the insertion point. So why had the Old One passed on the opportunity?

Sarah and Rakkim eased out the side door and into the stairwell. It had been three days since he'd woken up in the hospital and had his halting conversation with the Old One. Rakkim was dressed in some new clothes she had bought in downtown Las Vegas, ugly clothes he wouldn't have been seen in back in Seattle—Spanish-style, black trousers with little balls running up the side seams, and a yoked Western shirt with red parrots embroidered on the chest. In a city of tourists, dress like a tourist. He still hated looking in the mirror. Her clothes were typically modern—blue leather, knee-length skirt and a short-sleeved comfort sweater that adjusted its weave depending on the ambient temperature.

"Why am I dressed like a matador?" said Rakkim.

"I thought it would cheer you up."

"You thought it would cheer you up."

"That too." She squeezed his hand. "How are you really feeling?"

Rakkim started up the stairs, taking them two at a time. Sarah was right behind him. They stopped at the eighteenth landing, the top floor, both of them panting. Rakkim gave it a count of five, then started back down. When they got to the bottom, they did it again.

"That's *enough*," Sarah gasped, back at the eighteenth-floor landing, "After lunch. We can run up Mount Everest. Or swim. Swim the Pacific."

Rakkim bent slightly forward, rested his hands on his knees. He spit into the dusty corner. There was a tiny spot of blood in it.

They walked down the stairs and out the door on the main level. Stepped out into the morning sunshine. Eighty-six degrees and no humidity. Hot-air balloons drifted in the distance, not the dull security blimps that ringed Seattle, but brightly colored balloons from which tourists could appreciate the landscape.

"I still don't understand why we're still alive," said Sarah as they cut across the green lawn to the sidewalk. "Why didn't the assassin just kill us? If Fancy had any proof of her father's part in planting the fourth bomb, it's gone now."

Rakkim glanced around as they walked. He hadn't been out-side since he was shot and the open air smelled clean. Vegas was beautiful—the air crystalline, the Spring Mountains to the west set in high relief against the deep, cobalt blue sky. Rakkim had never seen such clear skies, either at home or in the Bible Belt. If anything, the Bible Belt was more polluted than the Islamic Republic, due to their dependency on coal. He looked back at the hospital, shielding his eyes. There was no way to appreciate how big it was from the inside. Open too, with plenty of glass and a lobby that faced the street. He had never seen a hospital without protective barriers around it to guard against truck bombs.

"So what does the Old One hope to gain by keeping us alive?" persisted Sarah.

"He's keeping us alive now for the same reason he didn't kill us before—he's using us to find his vulnerabilities. Things he missed. Things that could implicate him." Rakkim took in the cars and buses cruising past, hydrogen-fueled and almost silent. Voice-activated too, the steering wheel an anachronism. "If Fatima Abdullah was a threat to him before, she's no threat now. The Old One must think there are other loose ends. Someone else who knows too much."

"Like my mother. *She's* the one he really wants to find."

"I still don't understand why the Old One didn't implant a tracker."

"Darwin didn't need a tracker to find us in Disneyland. He did it the old-fashioned way."

Rakkim kept silent. It was true, but he didn't have to like it.

They walked on, both of them picking up the pace, glad to leave the hospital behind. Casinos loomed before them as they reached the edge of the Strip, a cascade of neon laser light and fanciful designs. Arabian Nights. Renaissance Italy. Star Wars. Mandarin China. Dinosaurs and musketeers. The two of them were still mostly alone on the sidewalk, tourists from the nearby hotels preferring the elevated moving sidewalks that took them from casino to casino. Tourists from the Bible Belt and the Islamic Republic, plenty of Asians and Europeans too. Even a few Dutch fundamentalists—even stricter doctrinally than the Black Robes—haranguing other Muslims for their sins.

"We should contact Redbeard, let him know we're here," said Sarah. "We should warn Colarusso too."

"The last thing we want is Redbeard coming here to rescue us, and even if Darwin was telling the truth about using Colarusso's informant, it's too late for a call to do any good."

"So we do *nothing?*"

"For now, the Old One is giving free rein. No guards. No chaperones. For the time being, we should assume that anything that's easy to do is what the Old One *wants* us to do. So we don't run the first chance we get. We don't call Redbeard. We wait. We act on *our* timetable, not his."

"You said now," said Sarah, stopping to look at one of the storefront souvenir stands. Small plastic sci-fi robots did a preprogrammed ballet, excusing themselves in five languages as they banged into each other. "You said we do nothing *now.*"

"There was a busboy at the Blue Moon that I helped out once. Peter. He had ambitions, but there were . . . obstacles because of his bloodline."

"He was Jewish?"

"His grandmother was. That was enough. We had a regular customer who flew into the capital a couple times a year to visit family. Supervisor at the China Doll Hotel and Casino. I introduced them. Called in a favor. Peter has been working there for a couple years now. He's already a pit boss. Peter Bowen." Rakkim picked up a miniature Vegas skyline enclosed in clear plastic, intricately detailed, diodes flashing to mirror the laser show of the real thing. $2.99. The plastic skylines were the modern analog of the antique snow globes that Spider collected. Rakkim could still see the shattered World Trade Center on the floor of the deserted underground lair, and he wondered if Spider was safe. If he and his family had escaped the Black Robes.

"What's wrong?" said Sarah.

Rakkim put the skyline back. "You should go on a shopping spree. Hit all the sites. Follow all the usual procedures. Somewhere along the line you should stop in at the China Doll and say hello to Peter. He told me once that the border of the Nevada Free State was a semipermeable membrane. Easy to get in, but hard to get out. Undetected, anyway, but I'm sure Peter considers that more of an opportunity than an obstacle. Tell him we want to get across the border. Let him know that there's a very powerful local who's got his eyes on us, so he's going to have to factor that in. Tell him we'll pay whatever it costs. Knowing Peter, he won't charge us a thing. Make the offer anyway."

"Why don't I just offer him oral?" Sarah said brightly as she riffled through a rack of souvenir T-shirts. "It's a beautiful day, maybe I should suggest the full gulp."

Rakkim stared at her. "I was being patronizing?"

"Follow all the usual procedures? Peter won't charge us, but make the offer anyway? Just a micro patronizing."

"Look, use your own judgment in dealing with Peter. Just tell him we want to get to Seattle as soon as possible."

"Why aren't we going back to Southern California? We should try to locate any of Safar Abdullah's former coworkers, see if they have any information."

"We're out of our element in California. The only contact I had betrayed us. No, we go home. We'll talk with Redbeard. See if he's willing to help. Things haven't been going very well for him either. Maybe he's ready to take a chance."

"Why do you get to decide?"

"Fine. *You* decide. Consider the assets we have in California. The access to data. Consider our familiarity with the city.

The degree of back-channel communication we have with the local authorities. Consider our chances of finding people who worked with Abdullah twenty-five years ago. People who probably had nothing to do with his trip to China. Factor in that the Black Robes are on alert now. Go on, *you* make the call."

Sarah pretended to examine a T-shirt. "We'll go to Seattle." She slapped the T-shirt back on the rack, the hanger banging against the metal. "I just hate giving up."

"It's called a strategic retreat. That's what you do when you're getting your asses kicked and you want to regroup and try again."

Sarah fluffed her hair. "I think I'm going to do that shopping we talked about. Do you want me to walk you back to the hospital?"

"I got a card today from Darwin." Rakkim stared at the enormous black pyramid in the distance. The Luxor. Oldest casino on the Strip. "It was on my bedstand when I woke up this morning."

"What did it say?"

"'Please convey my apologies to Miss Dougan. I was a little overheated on the flight from Disneyland. I'm sure you understand.'" Rakkim kept his eyes on the Luxor. His doctor said it was scheduled for demolition next year. "What does Darwin have to apologize for? I asked you what had happened after I passed out, and you said you barely spoke on the flight."

"He's trying to upset you."

"It's working."

"What did he mean, 'I'm sure you understand'?" Her eyes flashed. "You see, I could ask the same kind of questions you do. That's what he wants." She faced him. "Darwin tried to scare me, and he *did* scare me, for a moment anyway. Mostly he repulsed me. The strangest thing though . . . when I think about the conversation now, I think Darwin made a mistake talking to me." She waved at the brightly clad tourists on the skybridge. "Darwin kept asking me questions, pretending to know more than he does. He has no idea what we're looking for. The Old One doesn't trust him with the whole picture, and it bothers Darwin. He feels insulted."

Rakkim smiled and she smiled back at him. Eager. From the pleasure she took in her insight, Darwin must have done more than try to scare her.

Sarah was serious again. "When you first meet Darwin, he's so mild and amenable that it's as if there's no one there. He's just so . . . *still*. Later though, when you get a really good look at him, you see that there's this massive ego at the center of him. An ego that can never be filled, never be satisfied. Most of us are defined by an emotional interaction. You can tell who we are by who we're responsible for. Who we care about. Who we *love*. Darwin, though . . . he's a universe unto himself. The one and only. That's why he seems so still, because there's nothing *but* him as far as his eye can see." She brushed her lips across Rakkim's. "Do you want to know a secret?" She bit his earlobe. "If I were the Old One . . . I'd be scared of Darwin."

"Let's go to your hotel," said Rakkim. "I can go back to the hospital later."

"Do you think you're well enough?"

"I'll just have to stay horizontal. No rough stuff."

Sarah showed the tip of her tongue. "Where's the fun in that?"

CHAPTER 52

After evening prayers

"Here." Darwin shoved Rakkim a stack of black, $100 chips. "Go ahead. It doesn't mean we're going steady or anything."

"Where's my knife?" said Rakkim. "I know you have it."

Darwin shook the dice. "I was going to keep it as a souvenir."

"I'll give you something else to remember me by."

"Sir?" The stickman at the craps table straightened his black bow tie. "Bets, please."

Darwin plucked a single chip off Rakkim's stack, tossed it on the pass line next to his own pink, $1,000 chip. "Now we're on the same side." Other than at Disneyland, this evening was the first time Rakkim had gotten a look at Darwin. He was clean-shaven, and supple as a snake. He tossed the dice. Seven.

Cheers from the table. The stickman paid off the winning bets. The table was crowded, people pressed against the railing, laying down bets and talking loudly to one another.

"Press it," said Darwin, letting ride his now doubled bet and Rakkim's. Another seven.

Cheers! Players from other tables wandered over, drawn to the energy, squeezing in, throwing down money. Darwin beamed, resplendent in a canary-yellow cashmere sport coat and black and yellow-checked pants—the perfect cosmopolitan, one of the moneyed world citizens who flocked to Las Vegas for deals and contacts and high-class sin. Rakkim wasn't sure if Darwin wanted to blend in, or if it was his true coloration.

Rakkim's bet had grown to $400, Darwin's to $4,000. Another seven. The crowd roared with approval.

"You're my lucky charm." Darwin put an arm around Rakkim. "I'm *glad* I didn't kill you."

Rakkim pushed him away. "What did you want to talk about?"

"I just thought after all the time we spent playing hide-and-seek we should have some fun." Darwin shook the dice. The people around the table leaned forward, mouthing prayers. Two Chinese matrons bedecked in jewels screeched encouragement. "I'm disappointed you didn't bring the little woman. She and I had quite a time while you were being cut on. She practically talked my ear off."

"She said *you* were the one doing most of the talking. I think she was bored."

Darwin kept rattling the dice. "You like to shoot craps?"

"Never played."

"Best game in the world. Pure action. You walk past a twenty-one table, it's all this polite banter with the dealer. People *sit* when they play twenty-one. They plot and practice their computer simulations for that half-percent advantage. Craps is raw aggression, hand-to-hand combat. People screaming, bumping each other, pleading with the dice. None of it does any good. No way to predict the dice. No system. No magic formula. It's all luck, and no way to know when it's going to end. And it *does* end. Once you work out the math, the longer you play twenty-one, the better your odds. Craps is the opposite—the longer you play, the more certain you are to lose. That's part of the appeal. When you hold the dice, you're the center of the world. All you can do is ride that hot streak. Ride it until you drop. And you always drop hard. No such thing as a soft landing in craps."

Rakkim yawned.

"Sir?" The stickman tapped the green felt.

Darwin threw the dice hard, bounced them off the far rail. Eleven. "Pay the table," he told the stickman as the crowd applauded. He had $16,000 on the line now.

Two expensive redheads at the far end of the table waved.

Darwin waved back. He was average height and weight, easily overlooked except for the energy that radiated from him. Energy that he would mask when necessary, to become the common man again, harmless as a pancake. Now he was a panther, loose and easy, utterly alert. A man who would hate to be surprised. Rakkim thought of Darwin's car rolling off the road that night in the badlands, the rage he must have felt. Seventeen werewolves slashed to pieces in the rain, and it wouldn't have been nearly enough. There was never enough for a man like Darwin. He must have stood by the side of the road afterward, the rain sluicing him clean . . . he would have known Rakkim was watching.

"What are you smiling at?" asked Darwin.

"You."

Darwin's mouth twitched, but he kept the appearance of good humor. He held out the dice to Rakkim. "Blow on them."

"Die."

Darwin rolled the dice. Snake eyes.

The crowd groaned as the stickman wiped everyone's bets clean.

"You broke my heart, Rikki," said Darwin.

"Don't call me that."

Darwin pocketed the rest of his chips, hugged Rakkim again. "Let's get a drink."

"They're still your dice, sir!" called the stickman.

Darwin walked away from the table, not looking to see if Rakkim was following. He sat at a table in the lounge, watched Rakkim approach. "You've got that slight limp thing down sweet," he said as Rakkim sat across from him. "That faint wince on the right step, as if you're trying to hide the pain. Nice touch. The old man probably buys it. I know better. You're not recovered, but you're close enough." Darwin smiled at the waitress, a petite thing in a short, frilly dress, her belly bare, a golden ring in her navel. "Double bourbon. The best small label you've got. Same for my friend here."

Rakkim started to reject the offer, but stopped. "You have Mayberry Hollow? The twelve-year-old?"

The waitress raised an eyebrow. "Yes, *sir.*"

Darwin watched her wiggle off. "You impressed her." He sat loosely in the booth, one foot up on the leather seat. The wall at his back. He could see the whole room from here. "I've been waiting for you to thank me for saving your life."

"Why?" Rakkim eased closer. "You were just following orders. That's what you do, isn't it?" He noted the faint tinge to Darwin's earlobes and knew he had hit a tender spot. "Maybe I should thank the Old One. He's the one holding the leash."

"There were plenty of times these last couple weeks I wanted to carve on you a bit. I'd be the first to admit that." Darwin had light gray eyes, widely spaced, and slightly upturned at the ends. Wolf eyes. "I've grown fond of you. A lovely, young killer, that's what you are. Reminds me of someone I knew a long time ago. That nonsense with the werewolves . . . nasty, nasty. Yeah, even if the old man hadn't asked me to bring you here, I'd have saved you back at Disneyland. I can change the rules when I want to." Darwin showed his teeth. "I can change them back again too. Anytime I want."

"What a sweet man. Can I buy you an ice-cream cone?"

"Haven't you wondered how SWAT knew where you were?"

Rakkim watched him. "I figured you must have called them in so you could play hero."

Darwin shook his head. "It was your old Fedayeen buddy Pernell. He heard about the million-dollar bounty the Black Robes were offering and grabbed it." He smiled. "Million for Sarah. You're not worth a thing to Ibn Azziz."

Rakkim shrugged. Kept his breathing level. Darwin was telling the truth.

The waitress reappeared, set their drinks in front of them and left.

Darwin picked up his glass, examined the color. Sipped. Smacked his lips. "You know your bourbon. I guess you picked that up in the Bible Belt. Never been there myself, but I hear parts of it are pretty enough." He savored another sip. "I already dealt with Pernell. *That's* what you should really thank me for. That was a pure favor to you."

Rakkim cupped his glass. "I didn't need you to take care of Pernell."

"What are friends for?"

Rakkim let the bourbon slide down his throat in a warm rush. "Must have been a real challenge, killing a cripple."

"No such thing as a crippled Fedayeen." Darwin watched Rakkim over the rim of the glass.

"Pernell must have gotten word that you got away. Probably heard about all the dead men left behind too. He was holed up in a local police station. Surrounded by badges. So there's the challenge you were wondering about." Darwin stuck a forefinger in the last of the drink, sucked it. "I told him you sent your regards before I killed him. Knew you'd want it that way." He leaned forward, pointed to the wall screen behind the bar. "Look what happened to your favorite mullah."

Mullah Ibn Azziz was being interviewed by a reporter from the state news agency. Ibn Azziz's face was heavily bandaged, one eye completely covered as he railed about terrorists and how only the hand of Allah had saved him from the Zionist devils.

"Kind of an improvement," said Darwin.

Rakkim spotted Lucas walking past the row of slot machines, silently cursed his bad luck. There must be a tobacco exporters convention in the city, "Did you do that to Ibn Azziz?" he asked Darwin.

"Don't insult me." Darwin banged his glass on the table for a refill. "If I had gotten the call, he wouldn't be showing off his wounds." He leaned forward, the skin stretched taut across his face as though what was inside could barely be contained. "I'd take him down at his mosque. I'd take him down in the middle of Friday prayers, right in front of the faithful. I'd shove a pork chop in his mouth and scamper off, and that would be that. I've told the old man, all he has to do is say the word—"

"Dave!" Lucas strode over, grinning.

Rakkim stayed seated. Not much chance that Lucas wouldn't notice him—not with his eyes. Lucas was a tobacco grower now, but had been a sniper in the civil war, had killed twenty-seven Islamic soldiers during the house-to-house battle for Nashville. He was still the best shot in Gage County, Georgia, a maker of cornhusk dolls in his spare time.

"Dave, I can't believe it." Lucas clapped him on the shoulder, sat down beside him, a fleshy good ol' boy in a badly cut blue suit. "I'm in town for the China Expo. What are you doing here?"

"Just . . . taking in the sights."

Lucas glanced at Darwin, then back at Rakkim, then tugged at Rakkim's goatee. "What's with the chin whiskers? You look like a billy goat or one of the towel heads around here." His laugh tapered off. "Oh, no. *Don't* tell me that."

"Lucas—"

"Christ o'dear, you're one of *them*." Lucas stood up, knocked the chair over. "They always tell us, watch out for spies, don't trust strangers . . ."

"I guess the joke's on you, peckerwood," said Darwin.

"I'm sorry," Rakkim said, before Lucas could swing on Darwin.

"They tell us to watch for strangers, but you weren't no stranger," said Lucas, still trying to make sense of it. "First time I met you, it was like you were kin." The bags under his eyes had gotten puffier in the four years since Rakkim had seen him. "You sat on my sofa and drank my whiskey. We went hunting together, fishing together . . . My niece . . . Jesus, my niece is *still* on me, asking when you're coming back."

"I wish I had a violin, so I could properly accompany this tale of woe," said Darwin.

Lucas stared down at Darwin. "Hey, shit-fer-brains, are you a spy too?"

Rakkim could see tiny flecks of light in Darwin's eyes. "No, Lucas, he's the guy who's going to kill me someday."

"Yeah?" said Lucas. "That true, mister?"

"It's a possibility." Darwin's right hand flexed ever so slightly.

"Well, sooner rather than later." Lucas turned to Rakkim. Unsure what to do now. He wanted to say something. To keep things going. To unleash his hurt and betrayal. Darwin would be happy to help him. To goad him into more trouble than Lucas could imagine.

"Good-bye, Lucas," said Rakkim.

"Don't leave, peckerwood," said Darwin, affecting a mock-Southern drawl.

"Good-bye," said Rakkim.

Lucas stalked away.

"Here." Darwin palmed Rakkim's knife over to him. He must have been waiting for the opportunity to gut Lucas with Rakkim's own blade. "You spoil all my fun."

Rakkim tucked the knife away. "You haven't seen anything yet."

The waitress brought fresh drinks.

Rakkim took a swallow. The last time he had tasted Mayberry Hollow, he was in Lucas's living room watching old football games. Lucas had years of Georgia football, all the way back before the war. The Georgia Bulldogs—leave it to the rebels to pick a dog as a mascot. There had been some good times with Lucas. The man knew how to tell a joke, and he laughed hardest when the joke was on him. Not this time, though.

Darwin sipped his whiskey. "What have you got on the old man?" He tapped his glass with a fingernail. "Must be something special, because you and the girl got him spooked."

"Hasn't he told you?" Rakkim tilted back in his chair. Darwin had good control, but from this angle Rakkim could track minute changes in the assassin's respiration by watching the tiny hairs in his nose. "Golly, I wonder what that means."

Darwin slid his index finger along the rim of his glass. "I don't need to know everything that goes on in the old man's head."

"Still, a man with your specialty . . ." Rakkim shook the glass so that the ice rattled. "It has to sting."

Darwin's mouth smiled. "Sometimes." He cocked his head, listening, then glared at Rakkim. "We'll have to continue the foreplay some other time, Rikki. The old man wants to talk with you. Chop-chop."

CHAPTER 53

After sunset prayers

"I love this time of the evening," said the Old One, resting his hands on the railing. "The wind dies down and there's this brief moment of stillness before the thermals bring the cool desert air rushing down from the mountains."

Rakkim surveyed the city spread out before them, a vast neon sea glittering in the night. They were alone atop the penthouse on the ninetieth floor of the International Trust Services building. Dozens of bright hot-air balloons drifted against the mountains, catching the last of the light. The Old One was younger than he expected; somewhere in his seventies, a distinguished Arab with a groomed white beard and a face like a hawk. Hint of a British accent. Dark blue suit, collarless linen shirt. A man comfortable with authority.

"It's a pleasure to meet you when you're fully awake. I remember getting a report that Redbeard had adopted some homeless urchin, and wondering what he was up to." The Old One inclined his head toward Rakkim. "I quickly realized Redbeard's wisdom. He and I aren't that different. We each seek allies, instruments to carry out our will. People we can mold and shape. Most of all we seek a successor to carry on our work. I chose to have sons to carry on my legacy. Redbeard chose you."

"I hope your sons worked out better for you than I did for Redbeard."

"You're much too modest."

Rakkim caught the slight change in intonation. The faint whiff of regret. "Your sons must have been quite a disappointment."

The Old One adjusted his cuffs. "Fortunately I have many sons."

"You're going to need every one of them."

The Old One didn't acknowledge the threat. "Do you believe in God, Rakkim? One who takes an active interest in the world? One who rewards submission and obedience?"

"I think God has better things to do."

"I used to say the same thing when I was young. At least I *hoped* He had better things to do. That way He wouldn't notice what I was doing." The Old One folded his hands. "You haven't lost your faith, you merely misplaced it. God has plans for you. That's why you're here right now. Why you didn't die when the police shot you. Why I had Darwin bring you here, and why I had your wounds tended. We are both chosen by God to do great things—a burden and a blessing." He peered at Rakkim with those deep-set eyes. "Some think me a devil and some think me the Mahdi, but I am *a* Muslim. As are you. We are brothers. We should not make war on each other."

Rakkim moved closer. "It's a little late for that."

The Old One was against the railing. Exposed to the night with only the stars above and the concrete far below. "Yes . . . it wouldn't take much effort to toss me over the side."

"Hardly any effort at all. Maybe you should have invited Darwin to join us."

"Darwin has never been allowed up here." The wind was picking up now, and the Old One faced into it. "Besides, you're smart enough to know what would happen to Sarah if a single hair on my head was disturbed."

"Yeah, but even so . . . it *is* a temptation."

The Old One didn't react. "Darwin told me he returned your knife. Quite a blade. They say the only thing more deadly than a naked Fedayeen is a naked Fedayeen with a knife, but then, I've always felt the Fedayeen were overrated. That image of the invincible holy warrior was necessary in the early days, but in spite of the training and those genetic cocktails, you're still only human. Of course, I'm speaking of the Fedayeen assigned to the strike battalions. A coup in Ghana? Muslims massacred in Rio? Russian Spetznats airlifted into Quebec? Send in the Fedayeen!" He wagged a finger at Rakkim. "You, though, you're a horse of a different color. You *and* Darwin."

"Equating me with Darwin is a mistake. I didn't think you made many of those. It only takes one, though, if the mistake is big enough." Helicopters dipped and soared over the city like dragonflies. "The unexploded nuke you left in China, that was a *serious* mistake. They don't make them any bigger."

The city lights blinked before the Old One. "It's not in China." Rakkim stared.

The Old One's eyes were calm as smoke. "The fourth nuke is in the South China Sea, somewhere off the coast of Hainan. Thanks to my own faulty judgment. You look surprised, Rakkim."

"I had expected . . . a denial."

"There should be no secrets between us. That's why you've been given free rein of the city, without being followed or restricted in any way. I have enough slaves. I require a free man."

"Of course."

"I anticipated your doubts. As with all things, they too shall pass." The Old One half closed his eyes, pained. "I *should* have planted the fourth nuke under the Vatican as my son Essam wanted. The blast would have set the Catholics irrevocably against the Jews . . . and Essam would be by my side instead of you." He shook his head. "Essam was the oldest son of the last wife I truly loved. First in his class at MIT. A brilliant boy. Essam wanted to detonate the nuke under Saint Peter's Cathedral, but I was worried about China's growing economic might. I said Shanghai and he was obedient. Now he is dead." The breeze rippled his fine white hair. "It was no windier than this when their fishing boat went down. Safar Abdullah, who had shepherded the fissionable fuel rods, Safar Abdullah, who was already dying, *he* was the only one to survive." He gripped the railing. "Surely Allah was teaching me a lesson in humility."

"You killed at least twenty million people that day. It's a little *fucking* late for a lesson in humility." Rakkim noted the minute tightening at the corners of the Old One's mouth—the profanity annoyed him.

"I've done whatever has been necessary to defend the faith. To *spread* the faith. As the Holy Qur'an commands—"

"Twenty million—"

"They died to restore the caliphate, as has been prophesied. The faithful who perished in Mecca are already in Paradise. The others . . . they are smoldering in hell."

Rakkim forced himself calm. *The man who shouts wins battles; the quiet man wins the war*, that's what Redbeard had taught. "If the bomb is at the bottom of the ocean, you have nothing to fear. So why did Darwin kill Marian Warriq? Why did he kill Fatima Abdullah? What are you afraid of?"

"I'm afraid of running out of time," said the Old One. "Redbeard has already cost me twenty-five years. That's how long it took me to put my pieces back into place on the chessboard. Allah loves a patient man, but I may not have another twenty-five years."

"If there's no proof—"

"Redbeard doesn't need *proof* to cause me grief—haven't you learned that much from him?" The Old One clasped his hands, the backs spotted and blue-veined, the nails yellowed. The hands of a mummy. "The president is dying. I have labored to assure that his successor will owe his allegiance to me. These are . . . tenuous times. Even without proof, Redbeard's digging up the Zionist Betrayal will spread doubt and confusion among the people. I can't allow my plans for a smooth succession to be jeopardized."

"I'm going to enjoy fucking you up."

"Open your eyes, Rakkim, and see what I am offering you." The Old One spread his arms to the Strip, and the whole world was there in perfect miniature—Paris, Rome, Pirate World, the Great Pyramid, Sugarloaf and Rio, Mount Kilimanjaro, Beijing, the Kremlin. "All you see and more can be yours."

Rakkim looked out at the world. He believed the Old One.

The Old One grabbed Rakkim's shoulder, and the current ran through both of them. "A great wind is rising. You can either *become* the storm or be swept away by it. I'm offering you a place beside me. Join me and nothing will be denied you. *Nothing.*"

Rakkim shook him off. "How . . . how about a case of Twinkies? They're supposed to be incredible, and I've heard there's a whole warehouse full of them somewhere. I mean, you did say nothing would be denied me, right?" Rakkim's teeth were chattering. "So, okay, a case of Twinkies and a . . . copy of *Batman* number one, for Sarah."

The Old One's laugh rattled. "I haven't thought of Twinkies in thirty years." His grin was smooth. "Ibrahim, my oldest son remaining, is not going to like you. He's going to be threatened by you, and no matter how much I reassure him, he will recognize that I prefer your company. You are not descended from the Prophet, all blessings upon Him, so you will never ascend to my place. These facts should soften his jealousy, but they won't. Ibrahim fears Darwin, but he will *despise* you."

"Your boy sounds like he's got marshmallows in his nut sack.

You might want to rethink this little campaign to restore the caliphate. You haven't got enough backup."

The Old One measured him. "That's why you're here, Rakkim. You and Darwin."

"Well, *that's* flattering. Are you trying to seduce me? Because if you are, you should know I'm going to end up breaking your heart."

"I'll take that risk." The Old One looked past him. "I wish you and Essam had met. He would have liked you. He wasn't afraid of anyone." His lower lip trembled. "Such a beautiful boy . . . now lost in deep, dark sea. I hate the ocean now. I used to swim every day, but I can't bear the sight of the waves anymore. I sometimes think that's the reason I chose to live in the middle of the desert."

Rakkim watched him. The tears in his eyes seemed genuine.

The Old One cleared his throat. "I've been waiting for you a long time. Same with Darwin. I searched for a retired assassin for years, someone off the books, someone who had broken his leash to the Fedayeen. I used all my resources, but it was only later, when I finally found Darwin, that I learned why it had taken so long." He leaned closer. "Assassins and shadow warriors are linked. Both are elite units of the Fedayeen, fiercely independent . . . and both ultimately betrayed by their leaders." The Old One smoothed his lapels. "Assassins average nineteen missions before they are terminated. If they survive that long, they become too dangerous, too resistant to control, mad with bloodlust. It's the great secret of the Fedayeen, known to no more than a dozen senior officers. Assassins aren't aware of this, of course, they believe the lie of the retired assassin, his identity unknown, living out his years like a pasha. It's not so. There *are* no retired assassins. Except for Darwin. He'd completed forty-five missions when they decided to kill him." His amusement was icy. "They waited too long."

"How do you kill an assassin?"

"Are you taking notes?"

Rakkim didn't answer.

The Old One nodded. "The Fedayeen sent *three* assassins to kill Darwin, experienced men told by their superiors that he had gone rogue." The red lights of the city were reflected in the Old One's eyes. "Darwin killed all three of them. Then he killed General Cheverton, head of the assassins unit. The man who had given the order. So you see, you and Darwin have something *else* in common."

The Old One was trying to impress Rakkim with his knowledge. A sign of his vulnerability or his ego. Rakkim wasn't sure which it was.

"Shadow warriors are extraordinarily valuable, even more useful strategically than assassins, but equally dangerous to the high command. Shadow warriors *always* go native. It's what makes them shadow warriors to begin with. The ability to blend into the environment, to assume the protective coloration of the enemy . . . well, really, what did they expect?" The Old One shook his head. "There are plenty of retired Fedayeen, but no such thing as a retired assassin. No retired shadow warriors either. You and Darwin, you're each one of a kind."

Far beyond the city's lights, beyond the mountains, Rakkim could see the stars. There was comfort in their unimaginable distance. Close enough to see, but too far to reach. He imagined God living out there among the galaxies. That's where *he* would live if he were God.

The Old One leaned against the railing. "That last mission of yours . . . what exactly happened? I've tried to find out, but all the files have vanished. It must have been something special. All I know is that you were gone for months. Much longer than anticipated. It was assumed you were dead. Then you were back. Untouched as always. If you were debriefed, no records survived. Then, a few days later, the two officers above you in the chain of command disappeared. Two top Fedayeen *gone*. As though they had stepped into a mist one morning. From the disposition of the body, Darwin made his displeasure with General Cheverton quite apparent, but no trace of these two officers was ever found. Still, the message was clear. Perhaps that's why they let you retire. Or perhaps it was Redbeard's intervention. He was more powerful then."

"Thanks for the conversation, and the nice view, but I'm a little tired. Still not fully recovered from my wounds. I think I'm going to take a nice warm bubble bath."

"Be careful. You wouldn't want to doze off in the tub. I hope you'll consider my offer."

"Sure, I'll give it the full ponder. Either way, you win, right? If I sign up, you gain a shadow warrior. If I pass on the deal, Darwin dogs me and eliminates anyone who might harm you. I find the evidence, he gets rid of it."

"There is no evidence."

Rakkim shrugged. "Twenty million people dead . . . you didn't even get what you wanted. Here we are all these years later, and you're still worried you won't make it. Pathetic."

"I've acknowledged my mistakes. I misjudged the spiritual resiliency of the Christians. I had lived too long in the city. I believed their faith was flabby and would be quickly discarded. I never imagined the great migration after Kingsley was elected, millions of Baptists and Pentecostals and Catholics trekking to the Bible Belt. I would have expected this from Muslims—did not the Prophet himself, all blessing upon Him, flee Mecca for Medina in his own hour of need? But *Christians*? It would not have mattered if Redbeard had died that day along with his brother. My men at State Security would have taken over, and Kingsley's days as president would have been brief. Then we would have crushed the Bible Belt. The nation needed to be unified then, and it needs to be unified now. No, the loss of the fourth nuclear weapon was an accident, but I take responsibility for underestimating the faith of the Christians."

"That's big of you. Still, you have to admit, that's a major miscalculation. Don't you wonder what else you might be wrong about?"

"Do you expect me to run and hide?" snapped the Old One, his mouth pinched. "When the West wallowed in greed and vice and vanity . . . I prayed. And paid the politicians. When the West banished religion . . . I prayed. And paid the ex-diplomats and journalists, people for whom *everything* has a price. There were times I thought I would never be able to wash myself clean. The nuclear attack merely toppled a rotten tree. Look at the map: China may dominate the globe now, but I've planted seeds in Russia too, and don't you think there were many already there who hated their borders being thrown open to the Zionists? No, Russia is ripe . . . South America is ripe. China remains resistant, but look at the map. Iran, Iraq, Indonesia, Pakistan, East Africa, Nigeria, the whole patchwork of believers awaits only a caliph to stitch them together. A caliph come to lead Muslims to greatness. The long wait is over, Rakkim. We'll start *here*."

Rakkim applauded, the sound ringing hollow across the penthouse. "Wow. That's a great little speech. I bet you don't get interrupted very often. You just build up momentum and roll right on forever. That kind of power is fine when things are smooth, but it can be a disadvantage. You get so used to having your own way and your own say that, when things fuck up, and things *always* fuck up, you don't know what to do. That instant of doubt shakes you. Not so that anyone can see it, you're too good for that, but you know, and it scares you. So you call in somebody like Darwin, but he's hard to control. You can't even invite him up here, because he might do something you haven't anticipated. I bet you haven't even told him what you told me tonight. Am I right?" Rakkim wagged a finger. "See, that could be another mistake. It's dangerous telling Darwin what you're really up to, but it's even more dangerous to keep secrets from him. Assassins and shadow warriors . . . we take things personally. I'd watch out for him if I were you."

"Thank you for your advice." The Old One gave no indication of anger or any other emotion. Not now.

Rakkim smiled. "Well, it's been a nice view, a *really* nice view from the top of the world here, but I'm going to take that bubble bath."

CHAPTER 54

Before afternoon prayers

"Nervous?"

"Excited," said Sarah.

Rakkim checked the mirrors as they left the Joy Luck Boutique. The main mall was crowded, filled with eager shoppers from all over the world. Sleek oil barons from West Africa, technos from Japan and Russia, Arabs trailing their retinues. Tourists in the brave new world. No sign of anyone tracking them; in fact he hadn't sensed any stragglers in days. The Old One said they had free rein, but Rakkim always assumed he was being followed. Always assumed he was being followed by the best.

Sarah had gotten her hair styled at one of the fashionable shops in the Mangrove Hotel, had it cut and stiffened into layers of ringlets. Rakkim hated the flashy look, but it would wash out and allow her to change her appearance quickly. She wore Mylar pants and jacket, purple snakeskin stiletto half-boots, real attention-getters, but in one of the shopping bags Rakkim carried was a change of clothes and shoes.

"I saw Ibn Azziz on TV again, screaming about Zionists," said Sarah. "His whole face looks infected."

"It matches his soul."

"I know you don't think it was Redbeard," said Sarah, "but who else would have gone after Ibn Azziz? Redbeard must have heard he tried to kidnap us at Disneyland and wanted to send him a message."

"Ibn Azziz is too hard-core for messages. Redbeard knows that with someone like Ibn Azziz, you either kill him or turn them. Maybe another one of the Black Robes tried to assassinate him. Mullah Oxley had plenty of friends."

Sarah swayed to the music piped through the mall. Calibrated cash, that's what it was called, harmonies designed to give shoppers energy, to increase their pleasure and sensuality. Sales had increased 17 percent after the music service had been installed, but it was the subaudible program that really made the difference, a vibration tucked under the music that released endorphins in the brain. The music selection was changed every five days, but the subaudible stayed the same. The human constant. "Smile, Rakkim." She wiggled her hips, the Mylar outfit throwing off sparks.

Rakkim smiled. It wasn't an act or the subaudible, she was genuinely happy. Las Vegas didn't apply Web filters—yesterday she had walked into a toy store, picked up a wireless stuffed bear, and tapped into the Devout Homemaker site. There had been a coded message from her mother. Katherine was in Seattle! Sarah posted her intention to taste the recipe for victory radishes soon. They had spent the next half hour in the toy store, playing with nanobots, Sarah all the while keeping up a commentary on the history of toy soldiers and dolls with body functions and how it all meant . . . something.

Sarah danced for Rakkim beside the light fountain in the mall, and a couple of Chinese college girls loaded with jewelry mirrored her moves, the three of them dancing for each other while Rakkim stood transfixed. The Chinese girls finished with bows to Sarah, and she responded with a deep curtsy.

Sarah took Rakkim's hand as they strolled on, so happy she was buoyant.

"Strange to see college girls wearing old-fashioned jewelry," said Rakkim. "I thought the Chinese directed all their energy to the future."

"Retro-chic is all over the runways of Shanghai and Milan. Nigerian divas decked in safari outfits, French software designers dressed as peasants, fake mud and all. It's an attempt to reclaim one's heritage at a time when individualism is under attack." Sarah squeezed his hand. "I was writing a paper on the subject before . . ." She turned around, watched the two Chinese students slip through the crowds.

"What's wrong?"

"I'm not sure. Nothing. There was something . . . but, I don't remember what it was." Sarah shook her head. "Just trying to put the pieces together."

Wrist alarms buzzed around them, alerting the faithful that they had fifteen minutes before afternoon prayers. No one dashed for the exits; no one made the slightest attempt to interrupt what he or she was doing. In the Islamic Republic, Muslims would have responded or had the alarms turned off, not wanting to advertise their lack of piety.

Sarah tensed. "There's Desolation Row."

"Relax. Peter has done this before."

Sarah hesitated. "Do you believe the Old One? I know you're sick of talking about it, but why would he admit to faking the Zionist attacks, admit to a fourth bomb, and then lie about what happened to it? Why not just lie about *everything*?"

"The most effective lie is ninety-nine percent true. If we believe the fourth bomb is *really* at the bottom of the South China Sea, why keep looking? Why not just sign up for the caliphate and do whatever he says? No, we have to act as if he's lying and go forward."

"What if he's telling the truth?"

Rakkim kissed her. "Then the joke's on us."

Sarah ducked into Desolation Row. The chicest of the chic, deliberately transgressive, the mannequins hollow-eyed and gaunt, bare brick walls, stark lighting. The clothes themselves were flimsy and dull, flattering only the most perfect and youthful figure. No prices. The place was packed—mostly Asians and L.A. Catholics, plus a few blond Europeans. She wandered the aisles, fingering the merchandise with the distant show-me expression affected by those to whom price was irrelevant. He went back outside. Checked the reflections in the windows.

In a few minutes, Sarah would go into changing room 9. Instead of slipping into something from Desolation Row, she would change into the casual clothes they had brought. Rakkim would show up a few minutes later, loudly complaining. When she called him in to help her, the two of them would slip through a false panel in the changing room and into the maintenance corridor. Peter would be there. Fifteen minutes later they would be lifting off in one of the hot-air tourist balloons. Only this one would go off course, drifting into the Islamic Republic. Peter said it happened all the time. Wind currents were unpredictable, part of the charm of the balloons. A car would be waiting for them when they came down, gassed up and legally licensed, its GPS unit programmed to show every back road in the country.

"Rakkim?" Sarah's eyes were wide. "I want to show you something." She led him back into the store. "There's a woman beside the shoe display. An older Chinese woman shopping with her granddaughter."

Rakkim pretended to examine a blouse. "She's had some good cosmetic surgery. They tucked up the epicanthic fold, but maintained her ethnic integrity. She looks disgusted by the merchandise, but judging by the diamond studs in her ear, she can afford—"

"Look at her pendant."

"Nice. Plain, but nice."

"That's *all* you see?"

Rakkim moved some ugly tops around. "It's a small, copper pendant with Chinese writing on it. Looks old. What am I missing?"

"I'm not sure." Sarah kissed him. "Go wait for me outside."

"What about Peter?"

Sarah gave him a little push. "Now, *go*, let me shop in peace."

Rakkim heard other women laughing as he stalked out. He found a coffee bar. Men were sprawled on small metal chairs, packages on their laps, looking dazed and exhausted. He ordered a double espresso. Ten minutes later . . .

"Rakkim!" Sarah beckoned from Desolation Row. "I need you to help me decide."

Rakkim walked into the store. The Chinese woman stood at the counter with her granddaughter, the counter overflowing with clothes. He followed Sarah inside changing room 9, tossed the bags into a corner.

Sarah closed the door behind him. They quickly changed clothes. Slid back the panel.

Peter stood with his arms folded. Another man and woman beside him. Body doubles. "Glad you could make it."

Sarah and Rakkim stepped into the corridor. The man and woman quickly put on their former outfits, then slipped into the changing room.

Peter replaced the panel, locked it. He spoke into his cell, and a moment later bio-emergency sirens went off all around them. In the crush to the exits, anyone monitoring the mall security cameras would be fooled by their body doubles.

Peter led them down the passageway.

* * *

"It was too easy," said Rakkim.

"Would you prefer we got caught?" said Sarah.

Rakkim watched other tourist balloons drifting far below, massive orbs stenciled with adverts, iridescent in the sunset. Peter had taken their own balloon to a higher altitude, letting the eastern airstream push them toward the California border. Rakkim shivered, pulled the hood of his heavy jacket tighter. Maybe he was just uneasy being up here in the sky, transitory as a dust mote, completely vulnerable. One handheld missile from below . . .

"You should be used to getting away," said Sarah, sitting cross-legged on a heated cushion. "Disappearing . . . that's one of your specialties, isn't it?"

Rakkim followed the nearest balloon, caught by the thermals, rising slowly. "Yeah, and keeping track of things, planning every detail . . . that's the Old One's specialty."

Sarah tapped away on the cell she had borrowed from Peter. Latest model from China. Full data bank access. Untraceable.

If Rakkim squinted, he could make out the skyscraper where the Old One had offered him the world last week.

Peter broke away from the trusted guests he had invited along for cover. He sidled over, nodded at the Las Vegas skyline in the distance. "Nice view, eh?"

"Any word from our body doubles?" said Rakkim.

"They're driving south toward Arizona," said Peter, still looking toward the city. "Sarah's double said they've had a succession of trailing vehicles, all makes and models. They never get too close and peel off after five or ten miles and are replaced by another. Somebody knows what they're doing."

"Good," said Rakkim. "That's good."

"Thank you, Peter," said Sarah, not looking up from the cell screen.

"Casino management is all about the incurring of debt and

the repayment of same." Peter glanced at Rakkim. "I owed Rakkim."

"Note the past tense," said Rakkim.

Peter smiled. "I'm going to own the place the next time you two visit." The breeze barely moved his lustered hair. "I have a car across the border tracking our progress. It'll be waiting for you when we touch down. I'll call in our location to the authorities after you leave. Even doing the legal limit, you should be in Seattle in two days." He bowed to Sarah, ambled back to the pair on the other side of the balloon.

Sarah waited until Peter was out of earshot. "We're not going to Seattle. We're going back to L.A."

"What are you talking about?"

"The Old One lied to us, just like you said. The fourth nuke wasn't lost off the China coast. It's on the mainland." Sarah had that hard, wide-eyed stare, her brain working overtime. "I just . . . don't know where exactly."

Rakkim sat beside her. "Are you okay?"

"Like Redbeard always said, keep your eyes open. Pay attention. Life's a puzzle. You get new pieces, the picture changes. Don't be afraid to take a fresh look. *That's* what happened, Rikki." Sarah gazed past him. "Fancy's scar . . . it wasn't from a tracheotomy. It was too round. Too perfect. I wondered at the time if she had done it deliberately. Scarification is popular with certain subcultures—"

"Tracheotomies are popular with junkies who overdose."

"That's the old puzzle. I got a new piece at the mall and it changed *everything*."

Rakkim glanced around. Peter and the others were on the far side of the balloon gondola.

Sarah took his arm. "The Chinese woman in Desolation Row wore a medallion the exact same shape as Fancy's scar, resting at the same place at the hollow of her throat. She said it was a good-luck amulet from the village where she was born. The spot on the throat is the precise intersection of five different energy meridians in Chinese medicine." Sarah squeezed him tighter. "Fancy's scar is a *radiation* scar. Her father must have bought her the medallion on his last trip, and it picked up traces of the radioactive material he was transporting. He probably didn't realize he had radiation poisoning until—"

"You spent five minutes with this Chinese woman—"

"Five seconds would have been enough. I knew there was something about Fancy's scar that bothered me. I just didn't have enough data."

"You still don't have enough data."

Sarah showed him the cell screen. A round, gray scar with two small pink spots. She zoomed out and Rakkim saw a man's abdomen with several identical scars running down from his sternum to below his navel.

"Buttons?" said Rakkim.

Sarah nodded. "Silver buttons from a military dress uniform. Probably from Chernobyl or some other hot spot, then were sold and reused by this man's tailor." She zoomed in closer. Closer. The scar filled the screen. The edges had tiny bubbles with faint striations toward the center. "I saw the same stippling on Fancy's scar."

Rakkim stared at the screen. "It was dark at Disneyland—"

"There was moonlight, and I was right beside her. I *know* what I saw. I just didn't know what it meant at the time. Now, I do. The Old One's son may have drowned in the South China Sea, but Fancy's father made it to land. So did the fourth bomb."

"Why . . . would he buy her a souvenir on the most important mission of his life?"

"Because that's what fathers do when they go away," Sarah said quietly. "They buy a memento for their daughter, so she knows he was thinking of her when he was away. That's why

Fancy would have kept the medallion, even after she realized it was ruining her skin. I know *I* would have. If that was the last thing my father had given me, I would have kept it no matter what."

Rakkim remembered the snapshot of Sarah and her father that he had found in her music box, Sarah as an infant resting in her father's arms. He remembered the expression on her face when he'd handed it back to her. So happy she couldn't stop crying. She said it was all she had left of him. Rakkim didn't have anything. Any keepsakes, any photos of his mother and father, had been lost along with everything else before he met Redbeard. Except for the key. A key to the house he'd grown up in. A few days after Redbeard had brought him home, Rakkim had flushed the key down the toilet. He couldn't remember now if it was because he thought he had a new home   or if he was afraid that Redbeard would use the key and all it represented against him.

"The Chinese woman said every village has their own distinct medallion," Sarah said. "When we find the medallion, we'll know where he was on that last trip. We'll know where he planted the fourth bomb."

"Fancy's girlfriend . . . Jeri Lynn. She'll know where the medallion is."

Sarah smiled. "You believe me."

"You haven't been wrong about anything important since I met you."

"We still have to find Jeri Lynn."

"That'll be the easy part." Rakkim hesitated. "If the medallion was so important to Fancy, Jeri Lynn might have buried it with her. She's been dead over a week. You better be ready to dig her up, because that's what it could come down to."

Sarah's eyes blazed now in the setting sun. A cold fire. "I'll do whatever is necessary. Just like you."

CHAPTER 55

Sunset prayers

Rakkim and Sarah walked up the apartment steps just as two women came out the front door. They embraced. "You take care of yourself, Jeri Lynn," said the pregnant blonde.

"If I don't, who will?" said the short brunette. She waited until the blonde eased down the steps. "You here for Fancy's wake?"

"Yes, we are," Sarah said quickly.

"Come on in," said Jeri Lynn. "There's mostly just cheese balls and orange soda supreme, and the sherbet is melting." She tried to smile. "I guess you didn't come for the food—" Her mouth formed a big O. "That isn't . . . ? Cameron? Cameron!" She barreled past them, scooped the kid up, and swung him around as if he were a stuffed animal. She waved to Sarah, tears in her eyes. "Come inside, honey, you made my day."

Sarah and Rakkim followed them into the living room. A couple of other women sat on the couch—a chubby teenager with a baby on her shoulder, and a henna redhead, with a face like a plow horse, looking through a photo album and clucking.

"Girls, this is . . . Sorry, I didn't catch your name," said Jeri Lynn.

"I'm Sarah and this is my friend Rakkim."

"Little mama's Ella, and that's Charlotte," said Jeri Lynn.

Pleased-to-meet-you all around. The baby let out a deep, rumbling fart and everyone smiled. His mother patted him on the back. "Feel better now?" She stood up, popped a cheese ball into her mouth from the paper plate on the coffee table. "We got to go home and start working on dinner." She kissed Jeri Lynn. "I am just *so* sorry."

The henna redhead closed the album. "I should get going too." She gave Jeri Lynn's arm a squeeze. "She was a sweet, sweet girl and we'll all miss her."

Jeri Lynn walked them to the door.

The previous night Rakkim and Sarah had driven into Los Angeles and headed straight for Disneyland. It took them a few hours to find someone who could tell them about Fancy's girl-friend, and even then, they only got a general idea of where the two of them lived. Someplace on the outskirts of New Fallujah, almost to Orange. None of the other rent-wives had ever been invited to visit. It seemed to annoy them. Rakkim wanted to can-vass the supermarkets and drugstores with Fancy's picture, but Sarah had a better idea. She said they should wait until tomorrow, get some rest, and then go back to Long Beach and pick up Cameron. The kid who said he would be waiting for Fancy every day at St. Xavier's Church. Noon. Sarah said that way they could drive around New Fallujah until Cameron recognized the apart-ment. Showing up with Cameron would open the gates.

Jeri Lynn came back, waved them toward the couch, a short woman with frizzy hair, smooth skin, and exhausted eyes. "Sit down. I see people standing up in the house and I think they're bill collectors." She had a brave smile. "You aren't bill collectors, are you?"

Sarah and Rakkim sat on the lumpy, corduroy couch. It was still warm from the other two. The living room had a few pieces of cast-off furniture, a small wall screen, and a giveaway hologram of President Kingsley on one wall. A family holo of Fancy, Jeri Lynn, and three kids was on the cabinet, the kids in shorts and matching tops. They looked happy. Dried cereal was ground into the lime shag carpet. Chocolate-Soy'Os. Breakfast of Champions. A wooden salad bowl on the coffee table contained a couple hun-dred dollars in crumpled bills, along with a few sympathy cards.

Jeri Lynn grabbed Cameron, rubbed his hair. "Damn, I wish

Fancy was here to see you." The hem of her black dress had been altered too many times and was coming loose. She didn't seem to care. She pushed the tray of cheese balls at them. "Eat something, will you?" She plopped in a chair across from the couch. "How did you folks know Fancy? Do you live in her old neighborhood?"

"We . . . we were with her when she died," said Sarah. It was probably a good idea to get it over with, but Rakkim would have approached it more obliquely.

Jeri Lynn looked back and forth between them. "You were the ones asking around for her that night."

"Yes," said Sarah.

"Cameron, why don't you go in the kitchen and fix yourself something to eat?" said Jeri Lynn. "I know you're hungry."

"I'd rather take a shower first," said Cameron. "If it's okay?"

"Second door on the right. Let me know when you're done and I'll get you some clean clothes. You're about Dylan's size." Jeri Lynn waited until he had disappeared into the bathroom. "I appreciate you bringing him here. Fancy . . . she had a real sweet spot for him. Always talking about bringing him here to live with us." She arranged her black dress, blew a strand of hair that fell over her face. "What do you want?" she said to Sarah. She had hardly looked at Rakkim since they'd arrived. "You must want something."

"We're very sorry for what happened," said Sarah. "Fancy was—"

"My kids are coming home from school in about an hour. I don't want you here upsetting them. They've already been through enough. Cameron can stay. The kids like Cameron."

"The men who killed her . . . they were trying to stop us—"

"I haven't even been able to bury her." Jeri Lynn twisted the gold band on her left ring finger. "Her body is in a cooler at the funeral home, waiting for me to come up with the money to bury her properly." She glanced at the bills in the wooden bowl.

"We would—"

"The local mosque wouldn't help us. They said Fancy wasn't a Muslim anymore. I don't blame them. She prayed at home, but she was too ashamed to go to mosque. Muslims have their rules. Body has to be buried within twenty-four hours. Fine." She kept twisting her ring. "Catholics are no better. I'm Catholic, but I'm not their kind of Catholic. So they won't bury her." She looked at Sarah. "My kids keep asking when they can put flowers on her grave, and I keep telling them soon." She kept her eyes on the holo portrait of her and Fancy holding hands. "We had a good life before you people showed up looking for her. Not a perfect life . . . She hated what she did and so did I, but that was her night self. That wasn't who she really was, that was just a game she played. The rest of the time, we were a family and we were happy. We were *happy*."

"We'll pay for the funeral," said Sarah. "No strings."

Jeri Lynn didn't react.

"Did Fancy own a necklace from when she was a little girl?" said Sarah. "A small, round medallion with Chinese characters on it?"

"What do you want that thing for?" said Jeri Lynn. "It's not worth nothing, except to Fancy."

"Could I please see it?" said Sarah.

"It's not for sale, I don't care how much money you got. Fancy's going to be buried in her favorite dress. In her favorite shoes. She's going to be buried with her hair fixed just right, and her makeup perfect . . . and with that medallion around her neck."

"That medallion is part of an investigation," said Sarah. "That medallion—"

"What are you, cops? The cops are the ones who killed her."

"Cops didn't kill her," said Rakkim.

Jeri Lynn stared at him.

"His name is Darwin," said Rakkim. "I saw him do it. I tried to help, but—"

"The police shot Rakkim," said Sarah. "He almost died."

"Why did this Darwin *do* it?" Jeri Lynn's face was flushed.

"That's what he does," said Rakkim.

"Could we please see the medallion?" asked Sarah. "Help us, Jeri Lynn."

"Jeri Lynn!" Cameron stuck his dripping head out of the bathroom door. "Can I have some clothes, please?"

Jeri Lynn got up with a sigh, walked down the hall toward the bathroom.

"We know the medallion is here," Rakkim said to Sarah. "At a certain point we have to stop asking."

Sarah placed a small pile of $100 bills in the wooden bowl. "We're not at that point yet."

"You're the one who thinks the medallion is the answer to all our prayers."

"I said not *yet*."

"I was remembering when we first met, Maurice," said Redbeard. "You were adjutant to General Sinclair. I saw this tall African with the bearing of a king and wondered if you'd last a year with all the officers arrayed against you. The things they said behind your back . . ."

"It couldn't have been worse than the things they said to my face," said General Kidd.

Redbeard had shown up unbidden and unannounced at the small conservative mosque, the only white face among the Somali worshipers. He and General Kidd now sat cross-legged on rugs spread under a wisteria tree, eating dates and sipping strong, sweetened coffee that Kidd's youngest wife brought them. No bodyguards in sight. None needed.

"We've seen a lot of history." Redbeard spat out a date seed. "You and I sailed some dangerous waters together, yet I feel the worst of our voyage still lies ahead."

"The nation has gone off course, Thomas." Kidd blew across his cup. "We were to be a light upon the world. Now, we might as well be kaffirs, the way the young people behave. They are soft and given to indolence and idolatry."

"The young should be given time to find the way."

"The young should be *instructed* in the way."

Redbeard slurped his coffee. "Would you want Ibn Azziz to do the instructing?"

Kidd popped a fat date into his mouth, chewed slowly. "I heard you had a death in the family. The men responsible . . . they are dead?"

"The men who stole her from outside her mosque are dead. Killed by the man who sent them before I could find them. As if I needed to question them to know who was responsible." Redbeard tore at his beard. "Allah has given you a choice. You can keep your oath and stand beside your president, or you can become the sword of a mullah who abducts and murders devout women. A mullah who takes refuge in the Grand Mosque with a hundred bodyguards. Is the protection of Allah not enough for him?"

Kidd's face was a mask, but his eyes betrayed his turmoil. "I love President Kingsley as my own father, but he is old. He is dying."

"We're all dying, Maurice."

"Did you come to tell me that, old friend?"

Redbeard reached into the basket of sweets, smiled. "I came for the dates."

Rakkim had just finished checking the street again when Jeri Lynn came back. She was carrying a small, red enamel box.

"God bless you," said Sarah.

"Don't get excited yet." Jeri Lynn sat down beside Sarah, opened the box. "Fancy said her daddy give this to her when he came back from China that last time." Jeri Lynn took it out of the box, dangled it by the black woven-fiber cord, the beaten-copper amulet decorated with Chinese ideograms. The amulet slowly turned as she held it up. "Fancy said she didn't take it off for years, called it her good-luck charm, but then I guess her luck turned. She was older then and it made the skin underneath flake off, and things went downhill from there. She said she thought it was a judgment from Allah, because of the way she was living, so she put it away for safekeeping. I used to see her wearing it sometimes, looking in the mirror and smiling." Jeri Lynn tucked it back in the box. "It's not much to look at, but Fancy loved this necklace."

Sarah made no move to take the box.

Jeri Lynn replaced the lid. She looked at Rakkim. "Cameron told me some things about you. He said he saw you kill a man with your bare hands. Said he never seen anything like it. I want your promise. I want you to promise that if I give you this medallion, you're going to find this Darwin. You're going to find him and you're going to kill him."

"It could take a while," said Rakkim.

"Just promise that you'll do it. I'm not asking for a schedule."

"I promise."

Jeri Lynn turned to Sarah beside her. "Can I trust him to keep his word? Fancy never had much luck with men, and I had even less."

Sarah stared at Rakkim. She was thinking about what he had told her about the assassin. That he had no chance against him. "I trust him."

Jeri Lynn handed her the case. "I hope this does what you think it will."

Sarah tucked the box away.

"I don't know if it makes a difference to you, but I would have killed Darwin anyway," Rakkim said to Jeri Lynn. "I would have killed him for Fancy and a few others he's butchered. I made up my mind about that a long time ago."

Cameron wandered out from the back of the house. His hair was combed. He was wearing clean pants and a frayed L.A. Ramadan 2035 T-shirt. He sat in Jeri Lynn's lap and didn't even look embarrassed. "You sure I can stay?"

"Long as you want, baby." Jeri Lynn put her arms around him, but kept her eyes on Rakkim. "You keep your promise, and if you can make this Darwin suffer, that's all the better. Make it *hurt*. Make him howl so loud the demons in hell will know he's on the way."

CHAPTER 56

Before noon prayers

"You said we were to meet *tomorrow*," said Professor Wu. He looked from Sarah to Rakkim, unsettled by the lack of harmony a broken engagement engendered. "We were to meet at the King Street Café, not here. Not at my home. We were to have dim sum, Sarah, and—"

"Could we come in, Professor?" said Rakkim. "I'd rather not stand out in the cold."

Wu glanced at Sarah, disappointed, although she wasn't sure if he was annoyed at their unannounced arrival or at Rakkim's interruption of him. Wu backed away, waved them inside. "Please." He led them into a small, sparsely furnished living room, moving slowly. The bare spot at the back of his head had expanded in the years since she had last seen him and now encompassed most of his liver-spotted skull. He waited for them to sit on the clean but threadbare sofa, then excused himself, said he had to retrieve the photos of the medallion that they had onlined him.

Rakkim and Sarah had driven straight through from Southern California, keeping to the main roads, lost in the traffic. According to a jeweler in Long Beach, Fancy's medallion was slightly radioactive. Not enough to pose a danger, but still more proof of its connection to the planting of the fourth nuke. The trip had been uneventful, except for a multicar accident in the Bay Area that threatened to detour them into San Francisco, a rabid fundamentalist stronghold. Terrible place, the old Golden Gate Bridge renamed for an Afghan warlord and decorated with the skulls of homosexuals purged after the transition. A section of the bridge had collapsed two weeks ago. Zionists or witches blamed. Any cars entering the city would be searched. Cells with picture capability or Web access would be confiscated, women dressed immodestly beaten. If Rakkim and Sarah's forged marriage papers had been questioned, they would have been arrested for suspicion of fornication, and worse.

It had been raining in Seattle for the last five days, a cold, steady downpour that drove people off the streets and sent cars sliding into ditches. Sarah missed the heat and freedom of Southern California, but it was still good to be home. Or what passed for home. A warehouse in the industrial section south of the Sheik Ali Mosque. Another one of Rakkim's hiding spots. Three days ago she had sent photos of the medallion to Wu, a Chinese scholar dismissed a few years ago during a bout of campus politics.

Wu shuffled back into the living room, slowly lowered himself into a reading chair. His fingers curled against the leather arms of the chair. His neck was so thin it could barely support his head. "Tuesday is the best day for dim sum at the King Street Café," he said, Adam's apple bobbling. "Madam Chen is only able to work one day a week, but her spring rolls with black mushroom are still the best in the city."

"Perhaps next time," said Sarah.

Wu had a laugh like the bark of a seal. He looked at Rakkim. "A brilliant student, but she seemed to delight in flouting proper procedure. Always going her own way."

"I'm shocked," said Rakkim.

Another laugh from Wu, and then his expression slumped. "I'm sorry to disappoint you, Professor Dougan, but I am unable to help you determine the origin of the medallion. There are tens of thousands of small villages in China, and each one of them takes pride in minting their own medallion to celebrate the yearly plum festival."

"No apology necessary," said Sarah, trying to hide her disappointment. "I didn't realize the enormity of the request."

Wu clung to the arms of the reading chair. "I did what I could. The medallion commemorated the 2015 plum festival, the year of the sheep. The workmanship is crude, but that's part of its charm to collectors. I assume that's where you got it?"

"Yes," said Sarah.

"The collector had no idea what village it came from?"

"No," said Sarah.

Wu nodded. "The slogans on your medallion, *longevity* and *prosperity*, are a common hallmark of such items, I'm afraid. From the style of the ideograms, I would guess that it came from Sandouping, Yichang, or perhaps the Hubei province, but again, that is a lot of ground. China is vast." He lowered his eyes. "I deeply apologize."

Sarah clasped her hands in gratitude. Those three areas were all in the vicinity of the Three Gorges Dam, and the date, 2015, was the year the other bombs had been detonated. She stood up, bowed. "Professor, we appreciate your help."

"Very little help." Wu struggled to get to his feet. "A retired professor enjoys nothing more than to be called upon by a favorite pupil." His eyes sparkled. "Other than sharing lunch with her and her companion."

Rakkim helped him up. "Thank you again, sir."

"I wish you could have waited," said Wu, walking them to the door. "I still haven't heard from Master Zhao."

Rakkim stopped. "You forwarded the photos of the medallion?"

"Of course. When I realized my own poor knowledge was insufficient—"

"We asked you not to do that, Professor." Sarah felt Rakkim's tension, his eagerness to leave. He had been the one who had insisted they drop in on Wu unannounced.

"I thought . . . well, often collectors have been known to import historical objects without permission, but this is of such recent origin . . ." Wu looked from one to the other. "I was trying to help."

"How many people did you send the photos to?" said Rakkim.

"Six." Wu grimaced. "Including my son, Harry Wu, adjunct professor at the University of Chicago, who could not be bothered." He caught himself. "I hope I have not caused a problem. Master Zhao may still be of use to you. He is quite knowledgeable."

"There is no problem at all, Professor," said Sarah. "May you be well."

Rakkim lightly clasped Wu's hand, felt the man tremble. "Professor, Sarah and I would like to invite you for dim sum a month from now. The fourteenth. That's a Tuesday too." Rakkim smiled. "We'll see if Madam Chen's spring rolls are as good as you say. We'll meet you at the King Street Café at one p.m. on the fourteenth."

"Wonderful!" said Wu, beaming. "I'll bring my appetite, if you bring yours."

The two of them were driving away before Sarah spoke. "I doubt that the six people Wu contacted will be in touch with the Old One."

"They don't need to. The Old One probably has all kinds of triggers scattered throughout the academic world. Computers, databases . . . A keyword in a query, that's all it takes."

Sarah cursed quietly, then stopped. *"That's* why you made the lunch date."

Rakkim nodded. "This way, if Darwin comes calling, he'll want to keep the professor alive." He checked the rearview. "If things go right, by next month the Old One will have other priorities."

"Thank you, Rikki."

"Yeah."

"There's another way we can find out what village the medallion came from. You're not going to like it though."

Rakkim laughed. "Why, is it *dangerous*?"

Her eyes were bright. "Worse."

CHAPTER 57

After sunset prayers

"Ambassador, may I present Sarah Dougan and her escort, Rakkim Epps," said Soliman bin-Saud.

Ambassador Kuhn nodded to Sarah, then Rakkim. "Welcome to our tiny bit of Switzerland." He was a short, round man with an upward-curling, waxed mustache and watery blue eyes. An ornate red jacket with gold piping and full-cut black trousers gave him the appearance of an overfed bird. He gave a wan smile to bin-Saud. "A pleasure to see you, Soliman. Pity your esteemed father could not join us."

Bin-Saud plucked a canapé from a tray offered by a liveried waiter, nibbled at foie gras wrapped in rose petals. Bin-Saud was a handsome Arab with a perfumed, square-cut beard, dark eyes, and lips that were too soft. "Matters of state called. I'm sure you understand." He took another canapé from the hovering waiter, offered it to Sarah, holding it just above her lips. "You *must* try it, darling."

Sarah took one from the tray. "Ummm, it is good. Rakkim?"

Rakkim waved the waiter away.

"Forgive my guest's impertinence, Ambassador," said bin-Saud. "Mr. Epps is Fedayeen, and as you know, they are creatures of simple pleasures."

"Oh, my, yes, fearsome beasts from what I've heard." The ambassador studied Rakkim. "Can you *really* kill a man with one finger?"

Rakkim reached out too quickly for the ambassador to react, twisted the left tip of his mustache. "There, that's better."

The ambassador stepped back, eyes wide. "Come . . . come with me, Soliman. You really should sample the hummingbird in aspic." Kuhn nodded to Sarah and Rakkim. "Please enjoy yourselves."

Sarah watched the ambassador and Soliman make their way across the room. The ambassador glanced back once, hurried on. She pretended she hadn't enjoyed what Rakkim had done.

The party was crowded with perhaps three hundred guests, laughing and eating and drinking, ambassadors and diplomatic staff from almost every embassy in the capital of Seattle. Nigerians and East Africans in a blaze of color, Brazilians and Argentineans in Western formal attire, Swedes and Norwegians, and Australians, some Sarah recognized from past events she had attended with Redbeard, but plenty of new faces. Though they had no formal diplomatic relations, there was even a representative from the Bible Belt, an older man with a mane of gray hair, wearing a black frock coat like a country preacher.

"Soliman looked happy to see you tonight," said Rakkim. "You don't meet many Saudis who kiss ladies on the hand. And so elegant. How many pounds of emeralds do you think were sewn into the hem of his robe?"

A waiter offered alcoholic and nonalcoholic champagne. Sarah opted for non. He didn't.

"Soliman did me a favor inviting us to come here tonight," said Sarah, sipping her drink. The bubbles tickled. "When his father finds out, he'll get in trouble, because his father thinks the Swiss are libertines. Besides, would you rather we went to Redbeard for help?"

"I just don't like him."

"That's okay, he doesn't like you either."

Bin-Saud's father was right about the Swiss: they *were* libertines. Decadent and agnostic and rich beyond counting. Strictly neutral for the last six hundred years, they dealt with every government regardless of politics or religion, and they made money from them all. The Swiss had no allies, no enemies—they only had clients. A string quartet played Mozart, making sure that no one's sensibilities would be offended. The party featured trays of crab and prawns and caviar for the Chinese and Russians and South Americans, trays of halal delicacies for the faithful. *Everyone* got to partake of the euphoria generators in the air-conditioning, the microscopic mist of neurotransmitters and pheromones, a boon to relaxation and feelings of intimacy.

Sarah felt a little light-headed. Her bare shoulders tingled and she could feel every inch of the body-hugging formal dress she had bought today in the modern district. She wished she and Rakkim were someplace alone. "What is it, Rikki?"

"I don't know."

"You're restless."

Rakkim exchanged glasses with a passing waiter, used the opportunity to scan the room. "I feel like we're being watched."

"I'm sure we *are* being watched. That's why people come to

embassy parties: to look at other people and try to figure out what they're really up to."

"I don't mean like that."

"Well . . . we won't stay long then." Sarah felt the Chinese medallion tucked into a pocket of the gown. "Rakkim . . . when you promised Fancy's girlfriend that you would kill Darwin, you were just saying that, weren't you?"

Rakkim nodded as he took in the room.

"You were just making sure she would give us the medallion?"

"I've already told you that," said Rakkim.

Sarah stared at him and couldn't decide if he was telling the truth. "Dance with me."

"Living dangerously, are we?"

"No." Sarah took him by the hand, led him through the crowd. "I spotted the Chinese ambassador dancing with one of his concubines. The old letch has been giving me the eye since I was fourteen."

A tray of tiny curried eels passed by at eye level, and Rakkim wished he could join them curled on their beds of ice.

Anthony Colarusso sat at the kitchen table in his boxers, slathering peanut butter onto white bread and wishing that Marie had stocked up before she'd left. The knife banged against the glass sides of the jar. Almost out. He had been living on peanut butter sandwiches and takeout ever since she and the kids had gone into hiding. The bread tore under his rough handling and he shook his head. Should have heated the peanut butter in the microwave, but he was no cook.

"Toast the bread, Pop, you won't have that problem."

Colarusso jumped up, knocked the chair over.

Anthony Jr. stood in the doorway from the cellar, laughing.

Colarusso ran to him, smacked him a couple times while the kid pretended to be hurt. "Trying to give me a heart attack, you little shit?"

Anthony Jr. put him in a bear hug, lifted him off the ground. Colarusso outweighed his son by eighty pounds, but the kid swung him around as if the beefy detective were one of those ballet dancers with the short skirts.

"Put me down!" Colarusso stood there in his polka-dot boxers, hands on his hips. "How did you get past Ames and Frank?" He picked his police-issue off the counter, thumbed the safety as he peeked out the kitchen window. "They're supposed to be watching the place."

"Come on, Pop, I've been sneaking in and out of this house since I was twelve. Couple of uniforms aren't going to spot me." Anthony Jr. sat at the table, ran a finger around the rim of the peanut butter jar, and put it in his mouth. "Couple of uniforms aren't going to spot the guy who came to our front door either. Even if they do, they're not going to stop him."

Colarusso stayed standing. "You're supposed to be with your mother and sisters."

"Eight days with Cousin Charlotte was like eighty years in purgatory. She's even a worse cook than Mom, and all she does all day is knit sweaters for dolls." Anthony Jr. dipped into the peanut butter again. "They're safe, don't worry. A Christmas card once a year isn't much of a connection to follow. Besides, this guy at the door, it was *you* he wanted."

Colarusso hefted the pistol. "Well, I'm here if he wants to come knocking again."

Anthony Jr. looked up at him. "I'm here too, Pop."

"You've been taking dance lessons, Ambassador," purred Sarah.

"No, but I have lost a little weight," said Lao, the Chinese ambassador, dipping her, using the occasion to lightly bump bellies. A short, round, middle-aged man in traditional garb, silk slippers on his feet. A player almost since the changeover, Lao was a deadly trade negotiator for one of the two current superpowers.

Only the Russian ambassador carried as much heft in the capital, and he had been called back to Moscow. "I believe it's changed my center of gravity for the better."

"Yes, I can definitely tell."

"I was a bit surprised to see you here tonight with Soliman." The mascara didn't make Lao's eyes any less piercing. "A nice boy, but I thought you had sent him on his way."

Sarah smiled. "We're just good friends."

"Of course, you are." Lao nodded toward where Rakkim hung on the periphery. "I see Redbeard sent along a bodyguard. It's really not necessary. One of the many delights of the Swiss embassy parties is the minimal need for security. We *all* have an interest in maintaining a place for civilized pleasures without the petty concerns of state."

"I'll remember that next time, Ambassador, but you know my uncle. *Nothing is more dangerous than a place of safety.*"

"Does he insist you take your bodyguard to your soft, warm bed?" Lao laughed at his wit, eyes glittering. "Forgive me, Sarah. Chinese women are bold, and I forget the sensibilities of Islamic women."

"Eighteen years in the capital and you forget?" Sarah gently chided him. "You're a naughty boy, Ambassador."

"Getting more naughty every year," said Lao, spinning her faster. The light caught the sheen of sweat on his forehead. He smelled like lilacs. He slipped a fan out of a voluminous sleeve, waved it rapidly. "I do believe that Ambassador Kuhn has turned up the euphoria mist. I feel positively giddy."

Sarah was grateful for the break in the music and strolled over to a quiet corner of the ballroom. "I have a favor to ask."

Lao's flirtatiousness was gone.

"I have a piece of jewelry I want to show you. A medallion from your own country. A small-town piece honoring the yearly plum festival." Sarah laid the medallion in his hand.

Lao looked it over, shrugged. "It's of no value. No *apparent* value."

"I'm trying to find out what village it came from."

Lao slipped the fan back into his sleeve, showed her a hard smile. "I'm a city boy."

"I'd like you to keep the medallion," Sarah said, closer now. "When you find out the village it came from, I think you should have the authorities start a search. There's something in the vicinity of the village . . . something of great interest to all of us."

Lao waved the fan, covering his mouth. "What *exactly* am I looking for?"

Sarah closed his hand around the medallion. "Radiation."

CHAPTER 58

Before noon prayers

Rakkim woke up, rolled into a fighting stance.

Sarah closed the door behind her, swept into the room wearing a dark blue chador. "I didn't want to wake you when I left." She looked proud of herself for slipping out so quietly. She deserved to be.

They had taken a circuitous route back to the warehouse after the embassy affair. Rakkim was still certain that they had been watched at the party, but he was just as certain that they hadn't been followed. Still exhilarated by the euphoria mist, they had made love for hours, tearing at each other, more interested in friction and heat than intimacy. She had dozed off afterward, but he had lain awake thinking of Mardi. She had disappeared from the Blue Moon two weeks ago, just as he had told her to do. Her cell was not in service, which was smart. She had done everything right. He hoped it was enough. Tired now, the bed warm and Sarah curled beside him, he had fallen asleep as the call to dawn prayers had echoed down the cobblestones. And dreamed of Mardi and Darwin nuzzling and sharing drinks at the Blue Moon while Rakkim struggled to make himself heard.

"You look so happy," said Rakkim. "Did you call the Chinese embassy?"

"Ambassador Lao is unavailable, which isn't surprising. Even if they recognize where the medallion came from, it will take a while to search the area." Sarah took off her head scarf, tossed aside her robe. She had a sheer slip on underneath, her nipples puckering the silk. "That's not why I'm happy. I went to mosque and accessed the Devout Homemaker site. My mother left me a message." Her cheeks flushed as she sat on the bed. "We're meeting her this afternoon. She wants you there too." Sarah played with the sheets. "I can hardly wait. I mean, I'm afraid too, but . . . it's been so long."

"Where are we supposed to meet her?"

Sarah lay beside him and cocked her leg across him. "I don't know . . . but *you* do." She kissed him, her face cold from being outside. "My mother must have found out that we're together. *Remind your companion to put his best foot forward.* Must be code. She wanted to make sure I wasn't a poacher." Sarah's head was on the pillow beside him as she slid her hand under the sheets. "Do you know what that means?"

Rakkim felt as if he had stepped off the edge of the world. "I think so."

Ibn Azziz lay back as the hypodermic needle penetrated the infected abscess under his ruined left eye. The pain was incandescent. He felt warm fluid draining down his cheek, smelled the stink of rotting tissue, and for the thousandth time he silently cursed Redbeard's housekeeper for what she had done to him. His hands clenched, but not a sound escaped his lips.

The doctor started trimming away the dead flesh around the raw socket. The last thing that eye had seen before the old hag had clawed it to jelly was her determined face as his bodyguards stabbed her again and again. He wished he hadn't given her body back. He should have heaved her into the sewer or left her in a cornfield for the ravens to pick at. He had been merciful to one who didn't deserve mercy. Never again. Ibn Azziz had been in touch with the ayatollahs in San Francisco and Denver, two of the most devout cities in the country. They were ready to follow his commands at a moment's notice.

His good eye blinked rapidly, uncontrollably, tearing as the doctor began to drain another abscess, a deeper pocket under his nostrils that went almost to the bone. The pain rolled through him like a great tide pulled from the sea by the moon. If there was one great gift Allah had given Ibn Azziz, it was the ability to bear suffering. It wasn't that he didn't feel the pain, it was that he knew pain was a road to Paradise. Ibn Azziz hissed as the doctor applied antiseptic, lips fluttering with ecstasy.

Rakkim pushed open the door to the barbershop, held it open for Sarah. He had walked past the storefront five minutes earlier, glanced inside to make sure that Elroy was in back.

"Haircut?" said one of the barbers, looking up from his magazine.

Rakkim jabbed a thumb toward the shoeshine stand. "Need to put my best foot forward."

"Wondered if you were going to figure it out," said Elroy as Rakkim sat down in the chair, put his feet up. Elroy pulled brushes and polish out of his kit, still grumbling. "I told Spider he'd have to give you more hints."

Sarah sat beside Elroy. "Where *is* she?"

"Nice to meet you too." Elroy smeared black polish on Rakkim's boots, worked it in. "Okay, I give up, you clouded my mind with your beauty. She's in the parlor with Professor Plum."

"*Clue?*" Sarah laughed. "How do you know about Clue?"

"Clue, Scrabble, Risk, Big Business, Candy Land—we play all the old games in my family." A brush in each hand, Elroy smacked Rakkim's boots in a steady rhythm. "I could bankrupt your ass in Monopoly in less than an hour. Guaranteed. I'll play you for a hundred dollars, real money, and spot you both utilities."

Rakkim had no idea what they were talking about.

Sarah sat back and let Elroy continue.

Rakkim watched the brushes fly. "Your family's all right?"

"I'm sharing a room with four brothers instead of two. Refrigerator keeps cutting out. The computers are up and running, that's all that matters. That . . . and we're together. We're safe." Elroy leaned back, examined his work. The boots were obsidian bright.

Rakkim gave him a twenty. "They look great."

"Twenty bucks? Sucker." Elroy tucked the bill away. "There's a fix-it store around the corner," he said quietly. "It's closed, but if you go down the alley, Spider will let you in. *She's* there too." He eyed Sarah. "You look like her. Some people get all the luck."

"Thank you." Sarah kissed Elroy on the cheek. "The utilities? Worst properties on the board. I'll spot *you* the utilities, if you give me the three light blues. I'll even let you land there rent-free twice."

"No deal, lady." Elroy nodded at Rakkim. "Thanks for letting me meet the brains of the outfit, tough guy."

Rakkim and Sarah went out the back of the barbershop and started down the alley. A few abandoned cars, windows broken out. Boarded-up buildings. Dog shit and graffiti and soggy cardboard boxes. Typical run-down Catholic neighborhood.

"I like him," said Sarah.

"He likes you too." Rakkim heard a faint tapping and turned around. Looking. As though he had dropped something. They weren't being followed. A door at the rear of the fix-it shop opened and Sarah stepped inside. Rakkim backed in, taking one more look outside, and the door closed behind him.

Spider shook his hand. A gnome in the dimness of the shop, his curly hair under a watch cap, his smile nearly hidden by his full beard. Nearly.

"I want to see my mother," said Sarah.

Spider opened another door, a door to a small workroom. She was standing inside, waiting. Katherine Dougan. Older than the pictures of her that Rakkim had seen, and she had clearly spent a lot of time outdoors, but definitely *her*.

For all her prior eagerness, Sarah just stood there, staring back at her mother. Neither of them moved. Finally Sarah took a small step and her mother rushed toward her, held her, the two of them crying now, hanging on to each other, tears streaming down their faces.

Rakkim turned to Spider, who shrugged, embarrassed.

Katherine held Sarah back, taking a good look at her, staring at her hair, her face, her body, taking in her height, her skin, drinking her up.

Sarah laughed. Did a slow pirouette.

Katherine hugged her again, the two of them sobbing. They still hadn't said a word.

Rakkim looked around the workroom. It was grimy, but a new Chinese laptop with a couple of satellite nodules was poking out of a case. Straight-off-the-shelf legal in Las Vegas, but a major felony in the Islamic Republic. Ten years minimum. *If* you gave up your source. A whisker-thin monitor taped to the wall showed eight camera views. Two of the alley in both directions, two of the street the same way. The other four views were from high up, showing a panoramic view of the whole sector. If anyone was coming that didn't belong, Spider would have plenty of time to get them all out of here.

"How did you find her?" Rakkim asked Spider.

Spider's right eye twitched. "How long has Redbeard been looking for her? And that other one . . . how long has *he* been looking for her? Twenty years?" Spider's mouth jerked with pleasure. "It took me three weeks. Not that I didn't have some advantages." He glanced over at Katherine and Sarah. They were talking quietly now, their hands still on each other, as though if they broke contact, one of them would disappear.

"Was she in Seattle the whole time?" said Rakkim. "I can't believe—"

"Don't be an idiot." Spider checked the surveillance monitor every six seconds as if he had a chronograph inside his head. "She was in a safe spot. I have to give her credit. If she hadn't communicated with Sarah, I doubt that she would have ever been found."

"You tracked her through her uplink? You told me she was bouncing all over the world."

Spider smiled. *Way* too many teeth. "It was impossible to track the call she made to Sarah at the Mecca Café, but I did some backtracking. I pulled the accounts of every business in the vicinity of the café, spreading out in concentric rings. It took a while, but I got a pattern of contacts between them going back over a year. I did some logarithmic analysis . . ." He looked pained. "I'll try to keep it simple. The signals were bouncing all over the globe, but they all started at a certain satellite. Except there was no satellite at the point of origin. What I finally realized is that the satellite used for the original uplink was an old regime satellite in a highly degraded orbit. No one uses that satellite anymore. Once I figured that out . . . well, it was just a matter of research and triangulation."

"You did all this while you were escaping from the Black Robes?"

"I intimidate you, don't I?" said Spider.

"A little."

"Shall I make you feel worse?" Spider shifted his eyes, checked his screens. Rakkim barely noticed anymore. "Elroy is smarter than I am. I can barely keep up with him. I've got a seven-year-old daughter . . . in a few years, she's going to put Elroy in his place."

"Benjamin?"

"Yes, Katherine," said Spider.

Rakkim stared at Spider. He had never heard the man's given name used before.

"Show them, please," said Katherine.

Spider touched a key on the laptop. They huddled around him.

On-screen there was a flicker of gray, then the image of a man sitting in a chair. "My name is Richard Aaron Goldberg." One of the most recognized faces in the world, the Zionist team leader who had planted the nuclear bomb that had devastated New York City. His digital confession familiar to every schoolchild, a digital played endlessly on the anniversary of the attack. "Eleven days ago, my team—"

"No, no, no. Your body language is wrong. How many times must we go over this? You have to maintain a back arch. And jiggle your leg slightly. You're under duress, remember? Try it again."

"That voice . . . is that Macmillan?" said Rakkim.

"My name is Richard Aaron Goldberg. Eleven days ago—"

"You're not maintaining pupil consistency. It doesn't matter if they're slightly dilated or not, what matters is consistency. It's the change in size that denotes a lie." A spindly man with thick glasses stepped into the frame, placed a hand on Goldberg's diaphragm. "Use the breathing techniques I taught you." He backed out of view.

"Oh my God," said Sarah.

Goldberg cleared his throat. "My name is Richard Aaron Goldberg. Eleven days ago my team simultaneously detonated three nuclear weapons. One destroyed New York City. Another destroyed Washington, D.C., and the third left the city of Mecca a radioactive death trap. Our intention . . ." He placed a hand on his shaking knee. "The plan was for radical Islamists to be blamed. To drive a wedge between the West and Muslims, and to create chaos within the Muslim world itself." A trickle of sweat rolled down the side of his face. "I think . . . I believe we would have succeeded had it not been for some bad luck." He lifted his chin slightly. "My name is Richard Aaron Goldberg. My team and I are part of a secret unit of the Mossad."

The sound of clapping. "Better. I particularly liked the sweat bead. Now, do it again."

The screen went gray. No one spoke for a long time. The storefront above them creaked and groaned.

"Was what we just saw . . . was it real?" Rakkim asked finally.

"It's real," said Katherine. "My husband gave it to me the night before he was murdered. The download was hidden in a strand of prayer beads."

"Things like that can be faked," said Rakkim.

"Anything can be faked, but that was the FBI's master interrogator walking Goldberg through the confession," said Spider. "Lorne Macmillan, one of your glorious heroes of the new Islamic Republic."

Sarah stared at the blank laptop screen. "It's like . . . it's like seeing Jack Ruby standing around with Oswald, the two of them rehearsing their encounter in the Dallas garage." She shook her head. "'I'll step out of the crowd of photographers, Lee, and you'll stop and act surprised—'"

"Who's Jack Ruby?" said Rakkim.

Spider moved closer to the surveillance unit. "Don't like that white car." He waited. "No . . . never mind, it turned off onto Madison." He kept watch.

"Why didn't you tell me about this?" Sarah demanded.

"I . . . I couldn't," said Katherine, coloring. "I was afraid something might happen to you and—"

"You didn't trust me," said Sarah.

"Your father always said it was best not to let the right hand know what the left hand is doing," said Katherine. "He didn't even tell Redbeard."

"You didn't *trust* me," repeated Sarah.

"You can hate me later," snapped Katherine. "Right now, we need to show Redbeard a copy of this. How did you put it, Benjamin?"

"Speed and distribution," said Spider. "We got to get the message to as many people as possible, as fast as possible. Otherwise the official disinformation will drown us out. I thought about hacking some of the major net sites like *whatdoido-imam.com* or *faithful-jobsearch.com,* but I can't do it on my own. Redbeard can help us bypass some of the crash triggers, and I'm not even sure those are the best places for us. We really need to go international with this."

"I don't know if I could ask Redbeard to do that," said Sarah, unsteady and still angry. She had been prepared intellectually for the truth about the Zionist Betrayal, but to actually *see* it . . . Perhaps she was a littler raw from meeting her mother after all these years. "He knows what could happen if this . . . grotesque bit of history got out."

"I'm not asking *you* to do it, dear." Katherine was all hard edges and determination. "I'll ask Thomas."

CHAPTER 59

Before noon prayers

"The prodigal returns," said Stevens, the pockmarked dandy who had fetched Rakkim from the Blue Moon after the Super Bowl. It seemed years ago. Stevens's hair was glossy and sleek, his suit perfectly tailored. His shoes gave him another two inches of height. His eyes had the glimmer of a man with secrets. "You don't look so happy to see me, Fedayeen."

"Just surprised."

Stevens wanded him, rapping him sharply between the legs. "Sorry. Have to make sure you're not carrying something dangerous in your privates. I guess there's nothing there."

The guards who had brought Rakkim to Stevens laughed, then went back to watching Sarah and Katherine being checked by a female security officer. Katherine was cloaked in a black burka, only her eyes visible through the eye slits.

Rakkim kept quiet as Stevens continued his rough patdown. Security at the villa had always been layered, but this was hermetic. They had already gone through two security screenings—testing for biologicals, electronic devices, and explosives. The download of Richard Aaron Goldberg's confession rehearsal was inert and set off no alarms.

"It's good you're back," Stevens said. "Redbeard has enough on his shoulders."

"Since when does Redbeard confide in *you*?" said Rakkim, still aching from the wand.

An alarm went off, the guard checking Sarah stepping back. Rakkim stared at the blinking bioscanner and silently cursed himself for his lapse in judgment. The Old One hadn't implanted a tracking device in *him*, he had implanted one in Sarah while she slept, a biochip undetectable by her wrist alarm or the first two layers of the villa's security system. No wonder they had been allowed to escape from Las Vegas. Floating above the desert like a soap bubble . . . a pinprick away from a hard landing.

While a technician neutralized the pinhead-size chip from behind her ear, Rakkim called Spider, warned him and Elroy to stay away from the barbershop. Then he called Peter and Jeri Lynn and Professor Wu. Peter answered from the casino. Said he appreciated the call and quickly hung up. Jeri Lynn said she had wanted to warn them, but she had no way of getting in touch. Said Darwin had awakened her from a sound sleep, sitting on her bed, bouncing her youngest daughter on his hip. Jeri Lynn's voice quavered, wondering how he could have known *this* was her favorite child. She had told Darwin everything she knew, and he had left as suddenly as he'd appeared. No answer from Professor Wu.

Sarah walked over as he put away his cell. "Our body doubles . . . they were followed from the mall. Their car was tracked all the way into Arizona. *Why?*"

"To convince us we had outsmarted him. The Old One needed us then to find any loose ends he might have missed. Like the medallion."

"He thought we were more useful than dangerous. That's why he didn't kill us." Sarah scratched behind her ear. Caught herself, disgusted. "He knows better now, doesn't he?"

"He knows about the medallion, but not about the confession download. That's our great advantage."

The doors to the inner area of the villa hissed open. Unequal air pressure prevented biological or gas attacks. Redbeard stood waiting inside, his expression grim. He was dressed more stylishly than usual in an unbelted white tunic and trousers, embroidered slippers on his bare feet. Rakkim would have been happier to see Angelina, but she was probably preparing a feast. No cooking smells though. Sarah, Rakkim, and Katherine walked inside. Stevens started to follow, but with a subtle hand gesture Redbeard ordered him to stay. The doors slid shut behind them again. "Thank you for bringing Sarah back," Redbeard said to Rakkim. "Perhaps next time you could simply leave a trail of bread crumbs for the Old One."

"I see you've put Stevens in charge of security," gritted Rakkim. "Has he gotten his own room at the villa yet?"

"I'm sorry, Uncle," interrupted Sarah. "I know I've disappointed you, but I had to—"

Redbeard embraced her. "You're safe, that's all that matters." He looked at Katherine as he clung to her. "Who is this devout woman you've brought into our home?" He froze as Katherine pulled off her head covering, but there was no surprise in his eyes. Rakkim saw something else. "Welcome . . . welcome home."

"It's good to see you, Thomas." Katherine inclined her head. "I made some mistakes."

"So did I," said Redbeard.

Sarah looked at Rakkim. He raised an eyebrow.

"We need your help," said Katherine.

"We can talk in my office." Redbeard led the way, glancing at Sarah. "Did you find what you were looking for?"

"I'm not sure," said Sarah. "That's not why we're here. Katherine is the one with the real treasure. She took a very great risk coming here, but you know that."

"I never gave up looking for you," Redbeard said to Katherine, the two of them side by side now. "If you only knew how much I—"

"I should have contacted you after I realized . . ." Katherine hesitated.

"After you realized I didn't murder my brother," finished Redbeard.

Katherine nodded.

"I don't blame you," said Redbeard. "James told me he had
come into possession of something very dangerous. A danger to
him and a danger to the country. James loved me, but he wouldn't
tell me what he had. Not yet, that's what he said. *Soon, Thomas.*"
His eyes shimmered. "Ten minutes later, he was dying in my arms.
No, you did what James would have wanted you to do. Keep the
secret safe. Trust no one."

"It wasn't just that," said Katherine. "I didn't . . . trust myself."

Rakkim stared. He had never seen Redbeard blush.

Redbeard opened the door to his office, ushered them inside.

"Where's Angelina?" said Sarah. "I keep waiting for her to
appear, pretending to be angry, telling me what a disobedient
child I've been."

"I'm looking forward to seeing her too, Thomas," said Katherine. "She knows how grateful I am to her, but I want to tell her in
person."

"Is she still at mosque?" said Sarah. "She should be back . . .
What's wrong, Uncle?"

The screen flickered and went blank as the flashload finished.
They had watched the eighty-three-second rehearsal three times.
No one had said a word. The only sound was Sarah curled on the
couch, sniffling about Angelina while Katherine patted her back.
Rakkim tried to focus on Redbeard, tried to gauge his reactions as
he watched the wall screen.

Rakkim could still feel Sarah's sobs reverberating in his
chest. He had held her after Redbeard had given them the news,
held her and let her do the weeping for the both of them. He
had been nine years old when Redbeard had brought him home.
Angelina had raised him, or come as close as anyone could to

accomplishing that. He missed her already. Missed the clean smell of her, the imported soap that was her one extravagance. Someday he would go to mosque and pray for her. She who needed no prayers to guide her into Paradise. He would pray for her anyway. In hope that she would someday intercede on his behalf. Could even Allah himself refuse her?

"It's real, Thomas," said Katherine, breaking the silence.

"I never believed that Macmillan slipped in the shower and broke his neck. 'The hero who broke the Zionist ring,' that's what they called him. The nation was in mourning for a week. James and I were part of the honor guard at his funeral." Redbeard stared at the blank wall. "I'm glad you're here . . . but, I wish you had not brought this with you."

"We need to get this out." Sarah swiped at her eyes. "We need your help to flashload it everywhere, before it can be discredited. People have to see it with their own eyes, hear it with their own ears, before the media twist it."

Redbeard removed the flashload, tossed it to Rakkim. "I'm not going to help you destroy the country. I took an oath to protect it. So did you."

"The country was built on a lie," said Rakkim.

"What country wasn't?" Redbeard's eyes were icy. "Tell him, Sarah. You're the historian. Tell him about the former regime."

"I know they didn't burn fornicators and witches," said Sarah. "They didn't stone girls to death for running away from husbands. They didn't cut off the hands of thieves—"

Redbeard snatched Rakkim's hand. "*He* kept his hand." Rakkim took his hand back. "The law is hard, but there is room for mercy. Don't tell me about the old days, girl, I lived through them. Drugs sold on street corners. Guns everywhere. God driven out of the schools and courthouses. Births without marriage, rich and poor, so many bastards you wouldn't believe me. A country without shame. Alcohol sold in *supermarkets*. Babies killed in the womb, tens of millions of them. I was a Catholic then. There were politicians who voted to allow this and took Holy Communion afterwards. Do you know what Communion is? These politicians knelt for Communion and there was no shortage of priests eager to place the host upon their tongues." Redbeard shook his head. "We are not perfect, not by any measure, but I would not go back to those days for anything."

"They weren't afraid," said Sarah. "Look at the old videos, the movies . . . they weren't afraid. Look around you, Uncle, go out on the streets—people are scared. Afraid they're going to do the wrong thing, say the wrong thing, *think* the wrong thing. Yes, the Americans were drunk on freedom. Yes, they lacked shame, but they did glorious things too with that freedom. Breakthroughs in science and medicine. Inquiries into the mysteries of the universe. Wonderful things. Noble—"

"You both are missing the point," said Rakkim.

Katherine stared at the ground-zero photographs of New York, Washington, D.C., and Mecca that dominated the office.

"James must have felt the same way I do," Redbeard said to Katherine. "He had the flashload, but he gave it to you for safe-keeping. He didn't even trust the president with it. Not until he was sure they had a common strategy. James would have wanted to use the flashload to rein in the fundamentalists, but he would never have put it out for the world to see. He wanted to save the Muslim nature of the state. Just as I do."

Rakkim put his hand on Redbeard. "It's not about what system is better. It's too late for that. The flashload is all we have now. I met the Old One. I talked with him. You can't stop him anymore, and he knows it. The president is in failing health. Once he's gone, the Old One will make his move. He has men in waiting to replace the president. Politicians, judges . . . he *told* me so. Men close enough in line that it wouldn't even take a coup. A legitimate transfer of power . . . legitimate enough.

That's if the Old One doesn't get tired of waiting and it's the president this time who slips in the shower and breaks his neck."

"His name is Hassan Muhammed," snapped Redbeard. "He's always been a liar."

"I don't think he was lying this time," Rakkim said. "I met him in Las Vegas. He summoned me to the top floor of a huge office building, one of his vast properties. Just the two of us up there, the city spread out like a magic carpet."

"Did he offer you a place of honor beside him? Did he offer a fat slice of the world?" Redbeard tugged at his beard. "I'm no mind reader. It's always a wise strategy to appeal to a man's vanity and greed. His only mistake was making the offer to the wrong man."

Rakkim ignored the compliment. He could see the turmoil beneath Redbeard's bravado. "The Old One talks of a tolerant caliphate, a weaving of the disparate strands of Islam, a harmony of believers. He even leaves room for Christians. He sounds as moderate as you, but, once he has control, do you trust him to maintain his tolerance? If he was willing to kill millions in the nuclear strikes, if he was willing to pollute Mecca itself with radioactivity . . . do you think there is anything he *wouldn't* do to maintain power?"

"Rakkim is telling you the truth, Thomas," said Katherine. "You know he is."

Redbeard nodded and no one dared speak. "Tell me what you want me to do," he said finally. "If we are to be crushed by the truth, so be it. Allah *must* be on the side of truth."

"Thank you," said Sarah.

"Don't thank me," said Redbeard. "I already have enough doubts. You start thanking me, I *know* I've made a mistake." He narrowed his eyes at Rakkim. "What were you and Sarah doing at the Swiss Embassy Tuesday night? Stevens got there five minutes after the two of you disappeared. If I had said no to your request, were you planning to emigrate?"

Rakkim had sensed that he was being observed. He was relieved that it was one of Redbeard's informants. "This is my country. I'm not leaving."

"Good. We'll all stay and fight then." Redbeard's expression darkened. "We may get our chance sooner than we expect. Your friend Detective Colarusso had a visit from the Old One's assassin. Colarusso wasn't home and his son had the good sense to keep the security door locked, but you *are* right, things are coming to a head."

"I'll call Colarusso when we're finished here," said Rakkim.

"You don't have to leave. Your rooms are just as you left them," said Redbeard. "I hope you intend to stay with us, Katherine," he said gently. "This is your home too."

"I'd be honored," said Katherine.

Redbeard pulled Rakkim close, and Rakkim smelled the fatigue on him. "I don't see you for weeks, and almost the first thing you say to me is to ask if Stevens had a room at the villa. Haven't I taught you *anything*? You let your pride speak instead of your wits. Rather than see Stevens as a rival, you would do well to look upon him as an ally. He was the one who retrieved Angelina's body from the Black Robes. He was the one who walked into that nest of vipers alone and demanded that Ibn Azziz turn her over. From what I was told, the boy cleric's bodyguards wanted to cut Stevens to pieces, but Stevens didn't back down, and in the end Ibn Azziz gave him the location of the body. Ibn Azziz admitted nothing, of course, but we got her back in time for a proper burial."

"I'm sorry, Uncle."

Redbeard let him go, smacked his hands together. "Now, how can I help?"

Rakkim smiled. "Are you handling security for the Oscars?"

CHAPTER 60

Before sunset prayers

Rakkim strolled through the front doors of the Blue Moon, hoping to draw the attention of anyone looking for them and keep it away from Sarah. The crowds were light midweek, and he had taken his time on the walk from the monorail, stopping a few times to look into shop windows.

"Boss!" Albert came from behind the bar, beat him on the back. "Where you been?"

Rakkim pointed toward Mardi's regular booth in the back. He couldn't see her, but he knew she was there. "Bring us a couple, will you?"

Mardi looked up from her paperwork as he approached, blond and brassy. She had lost weight.

"Don't be mad."

"Why would I be mad?" Rakkim sat down opposite her. Sat so he could see and be seen from the front of the club. "All I can do is try to save your life."

"I was gone for almost two weeks. I thought I would go nuts."

"You brought Enrique with you."

"I had to have *something* to do." Mardi looked around, annoyed. "Who told you that? What, you get to scamper around the countryside with the Muslim princess, and I'm supposed to hide out by myself?"

Rakkim laughed. "Scamper?" He shook his head. "You probably don't have to worry about Darwin coming around, not anymore." People were slowly filling the club, moderns with bright clothes and etched hair. The call to evening prayer undulated through the streets, faint as a buoy tolling in fog, warning sailors from the rocks. "I heard Enrique got promoted from busboy to waiter when you got back."

Mardi beamed, shook back her hair. She had gotten some sun, and a thin, gold bracelet on her left wrist, and she would have needed her back oiled while she was away. She had a beautiful back, lean and finely muscled, two dimples at the base of her spine. "It was a very good vacation."

Albert delivered a couple of fruit slushies, lingered for a moment, then walked away.

"I missed you," said Mardi. "Hey, I didn't mean to embarrass you. I was just being polite."

"I'm not embarrassed and you're not polite."

"It's happened, hasn't it?" said Mardi.

"What?"

"You've got a mission. I used to see the same look on Tariq when he got word. I'd glance over at him and he would be so . . . calm, so utterly poised, that I knew he was readying himself. Getting ready for whatever fate had in store for him. No fears. No regrets—"

"Building strong the ship of death."

"Yes, that's exactly what Tariq used to say. There was no room for me on that ship, no room for anyone." Mardi watched him with those cool blue eyes. Sometimes when they had made love, there would be an instant when her eyes would tender up. It wasn't anything he did, it was something she allowed to happen. Letting go of the memory of her husband, or maybe it was feeling his presence in Rakkim. That Fedayeen self-assurance, like a scent you all give off, she had said. "You got yourself another mission."

"Yeah, I did."

Mardi pushed her drink around the table, but didn't pick it up. "I only met Sarah that one time, and I didn't much like what I saw, but Rakkim . . . right now I feel sorry for her."

"This is a lovely spot, Thomas."

"You're the only one who calls me that anymore," said Redbeard. "I like it."

Katherine trailed her hand in the tiny waterfall at the center of his garden, the very heart, just the two of them. "I always wanted a water garden."

"I remember," said Redbeard.

"I love the sight and sound and smell of it. The way it teems with life." Katherine lifted up her arms; let water run down her bare arms, the late-afternoon light turning her skin coppery. "Birds and frogs and lizards and fish. Moss underfoot, leaves brushing against your face. Like making love to the earth."

"I never thought of it quite that way."

"Close to God, is that better?" Katherine smiled, watched a leaf spin wildly in the current, caught in a minor eddy. "You did a good job with Sarah."

"Angelina did a good job."

"No . . . there's a lot of you in her. She's a fighter."

"Like her mother."

"Yes, like me."

Neither of them mentioned James. He was many fine things, but James was not a fighter. Not like Redbeard. Or Katherine. "Do you ever wonder?" he started. "Do you ever—"

"Yes, I do."

Redbeard nodded, reluctant to continue. It was good enough sitting here in his favorite spot, just the two of them. As he had dreamed about forever.

"I could never have betrayed James," said Katherine. "Neither could you. I tried not to look at you. I thought that would help."

"I thought you didn't like me," said Redbeard. "I didn't realize until you came home yesterday . . . I didn't know how you felt."

"That's why we were so awkward and nervous around each

other, misreading every innocent comment. Our minds were guilty. We were lovers in our imaginations, adulterers without ever touching." Katherine scooped a rusty Coca-Cola bottle cap out of the water, held it up dripping. "It seems like only yesterday."

"It's too late, Katherine."

"I know that."

"He was my brother. I loved him. I felt so . . . dirty with the thoughts I had. I used to worry that he could see into my mind. Then, when he died . . . I used to . . . I used to think . . ." Redbeard was crying, his big frame lurching from trying to hold it back. "I used to think that maybe *I* had done it. That the reason I didn't see the assassination coming, the reason I didn't react quicker . . . maybe I *wanted*—"

"Shhhhh." Katherine was half his size but seemed larger as she pressed his face against her. "You were shot three times and you still managed to bring down his killer. If you wanted James dead, there were easier ways to do it."

"I was supposed to protect him," Redbeard croaked.

"We do what we can and leave the rest to God."

"I'm sorry, Katherine. I wish . . . I wish we had time."

Katherine flipped the bottle cap to him. "There must be others where *this* came from. Have we got time enough for *that*, Thomas?"

Sarah's horse sneezed, and she spurred it forward, hanging on tight. Horses made her nervous. "I just want you to know what you could be getting yourself into."

"Let me tell you a secret," said Jill Stanton, their horses side by side as they trotted through the outskirts of a neighbor's ranch. "I've been out of the public eye for fifteen years, but when you've been famous, *really* famous, you can get away with almost anything. Rape, drugs, theft . . . even murder sometimes." Green grasshoppers flew around them as the horses barreled through the brush. "After the Oscars next week, I'll be interviewed on every network. I'll *lead* every special report. You watch me, honey, I'll be the best innocent victim you ever saw. Don't worry about me."

Sarah barely had control of her horse. She had approached Jill's neighbor earlier, rented a horse, then had him call Jill for her. Rakkim had checked the area, hadn't found any lurkers, but he was cautious, as always.

"You're holding the reins too close," said Jill. "Give the horse room or you'll spook her."

Sarah loosened the reins. She was itchy and sweaty and couldn't wait to get off. "I can't tell you what's going to happen that night . . . it's going to be very big though."

"I wouldn't want to know. I'm the innocent victim, remember?"

"Jill, this is important. *Everything* is going to change."

Jill laughed, and her face in the setting sun showed every crease and wrinkle. "If I had a dollar for every time I heard that . . ."

CHAPTER 61

After sundown prayers

"Idolatry!" Ibn Azziz shrieked to the tens of thousands milling in front of Crown Prince Auditorium. Most of them were moderns and moderates, here to cheer the movie stars inside on Oscar night, the movie stars shown on the three-story-high screens outside the auditorium. Thousands though were hard-core supporters of Mullah Ibn Azziz, bused in from mosques all over the country. "This is a celebration of idolatry!"

"Idolatry!" responded his supporters: women in black burkas

clacking smooth stones together, men in jellabas, flogging themselves with chains. They surged around Ibn Azziz's bodyguards trying to touch him, seeking his blessing. "Idolatry!"

The moderates and moderns in the crowd roared whenever their favorite stars appeared on camera, but their voices were drowned by the rage and intensity of Ibn Azziz's supporters. A police line five deep surrounded the entrance to the auditorium, a phalanx of uniforms staring straight ahead through their face shields. Dozens of helicopters circled overhead, searchlights playing across the crowd. The Academy Awards were always televised from Los Angeles, but this year, on the twenty-fifth anniversary of the founding of the Islamic Republic, the president had decided to host the event from the capital. To not only show the whole world the tolerant face of Islam, but also lend his political support to one of the republic's largest economic drivers.

The rage of the fundamentalists was largely manufactured by Ibn Azziz for political gain. As usual, most of the nominated films told uplifting stories of good Muslims overcoming temptation through moral strength. *Flesh or Faith*, considered a shoo-in for Best Picture, was the tale of a beautiful Muslim girl from a poor family engaged to marry a rich Catholic who owns the home they rent. At the final hour, a visit from an angel turns the girl back to the true faith and leaves the groom alone and humiliated at the altar. *Miracles Inc.*, another highly acclaimed film, used state-of-the-art computer imagery to suggest the holographic wonders and delights of heaven itself. Like all Hollywood creations, the production values were flawless, the acting mesmerizing, the message trumpeting modest devotion. Rather than assuaging Ibn Azziz, Hollywood's piety was seen as a threat, the cleric declaring that time in movie theaters would be better spent in mosques.

"To *hell* with these immoral images! To *hell* with the false gods of Hollywood!" shouted Ibn Azziz for the cameras as he was bumped and jostled. His face was still swollen and scratched from

Angelina's fingernails, his ruined eye a ragged hole in his skull. "Tonight we show the world that Muslims will not abide such sacrilege in the capital itself!"

The crowd of fundamentalists moved forward, chanting, the crashing of stone on stone providing a potent beat. A tremor ran through the line of uniforms, the rows of armored police squaring up.

Rakkim and Stevens easily passed through the first three checkpoints, but they hit trouble at an unexpected one deep within the amphitheater. Two presidential Secret Service agents refused to accept Rakkim's credentials without further confirmation. A potentially disastrous delay. He and Stevens should have had a half hour to get into position, but the top box-office actress in the world had thrown a fit at Jill Stanton's career retrospective bumping up against her own musical number. The star, who had a marginal voice in spite of all the audio engineers, had insisted the retrospective be moved ahead a segment so Jill's superior talents wouldn't overshadow her. They had no more than fifteen minutes to get into the main control room.

Rakkim held out his credentials. "Check my ID. Do an iris scan to confirm my identity. I'm *cleared*. Redbeard himself signed off."

The agent with the sandy hair shook his head. "*I* didn't clear you."

The bald one had moved into perfect position, back a few paces, hand on his pistol.

"Stevens, you can pass," said sandy hair. "Mr. Epps, wait here for my supervisor."

Stevens stood his ground. "You two shouldn't even be here. Interior of the amphitheater is State Security's responsibility. You don't have jurisdiction."

"We don't have to explain anything to you," said sandy hair.

"The president requires at least six possible exit routes, fellas," said the bald one. "We have to secure each and every one of them."

The live-feed screen at the checkpoint showed the mass of fundamentalists stopped three feet away from the police line. Chains were flying, faces contorted as the hard core shouted for the police to join them.

"Give me your cell," said Rakkim. "You can talk to Redbeard himself."

"Fuck Redbeard," said sandy hair.

"Come on, Marx," said the bald one, still keeping a watchful eye. "What can it hurt?"

"Is Redbeard the fucking president, Beason?" said Marx. "No, he's not. Do *we* work for the fucking president? Yes, we do." He looked at Stevens. "You going or staying?"

"Go ahead, I'll catch up with you when their supervisor shows up." Rakkim tugged at Stevens's jacket as though straightening it, passed him the digital download.

"Are you sure you have enough men deployed, Chief?" Redbeard said into the limo's phone.

"As I told you—"

"I know what you told me, I also know what I'm seeing on TV, and it looks to me like you don't have enough men." Redbeard could feel Sarah's tension as she sat beside him, watching the chaos in front of the auditorium.

"I guess I could call in the overflow—"

"I thought you would have already done so. I gave you intel yesterday that Ibn Azziz was going to make trouble." Redbeard slammed down the phone, looked at Colarusso. "Your boss is an ass."

"Never had a boss who wasn't," Colarusso said from the jump seat facing them.

Anthony Jr.'s voice came over the intercom from the driver's seat. "Anything I can do?"

"Stay put," both Redbeard and Colarusso said at the same time.

Colarusso shrugged. "The kid hears there's trouble, he wants to be first in line."

"Proactive . . . I like that," said Redbeard. "With proper training, there's no limit to how far he could go." Redbeard looked out the smoked windows. "Hate to see a young man with such obvious talent get shunted into the Fedayeen."

"Maybe we could talk about that," said Colarusso. "After this business is over."

Redbeard let the offer linger as he watched the street. They were part of a long line of identical limos strung along the back streets behind the auditorium. Limos reserved for second-tier celebrities and minor industry honchos. The stars' limos were in the parking garage under the auditorium. A lousy place to be if you had to make a hasty exit. Redbeard had two doubles at the event. One in a secure VIP lounge inside the auditorium. Another in a command limo with Redbeard's regular driver.

Redbeard picked up the phone again, punched in a nontraceable number. Luc picked it up on the first ring. Crowd noise on the other end as Luc squeezed through, making his way toward Ibn Azziz. "Do it," said Redbeard, clicking off. He settled back into the plush seat. Smiled.

"I'm going to walk the area," said Colarusso. "I know the uniform working traffic control for this sector. I'll bring him some coffee."

"It was a pleasure seeing you again, Detective," said Redbeard.

Colarusso got out, leaned over, poked his head inside. "My boy is a good driver, you don't have anything to worry about."

"Inshallah," said Redbeard.

"Yeah, whatever," said Colarusso, the door closing with a heavy thunk.

Their gray limo was like all the others in line, only it was fully armored, the glass bulletproof and bomb resistant, the air recirculated in case of tear gas or worse. The armor was important but the anonymity was better. If one's enemies know where you are, no matter how well protected you are, you can be gotten. Better to be a chameleon than a turtle. The limo was as safe a place as there was around the auditorium—he was still glad he had insisted that Katherine not join them. Someone needed to have a copy of the download in case things went bad. That's what he had told her anyway. He had told Sarah the same thing, ordered her to stay away, to go into hiding until things were clearer. She had kissed him, told him she loved him . . . and then said she was a grown woman who had survived two months on her own, two months with a Fedayeen assassin trailing her. She could handle a night at the Oscars.

Stevens hurried down the hall. One of the monitors set into the wall showed that skinny young actress accepting her Best Supporting Actress award, her voice high-pitched and with the hint of a lisp. He walked even faster. His new boots were a little stiff, but they were French. Well worth a few pinched toes. A right at the next split in the corridor, deeper into the labyrinth. Never should have left Rakkim back there. He touched the download in his pocket. He didn't know what it was, but he knew what to do with it. Redbeard had said if either of them were caught with it, they would be executed, then offered him a chance to say no. He smoothed his pencil mustache. If Redbeard said to dive into a blast furnace, Stevens might ask for a cold drink first, but he would jump. He and Rakkim were supposed to take over the control room and lock it down. The download went into the preview bay of the central control panel. Redbeard had put a mock-up on the computer, run Stevens and Rakkim through the drill a few times. It was a simple procedure. When the preprogrammed career highlight reel started, one of them would switch the main feed to preview mode and the download would play. A trained chimp could do it. So why was Stevens's heart pounding?

It must have killed Rakkim to get paired with him. Fedayeen thought they were God's gift. Now look at him, stuck back there with those Secret Service yobs. In spite of his height, when he'd turned eighteen, Stevens had been accepted in the Fedayeen . . . but a broken ankle the first week of training had sidelined him. He got another chance after the ankle healed, but he came down with hypothermia during winter maneuvers and that was that. The only luck he had was bad luck. Except when it came to women. Stevens touched his nose. It had healed nicely, with just the faintest sign of the break. Stevens had insisted on that, against the wishes of his plastic surgeon. Women loved a man with a broken nose. He wished Rakkim were with him. Not that he needed him. To *show* him.

Kerenski and Faisal were outside the control room window, natty in their dress blazers.

"Redbeard wants the two of you shifted out front to reinforce the cops," said Stevens. "Report to the watch commander, but maintain your autonomy."

"Who's minding the store back here?" said Faisal.

Stevens glanced into the control room; saw a half dozen people hunched over their consoles. Two young women, one a modern with blue-tipped hair. *Very* cute. "I am."

"You're welcome to it." Kerenski nodded at the wall screen where the skinny actress was droning on with her acceptance speech. "This is one boring assignment."

"Doorman . . . isn't that a little below your pay grade?" said Faisal.

"Redbeard didn't like the way I looked at his niece." Stevens grinned, ran a fingernail along the curve of his sideburns. "Or maybe he didn't like the way she looked at me." His expression hardened. "Key combo?"

Faisal hesitated. "Three nine nine."

"Go on," said Stevens. "I'll expect an action report a half hour after the broadcast." He watched them double-time it down the corridor until they disappeared from sight. Turned and saw the cute modern in the control room watching him. He waved at her through the bulletproof glass and she went back to work, cheeks coloring. Another glance down the corridor. Still no Rakkim. His loss. The glory would all be Stevens's.

It had been an honor to be selected by Redbeard for a secret assignment, but to be the one to initiate the action . . . Stevens unconsciously stiffened to attention. He had dreamed of doing brave deeds for as long as he could remember. A childhood playing Arabs and Crusaders, Stevens always taking the part of the outnumbered Arabs making a last, desperate stand against the desecraters of the holy places. He smiled at the memory. To put his life on the line for his country was a blessing he had received many times since joining State Security, but this was different. He could tell from the tone of Redbeard's voice. The way his hand had shaken slightly as he'd laid it on Stevens's shoulder. Whatever Allah required of him, Stevens was eager to meet his destiny. A final check for Rakkim, and Stevens stepped to the door, punched in three nine nine.

Heads lifted from their consoles, and quickly returned to work. Except for the cute girl who had been watching him before, lingering . . . and a man standing behind the consoles, hands clasped behind his back. Producer. Better get that settled. ASAP.

"I'm Stevens," he said, shaking hands with the producer. "I'm taking over the room. Order of Redbeard, director of State Security."

The producer trembled. "Is there a problem?" He checked the screen showing the crowd of Black Robes milling around, bullhorns booming. "Surely we're not in any danger?"

Stevens moved to the preview bay, slipped the download in. "Lock in the override. I'll be running the preview in a few minutes."

"But, that's . . . that's my job," said the producer. "Just tell me what you want me to do."

Stevens could see the cute girl watching him; saw the pulse in her throat throbbing. "I want you to get your people out of here. You can stay. You and the modern with the blue hair. I'll need you to run things. You can do that, can't you?"

"Yes . . . of course. We'll go with a straight three-camera—"

"Just tell the rest of them to go to the nearest staff lounge." Stevens waited until the others left, the door locking into place. The modern with the blue hair kept glancing over at him as she pretended to work. She had a great smile. He leaned close to the producer. "The girl . . . what's her name?"

"I really don't know. I was called in at the last minute when the regular producer got sick." The man looked as if he was about to cry. "We're not in any danger, are we?"

"Relax, you're in good hands here," said Stevens. "What's *your* name?"

"Darwin."

Stevens sat down at the preview bay, kept his eyes on the live shot. The skinny actress seemed to be winding down. Just a few more minutes until Jill Stanton's career retrospective. "Okay, Darwin, you just do your job and I'll do mine."

CHAPTER 62

After sundown prayers

"Call your supervisor." Rakkim stepped forward. "*Call* him."

Beason centered the pistol on Rakkim's chest. "I *will* shoot you, Mr. Epps."

Marx, the sandy-haired Secret Service agent, whipped out a pair of clear jelly-cuffs from his belt. "You're under arrest."

Beason pressed a finger to his earpiece, listening. "Hang on . . ."

Rakkim put his hands out, inched back just enough so that when Marx went to slip on the cuffs, he momentarily blocked Beason's line of fire. Rakkim twisted the cuffs away, slapped them around Marx's throat. He kept the agent in front of him.

"What are you doing?" said Beason, trying to get a clear shot.

"Drop your weapon." Rakkim hung on to the back of Marx's jacket, using him as a shield and preventing him from reaching the gun in his shoulder rig.

Marx wasn't interested in his gun though. He clawed at the cuffs locking around his throat. Made from a viscous memory-polymer, the cuffs tightened automatically around the wrists of a suspect, stopping just short of pain. Around the neck they strangled.

"Let him go, Mr. Epps!" said Beason, the gun wobbling now. "We're leaving anyway."

Marx's eyes bulged as he tore at the cuffs, his knees buckling.

Beason placed his pistol on the floor.

Rakkim pinched the release point, peeled the cuffs away. They left a deep red line around Marx's neck. Rakkim passed him over to his partner.

Beason struggled to hold him up, Marx gasping, trying to suck in air. "You didn't have to do that," he called after Rakkim. "We're shifting to Quadrant B. Now, how am I supposed to explain the ligature around his neck?"

"Don't worry," said Redbeard. "Rakkim can take care of himself."

"I know." Sarah didn't sound convinced.

The TV in the limo showed Ibn Azziz making his way toward the police line to join his followers. Spotlights raced across the crowd as he urged them on.

Redbeard leaned forward slightly. Any moment now . . .

Ibn Azziz jerked, his face suddenly slack as the camera zoomed in. He clutched at his stomach, bent slightly forward. Those around him turned, stepped back, even his bodyguards, as

Ibn Azziz lost control of his bowels. The cameras caught him in the white glare, shoes spattered with his own excrement, robes soaked. The newscaster on the voice-over giggled, and the crowd started laughing too. The police line rocked with jeers, and even some of the fundamentalists joined in as the image of Ibn Azziz loomed over the auditorium, mouth working like a hooked fish as he emptied himself. For an instant Luc was caught by the cameras . . . smiling.

Redbeard's laugh boomed within the limo.

The broadcast was in the middle of a car commercial when Rakkim reached the control room . . . and saw Darwin inside, giving a jaunty wave from the other side of the glass.

Comprehension like a strobe light. Darwin. A girl with blue-tipped hair working the control panel, sobbing as she called in camera shots, her back toward . . . toward the table behind her. Stevens sitting in a chair placed atop the table. Silvery tape across his mouth. Arms and legs taped to the chair. A wire around his neck, connected to the boom in the ceiling. Plenty of slack in the wire. But not enough to reach the floor. Enough slack to snap his neck. Full-glide casters on the chair. A sneeze could send it over the edge.

"Door's open." Darwin grinned, one hand on the back of the chair, rolling it back and forth. "Come on in, Rikki. The water's fine."

Redbeard watched the commercial for the new Ford Pilgrim, thinking of the cars of his youth—the land-yacht Lincoln his proud father had rolled home in one day, his mother's minivan that smelled of spilled Coke, and the greatest car in history, the Mustang convertible he'd driven in college. He had been a wild Catholic boy in those days, in love with speed and the wind howling around him. That was before his conversion. Before his brother married Katherine. Redbeard felt a great weariness permeating him. It wasn't his memories bearing down upon his chest. It was the *other* thing. That which the doctors had been helpless against, their faces long, eyes averted.

The television cut back to the action inside the auditorium, movie stars chatting among themselves, one eye cocked for the camera.

Sarah checked her watch, but didn't say anything.

Too late for second-guessing. Redbeard focused on Sarah instead. She looked so much like her mother. If he and Katherine had been the ones to marry, would they have had a daughter who looked like her? Probably not. Better Redbeard didn't pass on his ugly genes. Still . . . he couldn't help wondering.

"What is it, Uncle?"

"I was just thinking how beautiful you look."

Sarah furrowed her brow. "A compliment from *you*? Are you sick?"

Redbeard eased back into his seat. "Never felt better." He thought of Katherine again. He had thought of little else since she'd taken off her burka disguise last week. All the time lost. All the things he could have done, should have done. When he'd told Katherine of his regrets, she had pressed a finger against his lips, said, what makes you think it was all up to you? She was right. Which made the regret so fresh that he felt the ache. The burning. No, not *now*. Not yet. Redbeard breathed deep. Inhaled the warm leather memory of that Mustang convertible. He had done the right thing. *They* had done the right thing. Katherine was his brother's wife. There was honor in love denied.

Sarah grabbed his hand. "Here's the head of the Academy. They're about to start Jill's introduction."

Redbeard wasn't interested. He had already seen the download. Now the rest of the world could see it. Let Malik bin-Hassan choke on the truth. *The Wise Old One.* Horseshit.

Redbeard looked out the window as the pain in his chest twisted, sharper now. Insistent. He had spent too much of his life thinking about Hassan Muhammed. It had been necessary, absolutely necessary, but the man wasn't worth another instant of his attention. Allah would deal with the old fraud in his own good time. "Sarah?"

Sarah turned away from the television.

Redbeard tried to speak but the pain was too intense.

"Uncle?"

"Do you . . . still want to marry Rakkim?" Redbeard asked.

She looked surprised, lowered her eyes for an instant, but only for an instant. "Yes."

Redbeard nodded. All pain was bearable when Paradise was at hand. "I would like that too."

"We have your blessing?"

Redbeard drank her in. Her face sparkled. Stars flickered around her. Oxygen deprivation. So this is what dying is like. A galaxy of love and Sarah at the center of it.

"Uncle? Do we have your blessing?"

"Mine and your mother's. With both our hearts. With both our souls." Redbeard smiled. It seemed as if he had been waiting all his life to say those words. *Our* hearts. *Our* souls. His vision was narrowing. He could no longer see Sarah, but he felt her kiss his hand. Felt her hold it against her soft, warm cheek.

"Grandma, what a big *knife* you have," said Darwin.

Rakkim laughed. It was a good line. No one but another Fedayeen would have seen the knife tucked up against the inside of his forearm.

Darwin shoved the chair, stopped it just short of the edge. His eyes never left Rakkim.

"Camera five, tighten up," whispered the girl with blue hair into her throat mike. "Camera one, prepare to go wide."

"Who's the asshole in the chair?" asked Rakkim.

"He's the asshole who's going to die if you don't put away the blade." Darwin grabbed Stevens's ear, twisted. "When a man's neck gets snapped, he ejaculates like a fountain. It's a real floor show." Stevens bit his lips shut as Darwin kept twisting. "You ask me, God's a fucking maniac."

"God's not the only one." Rakkim held his palm out, the knife perfectly balanced in the center. A drop of blood oozed around the tip. It was a doable throw, but Darwin was fast and if he missed . . . He flicked his wrist and the knife stuck in the door behind Darwin.

Darwin seemed disappointed. "I looked at the download your buddy here brought. No wonder the old man was upset."

The girl with blue hair sniffed as she worked the board. "Camera two. Camera eight. Pan the first row, camera four."

"You ready, Karla?" said Darwin.

Rakkim cocked his head. "You're going to run it?"

"Soon as they start the retrospective." Darwin spun the chair across the table, the wire tugging at Stevens's throat. "Just wish we had some buttered popcorn."

Rakkim moved closer.

"I kept asking myself, why does the old man want Rakkim so badly when he's got *me*? What's he up to?" Darwin shrugged. One of the casters on the chair squeaked; Stevens was wild-eyed. "If I wanted to be kept in the dark, I would have stayed in the Fedayeen." Thunderous applause from the monitors all around them, eight different camera angles, and live feeds from remotes all over the world. Movies, the universal language. "You ever get bored with it all, Rakkim? You ever ask yourself, what's the point?"

"Never. My life is sunshine and kitty cats."

Darwin patted Stevens's hand. "Look at this . . ." He broke one of Stevens's fingers, and Stevens lunged against his restraints, screams muffled by the tape across his mouth. "There was a time when that snapping sound would have given me a happy tingle." Darwin broke another finger. "Now, it doesn't mean a thing."

Rakkim inched closer. Stevens had fainted.

"I had a good time with a handsome policeman a few weeks ago . . . but it didn't last." Darwin toyed with his own knife. "It never lasts."

"Maybe you should kill yourself," said Rakkim. "Put yourself out of your misery."

"You're the most fun I've had in a long time—that's why I let you live." Darwin lightly outlined Stevens's eyes with the tip of his knife. A beadwork of red goggles. "I saw you at the embassy party . . . did you know I was in the balcony? The old man said I should stop you. Take you down right there." The knife traced Stevens's mouth. Blood reddened his lips. "The Swiss have lousy security. It's as if they don't care, or maybe they're just arrogant. That happens when you win for a thousand years. I saw you down below and I thought, why not let things play out a little longer? Let the old man wonder what *I'm* up to for a change."

"Cuing the download," said Karla.

Rakkim took a small step perfectly timed to the rhythm of her voice. Darwin missed it.

"Craps players, that's what we are. None of that card-counting drudgery for us. A man could go crazy playing it smart." Darwin whipped the chair, flung Stevens around. "A couple of go-for-broke boys, that's what we are, and it's going to get good and messy after the world gets a look at the download. We're going to throw the bones, Rikki, and not care how they land."

"*Jill Stanton began her career playing a cheerleader in the little-seen* Eyes of Texas, *but within five years she was the most recognized face in the world.*" The retrospective had started, the Oscars' website address crawling across the screen, inviting viewers to log on to download the proceedings. If Spider had done his job . . .

"During the old regime's last days, it was Jill Stanton's courageous stand at another Academy Awards presentation—"

Rakkim heard Richard Aaron Goldberg's voice.

"I bet the old man just spilled his tea in his lap." Darwin frowned. "Get back."

Rakkim didn't move. He just needed another step. "I bet there was a time, not too long ago either . . . I bet there was a time when I couldn't have gotten this close."

"Oh, you're not nearly close enough." Darwin pushed the chair to the edge of the table, Stevens's head flopping. "Stand down, Rikki. You wouldn't want me to forget my manners. You've seen what I can do. If I wasn't on my best behavior, I would have butchered the whole crew and put their heads in the window like jack-o'-lanterns for you."

Karla sobbed, covered her mouth.

"R We Having Fun Yet, Darwin?" Rakkim waited for him to blink.

Darwin smiled. "I don't like repeating myself."

"You repeat yourself all the time. That's your problem. It's all the same for you. Just death and more death. No wonder you're bored."

"You're not maintaining pupil consistency. It doesn't matter if they're slightly dilated or not, what matters is consistency. It's the change in size that denotes a lie."

Banks of monitors showed the crowd outside the auditorium growing silent as they stared up at the JumboTron.

"I'd love to talk some more with you, but I've got plans for the evening," said Darwin. "You'll have plenty of time to come after me when all this settles down, but here's the good part. Next time you're going to have a sliver of doubt about me. Now, I'm a monster, but next time you're going to remember me as Darwin, who did some outlandish things, but let you live—"

"Outlandish? Is that what you call it?"

Live video feeds flashed on mobs forming in Chicago and Denver . . . Oscar parties turned ugly . . . cars burning, horns blaring . . .

"Look what we've done. Isn't it *beautiful*?" said Darwin. "I could have killed you but I didn't. I could have killed Jeri Lynn and the kiddies, but I didn't. Knowing that about me, it's going to change things between us. Deepen them."

"Why don't you stay?" Looking into Darwin's eyes was like falling forever into darkness, but Rakkim didn't turn away. "Stay and we'll find out."

Darwin shook his head. "I don't want to rush it. This is the best time I've had in years. Come on, admit it, you're enjoying yourself too. Say hello to the little woman for me. Tell her I can't wait to see her again."

"My name is Richard Aaron Goldberg. My team and I are part of a secret unit of the Mossad." Clapping. *"Better. I particularly liked the sweat bead. Now, do it again."*

. . . wobbly footage of looting in Rio and Lagos, rage accelerating . . . a newsman hit by a brick in the middle of a live remote . . . the Eiffel Tower obscured by smoke.

"Don't go," said Rakkim. "Stick around. What are you worried about?"

"Why, *you*, silly. I'm worried about you." Darwin shoved Stevens off the table.

Rakkim dove for the chair, caught it just before the wire around Stevens's neck snapped taut. He glanced behind him, but Darwin was gone. Rakkim carefully set the chair on the floor. Stevens had the same raw ligature mark on him as the Secret Service agent.

. . . the crowd outside the auditorium tore at each other now, wailing at the night sky and the dying stars . . .

*   *   *

Other limos were peeling out of line, racing down the streets. Some with their lights off in their haste, leaving their clients milling around on the sidewalk.

"Stay put, Anthony," said Sarah. Tears ran down her cheeks, but her voice was firm.

"I'm not going anywhere until Rakkim shows up, don't worry," said Anthony.

Sarah arranged Redbeard's hands in his lap so that it looked as if he were praying. She wiped her eyes. Impossible to believe he was dead. The TV cut to the Oscars' host standing nervously onstage. He made a joke but there was no laughter. A camera caught the audience bolting for the exits, then cut back to the host. Jill was there too, weeping, her hands outstretched—it was as good a performance as Sarah had ever seen her give, just the right mix of shock and confusion.

Pounding on the roof of the limo and Sarah jumped. Colarusso. She rolled the window partway down.

"Get out of here while you can," said Colarusso.

"Rakkim's not here yet. Why don't you get in?"

Colarusso shook his head. "I got to help out the uniforms. Command structure is barely holding together."

"Pop, get in," said Anthony Jr.

"Duty calls and all that shit, Junior." Colarusso pounded the roof again for good luck and then walked across the street.

The TV went blank, then cut to a news anchor blabbering about how their broadcast had been hijacked by Zionists. Even *he* looked as if he didn't believe it.

Sarah's cell rang. "Rakkim?"

"We *did* it," said Spider, voice cracking. "The Oscars' website got seven million hits before it crashed, but by then it was too late. Every hit transferred a worm back, sent the download on to everyone in their address book. A chain-letter bomb hot off the grid. Gotta go!"

Sarah shut the cell. Rested her head against Redbeard's shoulder.

Satellite feeds hijacked the broadcast now. Riots in Chicago and Mandellaville, roads snarled in Paris and Baghdad and Delhi, streets littered with glass and bodies, mosques burning. Complete curfew called in San Francisco, Mayor Miyoki railing against treasonous Hollywood Jews, the Castro District imam calling for jihad.

Ten minutes later, the security lock on the doors beeped and Rakkim slid into the backseat. "Get us out of here, Anthony." He kissed Sarah. "Redbeard, I hope . . ." His voice trailed off.

Sarah took his hand as they pulled into traffic.

Through the windows of the limo, they could see the glow from the fires burning all over the capital.

EPILOGUE

Nine months after the Oscars

Allah is great.

Rakkim emptied his mind as he stood within the mosque, putting the world behind him. He faced the qibla, pointing toward Mecca, his attention on Allah. He brought his hands to his ears, palms forward, thumbs behind his earlobes. Speaking in Arabic, he recited his salat, the ritual prayer.

> *Allah is great.*
> *I bear witness that there are none worthy of worship except Allah.*
> *I bear witness that Muhammad is the Messenger of Allah.*

I seek refuge in Allah from Satan, the accursed
In the name of Allah, the infinitely Compassionate and
   Merciful,
Praise be to Allah, Lord of all the worlds.

At the end of his devotions he sat back on his haunches, hands on his knees. To complete the prayer he looked over his right shoulder and acknowledged the angel recording his good deeds, then looked over his left at the angel recording his bad deeds.

Now was the time for personal prayers, but Rakkim had none.

The worshipers at the Sword of the Prophet Grand Mosque stirred as Ibn Azziz started to speak, a whisper of anticipation that echoed off the spotless mosaic interior. Over twenty thousand believers packed in, eager to hear his sermon. Rakkim had arrived hours early to get a spot, passing through security and a series of patdowns. Rakkim had been coming to hear Ibn Azziz every day since he'd arrived. He knew the strengths and failings of the one-eyed cleric's bodyguards and had picked out at least a dozen operatives of the Black Robes salted among the faithful. Rakkim sat within the vast throng, aware of Ibn Azziz's exhortations, but focused more on the man's intonation, his facial expressions, his abrupt gestures. He was a powerful speaker, his intensity palpable, and the crowds were even larger now than when he had first arrived, hard-liners streaming into the city by the thousands, heeding his call.

Rakkim had been attending prayers at the Grand Mosque for thirteen days. The day before yesterday, he had spotted Darwin among the devout. Rakkim had offered up no personal prayers to Allah, but Allah had answered his heart's desire anyway.

The world had shuddered in the months after the Academy Awards, changed in ways that none of them could have foreseen.

There had been riots in a hundred cities around the globe, but infinitely more disruptive had been the quiet questions in a billion minds as they watched the download over and over: If the Zionist attack had been a lie . . . what else was a lie?

At first, the community of Islamic nations had joined President Kingsley in denouncing the interrogation-rehearsal download as a Zionist hoax or a plan by the Bible Belt to threaten the legitimacy of the government in Seattle. Experts were trotted out to explain how such digital manipulations were easily done, and news commentators offered their own sage advice. Talk-show comedians mocked the idea that Lorne Macmillan, the FBI agent who had broken the Zionist plot, would have been part of such a deception. They might even have held the day. The experts might have swayed public opinion. Except that ten days after the broadcast, the Chinese government broke the news of what they had found in a cave near Yichange, along the banks of the Yangtze River.

Carried live around the world, the news conference showed the fourth nuclear bomb surrounded by men in protective gear. Traffic on the freeways slowed, then stopped, as people were riveted to their video cells. Found thirty-seven miles north of the Three Gorges Dam, far enough away that it was never within the security perimeter, the fourth bomb was much more powerful than the ones that had devastated New York and Washington, D.C. It wasn't just the bomb that proved the truth of the download; the bodies of the three men dead of radiation poisoning were found in the cave. DNA and forensic tests established that all three were known Muslim terrorists with prior arrest records. Not a Jew among them. Two had spent time at Guantánamo and been released by court order. The third was Essam Muhammed, the ringleader, a former student at MIT, a physicist arrested at a minor demonstration years before he died.

Hassan Muhammed, the Wise Old One, disappeared from his

Las Vegas redoubt a few days before Interpol arrived. Billions of his assets had been confiscated around the world, but investigators felt they had only scratched the surface. The Muslim nations were as outraged as anyone else, demanding that he be called to account for the desecration of Mecca with a dirty bomb, calling on all Muslims to aid in the search for him. Though there was a worldwide arrest warrant, the Old One remained free, rumored to be in Switzerland, Kuala Lumpur, Pakistan. A hundred places and no place at all.

Someday Rakkim hoped to meet him again. Ask him if he still enjoyed the sunset. Ask if the view was still as grand from where he stood as it had been from the ninetieth floor? Rakkim had other business though, matters that required his immediate attention.

"Islam makes demands upon us," shouted Ibn Azziz, arms flailing. "As adult males we are instructed to prepare ourselves for conquest, so that the strictures of Islam are obeyed in every country in the world. *Every* country!"

Strung out on either side of him, Ibn Azziz's bodyguards glared at the crowd, looking for any sign of evil intent. A neon sign perhaps. Or a hand raised, seeking permission to assassinate their mullah. The entrances and exits were heavily guarded too, but like most weaklings, Ibn Azziz confused sheer numbers with skill. Two of his bodyguards were ex-Fedayeen, quiet men and formidable fighters certainly, but they were only two.

Rakkim half closed his eyes and thought of sweeter things. His wife, Sarah, was pregnant, swelling in her fifth month. His *wife*. Blessings on Redbeard . . . wherever he was. Katherine a doting grandmother. She and Spider . . . Benjamin, had lunch regularly, a most unlikely friendship. Colarusso remained a detective, had turned down a promotion, saying the country needed good cops more than another mediocre paper pusher. He was right, as usual. Anthony Jr. had rejected his appointment to Fedayeen, had instead taken a posting with State Security . . . working under the acting director, Stevens. Rakkim stifled a smile. Though they might still work together, he and Stevens *still* didn't like each other.

Perhaps the greatest blessing was the health of President Kingsley. Reported near death for years, he had been reenergized. Initially fooled by his advisers about the integrity of the rehearsal confession, he had accepted the truth . . . and dismissed his advisers. Acting quickly, Kingsley granted the nation's Christian minority expanded rights and rescinded the hated religious tax upon them, thus saving the country from disintegrating into a thousand warring fiefs. He had even granted amnesty to the Jews, a courageous move that brought the hard-liners into open revolt. General Kidd and the Fedayeen had stood beside the president in the hour of need, and the Black Robes and their supporters had retreated to strongholds in San Francisco, St. Louis, and Cleveland. While the internal battles were far from settled, Kingsley's greatest triumph had been the avoidance of open warfare with the Bible Belt. For years Kingsley had maintained a backdoor channel with the president of the Bible Belt, and their relationship had prevented hotheads on both sides from initiating a conflagration. Through his own contacts in the Bible Belt, Rakkim had done his small part to continue the dialogue between the two nations.

"Only those who know nothing of Islam—and I include especially the Arabic appeasers who dwell in our holiest cities—say the Muslims seek peace," said Ibn Azziz, his voice hoarse and cracking. "Those who say this are fools or worse."

The faithful in the mosque nodded in agreement. Darwin knelt near one of the far exits, hands clasped.

Even knowing the growing danger Ibn Azziz presented, Sarah had been angry with Rakkim when he'd left to go to San Francisco. She said his place was with her and with the baby.

He told her he would be back in time to see their child born. He gave her his promise. She was still angry. He didn't blame her.

"Should we Muslims sit back until we are devoured by the unbelievers?" demanded Ibn Azziz. "I say, put them to the sword and scatter their bones! I say, whatever good exists is thanks to the sword! Compromise with unbelievers is a defeat for righteousness! The sword is the key to Paradise!"

The believers sprung to their feet, roaring, "God is great, God is great, God is great," louder and louder until it seemed the dome of the mosque itself would shatter. As their voices faded, Ibn Azziz blessed them and disappeared into the back of the mosque. The crowd squeezed through the exits into the streets. Darwin took his time. Rakkim kept him in sight, following at a distance, making no effort to close the gap between them.

The crowd thinned out over the next half mile, dissipating into the maze of side streets. A rain was falling, a cold drizzle that soaked the robes of the faithful, forcing them to walk with their heads down. Not Darwin. Not Rakkim. Twice Darwin looked behind him, but Rakkim always kept a cluster of other believers in front of him, screening him from sight.

Darwin turned south off Union Street, continued on a twisting path deeper into the underbelly of the city, the apartment buildings decayed, many of them crumbled into bricks and rebar. Rakkim had followed Darwin into the sector after spotting him that first time, followed him and lost him. Not today. This time he saw Darwin dart into an abandoned church. Rakkim circled the church, the hood of his robe low around his face. He expected Darwin to slip out and continue on his way, but glimpsed him instead through a broken stained-glass window, Darwin climbing the stairs to the second floor of the church, taking the steps two at a time. Rakkim hurried to a side entrance before Darwin achieved the high ground and the greater visibility it offered.

The church was quiet and cool inside. Bright pieces of broken glass on the floor and ripped hymnals. A wooden crucifix splintered. The pews chopped up for kindling. An old fire pit where the pulpit had been. Empty cans and bottles. Obscene graffiti on the walls. Rakkim moved silently across the room toward the stairs. He heard creaking above as Darwin walked across the floor.

Far away, he heard an ancient streetcar rumble down Union Street, a tourist attraction for a city that no longer had tourists. Rakkim checked his watch. Fifteen minutes later another streetcar clattered down Union, this time the conductor giving a few rings of his bell. Fifteen minutes after that, Rakkim moved quickly up the stairs in time with the passing streetcar. His knife was part of his hand.

At the top of the stairs, Rakkim suddenly jerked back and Darwin's knife stabbed from the doorway, pierced the air where Rakkim should have been. Darwin kept coming, and Rakkim was off-balance, almost falling down the stairs. He regained his footing as Darwin vaulted toward him, Rakkim retreating.

"Where are you going?" said Darwin, knife twitching side to side like a divining rod. "What a surprise it was to see you at the Grand Mosque. I almost waved."

Rakkim felt out of breath, his chest tight. He forced himself to relax his grip on his knife.

"Are you okay, Rakkim? You want to take a break? Have some tea?"

Rakkim shrugged off his robe, the two of them circling each other. "What are you doing in San Francisco?"

"Same thing you are. Getting ready to kill Ibn Azziz."

Stained glass crunched under Rakkim's feet. Saints or prophets . . . he didn't look. Rakkim kept his eyes on Darwin. "The Old One take you back? Forgive and forget?"

"The old man doesn't do either. He didn't send me—" Darwin's knife flicked forward, and Rakkim pivoted, slashed at him. "I came here on my own."

They each took a step back. Noticed that they had identical cuts along their chests. Bowed.

"Blood to blood," whispered Darwin.

"Blade to blade," Rakkim returned the salute.

"I recognized you the moment I first saw you," said Darwin. "I knew what you were."

Rakkim didn't answer.

They moved across the church, stepping carefully, knives writing their names on flesh. They cut each other a dozen times. Not deep. Scratches mostly, but this was not a training exercise. Not a game. They were going for the killing cut. An artery. A tendon. A skull stab. Darwin's eyes stayed calm, his steps smooth, but Rakkim was no longer the only one out of breath.

Darwin half crouched, blinking away blood from a slash across his eyebrow. He switched the knife into his other hand.

Rakkim kicked aside a rat carcass. "I know who you are, too, Darwin. I know how you think."

"I feel sorry for you then, Rikki. I wouldn't—" Darwin launched an attack that cut Rakkim across the right arm, but the flurry left him momentarily open, and Rakkim drove his blade into Darwin's thigh. Darwin circled, ignoring the wound. "Knowing how I think . . . I wouldn't wish that on my worst enemy."

Rakkim advanced on him. "You don't care who wins or loses. Fundamentalists . . . moderates, Catholics and Jews, they're all the same to you. You just want to kill somebody . . ."

"Somebody important. Hard to kill. Like Ibn Azziz. Like you. The *challenge*, that's what it's all about. The only sin is not living up to our true nature. You know that, Rikki."

"I told you not to call me that."

Their knives darted back and forth, a sharp whisper in the

church as they circled, mirroring each other's moves. Their blades rarely touched, it was all feint and counterattack. Darwin bled from a dozen cuts on his hands and arms and face, none of them deep enough to slow him. Rakkim had been cut too, and Darwin was learning his rhythm, anticipated him more often, waiting for the killing opportunity.

"I was trained to snuff out great men. Generals and ayatollahs, popes and princes." Darwin shook his head. "I've squandered my talents since leaving the Fedayeen, but you . . . you made me re-examine things."

Rakkim closed in, forcing the battle. He had to. Time favored Darwin.

"After I kill you, I'll kill Ibn Azziz." Darwin backed up almost to a fallen statue of Jesus with his head broken off. "After I kill him . . . I'll kill the president. Maybe I'll even kill the old man. Would you like—?" He stumbled against the statue and Rakkim lunged. The stumble was faked though, and Darwin's blade slid into him and back out again.

Rakkim clutched his side, gasping.

"Ouch." Darwin laughed. "Do you know your Bible? Jesus got stabbed in the exact same place by a Roman centurion. Poor Jesus. Poor Rikki. Does it hurt?"

Rakkim felt blood leaking through his fingers.

"Don't die on me." Darwin spread his arms wide. "Not *yet*."

Rakkim laughed. Took his hand away from his side. Letting the blood flow.

"What's so funny?" said Darwin.

"You think you're this world shaker, this history maker . . ." Rakkim hung to an overturned pew. "You're *nobody*. You'll sink without a trace."

Darwin bobbed gently, a cork upon the waves.

"Who's going to weep for you, Darwin?"

"It doesn't matter. I won't be listening."

Rakkim winced, doubled over.

"I'm the one who's going to take your pain away." Darwin moved in. "I'm the last face you'll see. The last voice you'll hear. That *has* to mean something."

Rakkim sprang up at him, nicked his throat, and Darwin tumbled back against a pillar. Rakkim felt warmth along the back of his head as blood soaked his scalp.

"Almost fooled me." Darwin leaned against the wooden pillar, pressed three fingers against the side of his throat. "Another inch and you would have done some damage."

"Move your hand and let me see."

Darwin smiled. "Come a little closer."

Rakkim shook his head.

"You don't look so good, Rikki. Maybe you should sit down and rest."

Rakkim wobbled. He rolled the knife across his knuckles, almost dropped it.

"Are you afraid to die, Rakkim?" Darwin waited in vain for an answer. "I know about the baby. Are you sure it's yours?" He was pressing so hard against his neck his fingers were white, but still utterly alert. Knife poised. "Fatherhood . . . such a false refuge. Children suck the life out of a man. You can see the future in their greedy eyes."

"It's . . . it's the only future we have." Rakkim watched him.

"I'll tell Sarah you said that when I slice the baby out of her . . ." Darwin heard the distant ringing of the streetcar, distracted for an instant. "I'll tell her—"

Rakkim hurled the knife into Darwin's open mouth. Pinned him to the pillar.

Darwin thrashed against the beam, the knife cutting into his brain stem. A gush of blood as he tried to speak. Eyes wide. Lips working against the hilt of the knife.

Rakkim stood over him. Watched him die. Darwin's eyes

seemed to flare one last time before going blank, and Rakkim's gaze never left him. Wanting to make sure. When Darwin stopped moving, he tore the knife from his mouth.

Darwin slid slowly down the pillar, left a smear on the wood.

Rakkim wiped the knife clean on Darwin's tunic. He was dizzy now, bleeding from a dozen places, but he had spray-stitch in his robe. He would heal. He would survive. In a few days . . . a week at most, he would be well enough to return to the Grand Mosque. Well enough to kill Ibn Azziz. Well enough to return home to Sarah.

Rakkim looked down at Darwin's body. The Holy Qur'an taught that two angels hovered around each believer. One angel sat on his right shoulder recording his good deeds; another angel sat on his left recording his evil acts. Rakkim had never felt the weight of either. Not once in his life. Now, however . . . perhaps it was blood loss . . . a smile creased his face at that thought . . . now, for the first time, Rakkim felt the flutter of wings, felt the softest touch against his right shoulder, enfolding him now in a feathery, loving embrace. His surprise . . . his surprise was exceeded only by his joy.

ACKNOWLEDGMENTS

I would like to acknowledge my debt to Simone de Beauvoir, author, philosopher, and atheist, in the inception of this book. When asked by a journalist how it felt to have created a body of work that negated the existence of God, de Beauvoir responded, "One can abolish water, but one can not abolish thirst." I wrestled with this insight of hers for many years, and hope this book is worthy of the struggle.

The following websites in particular provided background information used in the writing of this novel:

> www.askimam.com
> www.islam.com
> www.techcentralstation.com
> www.virtuallyislamic.blogspot.com
> www.memri.org
> www.islamworld.net

In addition, *Tactics of the Crescent Moon: Militant Muslim Combat Methods* (Posterity Press) by H. John Poole, Michael Scott Doran's article "The Saudi Paradox" in the January/February 2004 issue of *Foreign Affairs*, and Abdul Hadi Palazzi's article "The Islamists Have It Wrong" from the *Middle East Quarterly*, Summer 2001, provided me with useful points of view.

My thanks to Colin Harrison, my editor and a man of many questions, for making the book richer and for not letting me blow the ending.

I am grateful to my agent Mary Evans for her strength and character.

Read on for an exciting preview of
Robert Ferrigno's gripping sequel to
Prayers for the Assassin,
coming soon in hardcover
from Scribner.

CHAPTER 1

Moseby needed to slow down. His haste stirred up a gray confetti of silt, disintegrating paper and pulverized glass from the neon sign that once flashed *Oyster Po'boys, Treat Your Mouth*. The tiny halogen beams on either side of his facemask bounced back from the confetti, the light made temporarily useless by his excitement. Moseby drifted in the warm water of the Gulf, waiting. He watched tiny bubbles from his respirator rise toward the surface. Plenty of time, no need to rush. He easily got three hours out of a two-hour tank. More if he stayed calm and clear.

The neon sign for Mama's lay in the street. The concrete block storefront canted, roof gone, the walls scoured clean by the tide. A couple of red leatherette stools lay on their sides, the floor carpeted with seagrass waving gently. He thought of the crowd at the LSU homecoming game last month, Annabelle on her feet beside him, cheering louder than anyone. He smiled around his mouthpiece. The cash register was sprung open on the counter, soggy bills hanging out like fingers from the till. Old money. Worthless. Mama's didn't hold any treasure. The oyster shack was a marker, an indicator that he was close to what he sought.

Moseby floated in place, listening to the sound of his own steady breathing. Easy to get spooked fifty feet under, a swimmer alone with the dead. It took patience to survive in the drowned city. More than patience, it took faith. Moseby pulled at the chain around his neck, lifted the small gold crucifix from under his wetsuit and brought it to his lips. He silently asked the blessing of Mary, mother of God. He asked her to intercede on behalf of all who had lost their lives in the city below, and he asked the dead for their permission for him to take what they no longer needed. A man could never pray too much. Particularly a man like

Moseby, who had much to atone for. He slipped the crucifix back under the suit, drifting, shivering in the warm water.

Unlike Moseby, most scavengers used electric sleds in their explorations, racing around at full power, churning up debris. Greedy, frightened men chopping their way through the city, so eager to get back to the surface that they ruined most of what they brought up. Hard, dangerous work under the best of circumstances. Equipment failed. Lifelines snagged. Floors and ceilings gave way. Walls collapsed. Jagged metal sliced through wetsuits, the rush of blood attracting the barracuda and morays that lurked in the mossy grottos of the French Quarter and the collapsed Superdome. More dangerous than anything else to the scavengers was the panic, the men disoriented by the darkness, and the fractured geometry of wrecked buildings. Gulping air, swimming frantically, they got lost in the concrete maze, adding themselves to the long list of dead.

The streets below were beyond the reach of sunlight, obscured further by thousands of automobiles leaking gas and oil even after all these years. Murkier still in the houses and restaurants and grand hotels where the easy spoils lay. Afraid of the deep, the scavengers used ever more powerful lights, blinding themselves, losing all perspective in the undersea tableau. Men had died for a crystal doorknob they mistook for a massive diamond, gotten trapped reaching for a sterling punch bowl far out of their grasp. Frightened of the dark and the loneliness, frightened most of all by the ghosts. Commuters floating in their vehicles. Lovers in their hotel beds or huddling in the lavish bathrooms where they had taken cover. Hard to pluck a gold Rolex off a bony wrist under those watching eye sockets. Hard not to hurry, to drop the goods and fumble to find it again. Easy to breathe too fast, to let the nitrogen build up in the bloodstream, to over-estimate their air supply. This year alone sixty-seven men had died or disappeared searching for loot. Most scavengers focused on the Mardi Gras district—the fancy stores and tourist emporiums had been picked over, but their familiarity offered some illusion of safety. Not Moseby.

His crew worked the untouched areas, the mansions and banks and businesses outside the central core, places where the flood had been most ferocious, leaving behind a deadly jumble of concrete and steel and twisted rebar. They were the most successful crew working the city, bringing up gold coins and jewelry, carved stonework and vintage brandy, Creole memorabilia and steering wheels from classic cars—most of them sold to collectors in Asia and South America. Moseby trained his men himself, taught them as much as they could handle. The men were careful . . . but they still died. Not as often as the men working the safer parts of the city, but often enough. Too often, for Moseby. That's why he dove alone today. Men had the right to risk their lives to feed their families, but Moseby wasn't seeking treasure today. At least none that would be sold or bartered.

Moseby switched off his light. Gave in to the darkness. Waiting. Moseby closed his eyes. Waited. When he opened them again, he could see. Not clearly, even *his* eyes weren't that good, but he could see. Now that Mama's had oriented him, the shapes and shadows seemed laid out before him, the messy grid on the city's outskirts, St. Bernard's parish, where the levee had failed first.

The old government had raised the levees two times after Hurricane Katrina inundated the city. Raised it higher and higher, trying to keep up with the rising sea level and the ever more powerful hurricanes. September 23, 2013 . . . thirty years ago, Hurricane James, a category 6 hurricane, predicted to miss the city, had suddenly veered west in the middle of the night, and struck New Orleans at sunrise. The levees gave way as though made of tissue, the waters of the Gulf covering the city under fifty feet of water. Most of the estimated three hundred thousand dead were stuck in traffic trying to flee. Hurricane James was the most violent storm ever recorded. Until Hurricane Maria two years later.

Moseby glided over the road, his no-wake flippers almost living up to their name. Brightly colored fish ignored him, twisting and turning as they darted past him, weaving in and out the open windows of the barnacle-crusted vehicles strewn below, many of the cars overturned by the force of the water when the levees broke. The houses in the immediate area were small and falling down, but the land rose slightly toward the north, the houses larger, many of them surrounded by walls. This was where Sweeny would have lived.

Anabelle couldn't remember much from her visit to her eccentric uncle's house—she was barely five—but there had been an ancient banyan tree in his backyard dripping with Spanish moss, and a swing set already rusted, squeaking loudly, one leg of the swing set lifting off the ground as she rhythmically pumped away. She remembered Sweeny taking her and her mother to a local po'boy joint, a hole in the wall specializing in oysters drenched in fresh lime juice, bourbon, and Tabasco. Sweeny said he ate two po'boys for lunch every day, her uncle proudly watching as his niece devoured one of her own, smacking her lips with pleasure in spite of the blistering hot sauce. Moseby had spent months searching for New Orleans take-out joints specializing in the cajun delicacy, months of scouring local guidebooks and newspaper articles. Last week he got lucky, ran into an old timer . . . a regular at Mama's in the old days.

Moseby's eyes adjusted even further to the dim light. Anabelle said if it had been him instead of Jonah swallowed by the whale, Moseby wouldn't have needed divine intervention to find his way out. He checked his watch. Plenty of time. Plenty of air. He passed over a small backyard, a line of laundry drooping but still standing. Shirts and pants and dresses, their colors faded, eaten through with time, ragged pennants rippling in the current. Another yard, the screen door thrown open, torn half off its hinges and Moseby wondered if the family inside the house had made it out alive, had clung to a boat, a skiff, an inflatable swimming pool . . . he wondered if they had gotten lucky, awakened from a nightmare before dawn and raced ahead of the raging floodwaters.

Anabelle had said her uncle's house had been large, with a high stone fence and white pillars, a rich man down on his luck, his house the remnant of his fortune as the neighborhood sunk into squalor. She and her mother had never gone back for a visit, Sweeney had taken offense at something her mother said . . . or maybe it was the other way around. Either way, her uncle and the house were a dim memory. The marble bust of the woman . . . that was a different story. Anabelle remembered it vividly. The stone queen, that's what she had called her. A beautiful woman with a head full of tight curls, her expression distant and dreamy, as though she had seen something that no one else had ever seen, and the sight had changed her. The world would never be quite fine enough for the woman now. Anabelle said she thought the stone queen must have seen into heaven and couldn't wait to go there. Moseby knew better. He and Anabelle had sifted through photos on the net until she narrowed down what she remembered. If she was right, the statue was Greek, probably early classical, in the style of Aphrodite of Melos. Priceless. Moseby was going to surprise Anabelle with it for their anniversary tonight.

A grove of trees had been flattened by the flood, thrown together in a tangle, and beyond the fallen trees, a huge banyan, squatting in place, leaves long gone, its branches sharp. A crumbling stone wall . . . Moseby angled lower, straining to see, not wanting to use his light until he absolutely had to.

The stone wall was festooned by spikey, brightly colored sea anemones, completely covering the south wall where the offshore flow brought the densest stream of nutrients. He jerked back as a sea snake poked out from a hole in the crumbling wall, tracked him with its tiny eyes, working its fangs as it undulated toward him. Yellow with red stripes, four feet long—five feet, six feet at least. Moseby drew his knife as he watched the snake, playing with it now, the flat of the blade making lazy rotations around his index finger. The spinning blade gathered the faint light, flashed in the darkness, and the snake inched closer, attracted. Moseby kept the blade moving, calling it closer. Sea snake venom was more deadly than a cobra's, that's what the old timers said. All Moseby knew was that three divers had died last month from snakebites, died ugly, puffed up until their skin split. Fifty years ago there hadn't been sea snakes in the Gulf, none like this, anyway, but the water was warmer now, the snakes migrating toward rich pickings . . . just like Moseby. The snake stopped, faced off with him, then retreated back to its grotto in the stone wall.

Moseby watched for another minute, then slipped his knife back into its sheath, moved on to the house. He slipped gently through a picture window that had been blown out, scattering fish with his presence. They returned just as quickly. He switched his face mask lights on to the lowest setting, bounced the beam off the ceiling. He saw well enough to navigate.

Tables and chairs lay jumbled below, the carpet thick with mud, sprouting sawgrass. Paintings on the wall hung askew, their surfaces occluded by a dull blue-gray fungus, gilt frame eaten by woodworms. Fish returned, nosed around him. Moseby lightly wiped a gloved hand across the surface of the largest painting . . . the paint rolled off in tiny droplets, spun lazily around him as the fish gobbled them down. He swam on through the house, limpets dotting the walls and ceiling. Crabs scuttled in the debris, hiding themselves from him.

Moseby hovered in the doorway of the master bedroom. A huge bookcase had fallen, scattered volumes. Pages swollen, the books gaped on the carpet. The Greek bust lay among the books, toppled off its display stand, a place of honor, evidently. He moved inside, eager now, his movements stirred the top layer of mud, but he didn't care. He wrenched the bust from the pile of books, sent the sodden pages free of their rotten bindings, fluttering around him. He cleared away the fine moss that covered the statue's features, taking off his glove to feel the smooth marble, not satisfied until she was clean. Moseby looked into her face. She was everything that Anabelle had described: strong and beautiful, but most of all possessed of secrets that had cost her greatly. The wisdom of time. He ran a finger along her cheek. Even buoyed by the water, the bust was heavy, maybe one hundred fifty pounds, but he tucked it under one arm, somehow comforted by its heft. He swam for the window, his kick powerful, leaving clouds of pages in his wake. All those lost words . . .

His wrist tracker guided him back to where his boat was anchored 1.3 miles away. He could have tagged the bust and returned for it when he got to the boat. Would have been easier, but the idea of putting aside the sculpture even for a few minutes, after all this time searching for it . . . Moseby couldn't do it.

He swam on, occasionally shifting the sculpture from arm to arm, more excited than fatigued. By the time the bottom of the boat came into view, he just wanted to load up and be gone. He carefully placed the bust on the hydraulic shelf at the stern, the stone queen's face gleaming in the sunlight after all those years underwater. Moseby tore himself away from her gaze, grabbed a handhold and pulled himself quickly onto the boat. Pushed back his face mask. He sensed trouble and turned.

"Nice morning. A little hot, maybe . . ."

Moseby stared at the man in shorts and a bright Hawaiian shirt leaning against the command console, cleaning his fingernails with Moseby's boning knife. A big, muscular bruiser, sweating in the heat. Tufts of short red hair blossomed across his skull. Small, cruel eyes, tinged with pink, made worse by the intelligence within. Large, flat, uneven teeth. An albino ape raped by a wild boar would birth something like this man . . . and then abandon it in disgust.

Moseby stood on the deck, dripping water. "What are you doing on my boat?"

The man wandered over to check out the statue. Whistled. "You carried that thing by yourself? You're a lot stronger than you look." He grinned those crooked teeth, idly adjusted the machine-pistol slung around one shoulder. "I best watch my manners."

"I asked you a question."

"You know who I am?" the man said softly, working the curved tip of the boning knife deep under his thumbnail. Coarse red hairs on his knuckles waved in the breeze.

"Yeah."

The man flicked something from under his nail with the knife, looked up at Moseby. "Then you know I don't need to give you any explanations."

Moseby had seen the man on video more than once, Gravenholtz . . . Lester Gravenholtz. He was usually standing behind the Colonel at news conferences, rarely acknowledged, but always there. The Colonel was a bona fide war hero, known as the savior of Knoxville for his tenacious defense of the city. *No retreat, no surrender, no prisoners*, his motto and his battle cry. At the height of the battle he had personally executed nineteen deserters, live broadcasting the slayings to his troops. A local warlord now— plenty of those in the Bible Belt, where any central authority was always suspect—but the Colonel was the most powerful, a law onto himself, with six thousand men at arms, and ten times that many irregulars. The Colonel commanded more men than the Tennessee governor. Better equipped too. Lester Gravenholtz had been with the Colonel since the beginning, more imp than guardian angel, an inciter of atrocities and vengeance for its own sake. Two years ago, President Jackson himself had signed a federal arrest warrant for Gravenholtz, citing multiple examples of rape and murder, sedition, and the sacking of the government armory in Vicksburg. The Colonel had hanged the federal prosecutor who attempted to arrest Gravenholtz. The thirty members of the prosecutor's armed detail had defected, and become part of the Colonel's private army.

In the distance, Moseby spotted two stealth helicopters just above the treeline, completely silent, their props wafting the branches. He didn't react, turned, and watched the water. Not one man in a thousand would have noticed the choppers. Not one in a million would have known what they were: Chinese, Monsoon-class, Model 4s. A skilled pilot could insert a Model 4 into a piney woods bog and not upset a bullfrog's lovesong. Day/night optics capable of counting the pores in Gravenholtz's nose from this distance. Laser-sighted armaments. The Chinese didn't export the Model 4s. The president himself had only a Model 3, a gift from the Chinese premier on his last official visit. So what were the Model 4s and Gravenholtz doing *here*?

"Fancy birds, huh?" said Gravenholtz.

Moseby pretended not to understand.

"If you're nice, I'll give you a ride." Gravenholtz tossed the knife, chunked it deep into the teak railing an inch from Moseby's hip. "Heckfire, I'll give you a ride even if you're *not* nice."

Moseby bent down, lifted the stone queen off the shelf and gently set it down on the deck. "No thanks."

Gravenholtz spit on the deck, wiped his mouth with the back of his hand. "What makes you think it was a *request*?"

Moseby plucked a strand of seaweed off the stone queen's shoulder, kept his attention on her. He didn't need to look at Gravenholtz to sense him closing in.

"The Colonel wants to see you. *Now*. I'll round up your crew later."

"Tonight's my anniversary." Moseby picked tiny bits of sand and moss off the stone queen's marble surface. "The Colonel will have to wait."

Gravenholtz's laugh was a humorless bark. "You believe in God, Moseby?"

Moseby kept working.

"Better to believe in the Colonel, because God can't help you now."

"You're going to stink up hell when you burn." Moseby gently removed a bit of grit from the stone queen's right eye. "Glad I'm not going to be there to smell it."

Gravenholtz pointed the machine pistol at Moseby's head.

"You didn't come all the way here to shoot me." Moseby pulled tiny snails from the stone queen's hair, the perfect spiral of their shells one of the infinite proofs of God. He flicked the snails over the side as he worked on the stone queen, his hands steady, unhurried. "You're here because the Colonel needs me for a project of some kind. Something special. Something he thinks only I can do. I wouldn't want to be you if anything happened to me."

He looked up at Gravenholtz. "Pick me up tomorrow morning after breakfast. If I like the Colonel's business terms, I'll send for my crew. I'll meet you tomorrow—"

Gravenholtz fired a burst into the stone queen, her head shattering into a thousand pieces. "I know where you live. I'll set my bird down in your backyard." He beckoned and the Model 4 streaked toward them.

Moseby stared at the shattered stone queen. Stood up. He pulled a shard of marble from under his eye, felt blood trickle down toward his lip.

Gravenholtz laughed again.

Moseby tasted blood. Christ had commanded his followers to turn the other cheek, to love those that cursed them, but Moseby knew his own limitations.

CHAPTER 2

Tariq al-Faisal didn't walk like the Christian he pretended to be. It was the walk that had drawn Rakkim's attention from a block away, long before he recognized the man. Al-Faisal in Seattle? The recognition made Rakkim's palms itch. Money, that's what the Cajun fortune-teller outside New Orleans would have said. She'd peer up from her table on the beached Delta Queen riverboat, rub his itchy palm and say, you've got *beaucoup d'argent* coming your way, child. Rakkim smiled. He knew better. Seeing al-Faisal here was worth more than silver or gold.

At least Al-Faisal had the externals of his pose right: high-ride trousers, cuffs rolled, fingerless gloves, even the St. Paul's Academy ear stud, which was a nice touch, but his walk kept reverting to type. He led with his chest as he stormed past the statue of Malcolm X on the corner, shoulders set, the gait of a Muslim fundamentalist certain of his place in the universe. Christians in the Islamic republic, no matter their station in life, moved from their hips, gliding, heads swiveling, alert for disapproval. *Kaffir-*

walk it was called in Rakkim's shadow warrior training, that elite branch of the Fedayeen, the deepest of deep-cover operators sent behind enemy lines, into the Bible Belt.

Rakkim sauntered along, taking his time. Like al-Faisal he pretended to be a Christian, but the Pope himself would have given Rakkim communion without a second thought. Invisible as a stolen kiss, that was the shadow warrior ideal.

Rakkim remembered practicing the Kaffir-glide for hours, days, weeks, remembered being jerked from sleep by his instructor, beaten if his first step was wrong. Homegrown Christians were easy enough to mimic, but Bible Belt patterns had been much more challenging and failure had cost more than one shadow warrior his life. Rakkim had been the best in his unit, able to pivot seamlessly between a Gulf Coast shuffle and an Appalachian hitch-along. He had lived for months in the Belt without rousing suspicion, sung hymns in a tiny church, tears rolling down his cheeks, worked on shrimpers, and done double shifts at a silicon wafer factory outside Atlanta, guzzling beer and pigs' feet afterward.

Al-Faisal eyeballed a new green Lamborghini curbed in a valet parking area. Ran a finger over the perfect finish as he walked past. Pathetic. A Christian wouldn't *dare* touch a vehicle with a Qur'anic inscription etched into the windshield. His three bodyguards were better trained, ex-Fedayeen from the look of them and the way they slipped easily through the crowd. They maintained a shifting perimeter around al-Faisal, a rough triangulation, two ahead, on either side of the street, another lagged behind, hoping to pick up a tail. No eye contact between them, just three moderate Muslims, seemingly part of the crowd, but the same barber had cut their hair, his distinctive scissor-work easy for Rakkim to read. Details, boys, details.

It must be an important mission for an important Black Robe like al-Faisal to leave the safety of New Fallujah. A mission too important to trust to an underling. Too important to trust phones or satellite communications. No, just like the old days, the most important conversations could take place only where no one could listen in. So what are you here to talk about, al-Faisal? And whose ear will you be whispering in?

A fat fundamentalist businessman nearly collided with Rakkim, cursed him, his coarse gray robes billowing as he barreled off for sundown prayers. Rakkim didn't even break stride, the businessman's wallet cupped in his palm. He dropped the businessman's money into a war-widows alms box a block later, turned in the wallet and ID to a passing policeman who half-heartedly thanked him for his citizenship.

Rakkim stayed far behind al-Faisal, loose-limbed and easy, enjoying the game. Perhaps enjoying it too much. Lifting the businessman's wallet? He was definitely in a playful mood today, almost eager for something to go wrong, something that would allow him to put all his skills to use. He flexed his right forearm, felt the Fedayeen knife tucked flat against the skin, ready to snap forth with the proper movement. He had seen al-Faisal only once before, glimpsed him two years ago in New Fallujah, the cleric haranguing a crowd on what had once been the Golden Gate. The Golden Gate . . . its new name, the Bridge of Skulls, suited it better. Rakkim flexed his right forearm again. Felt the blade slice an errant hair. For those with memories, there were always scores to be settled. Odd thoughts . . . Shadow warriors killed only as a last resort, but Rakkim wasn't a shadow warrior anymore. He was something else now, and whether it was more or less than before, he hadn't decided.

People filled downtown Seattle, poured out of the office complexes, commuters heading toward the monorail, students jostling toward the sin spots of the Zone, the faithful hurrying to prayers. A crowd of contrasts split along religious lines, rather than age or occupation—the modern and moderate Muslims in casual and business attire, the fundamentalists robed, prayer beads clicking away, while the blue-collar Catholics clustered together, staying with their own kind.

The air smelled of smog and salt water, hung heavy with the

aroma of coffee from the nearby Starbucks, clam chowder and jerked goat kebabs from the street vendors. The antiterror blimps ringing the city caught the rays of the setting sun, seemed to be on fire. Rakkim never tired of the beauty of the sight, to burn without burning . . . Two brightly garbed moderns chattered past, and Rakkim inhaled their perfume, the latest Italian cologne—*La Dolce Vita*, the sweet life at five hundred dollars an ounce. Moderns were so optimistic. Eager consumers enamored of their shiny, pretty things, the constantly upgraded gadgets. Their wealth comforted them, made them fearless as dreamers, eyes fluttering with the dawn.

Al-Faisal threw his arm around a stranger, pretending bonhomie, certain of his camouflage. Al-Faisal, another optimist, assured that Allah had already written his triumph in the book of days, fearless not as a consequence of his wealth but of his faith.

Ironic that the two opposite sides of the spectrum, moderns and fundamentalists, were the only ones in the Islamic republic certain that the future would be better, that their vision was destined to sweep away all others. The rest of country—the silent majority of moderate Muslims and Christians—they noticed the crumbling freeways and failing energy grid, an infant mortality rate worse than Nigeria's, and the regular outbreaks of cholera in Chicago and Denver. Let the fundamentalists and moderns trust in their hollow gods. Rakkim believed in the warmth of Sarah beside him, and the first halting steps of their son. He believed in unexpected friendships and laughter in the face of the inevitable. Optimism . . . a man had to close his eyes to remain an optimist, and there was no honor in that.

Optimism was for fools and children, that's what Redbeard used to say. Pray for victory, *plan* for disaster. Redbeard had been Rakkim's mentor. More than that, his uncle in all ways but blood. His tormentor, his taskmaster, his father-in-law, had he lived. Redbeard, State Security chief, lover of bone-crunch football and iced Coca-Cola . . . ferocious patriot, devout Muslim. Redbeard had died as peaceful a death as God granted, sitting in the back of a limo with his niece Sarah by his side. Not a day passed that Rakkim didn't wish Redbeard were still alive. The nation needed him now more than ever. Needed his strength and determination, his cool counsel when the world seemed ablaze. So did Rakkim.

News reports boomed from a kiosk, a holographic display showing troop movements along the border of the Mexican empire. Rakkim slowed. A commercial for cling-free chadors crawled along the bottom of the display while tanks rolled across the desert. Rakkim pretended interest, watching the bodyguards reflected in the display. The three of them did a slow pivot, scanning the crowd as al-Faisal hurried on. He still walked wrong.

Two college girls approached, moderates, their diaphanous veils only enhancing their beauty rather than masking it. Their eyes followed him—Catholics were forbidden fruit, their lust and volatility whispered about with fascination. Rakkim smiled back, kept walking, embarrassed at the pleasure their interest gave him. He thought of Sarah waiting for him at home, and for the millionth time was grateful for not being Catholic. Those fools so eager to confess. Who could keep up with their own sins?

Al-Faisal cut across the street, oblivious to the horns beeping around him. His bodyguards took their time, peeling off slowly.

Rakkim crossed at the signal, then stopped to buy an ice cream cone. Strawberry mango. He ambled after al-Faisal into the warren of small shops on the outskirts of the Zone, licking ice cream off his fingers.

The Zone was a moral free-fire district, where vice was tolerated and the police minded their own business. Creative, sordid, corrupt, a place of dance clubs and foreign movie theaters, of black-market electronics and stolen moments. A center of dangerous fun. No streetlights in the Zone, the only illumination coming from the neon signs and the dim interiors. Rakkim had lived in the Zone before he married Sarah. Had owned a nightclub, the Blue Moon. He knew the Zone, but the Zone didn't know him.

Music throbbed from every doorway, part of the unique signature of the Zone. While most of the city was off-limits to anything other than religious chants, the Zone took pride in showing off its freedom from any restraints. Russian pop, rock, world, Brazilian thump, Chinese techno, and Motown overlapped and merged in the Zone, became a dissonant heartbeat. Everyone walking down the street picked up the beat, feet moving faster, hearts racing, heads bobbing. Rat-a-tat-tat. Al-Faisal resisted, but even he was forced to give in, swinging his hands as his stride lengthened. He was going to have to ask forgiveness for such spontaneity, pray himself hoarse to atone for his inadvertent pleasure. Perhaps he would even sacrifice a white goat, slit its throat himself, then distribute the meat to the poor. There were always plenty of hungry mouths.

Al-Faisal half stumbled on a patch of blackened sidewalk, the concrete cracked and uneven. A suicide bomber had blown himself up on this spot Easter Sunday a year ago. The bomber had been trying to get into the Kitchy Koo Klub but the place was packed; he had to settle for taking out forty-three people waiting outside. A costly ticket to paradise. It had been a bad spring in the capital, with suicide bombers targeting the Zone, the death toll in the hundreds. Officially, Bible Belt zealots had been blamed, but ibn-Azziz, grand mullah of the Black Robes had been responsible. The president visited the Zones after the worst attack, cameras rolling, declaring the nation would not be intimidated. He also quietly ordered a Fedayeen commando unit to infiltrate New Fallujah and blow up ibn-Azziz's boyhood mosque. Ibn-Azziz blamed Zionists for the destruction, but the suicide attacks in the capital stopped immediately.

Al-Faisal turned abruptly and Rakkim thought for a moment that he had been spotted, but the agent turned back, ducked quickly into a tiny storefront, Chanaluski Digital Entertainment. That was a surprise. Chanaluski was a long-term resident of the Zone, a staunch modern and web hacker, a free thinker. He had spent many afternoons drinking khat tea at the Blue Moon, getting a pleasant buzz on. So what business did the Black Robes' emissary have with him?

Rakkim turned into the next alley, lost himself in the darkness. A glance back to the street, and he free-climbed the vertical brick wall, using just his fingertips and the toes of his boots, swiftly working his way up to the roof of the building next door. From this position he could see if al-Faisal left by the front or back door. Either way he would follow. Later he would have a chat with Chanaluski.

Rakkim waited. Watched as the three bodyguards took positions nearby, pretending to window shop. The trailing bodyguard stood in the doorway of the Crocodile Club listening to music, ignoring the three-hundred-pound bouncer, who told him to either come in or move on. The bouncer took a closer look at the man and retreated inside the club.

Rakkim perched in the shadows, noted how the bodyguards carried themselves. He caught his breath. Three short vibrations from the non-metallic transceiver implanted in his right earlobe. An emergency signal from Sarah. Three shorts was a call to meet her at the Presidential Palace. He waited. In three, two, one seconds he would get a repeat call to validate the signal. There it was. He hesitated, hating to back off from al-Faisal. No, he should go. He clambered down the wall, slid down the last ten feet. Pulled out his cell. Maybe Colarusso could tail al-Faisal. It wasn't a police matter, but Rakkim trusted Colarusso more than State Security. He took a look behind him as the phone beeped, saw al-Faisal hurry from the shop, going against the traffic flow now. He patted his right pocket, reassuring himself. He had gotten more than information from Chanaluski.

"What's up, Rikki?" said Colarusso.

"Later." Rakkim slipped the phone away. Checked his watch. If Sarah was at the Presidential Palace, she couldn't be in any immediate danger. Not likely, anyway. He walked after al-Faisal, slowed as he passed Chanaluski's storefront. The windows were one-way glass. LED Closed sign. He had intended to talk to

Chanaluski after following al-Faisal, but now . . . Something had changed hands in the store. He tried the door. Saw blood on the knob.

Down the street, al-Faisal increased his pace. Whatever he had gotten from Chanaluski made haste his primary concern. Equally focused, his two bodyguards fell in beside him, flanked him. The third led the way, breaking a path through the partygoers with his scowl and his shoulders.

Rakkim walked after them, keeping to the edges of the street, where he could make faster progress.

The taller of the bodyguards whirled around.

Rakkim shuffled along, hands waving, muttering to himself like another of the human gin blossoms that frequented the Zone, sloppy from bootleg alcohol. He sagged against a lamppost, pretending to breathe hard, sneaked a look toward al-Faisal.

The tall bodyguard stared right at him. Not taking his eyes away, he said something. The other flanking bodyguard stopped while the third bodyguard in front grabbed al-Faisal by the wrist, and dragged him down a side street. The flankers followed slowly as Rakkim hurried to catch up, slipping through the crowd with barely any contact.

This side street must have been picked as their rally point beforehand. Narrow, its few shops closed for the night, blocked off at the far end, a powerful German sedan idling behind the yellow construction barrier, waiting. A common vehicle in the capital, easily lost among the evening traffic.

Al-Faisal was halfway to the sedan, the two tailing bodyguards taking positions on either side of the alley as Rakkim approached. Their arms hung loose, their knives making tiny circle eights in the air. Like all Fedayeen, they were trained to be ambidextrous. The one on Rakkim's right kept his knife in his left hand, the one on his left held his knife in his right. That way they covered maximum space. Rakkim raised his own knife in a mocking salute. They didn't react, which spoke well for them. He might have learned something from seeing how they handled their blades.

"What's your hurry, al-Faisal?" Rakkim smiled. It wasn't a fake smile. Not a feint. Rakkim had no idea where his sudden good humor came from. No idea at all. "Stay and watch the fun. I'm all alone."

Al-Faisal stopped. Shook off his bodyguard at he glared at Rakkim.

"That's better." Rakkim smiled broader. He could see the two bodyguards out of the corner of his eyes, but he ignored them. "The last time I saw you it was Ramadan, two years ago. You were on the Bridge of Skulls." He strolled closer. "There was a boy . . . maybe eight years old. He had violated his fast. Ate an orange. Not a whole orange. Just one section." He could see al-Faisal's eyes narrow. "You remember the boy?"

Al-Faisal took a step back.

"You gave him three hundred lashes for his blasphemy." Rakkim rocked slightly forward. "He died at seventy-three. Must have been quite a . . ." Rakkim raced toward al-Faisal, his knife flicking out toward the two bodyguards as he sped past them. ". . . *disappointment*."

Al-Faisal's bodyguard grabbed him, shoved him into the sedan, jumped in after him. Slammed the door as the driver screeched away.

Rakkim grabbed for the door handle. Missed. Fell to one knee. He got up, watching al-Faisal's frightened face pressed against the glass of the back window. Then he walked back down the alley.

One of the bodyguards lay curled facedown on the pavement. He looked like he was sleeping. The tall one stood unmoving, still planted in the direction Rakkim had come from.

Rakkim circled around him, looked at the man. Late thirties, dirty blond hair. His jaw clenched. The effort it must have taken to stay utterly still. To tense all of his muscles. All of his *being*. Rakkim had stabbed each of the bodyguards in the upper abdomen as he passed. Stabbed them deep with the long, thin blade. Stabbed them in exactly the same spot. The fourteenth ganglia, a cluster of critical nerves. Instantaneous death. Except in very rare instances. Such as when the victim stayed perfectly still. So still that the nerve impulses still managed to make the leap across the cut tissue, the familiar pathways in service for a few moments longer.

The tall bodyguard blinked furiously as sweat poured into his eyes. Fear too, but he kept that in check. His tongue moistened his lips. "*How?*"

Rakkim didn't have an answer for the man. The bodyguards were combat Fedayeen, fierce fighters, hard to kill. Rakkim had made it look easy. Only one in a thousand qualified for Fedayeen, but only one Fedayeen in a thousand qualified to be a shadow warrior or an assassin. It wasn't the speed of his attack that had surprised him. Rakkim had always been fast, even for a Fedayeen. It was knowing *where* to strike that took him aback. Knowledge of the killing ganglia, the training required to deal the fatal blow . . . that was reserved for assassins. Rakkim hadn't even been aware of what he was doing until he was past the two bodyguards. He still didn't know how he knew.

A spot of blood appeared on the bodyguard's shirt. A tiny spot . . . but growing. The bodyguard twitched. Impossible to hold still enough. Even if he could, there was no fixing him.

Rakkim thought of asking him where al-Faisal had gone but stayed silent. The man wouldn't tell, and Rakkim wouldn't insult him by asking. The bodyguard might not have done the terrible things that al-Faisal had done, but he had facilitated evil, had protected evil. He had chosen. Fedayeen swore an oath to defend the president and the nation. When the troubles with the Black Robes had flared three years ago the warrior elite had been tested. All Fedayeen were Muslim, but it had been the recent converts who were the most devout, it had been the converts who had resigned and retired, the converts who had supported the Black Robes, declaring their fundamentalist doctrine the one true Islam. The great majority of Fedayeen had held fast to their vows, but there had been hard times, and it wasn't over yet. No, the bodyguard had made his decision.

The tall bodyguard's bright blue eyes were wide now. Hairs in his nostrils waved with even breath. He clamped his jaw tight.

Rakkim raised his knife in salute and this time he meant it. "Salaam alaikum. Go with God, Fedayeen."

The tall bodyguard exhaled slowly, eyes fluttering, weary now, as though settling down for a rest after a long race. He sank to the pavement, already dead.

Rakkim hurried toward the Presidential Palace and Sarah.

Not sure what to read next?

Visit Pocket Books online at
www.simonsays.com

Reading suggestions for
you and your reading group
New release news
Author appearances
Online chats with your favorite writers
Special offers
Order books online
And much, much more!

13456